A RHYTHMS OF REDEM

To Bring You Back

EMILY CONRAD

Library of Congress Control Number: 2021909802

This is a work of fiction. Names, characters, places, and incidents are either the products of the author's imagination or are used fictitiously. Any resemblance to actual persons, living or dead, businesses, or actual events is purely coincidental. Any real locations named are used fictitiously.

Scripture quotations are from The ESV® Bible (The Holy Bible, English Standard Version®), copyright © 2001 by Crossway, a publishing ministry of Good News Publishers. Used by permission. All rights reserved.

ISBN 978-1-7360388-0-2 (Paperback Edition)

ISBN 978-1-7360388-1-9 (Ebook Edition)

ISBN 978-1-957455-00-6 (Hardcover Large Print)

Edited by Robin Patchen, Robin's Red Pen

Author photograph by Kim Hoffman

Visit the author's website at EmilyConradAuthor.com.

For Danielle, my sister and my first biggest fan.
Your support means more than you know.

1

At the sight of the food trailer's next customer, Adeline Green coughed on the bacon-scented air. Tattooed Middle Eastern script ran down the inside of the man's left forearm. Half visible beneath his sleeve, an elaborately inked lion roared on his biceps.

She'd know those tattoos anywhere. In other contexts, half the nation would, since Gannon Vaughn and his band, Awestruck, had spent the last few years releasing one hit album after another. But only someone who had known him long before he'd grown famous, someone whose thoughts for him reached beyond his songs to a tragic shared history, would dare to imagine he would surface here, in a small tourist town in northern Wisconsin.

Was it really him?

Yes. His tattered baseball cap featured the mascot of their high school, two hours south of here. The numbers stitched on the side matched the year they'd graduated.

More than a decade had passed, but the events of those days remained painfully fresh.

At five-five, she had to look up at most men, but standing

inside Superior Dogs gave her the height advantage. The added stature, combined with his hat's visor, blocked eye contact while allowing her to study the man she never should've loved.

Though his hat wouldn't earn a penny at a garage sale, Gannon's T-shirt and jeans fit better than they had business doing, somehow looking expensive and out of place in Lakeshore, Wisconsin.

What was he doing here?

Maybe his mom had dragged him up for a quiet vacation. The food trailer dominated three of the parallel parking stalls along the curb on Main Street, serving customers who stood on the sidewalk. Adeline scanned the pedestrians but didn't spot Mrs. Vaughn.

Gannon stepped closer to the window and pulled out his wallet.

Her face burned as if she'd pressed her cheek to the grill. When she'd imagined their next encounter, she'd hoped to prove how well she was doing without him. To that end, she'd never planned to let on that she served hotdogs for a living. Or half a living, anyway.

Maybe if she played it cool, he wouldn't recognize her, and whenever they crossed paths in the future, she wouldn't smell like a beef frank. She gripped the metal windowsill of the food trailer, willing him not to place her. "What can I get you?"

The baseball cap's brim pointed toward the menu. "What do you recommend?"

His voice. She'd forgotten the way it resonated through her. Recoiling, she bumped into Asher, the owner who manned the grill in the cramped space behind her.

Ever the willing salesman, Asher braced an arm against the top of the window. "The Super Superior is our namesake. Hotdog—local, natural casing—topped with barbecue pork, cheesy macaroni, and bacon. Can't go wrong." He projected the description, and a few more tourists slowed.

Gannon glanced up. His hazel eyes seemed to note her in the dim corner between the grill and cooler, but he focused on Asher. "Sold."

Of course he wouldn't recognize her. Photos of her weren't plastered everywhere like pictures of him were.

If only the images had been wrong when they'd showed how well he'd grown up and filled out.

"And a water, please." Gannon lifted a twenty as a group of three lined up behind him.

Asher's plastic gloves crinkled when he removed them to take the payment. Handling money was her job. Any moment, he'd ask her to take over, forcing her from the shadows.

That couldn't happen. Gannon couldn't see her. Not now. Not like this. "I need a quick break."

Asher shot her a questioning look, the faint wrinkles on his forehead creasing. The line behind Gannon had grown to five people. Hundreds had come for today's event. The shops and art galleries along both sides of the quaint Main Street had coordinated special, lake-themed displays. Superior Dogs, which didn't operate in the cold, snowy months, depended on days like today.

"I'll be back soon." She'd make good on the promise right after Asher had cooked Gannon's order and sent him packing.

Asher waved permission, so she popped open the door opposite the serving window and hopped onto Main Street. No sooner had she shut the door and stepped away to cross the street than a blaring horn backed her against the side of the trailer. She pressed her hand to her chest as the car swerved past.

The trailer door clunked open, and Asher stuck his head out. "You okay?"

She gulped to return her heart to its place in her chest. People exiting the souvenir shop across the street peered in her direction, probably wondering why a grown woman didn't know better than to step into traffic. Beyond them, visible between buildings, the serene blue of Lake Superior beckoned her.

"So it's that bad."

Her eyes sank closed at the timbre of the million-dollar voice.

Multi-million.

Hoping she'd imagined it, she peeked. Sure enough, Gannon had followed her around the trailer to the street.

Adeline's fist tightened, knuckles pressing against her collarbone. She fixed a pleading gaze on Asher. If anyone could intimidate Gannon into leaving, it'd be her tall, imposing boss. But Asher assessed her and Gannon, then retreated, shutting the trailer door behind him. She should've expected that. Asher hated drama more than anything.

She had to escape. She took a step to cross the street, but a strong hand caught her arm. Her hair shifted with the breeze as a truck she hadn't seen flew by.

"Settle down, okay?" Concern that looked genuine enough filled Gannon's eyes. "You're going to get yourself killed."

"Ironic." She shrugged out of his grip, abandoned her plan to cross the street, and opted for the closer sidewalk. "Since when have you cared about people getting killed?"

He hadn't missed a beat when Fitz died.

"That's not fair, Adeline." He said her name confidently, as if perhaps he'd thought of her as often as she'd thought of him. If so, this encounter wasn't a coincidence, and walking away wouldn't ensure he'd leave her in peace in the future.

She turned. "Why are you here?"

He swiped his head as if he wanted to pull off the hat, but he left it in place, his brown hair sticking out underneath. "This is the first I could get away."

"In eight years."

His mouth tightened. "Since John said he saw you at Christmas."

Though she'd lost touch with the rest of the band, she still considered John, the drummer, a friend. When she'd seen him back home over the holidays, she'd wondered if he would mention their brief conversation to Gannon. As months slid by, she'd realized it wouldn't matter if he did. Gannon wouldn't be curious about her anymore, and seeing him again would accomplish nothing for her.

And yet, here he was.

"Christmas was seven months ago."

"Our schedule's crazy, and you moved to the middle of nowhere."

Excuses.

She couldn't do this again.

He lowered his face so the hat shielded him as a pair of college-aged girls passed. Gannon's voice may have made him famous, but now he also acted as a celebrity judge on a reality show. People might need prompting in this setting, but it wouldn't take much for them to recognize him.

And once they did, he'd be forced to deal with them.

Hope of rescue allowed her to take her first satisfying breath since he'd appeared at the window.

She moved back and pointed. "Look! It's Gannon Vaughn."

Heads swiveled.

He lifted his hands as if she'd pulled a gun. "Come on. Really?"

Still pointing, she stepped toward the college students. "Do you have a pen? I need an autograph."

"It *is* him!" A middle-aged woman hustled up. "Can my son send his demo? He and I never miss *Audition Room*. You're our favorite judge."

One of the students pulled a marker from her tote and advanced toward Gannon, but a man with thinning blond hair blocked both her and the middle-aged woman. He motioned the lead singer to cut down an alley. After a glance toward the food trailer, Gannon obeyed.

Adeline and the tourists stared after them. When had a bodyguard last ushered a client off Lakeshore's Main Street?

Or maybe the second man hadn't been a bodyguard. He'd looked soft around the edges. A friend? Someone Gannon worked with? It didn't matter as long as they were gone.

Except even in their absence, her peace didn't return. Maybe she'd been wrong to rebuff him instead of finding a way to get closure.

Closure? She scoffed, ran her hand over her ponytail, and headed back to Superior Dogs.

Some wounds never healed. She'd done the right thing.

On the narrow shelf by the window, steam wafted off a waiting Super Superior.

"He won't be back for that."

Asher arranged a bun in another cardboard boat, loaded a hotdog, and scooped on macaroni. "What'd you do to him?"

"Wrong question."

"Okay. What'd *he* do to you?"

"He killed my fiancé."

Asher held the hotdog in front of his customer but didn't hand it off.

Okay. She deserved as much blame as Gannon for what happened to Fitz, but she was doing her best to live a good life now. Meanwhile, Gannon pretended to deserve all the fame and fortune the world laid at his feet.

Face hot with shame—over the past, over mentioning it so carelessly—Adeline took the hotdog from Asher and completed the transaction with the man at the window. After the customer left, she glanced at her boss.

Still waiting for an explanation.

"I thought you didn't like drama."

With a grunt, he turned back to the grill. "He left a note in the tip jar."

The old pickle jar sat next to Gannon's abandoned food. A white slip swam among the crinkled bills. She plucked it out. When she read her name in Gannon's hurried scrawl, she could almost hear his voice again. Beneath, he'd left a phone number.

∿

"Good thing I insisted on coming." Gannon's manager draped his hand over the steering wheel of the rented sedan. "You'd think you'd never seen a fan before."

The fans hadn't erased Gannon's ability to entertain and manage a crowd.

Adeline had.

"So this is about a woman." Tim smirked. "Here I'd been thinking you were more or less immune."

Not at all. Gannon hooked the hat on his knee and pushed his fingers through his hair. He hadn't expected that seeing Adeline after all those years would revive every feeling he'd ever had for her. Too bad seeing him hadn't had a similar effect on her.

He'd hoped she'd forgiven him by now. Or at least come to a point of acceptance so they could talk, each giving and getting closure. Then they could both move on.

Considering her feelings, closure would be next to impossible. Considering his feelings, he might never move on.

I'm totally unprepared for this, God.

Tim checked the rearview mirror and followed the road around a bend, traveling steeply uphill. "Harper's going to be crushed."

The actress flirted, sure, but she had a boyfriend. "Harper knows she and I will never be more than friends, and Adeline's obviously not even that anymore."

"Fair enough, but we're not staffed for a full-scale inundation at the cabin."

"Lakeshore's population is what, five hundred?"

"Try eight thousand plus the campus, and there are other factors to consider."

He'd allowed Tim along for this kind of advice. Awestruck's manager was good at running interference, especially during scandals.

Yet Gannon had hoped he wouldn't need the help—especially not so soon.

He scratched his head again, then pulled the hat back on, an act of contrition to soften his next announcement. "Then you'll be glad I didn't leave her my number."

Tim frowned as he worked out the implication. "You left mine."

"I didn't know she'd make a scene." Or that at his first glimpse of her, he'd revert into the twenty-one-year-old kid he'd been when he'd last seen her. Every coherent thought had fled. He'd dropped the number in the tip jar, hoping that, if the first encounter didn't work out, they might have another conversation later. Still, he'd feel a lot better if he'd managed a single intelligent sentence when he'd followed her away from the food trailer.

She'd never use that phone number.

The road leveled out. Larger homes, spaced farther and farther apart, dotted the cliff. Soon trees and gates obscured views of the homes and the lake beyond.

Tim glared out the windshield. "You could've gone anywhere in the world to work on the album, and you picked this place instead of a nice, warm beach somewhere. Why the interest in digging up the one person in the world who hates you?" Tim gave him a look probably intended to shame him into relocating to the tropics to overcome his writer's block.

A lost cause. He wouldn't focus on a beach any better than

he had in LA. Not after John had come back from Christmas and hinted Adeline wasn't doing well.

He offered a wry smile instead of an explanation. "Other people hate me too." Though only Adeline's rejection stung like this.

Tim checked the mirrors again before turning off the main road. "True. And mostly people who love you cause the problems, don't they?"

Tim meant fans, but without them, Awestruck wouldn't exist. Gannon couldn't blame them for anything. He had caused himself more problems than anyone else ever could.

God, be merciful to me, a sinner.

Tim braked for the gate that blocked the drive. At the swipe of a card, the wrought iron parted. A carved sign labeled the property *Havenridge Estate.* Gannon had first heard the name two months ago, when he'd signed the rental agreement, securing the place indefinitely. Just inside the gate waited the guest house, a cottage about the size of the home Gannon had grown up in. A few more twists in the road landed them in front of the main residence, a sprawling three-story log cabin.

Tim cut the engine. "There's a lot on the line here."

"I know."

According to Tim, there always was, and even Gannon felt the pressure now.

The band's first contract would be up in less than two years. Afterward, Awestruck would be free to sign a new deal with the highest bidder. If they could maintain their momentum until then, the new contract would be their biggest payday yet, the stuff most musicians—and their teams—only dreamed of.

But if the next album bombed, Awestruck could tumble from the charts, and some other band would be right there to take its place.

Tim grabbed the keys. "I'd be the first to encourage you to let loose and have fun, but you and that girl? Nobody's got time to scale mountains of baggage that high. Especially not some-body due in the studio in a few months. Have your fun, sure, but don't get distracted by the past."

"Adeline isn't the past. She was the start. There's a difference."

"Label it however you want. Just stay focused." Tim got out and shoved the door shut.

Gannon studied the aspen and pine trees sheltering the cabin. The setting promised peace no place on earth could deliver. Tim was right. The future was on the line—his, the band's, Adeline's—but for any of them to move forward, he'd have to first fix what had gone wrong at the start. "Lord, give me strength."

2

A dog person shouldn't have this much trouble saying goodbye to a cat. Adeline held Nissa's carrier in one hand as she opened the door to the animal shelter with the other.

Heather, one of the few paid staff members, sat behind the front desk. Her sloppy bun of red hair bobbed as she stood. "The family's in one of the visitation rooms. Do you want to take her in?"

Adeline considered the lump in her throat and wished she could scratch the soft fur between Nissa's ears once more. The gray and white domestic long-hair cat had won her over by greeting her at the door whenever she came in. And her rumbling purr had comforted her through the barrage of memories Gannon's visit brought on.

But she'd had a week to put Gannon behind her again. She could cope on her own if it meant allowing Nissa to go to a great family.

"I'll introduce her." Maybe if she got a bad vibe, she'd put in an application to adopt Nissa herself. She could figure out the money later.

In the room Heather indicated, Adeline found a family she knew from church. Joe and Carrie Cullen sat in the plastic chairs against the wall. Their pretty seventeen-year-old, Olivia, had settled on the floor.

In a recognition ceremony for graduating high school seniors at church, Olivia had shared her plan to attend the local college while living at home, which meant she got along with her parents well enough. Adeline got along with them too. Still, if not for the way Olivia's blue eyes widened with adoration when she spotted Nissa, Adeline might not have been able to open the latch on the carrier.

The girl sprang to her feet, pushed her long hair over her shoulders, and gently transferred Nissa's weight to her arms. "Mom, look. She's gorgeous!"

They would love her to pieces. Much better than Adeline ever could.

The family—Joe included—focused on Nissa, so Adeline let herself out. She paused outside the door to gulp down her rising grief.

Had Gannon left town as quietly as she'd left Nissa? Had it been harder for him, or easier? She hadn't seen him or heard rumors about him since their encounter on Main Street. In a town this size, where no one could sneeze without everyone hearing about it, the silence meant he hadn't been around. Good. Their relationship had resulted in heartache and nothing else.

She'd put so much time and energy into distancing herself from the past, she shouldn't have harbored fantasies of confronting him once more. The past couldn't be righted, and she'd spend the rest of her life paying for it, even if Gannon refused to show remorse.

She passed the desk on the way to the exit.

Heather hopped up from her chair. "What do you think of a lab mix?"

Adeline hesitated. Nissa had been a comfort. A dog would be too, depending on what his issues were. Good thing her roommate also had a soft spot for animals.

"He's older and very mellow, but he's stressed here." Heather stepped from behind the desk. "He has allergies, and his meds aren't enough to control them because of the stress of all the barking and the strange environment. He kept licking his paws. We had to put him in a cone."

The barking got louder as Heather opened the room with the dog kennels. They stopped at the second chain-link gate, which contained a black dog with a graying face. He ambled forward, swaying as his tail whipped back and forth.

"The cone stops him from licking, but now he's whining and barking. Poor guy is going hoarse. He needs a calm home environment."

"I'm not home a lot during the day."

"He's used to owners who work." Heather swung open the door to let Adeline greet him.

The dog sat, the cone framing his sweet face.

She squatted and pet his warm head, her fingers tapping against the plastic.

Heather crossed her arms and leaned against the kennel. "A home will do him good. We'd adopt him out straight from your house to the new owner—less stress for an old dog."

Adeline looked into his brown eyes, which were edged with black and white lashes. A dog wouldn't hold her past against her, even if she whispered all the secrets she couldn't bear to tell another human. "How old is he?"

"Ten. We want to make sure his golden years are as good as they ought to be."

"What's his name?"

Heather chuckled. "See the bat-shaped marking on his chest?"

Adeline leaned to see under the cone. A clear white

marking stretched over his breastbone, bat-like enough to make the connection. "Don't tell me he's Bat Dog."

"No, but close enough. Adeline, meet Bruce."

GANNON'S PHONE sounded and displayed a picture of Harper English. She was requesting a video call. He leaned his guitar against the living room couch. If he'd finally broken past his writer's block, he'd call her back later, but all he could compose were more songs he likely could never use.

As a never-ending source of drama, Harper might spark an idea.

He pressed the icon to answer.

"Wow. A beard." Harper giggled. "How manly."

The week's worth of growth itched and made him feel like a caveman, but when he went back into Lakeshore tomorrow, he'd rather not be recognized. The trip into town was to see Adeline, and the longer he prevented Harper from learning about her, the better.

He pointed the conversation to her love life instead. "Things with you and Colton back on again?"

She lifted an eyebrow and looked away from the screen. Shadows lurked on her normally even skin, one at the back corner of her jaw, another on her temple.

"Are those bruises?"

She brought her big blue eyes back to the screen. "Maybe if you called me once in a while, you'd know."

"I'm up here to work. You know that. What happened?"

She made a face, then blew out a long breath. "Remember when you let me stay at your place?"

"Yeah," he said flatly. "I remember last week." He'd been in Wisconsin, and she'd had a fight with her live-in boyfriend, actor Colton Fremont. Gannon had given her access to his apartment to prevent her from wandering LA, drunk and upset. "And?"

"You were so worried what I'd do while I was drunk, you never thought to worry about me tripping down your stairs the next morning."

"You fell?"

"Little-known fact: I'm more stable drunk than sober."

Harper was many things, but she was never stable. Gannon kept taking her calls, trying to show her a better way.

"Did you get checked out? If I can still see the bruises a week later, that was a nasty fall."

"This is nothing. You should've seen me after the skate-boarding incident of '98."

Funny. He would've expected her to rush to the ER and flaunt the bruises for some sympathy from the press. She must've been embarrassed. "What about you and Colton?"

Her lids shaded her eyes, a frown playing at her lips in the perfect picture of sadness. "He's in Ontario with Leigh Wiles." She spoke as if Colton were vacationing with another woman, but Leigh and Colton were costars, in Ontario to film some dramedy.

"I take it you two didn't make up before he left."

"We did. But you do know how I met him."

On set. Colton and Harper had starred in a film together last summer. "That should reassure you. You were with Eric then, and you didn't cheat."

She sighed and focused her too-blue eyes on the screen again. He couldn't tell if she was looking at him or the inset of her own image. "But now Colton and I are together because we met then. What if he breaks up with me for her?"

"Have a little faith."

She moved close to the camera, and her perfect features covered his screen. "You know I only believe what I experience for myself."

Even that was iffy. She'd experienced plenty of problems because of her way of life, but still, she mostly disregarded Gannon's advice and his insistence that she needed Jesus.

"Anyway, I'm bored." On screen, the neckline of Harper's shirt shifted, exposing a bra strap. "I should come visit."

And play her games in person? No, thanks. She didn't need to show extra skin for him—or anyone else—to think her beautiful, but he'd seen how fast things went south when he disobeyed God in his relationships.

Never again.

"If you're going to get on a plane, use it to visit Colton."

"We could have a good time, you and I."

Exactly the kind of good time Tim wanted him to have. When would these two understand he wanted to honor God—and that was the only way to happiness? But they hadn't lived his life. They didn't know how wrong things could go when a human chose his own path.

He could explain that the only woman he could think about was Harper's opposite, a woman with long mahogany hair, cinnamon eyes, and a proven desire to repel rather than attract his attention. But Harper wouldn't let competition go unchallenged, so he kept his mouth shut. "I'm trying to work here. Call Colton."

ADELINE'S ONE-AND-THREE-QUARTER-STORY farmhouse stood a block off Main Street, tucked in among Victorians with pristine paint and gardens flowing with petunias. A misfit, her house featured chipping light blue paint and a weathered, sloping front porch. She'd planted a few tulips and daffodils, but now in July, her yard had reverted to a plain square of thin grass.

She parked in the gravel drive and gripped Bruce's nylon leash. "Home sweet home."

The dog thumped his tail twice and hopped out after her. She retrieved the dog food the shelter had provided, and Bruce followed her across the grass and up the creaking stairs, sniffing the whole way.

On the porch, she turned toward the view. Because of the slope of the land, she could see over the single-story pottery studio across the street to the lake four blocks away. This portion of Superior usually took on the sky's blue or gray instead of the emeralds and teals that glistened along some of the beaches. Today, a mostly sunny sky resulted in glittering, medium blue. No matter the color, the water exuded an unparalleled calm. If she couldn't count on anything else, at least Superior would always be there.

Bruce finished investigating the porch and looked to her for direction. Such an angel. She opened the screen door and led him through the living room and into the kitchen, which hadn't seen many updates in the last thirty or forty years. Still, the space was comfortable. Hers. Home.

Her roommate sat at the table with a cup of coffee and her laptop. Though Adeline had never been to California to see if the stereotype held true, she'd always thought Tegan looked like a surfer girl—blonde, athletic, and tanner than anyone else in Lakeshore.

Tegan set her mug down without peeling her attention from her screen. "Next time I'm considering teaching summer school, remind me—"

Bruce's nails clicked on the vinyl.

At the noise, Tegan abandoned her train of thought and laughed. "Who's this?" Within seconds, she was on her knees, scrubbing her fingers through a happy Bruce's fur.

Adeline relayed the story as she set down the dog food and sorted the mail. A couple of statements. Some ads. One envelope from the Downtown Lakeshore Neighborhood Association. She tore the association's letter open while Tegan dug out the water bowl they'd used last time the shelter had sent a dog home with her.

Tegan set the bowl in a corner for Bruce, chatting easily, but Adeline couldn't focus on responses when she read the first line of the letter.

Her gut churned like the time she'd been pulled over on Main Street. She'd known the siding and porch needed attention. She hadn't realized anyone else would care. If she'd known, she'd have found a way to repair them. Somehow.

Tegan sidled up beside her. "What's that?"

Adeline swallowed. "The neighborhood association has rules about curb appeal."

"Oh." Tegan's gaze roved over the interior of the house.

Adeline didn't have to look around to visualize it. The rest of the downstairs had refinished hardwood and new carpet, but she hadn't updated the kitchen. The vinyl was scuffed and yellowed. The plaster had cracked in a few places throughout the house, though she had at least applied fresh paint.

But the letter wasn't about the interior. The neighborhood association only cared about the aging exterior. "They're giving me ninety days to do something about the porch and the siding."

"Or what?"

"Fines." Big fines. Fines that got more severe the longer it took her to get the property up to standard.

"Can they do that?"

Adeline passed off the paper. Somehow, the fines—though they'd be problematic if they were levied—didn't bother her as much as being called out for not being up to snuff. She was doing the best she could.

If only her best had ever been enough.

"There's a statute or something meant to make Lakeshore appeal to tourists."

And tourists did love Lakeshore. The bed-and-breakfasts

and shops, like the pottery studio across the street, were peppered in among the homes and enjoyed bustling business from spring through autumn. In winter, deep snow and cold kept most visitors away, but some more adventurous types came for snowmobiling, ice caves, and cross-country skiing. Vacationers funded a significant portion of the town's economy.

And someone thought her house had become an eyesore to those all-important tourists.

How mortifying.

Tegan studied the letter while Adeline crouched to pet Bruce. The place did need improvements—more, even, than the letter required. A troubling water spot appeared on the ceiling of one of the upstairs bedrooms after rainstorms. One of the basement walls had cracked and shifted an inch. She would've done the repairs years ago, but working for Superior Dogs and as a secretary for the church left her living paycheck to paycheck.

"You really ought to charge me more for rent."

Adeline shook her head. Though the money did matter, the friendship had become more important. A teacher two years out of college, Tegan wasn't exactly making bank either.

"There's an opening for a career services coordinator at the college." The first time Tegan mentioned the position, Adeline had thought she'd done so to help lighten the workload for her friend who worked in the department. But as Tegan resorted to more of a sales pitch, Adeline realized she was the one Tegan wanted to assist. "You'd be advising students, and you'd even have a staff—a few students part-time, but still."

Adeline pressed her lips together. She wasn't about to turn her life on its head because of a one-time problem like the letter from the neighborhood association. "I don't have experience."

"You have a four-year degree in communications. Between that and working with people at church, I'm sure you have the background you'd need, and the pay is good. Plus, you'd help the students. You always have good advice for me."

"I like my jobs. Superior Dogs is just plain fun, and the church is important work." Besides, she could make a couple of thousand dollars another way.

Bruce licked her cheek, and she hugged him to her side as she drew a deep breath. "I'll sell my upright bass."

Even the warmth of Bruce nudging his head into her neck didn't ease the ache at the idea of parting with the instrument. She'd unloaded her electric bass guitar years ago because it prompted too many memories of her time as a member of a pre-fame Awestruck. However, she'd kept the classic double bass she'd learned to play in orchestra class, hoping the guilt over her mistakes with Gannon and Fitz would subside enough to allow her to return to playing for church, if nothing else. Eight years later, the thought of making her hope a reality twisted a knife of shame in her chest.

"Do you think a bass will cover all this work?"

"A nice upright bass is expensive. Besides, it needs regular service to stay in working order, so selling it will save money."

"Oh. Okay." Tegan slid the letter onto the table. "I always thought the bass was special to you, like you inherited it or something."

Tegan thought the bass was an heirloom? In a way, maybe. Both the bass and her connection with Gannon were an inheritance from her former self that she couldn't afford to keep, no matter what her feelings told her.

3

The last character of the Hebrew verse on Gannon's forearm was visible if someone looked for it, but his button-down covered the other ink that might give away his identity. He cleaned a pair of non-prescription glasses with the hem of his shirt before sliding them on.

Tim, who'd added a tie to his usual dress shirt, seemed intent on fitting in at the small church, even if his silence served as a complaint about giving up his Sunday morning for something he didn't believe in.

They mounted the stairs to the door, and Gannon reached for the handle. "You don't have to come."

Tim grunted and shadowed him into the building. He considered knowing the band's secrets part of his job. Since Gannon still hadn't told him more about Adeline, his manager was sticking close, probably hoping to piece it together.

At least this meant Tim would overhear a sermon.

The service already in motion, Gannon snagged a seat in the back without turning heads. He'd lost Tim somewhere along the way, probably in the tiny lobby.

Vestibule. The word hadn't crossed his mind in ages, but a

room that smelled like a one-hundred-year-old hymnal deserved the name.

Musicians took the stage to lead worship—three singers, a flutist, and a violinist. No Adeline. This was the only church in town that lined up with the beliefs they'd shared as teens. If she was present, why wasn't she on stage too? Back in the day, she'd been as passionate about bass as he'd been about guitar.

The first song started, and he fumbled open the hymnal. His home church was more contemporary, but the old songs were a blessing; focusing on the unfamiliar words meant setting aside thoughts of Adeline.

When the sermon ended and the pastor began the closing prayer, the old carpeting muffled Gannon's footsteps out of the sanctuary. Tim pushed away from the wall he'd been leaning against in the vestibule, and they advanced toward the exit, but the sound of children's voices turned Gannon's head.

A class of toddlers climbed the stairs from the lower level, perhaps to meet their parents in the lobby. Among them, three adults shepherded and hushed their young charges. A small girl in a purple poof of a dress held hands with Adeline.

Spotting him, Adeline froze. Her initial surprise drained to something less welcoming.

The little girl mounted the next step, then turned back to look at her guide.

"You've got to be kidding." Tim's voice came from over his shoulder, but the man didn't grab Gannon to pull him from the building.

And that was what it would've taken.

Gannon had been jealous of Fitz from the day he'd met Adeline. The two had already been dating a while when Fitz volunteered her to play bass guitar with the band. When Awestruck made plans to move to California and Adeline's parents forbade her from joining them, Gannon had hoped the distance would mean the end for Fitz and Adeline. Instead, the couple had seemed determined to last. Right before the band left, they announced their engagement.

Gannon had almost called off the move so he could stay, lay out his feelings, and change her mind about marrying someone else. But surely Adeline had known what she was doing. She was Fitz's girl, and because of it, Gannon should've known to stay away from her that Christmas he visited home from LA. But he hadn't, and he couldn't walk away now either, though frustration pursed her lips and narrowed those big brown eyes.

The little girl tugged her hand, and Adeline's expression softened as she dropped her focus. A lock of hair, which looked as silky as the last time he'd touched it, slid over her shoulder as she helped the toddler up the last of the steps.

The other adults took over ushering the kids toward the sanctuary while Adeline's gaze sharpened on him again. She kept her lips pressed shut until organ music trumpeted from the sanctuary. "You have a lot of nerve using church to get to me."

Without waiting for a response, she pushed open the door to the front walk and exited. In a moment, she had cleared the area visible through the glass. If he followed her out, was he in for a lecture? Or would she already be gone? He sucked in a deep breath and followed.

Adeline, already ten feet down the walk, pivoted back toward him, arms crossed and eyes blazing. "Are you stalking me?"

Behind him, Tim guffawed.

"I need God as much as the next guy."

"Even more." She planted her feet. "But you shouldn't be here."

Maybe not. His relationship with Jesus didn't depend on a church building or a sermon, and this confrontation hadn't been part of the plan. He'd meant to be on the road back to Havenridge by now, leaving Adeline, if she noticed him, curious, maybe curious enough to reach out to him, see what he was doing here. Instead, he'd set her more firmly against him.

"I know you can't see a reason, but we need to talk."

"If you think there's going to be a repeat of—"

"No." He couldn't get the word out fast enough. Did she really think so little of him? He struggled to stay calm, be the kind of man who deserved a chance. "We need to talk about Fitz. That's why I'm here, and I'm not leaving until we do."

Anger hardened her expression. "His name should not be in your mouth. Ever." With a shake of her head, she cut across the grass to return to the church without coming close to Gannon. "Just go back to LA."

As she went in, others exited, eyeing him with interest. Before he drew a crowd, he retreated to the car.

Tim steered out of the lot's back entrance, loose asphalt snapping under the tires. "Who's Fitz?"

Gannon sighed. "Before your time."

ADELINE MADE a beeline for the office.

Gannon hadn't left. He wasn't going to.

She pushed the office door shut behind her, but someone caught it. He wouldn't have followed her back inside, would he?

She'd make quite a scene if she locked him in the hall, and prying eyes and rumors would only make everything worse.

She pressed a hand over her pounding heart and stepped away from the door, allowing the other person entrance.

"Are you okay?" A crease marked the space between Tegan's eyebrows as she slipped into the office and finished closing the door. "Who was that?"

Adeline shook her head and clenched her teeth to stop from crying. At least he had given up for the morning.

"There's a rumor it's Gannon Vaughn." Tegan pulled out the

chair behind the desk and motioned for Adeline to sit. "People saw him with you on Main Street last weekend."

Gannon Vaughn. First and last name. The way people referred to him when they knew him as a celebrity.

Usually, any emotional talks with her roommate involved Tegan opening up and Adeline listening and offering advice. She wasn't ready to reverse that. "He's a guy I went to high school with."

"How in the world is this the first I've heard of this?"

Adeline cringed at the tone of offense in her friend's voice. "I'm sorry."

Tegan's expression softened. She leaned against the desk, studying her in the dim light from the window. "If you tell me where he is, I'll go beat him up for you."

Adeline laughed and blotted her cheeks with a tissue from the desk.

"Seriously. Who does he think he is, parading around, upsetting you? What did he want? I mean, high school was how many years ago?"

"I saw him a couple of times after graduation too." Understatement of the decade.

"I take it he's a jerk in real life?"

She tossed the tissue, grabbed a new one, and shook her head. Where would she even start the story about Fitz and Gannon? She'd tossed out a detail to Asher last weekend because she'd known he wouldn't press for more—he might not have even realized Gannon's identity—but as her closest friend, Tegan had a right to answers. "It's a long story."

"One you're not ready to tell." Tegan waited, but Adeline didn't disagree. "Okay. Well, anytime you want to talk, you know where to find me."

She did, but at the idea of sharing the details, panic pounded as it had on the lawn just now.

Once Tegan left her, Adeline laid her head on her desk and

focused on breathing. She'd been doing okay these last few years. Sure, the situation with the neighborhood association was a setback, but until Gannon had come, it'd been a long, long time since guilt had flooded her like water rushing into a sinking ship.

She could get back there, couldn't she? To a comfortable numbness? Working for the church often soothed the pain, even if it hardly covered her bills.

She forced herself upright and opened the church's email to take her mind off Gannon. A message from one of the committee chairs asked her to update an event on the calendar. Afterward, she moved on to typing up notes from a task force meeting. Halfway through that, the office door opened again.

"Adeline?" Pastor Drew was a tenor like Gannon but without the captivating grit or resonance.

Why did Gannon have to have such a fantastic voice?

The thought poked a hole in the hull of her composure. She slapped on what she hoped was a passably cheerful expression.

Drew's smile, dimples and all, answered. His side-parted blond hair was conventional enough to suit his role as pastor, but with boyish flare. When they'd hired him two years ago at the age of twenty-eight, there'd been an increase in single women at services. Someday, a bigger church would take notice of his talent and coax him out of small-town living. How many of those women would keep attending when an old, stooped pastor like their last one replaced him?

But romance wasn't for Adeline. She'd been on staff as the secretary before they'd hired Drew, and she'd stay years and years after.

A hint of disapproval tinged Drew's expression. "Not working on a Sunday, I hope."

"I was supposed to have these notes done before the service. It's for the music committee."

Amusement softened his expression. "Which you volunteered for because ..."

"I've always loved music." Her voice threatened to catch. Music committee was as close as she'd let herself get to playing again. Because of Fitz. Because of Gannon. And here came the tears again. Good thing Drew hadn't flicked on the light. "Besides—"

"You like to stay busy." Drew chuckled as he completed the line she used every time she took on yet another unpaid responsibility. He leaned his shoulder into the doorframe. "Since that's how you feel, I'm taking the high schoolers hiking along the lakefront this afternoon and need a female chaperone along. Small group, four or five kids. We're meeting at two in the lot." He lifted his eyebrows, hopeful.

"I never get tired of the lake." She threw in another smile for good measure. The hike ought to be a good distraction, and the lake always reminded her of how small she and her problems were.

Drew retreated into the hall. "Leave the office work for another day, okay?"

"Okay." She pulled her hand back from the mouse. She'd have to linger long enough to shut the computer down again. Hopefully by then the others would leave, allowing an escape free of more questions. But what if, when she made it to the lake, her problems looked as big as they felt right now? She might not even be able to see the water around all the turmoil Gannon had churned up.

4

*B*ruce would be a hit with the kids, hopefully halving any attention they might pay Adeline on the hike. The dog strolled beside Adeline to the church, rarely getting to the end of his leash until they stepped into the parking lot. There, he hopped and wiggled at the sight of Drew surrounded by over a dozen teens.

Hadn't he said to expect four or five? Why—

"Addie!" The cry rose from Olivia Cullen.

Bruce's tail rapped against her leg as a trio of girls charged forward.

Olivia gripped her forearm. "You know Gannon Vaughn? How could you keep that a secret?"

Sophie came up so fast, she bumped into Olivia. "How long have you known him?"

Amy, who hadn't run, arrived last. "Is one of his songs about you?"

The inundation of questions fed panic in her chest, and her eyes stung with tears. They were supposed to care more about Bruce than about her, and here they were ignoring the dog while they treated her like a celebrity.

And because of what? A relationship with Gannon she never should've had.

A whistle cut the commotion.

"Load up." Drew's tone struck such a commanding note that the girls trickled from her like a receding wave. He took up station at the van's side doors. "Squeeze in. Every seat's going to be full, so get comfy." Once the kids were in, he shut the door and joined Adeline away from the van.

She released the lip she'd been biting. "You said four or five students."

"You never said you knew a rock star." His eyebrows tented with both concern and apologies.

"I don't." Gannon hadn't been a star when they'd known each other, and life would be so much different—so much better—if Awestruck had never caught anyone's attention in the music industry. For one thing, Fitz would still be alive.

Drew's touch warmed her elbow. "Are you okay?"

She opened her mouth, but lie? To her pastor?

"Why don't you sit this one out?"

"All those girls."

One hand still on her arm, he freed his phone from his pocket. "Those girls wouldn't give you a moment of peace, and from where I'm standing, that's the greatest need. I'll call Tegan."

"And if she can't?" A silly question, since Tegan had been lounging around the house when Adeline left, perhaps exactly what Adeline should have been doing. But she'd made such a mess of her life, of Fitz's, that she needed to do good where she could.

Drew lifted the phone to his ear. A short conversation later, he put the device away again. "All set. She's meeting us at the trailhead. Go on and take care of yourself, okay?"

She nodded, averting her face from the van, where undoubtedly all those pairs of eyes were watching her. Weak.

She was weak for being so thrown by Gannon's appearance. And angry. What gave him the right to come in and upset her life like this?

Drew gave her a quick side hug. At the scent of his cologne, she realized they'd never touched before that day, let alone hugged. As a single, attractive pastor, getting close to the females in the congregation could start rumors. His choice to risk such a thing now meant she looked pitiful.

She gulped back another splash of guilt as Drew climbed into the driver's seat. He started the engine and, with a wave, drove a wide circle around her to the exit.

IF GANNON DIDN'T TAKE care of his voice and his body at a time like this, stress would leave him hoarse and useless.

Been there, done that.

Holding the phone in place with his shoulder, he picked an herbal tea and dropped it in his grocery basket. The light box bounced off the honey and settled next to the eggs.

He headed for the checkout counters, keeping the brim of his hat pointed toward the ground. He'd driven half an hour to this grocery store in hopes that people wouldn't be looking for him here.

"I don't understand why you don't do more to curb his behavior." His mom's voice through the phone sounded small, but she'd been going on about Awestruck's bassist long enough to convey how much the bad press was getting to her. "What Matt does reflects on you. On your message."

"I know." But Awestruck wasn't a Christian band. Though he, John, and Matt had started out claiming the same faith, Matt had given his up years ago. The Christianity card wouldn't stop his partying.

"You should fire him." Her clipped words brought back the

way she'd scolded him in high school when he'd snuck out for a gig while he was grounded. "He couldn't afford this lifestyle if Awestruck weren't funding it."

"He gets paid for being part of the band, like John and I do. And like me and John, he gets to decide how to live as long as he keeps up his part for Awestruck."

"And does he?"

Not as well as he should. Matt tended to miss interviews and rehearsals, but at least he arrived in good enough condition to play shows. "If he ends up broke, he'll be in even more trouble. Lack of funds won't stop an addict. This way, we can keep an eye on him."

"Doing things for him you wouldn't do for others, making allowances that make it easier for him to continue his addictions—that's called enabling."

"Was it enabling when we convinced him to go to rehab?"

"The trip to the ER did that, and a year later, he's back in the tabloids. It sounds like it's not just alcohol anymore."

It'd never been *just* alcohol. Matt's life was a blur of women, drugs, fast cars, and bar fights. But firing him wouldn't cure his addictions and turn him back into the active and fearless guy he'd been when they'd first moved to LA.

More likely, firing him would do what it'd done to Fitz—lead to his ruin.

Regret stirred in Gannon's chest. He couldn't have any more blood on his hands. "Do us both a favor, Mom, and stop reading the tabloids. They always make it out to be worse than it is."

Although, in this case, only marginally.

"I don't have to read anything. As soon as anyone hears anything about you, they ask me what I know. Like every time they see something about you and Harper."

"Nothing. Happened."

"That doesn't stop everyone from asking."

Gannon didn't have to ask who these curious people were. His dad had left back before Gannon had been born. Young, scared, and alone, Mom had turned to the church. They'd helped her practically and emotionally through her pregnancy and eventually led her to Christ.

He owed that community everything. His faith. The fact that he and Mom had a support system during his childhood. Even now, most of Mom's social circle involved people from church, and as his first fans, they were uniquely invested in him and his career.

Gannon neared the self-checkouts and slowed to scan the headlines. They featured little besides the latest royal baby and an ongoing celebrity divorce. People back in Fox Valley must be watching carefully to dig up a story about a partying rock star.

"I'll talk to Matt again, but I can't control him."

"I'll be praying."

"Thanks, Mom. Like I said, you're welcome to come up for a weekend." Hopefully, if she took him up on it, she wouldn't spend the whole time after him about Matt.

After they ended the call, Gannon scanned the tabloids one more time.

Did Adeline watch the same headlines as the people back home? If so, she had to be as leery as Mom about Matt and Harper. Or more so.

As if she hadn't had enough reasons to push him away.

As ADELINE REACHED for the TV remote, footsteps and voices wafted through the front door. She pulled her hand back into her lap. One voice was female, the other male. Other than that, she couldn't pinpoint their owners.

She slid her dinner, a steaming plate of homemade chicken pot pie, onto the coffee table and started for the door. Halfway there, she remembered her outfit. Athletic shorts and a T-shirt that had worn through in two spots on the shoulder.

She wouldn't mind friends seeing her like this, but Gannon had already shown up at both of her jobs. Surely it wasn't that much of a stretch that he'd try here next.

Bruce nosed the doorknob and peered back at her as if to ask what was holding her up.

What, indeed.

If the visitor was Gannon, did her appearance matter?

Even her most pulled-together outfit wouldn't impress him. He had everything and more, including a famous girlfriend. And she didn't want to impress him so much as show him she was living a life she'd prefer he not interrupt. Maybe these clothes did that as well as any.

But when she pulled open the door, she found Drew, his hair windblown from the hike. He bounced on his feet, attention on the boards of the porch while Tegan watched. He was testing the structure's integrity.

Adeline cringed and pushed her shoulder into the storm door, opening it.

Drew's gaze sprung upward, guilty. "Tegan told me about the letter."

Of course she had.

Adeline reached back inside for a leash and brought Bruce onto the porch with her. "I haven't gotten quotes yet, but we'll figure it out."

"Did you see the corner under that column?" Tegan motioned Drew toward the worst-looking part of the porch.

He took the three stairs down to the yard and crossed to the corner of the structure. "Sure enough."

Adeline drew an even breath, hoping to exude calm confidence. "I tried painting it last year to keep water and bugs from doing any more damage, but I guess that was a lost cause."

He braced a hand on the floorboards while he stuck his

head under the deck. "Hate to say it, but you need a new porch."

"You should see what the basement walls are doing, *and* the roof leaks." Tegan leaned on the railing. "The water seeps into the spare bedroom, and of course, there's the siding."

Adeline stepped up to the railing. She couldn't dispute Tegan's list of necessary repairs, but since when had her roommate tallied it all up? And why was she talking with Drew about this? "Unless there's a raise somewhere in this conversation, we don't need to get into it."

"I know." Drew took and released a deep breath. "I'm right there with you." On his way back toward the door, he turned and lifted his arms as if to embrace the lake. "At least you've got a great view."

The whole reason she'd invested in this fixer-upper. Pink laced the clouds over the lake, and the water answered with rosy highlights—serenity patiently waiting for her to lift her focus from her problems.

"How'd the hike go?"

Tegan laughed. "Fine, if you don't count all the pouting when I showed up at the trail and not you."

Drew chuckled. He petted Bruce as he rejoined them on the rotting porch, then shot Tegan a glance as he straightened. "I heard had an exchange outside church this morning. You seemed upset when I found you in the office. Then you looked like a deer in the headlights as the girls charged you."

She felt for pockets to hide her hands, but the athletic shorts had none. Did she look like a deer in the headlights now too? She cast a desperate look toward the lake. Still there. Calm and still. The clouds might be even brighter than before. "Thanks for having the sense to ask me to sit it out."

"Doesn't seem to have cured you."

She'd made pot pie, the ultimate comfort food, to help with

that. As if eating could erase the past any more than a beautiful lake could give a person peace.

He glanced at Tegan again. "You've never talked about him, but given the little I've seen, there's hard history between you."

Drew and Tegan must've planned this conversation together. Adeline pressed her lips shut and willed the tears not to rise.

Drew gave an apologetic smile, as if her struggle to maintain composure were completely evident.

Tegan neared, head tilted with sympathy. "We're here for you. It doesn't matter to us who he is."

Drew grinned. "Even a herd of high school girls couldn't drag a detail from me—if you choose to share anything, that is."

She hadn't shared anything as deeply personal as her history with Gannon since ... well since her history with Gannon.

Her secrets weighed on her, but she'd fought back by staying busy with good causes. If only busy were lonely's opposite, the distraction might've worked forever. But since Gannon had shown up, none of her old coping mechanisms were doing the trick anymore.

Maybe the time had come to implement a new strategy.

ADELINE FINISHED the last of her water and set the cup on the arm of her Adirondack chair. She, Tegan, and Drew had settled in the most solid corner of the porch, where they could look out at the lake and enjoy the summer evening. Bruce lounged nearby.

When they'd gone in for pot pie, the conversation had skipped from Gannon to home-cooked meals and had strayed from there. But as Drew finished the last gravy-coated piece of chicken and leaned back into his chair, he and Tegan exchanged another loaded glance.

Tegan interlaced her fingers and peered pointedly at Adeline.

She regretted every bite of food for the way her stomach clenched, but these two wouldn't let her stay silent forever. She started easy. "In middle school, when I had to pick an instrument, I elected upright bass."

Drew laughed. "I can just imagine."

"It looked as goofy as you're thinking." Her mom had pictures of her, maybe ninety pounds, lugging the instrument around. "I loved it. About halfway through our senior year of high school, the guy I was seeing, Fitz, joined a rock band with Gannon and John. Fitz asked me to play electric bass with them until he or Gannon could learn. They both caught on, but they preferred guitar, and I played well, so they kept me around."

Tegan, who sat on the porch and leaned on the railing, pushed her long hair back. "That's how Awestruck started?"

She lifted a heavy shoulder. The Awestruck the world knew wasn't the same one she'd been a part of. "We got some gigs, but no record deal. When we graduated high school, the guys decided to move to LA to try to make it, but my parents wouldn't hear of me canceling my college plans and going along."

"Can't say I blame them." Drew tapped the heel of his hiking boot on the porch.

"Gannon, Fitz, and John recruited another bass player. Matt replaced me. It was kind of last minute, but Matt jumped at the chance."

"So they went to LA and made it big without you." Tegan spoke wistfully, as if this fairytale would have a happy ending.

"It wasn't that simple. Before they left, Fitz, who had been my boyfriend for eight months, proposed. I said yes, and the next day, the guys got in their clunker of a van and set off."

Tegan slapped the porch. "You were engaged?"

"For a while." If the engagement was a revelation, other facts would be a shock. If not for Drew's calm demeanor, she might've tried to get out of sharing more. "They got day jobs in LA. Nothing fancy, just enough to cover rent. They couldn't afford trips home, but I talked with Fitz on the phone a lot. He was always full of promises of how things would be when they made it, always sure the dream was just another show or two away."

His hope hadn't been convincing, so when his tone dampened, she didn't do much to rekindle his faltering dreams. To her shame. "We grew apart, but I wasn't interested in anyone else and he was so down already. I didn't want to pile on by breaking it off. Gannon came home for Christmas about a year and a half after they'd left. He seemed optimistic, but ..." She shrugged, an ache in her throat. Did she have to get into this part of the story? Was this the time and place for confession?

No. Her story was shocking enough without getting into the part only she, Gannon, and Fitz knew. Oh, and God. Her vision blurred to gray, and she skipped ahead.

"A few months later, Awestruck was offered a deal on one condition: Fitz had to go. He'd gotten mono and had been struggling through shows. Though he was an excellent musician, he must've seemed like a weak link. Or something. I don't know."

Drew rubbed his thumb over his fingernail, something she'd seen him do while studying for sermons. "They went along with it?"

"The three founding members of the band had equal voting power. John wanted to wait for an offer that included all of them, so he and Fitz could've overruled Gannon, no matter how Matt, who had less say, voted. But it didn't come to a vote. Fitz took Gannon and the label trying to get rid of him hard, so he quit and came home. The others signed the deal."

"What happened with Fitz?"

"He broke it off with me. He had his reasons, plus he was seriously depressed—a lot more so than I realized at the time—and nothing I said or did ..." She stopped. She wouldn't paint herself to be a hero when she wasn't one. She was guilty. So guilty. "When Awestruck's first album came out, it was more than he could handle."

Drew leaned forward, elbows on his knees, while Tegan's eyes widened.

"He killed himself." And the only way she'd come to terms with his death and with her role in his downward spiral had been to build a whole new life where she didn't have to talk about the tragedy.

Drew's sigh washed into the air like a wave. "I'm sorry."

"Oh, Addie." Tegan climbed to her feet. Her shoulder bumped Adeline's chin as she awkwardly wrapped her arms around her.

Adeline couldn't relax into it. Couldn't feel comfort. She patted her friend's back and started to lean away, but Tegan gave her another squeeze before releasing her.

Drew fidgeted. "Why is Gannon here, after all this time?"

"I don't know." She picked at a snagged thread in her shorts. "Maybe fame isn't all it's cracked up to be. Maybe it's not an inoculation against regret."

"I'm sure it's not," he said.

Time and moving and acts of service had also proved ineffective. She blinked at her tears and lifted her focus once more to the lake.

The sun had set, and twilight blurred the line between the water and the sky. Having the lake almost always in sight was the one comfort she'd allowed herself, the one thing she clung to while everything else rotted.

But could she afford to keep this view? Did she deserve to?

Tegan tapped Adeline's foot with her toe. "His suicide is not your fault, Addie."

Her friend wouldn't say that if she knew the whole story.

The porch creaked as Drew shifted. "Maybe you should talk to Gannon. What he did to Fitz was awful, but Fitz died of a tragic choice that Gannon could never have anticipated. Neither of you should have to carry that weight. If he's here looking for forgiveness, this might be a chance for you to give it —both to him and yourself. God doesn't want us to spend years buried under guilt. Jesus came to set us free from condemnation."

The sympathy in his voice fed her tears. She busied herself with gathering the dishes. Her movement roused Bruce, and when she took the plates in, she brought him along. When she returned to the porch alone, Drew and Tegan stopped whatever they'd been quietly discussing. Tegan gave her another hug.

Drew patted her arm. "I hope I didn't say too much. I hate to see you hurting. And to think you've been carrying this for ..."

"Fitz died eight years ago." But she'd been carrying guilt much longer. The night that had changed everything, the one she'd skipped in her retelling, had been over a year before that. She'd been drowning in guilt ever since. For nine years.

"That's too long." He rested his hand on her shoulder for a moment.

Avoiding his eyes seemed like the easiest way to hide her doubts.

Had Jesus forgiven her? Maybe, but He shouldn't have.

Drew stepped back. "Thanks for letting us listen. I will be praying for you."

She nodded again, and he showed himself down the steps and away.

Back inside, Tegan finished the dishes while Adeline stopped at the dining table. She still hadn't decided what to do with the slip of paper with Gannon's number, so it sat under the letter from the neighborhood association.

She flipped the card between her fingers. Gannon's handwriting hadn't changed much since he'd scrawled lyrics in that red notebook of his in high school. Was this the handwriting of a killer? And how much responsibility did she deserve for Fitz's death?

Drew and Tegan had deemed her innocent because they didn't know the parts of the story she'd cut out, but since she'd skipped over them, those terrible details burned in her throat more intensely than ever before. If she gave voice to them, the sensation might stop. Or maybe this searing pain would only spread.

5

$\mathcal{T}$he air seemed as bent on freezing Gannon out of Wisconsin as Adeline was. When he took his guitar to the patio on Monday morning, the nip sent him back in for a sweatshirt—the only one he'd brought, since he hadn't realized July would be so cold. Farther south in the state, the weather wasn't like this. Either the lake contributed or being a couple of hours farther north made that big of a difference.

He reviewed the last set of lyrics he'd been working on. Yet another song about Adeline. The first in his collection of songs about her dated back to her time with the band over a decade ago. Some of them were his best work, but he'd never shared them because he could never muster the courage to ask Adeline if she'd mind.

He'd lacked the courage to face her at all.

He sighed and let his gaze wander the yard. A trail of broad, flat stones led from the patio by the house where he sat, through the lush lawn, to a second seating area along the cliff. A three-foot-tall stone wall separated the observation area from a one-hundred-foot drop to the lake. An island designated as a state park formed a green mass out in the water. Between there and the cliff, a sightseeing ship navigated away from its Lakeshore dock toward the lighthouse on the island.

From this distance, the tourists on the viewing decks were nothing more than dots of color.

The peace and inspiration he'd come for seemed equally far off, but pressure was mounting to write something worth recording. Even now, Tim was inside, arranging security for the grounds and a crew to set up a recording studio in one of Havenridge's offices. A recording studio Gannon currently had no use for.

He set aside his notes for the latest Adeline song and pulled his guitar closer. Maybe lyrics unrelated to her would come if he started with music.

He hadn't gotten far when his phone rang.

John was up and making phone calls this early on a Monday? That couldn't be good.

He answered on speaker. "What happened now?"

"How's the trip?"

"Just sat down to work."

"Huh." John fell silent a few beats. "How's Addie?"

Ah. John had always had his quiet way of looking out for her. When the drummer had returned from a visit home over the holidays, he'd mentioned running into her. "You should go see her," he'd said. "Button up the past. She could use that."

They'd been interrupted, and when Gannon brought her up again later, John had brushed him off saying, "She's okay. Getting by."

That Adeline might only be "okay" and "getting by" had gnawed at Gannon.

Until then, he'd told himself she was better off without him. Once he'd started worrying about her and the impact he'd had on her, his songs had dried up. He couldn't write about anything but her, which meant he had little for Awestruck's next album.

He'd prayed and prayed for other inspiration, but the only answer he could discern was that if he wanted peace and usable music, he needed to face Adeline.

So here he was, but what he'd seen since arriving hadn't comforted him. Adeline had let go of her dreams, and she clung to anger like a lifeline.

Gannon plucked a melody on the strings.

"So?" John prompted. "How's she doing?"

"She's angry."

"You blame her?"

"No."

"No?"

Gannon sighed.

John talked like he drummed; he drove at the beat relentlessly, but he left the words for someone else to fill in.

"I accept that I'm responsible for my actions, and I was wrong, but I didn't act alone. She's acting like I did, blaming me for everything."

"That's the trouble with you front men."

Despite years of decoding John's cryptic statements, Gannon didn't follow, so he waited.

"You think it's all about you. Adeline Green had dreams as big as ours, and she hasn't moved on any of them. She's barely scraping by, and it's not because she's mad at you."

"You think she's punishing herself?"

"It'd be great if she'd stop."

"Only God can change that."

"Well, you're all the way up there."

So he might as well try. "We've already fought in public twice."

"You have her number."

Because John, not Adeline, had given it to him. Calling when she would immediately hang up would solve nothing. "She can reach me too. I left Tim's number."

"How romantic."

"Who said anything about romance? This is about survival. I think you're right. She needs something, but if she won't speak to me, I can't help her, and I can't help Awestruck."

"Songwriting's still stuck, then."

"More or less." Gannon strummed his pick across the strings, then let his hand rest.

John's voice brightened. "Me and Matt should come up."

"You, sure, but Matt wouldn't help anything."

"He could use healthy ways to occupy himself." The false luster wore off his tone.

"Why?"

"He hauled off and punched a guy at a club. Avoiding charges cost a pretty penny."

Gannon rubbed the heel of his palm against his temple. If John knew, Tim did too, but he had said nothing. The guy really didn't want Gannon distracted. With that mindset, would Tim put Adeline through to Gannon if she called?

He went back to the melody he'd been circling. Matt's problem wasn't just having too much free time. The natural fearlessness that enabled him to try his hand at sports like rock climbing, surfing, BMX, and snowboarding seemed to have led to one risk too many, and now he was in too deep with all the wrong entertainments. "I'm not sure band commitments will straighten him out."

"Some accountability might. There are consequences for our choices, but everyone around us acts like there aren't. We've got to do each other the favor of speaking up when no one else will."

Matt was an expert at turning a deaf ear to their advice, but they could try. Besides, Awestruck had a couple of shows over the summer. It'd been months since the end of their last tour, and extra rehearsal time wouldn't hurt.

Gannon reached for his pencil, jotted down the first words in what might turn into a song about addiction. Maybe Matt could still benefit Awestruck after all. "All right. There weren't many private, gated rentals, so the one I got is huge. There's plenty of room for you guys."

"See you soon, then. Tell Addie I said hi."

Gannon hesitated.

"I'm looking forward to seeing what you've got for us." John disconnected.

That last part might as well have been a threat. John and Matt would expect more than old music and one song about Matt to work on. He needed to talk with Adeline again. The sooner, the better—and without an audience this time.

"Lakeshore Victory Church. This is Adeline." She cradled the phone with her shoulder, typed the last word in an email, and hit send.

No one answered her greeting.

"Hello?"

Drew appeared in the office door and crossed his arms.

"Hello?" Since no response came, she hung up and focused on the pastor. "What can I do for you?"

"I've been thinking about your problem."

She touched her throat, which still burned with unspoken truth. She needed to tell someone the whole story. Tegan would be a more appropriate audience than Drew, but what would her roommate think when she found out Adeline wasn't who she'd seemed all this time?

"We'd like to help you with the porch and the leak you mentioned."

Oh. That problem. "We?"

"The church. I called Chip this morning, and he swung by to take a look. He thinks a crew—volunteers from church—could get the old porch out in a weekend. The new porch would go in on weeknights or the following weekend. The whole thing would be totally free to you."

"I ..." She shook her head. "I can't ask them to do that. It's too much."

A click sounded like the main door. Someone must be early for the Monday afternoon Bible study.

Drew continued like he hadn't heard that or Adeline's refusal. "He climbed up on the roof. He said the shingles aren't too bad. He caulked a few places. If that doesn't stop the leak, let him know."

"Chip was on my roof?"

Drew grinned. "So you see, there's no way to stop us. The porch isn't behind locked doors either."

"But there are so many people who could use help with house projects. I'm employed and—"

"Don't tell me you could do the work yourself."

"I don't deserve this." In so many ways. "I'm healthy. I'm young."

"And you thought paint would fix rotting wood." He laughed. "You've done so much for everyone, and we want to help. Let us." He stepped backward into the hall, getting ready to leave.

"I really can't." At least they weren't also offering to paint too, but the porch was still too massive a favor to accept. "I think I have a way to cover the cost. Please don't go ahead with the work."

Something caught his eye—maybe Rosanne was approaching to make photocopies for the Bible study. He frowned at Adeline as if he wanted to continue the conversation but wouldn't with a witness. "Remember what we talked about."

"What we talked about?"

Drew gave Rosanne an odd, curt nod and turned for his own office without asking the longtime member how she was doing.

But it wasn't Rosanne.

Gannon, with broad shoulders, intense eyes, and each moment of their complex history, appeared in the doorway.

Yesterday, he had had a short beard, but today he was clean-shaven, revealing each of the strong contours that kept landing him on magazine covers. No wonder the press ate up anything he did.

His T-shirt left most of his arms exposed, and as he shut the door behind himself, she glimpsed the word *honor* on his triceps, woven into the mane of the roaring lion. Actually, she could see only the last three letters, but compliments of a magazine cover, she knew the rest.

He pulled the spare chair up to her desk. As he sat, he plunked a black motorcycle helmet beside her keyboard. He must not have worn it long because it hadn't flattened his hair, which fell across his forehead, unruly and begging for her fingers.

Her burning throat flared hotter at the thought.

He watched as if she'd summoned him and he wanted to know why. Had he somehow sensed her longing to confess the past? He'd been there. Talking to him should be easier than revealing her secrets to others. But confiding in Gannon, whom she never should've been close to, would deepen her betrayal of Fitz.

"No bodyguard today?" she asked.

"Tim's our manager, not a bodyguard. I don't have security up here yet, but he's bringing some on."

She was close enough to see the gold at the center of his irises and the blue-green surrounding it. In the old days, he'd always seemed to have a special reserve of attention for her.

Even now, the intensity of his focus on her belied his casual posture. "Once the guys get here, security will be more necessary."

"John's coming?"

"And Matt. But John will want to see you. He asked how you are."

"I'm good." She wiped dust from her keyboard with her fingertip. Gaze-avoidance didn't reinforce her words, though. She met his hazel eyes again.

"Why don't you play with the worship team?"

"I help with the kids during the service." Not every week, but often enough.

He nodded slowly. "You used to love playing."

"I haven't touched a bass in years. Not to play it, anyway."

Now, he was the one to look away. He seemed to take inventory of the file cabinets, the photocopier, the shelves of colored paper they used for bulletins. "This isn't where I expected to find you."

"You're here for another reason?"

"No, I knew you were here today. I called to make sure of it." He leaned forward, placing his forearm on the corner of her desk. "What I mean is, I didn't expect your life to turn out like this."

What right did he have to judge? To think her less-than? "What do you know about my life?"

"I know you're not using your degree. You're working two jobs and barely getting by. You quit music, even though you loved it."

He left so much out, all the good she did for this church and this community. How much Drew and Asher depended on her. The magnificent view she had from her own front porch.

The rotting porch that others offered to fix because she was a charity case.

The unsteadiness of emotion seeped into her chest. "You don't know me."

"But you think you know me."

She *did* know him. Why did she always bite when she saw something about him in the tabloids? And if an entertainment show mentioned him, why could she never change the channel? She couldn't get enough news of him, even though everything she heard and read and saw left her lungs stinging with anger. He joked around on *Audition Room*, obviously enjoying his life while dating beautiful women and probably behaving with them the same as he had with her.

The only thing she'd managed to resist was Awestruck's music. His voice struck her too deep.

"I know you much better than I'd like to."

He nodded, mouth tight. "I'll give you that. What happened when I came home that year never should've—"

"That's not what I mean." She spoke quickly, though doing so added gas to the fire blazing in her throat. "I mean, that too, but I'm sick of seeing you in magazines all the time. All the interviews and the awards and the TV show."

He hung his head and pushed what looked like tense fingers into his hair. When he sat back again, he leveled his gaze on her. "I'm sorry. I'm sorry about that night, and I'm sorry that in my guilt, I fired Fitz instead of facing him. God and I dealt with my sin a long time ago, and I told myself that was enough, but it wasn't because my actions involved you too. I never acknowledged that because God ... I knew He'd forgive, but you, after Fitz died ..."

"You thought God would absolve you free and clear."

He cleared his throat and studied his hands. "He did. Jesus Christ died so that God can forgive us when we repent. Free and clear."

If we confess our sins, He's faithful and just to forgive.

But what about the sins that were too bad to put into words? "So, just like that"—she snapped her fingers—"everything's good again." Her voice came out rough, as if she'd inhaled smoke.

He lifted his face. "I'm still a sinner. But I'm forgiven. And, Adeline ..."

He believed he was forgiven.

It wasn't fair.

Her eyes were hot, and she caught herself holding her breath to keep from adding air to her smoldering throat.

When he didn't continue, she met his gaze.

"All you have to do is ask, and you're forgiven too. Without doing anything. So if that's what all this is." He circled his hand, indicating the office or maybe the city. The life. "If you're trapped in some effort at doing penance, you're wasting your time and your potential. It's not what God wants for you, and it's not what Fitz would've wanted."

A tear fell, and she hated that show of weakness. Hated how much she wished he was right, how transparent her motives were to him. But there was no way Fitz, let alone God, wished her well. "How would you know?"

"About Fitz? Maybe I wouldn't. But you can't say what he was thinking or would've wanted either. He rarely gave hints about how deeply he struggled. I didn't connect the dots until after he died, but he dealt with depression the entire time we knew him, and I don't think the time he succeeded was his first attempt."

Her hands fell limp to her lap. "What?"

"He crashed his car once in California, and his explanation ..." Gannon winced and shook his head.

Adeline remembered that, how he'd strangely waited a day to tell her. He'd claimed he hadn't wanted to worry her. "He said the turn was sharper than he expected."

"He drove that road all the time." Gannon watched her, what he wasn't saying as loud as any words. "I saw his sister once a few years ago and learned he never had mono either. He disappeared on us because he'd been hospitalized on suicide watch."

Her blood ran cold. "No."

It didn't make sense. They'd known then that a label was interested in signing them. Fitz should've been as ecstatic as he'd sounded. She'd never for a moment doubted that illness had kept him from the stage at such a pivotal time.

And it had been an illness.

Just not the one she'd thought.

"He put on an act with all of us. Lied to all of us." Gannon's words washed over her like melancholy waves on a calm, cloudy day. One sentence after the other, slowly he carried her old beliefs about Fitz out to sea. "He was especially careful with you. While he was alive, I thought the way he brightened up around you was his way of keeping you from worrying about things like his grades or the band's prospects. Looking back, he was hiding his mental state most of all. I think he knew you'd read more into his behavior than we thought to."

Because she should've known. Should've helped. Her back ached with the effort of keeping herself from doubling over right there in her chair.

Gannon continued, and she listened, though she couldn't imagine how anything he had to say would alleviate the pain. The remorse. "What we did—especially what I did—piled on more wounds, but in the end, his choice wasn't based on one or two experiences, as awful as those were. He lost a war that had been raging for years."

"And that's how you justify going on to live your life. That he was depressed. That he had it coming." Two fat tears dropped, one to each cheek. She swiped them away.

His voice gained a gravelly edge. "That's not what I said or what I meant." He folded his arms, muscles tense. "This is how you've been coping all these years, isn't it? Penance and blame. Vilifying me and denying your own dreams to feel good about yourself."

She didn't feel good, though. Sometimes, when she volunteered for the umpteenth committee or cared for a rescue animal, the pain stopped. But good? No. Because Fitz was dead, and she could never have what she most wanted: a do-over so she could break up with Fitz when they grew apart. That way, she wouldn't have gotten between Gannon and Fitz. Gannon wouldn't have fired him. Maybe she would've ended up with Gannon or maybe she would've lost touch with both men that way, but at least Fitz would be alive and thriving with Awestruck.

He would be alive, right? Thriving? Eventually, someone would've learned his secrets and stepped in to help.

Maybe.

But those chances were dead and gone.

So maybe she had vilified Gannon. She was as guilty as he was, but going easy on him was one step toward letting her old feelings come back, and what good would that do? Their past was tainted beyond repair with sins she couldn't bring herself to confess.

She shook her head and stood. Since he'd plunked his chair in the walkway, blocking her exit, she turned her back on him and set her jaw as she waited for him to go.

A rustle signaled him rising, then he sighed, close in the small space behind the desk.

If she took a step backward, she'd run into him.

Gannon Vaughn, the man she'd thought so much about for so many years, was finally close, but they could never bridge the gap.

"You sought me out that night, not the other way around." His voice rolled with tightly controlled anger, but that faded as he continued. "I shouldn't have responded the way I did. For your sake, for Fitz's, for my own. But it was you, and I was nineteen, and I had liked you for years."

Guilt squelched the thrill his admission gave her. If only his voice weren't his strongest feature and she weren't so close to bawling, she'd stop him there. Or maybe she wouldn't. If she let him say this out loud, would the burning in her own throat stop?

Until the night he was talking about, she'd had nothing to feel bad about. She and Gannon had gotten to be good friends through Awestruck. Sure, she'd felt occasional moments of attraction toward him, but she was with Fitz, and she didn't want to be the kind of girl who'd end a good relationship over a fleeting, one-sided crush. When the band left, she and Gannon had mostly lost touch. Still, when she'd heard he was in town that Christmas, she'd been desperate to see him.

That should've been her warning that what had started as an innocent connection had grown across time and distance, like a ripple amassing into a tsunami.

"We were striking out in California," he continued, "and I wanted to feel good about something. None of that justifies my choices, but when you kissed me after that party and wanted the same things I did—"

"Enough." By now, he'd probably done much worse than sleeping with a bandmate's fiancée. But for her, that night had been the worst mistake of her life. It'd been so wrong, so incongruent with her beliefs. Gannon claimed to be ashamed of his behavior, but if he'd come to talk about it, he didn't know the meaning of the word shame. "We're in a church. The pastor's right down the hall. I won't rehash every detail."

Gannon's frustration was audible in his exhale. "Fine. Just tell me you haven't rewritten all of this, that your version doesn't involve me seducing you or forcing you or asking you to hide it from Fitz."

He hadn't done any of that. About a week after he'd returned to California, Gannon had begged her to tell Fitz because he didn't want to live with the guilt and deceit. She'd refused. Gannon had kept the secret, but then he'd fired Fitz.

At that point, she should've never breathed a word of it to Fitz. But shortly after he'd returned, he'd wanted to elope.

If she'd stayed quiet and married him, would he still be alive? Wouldn't that have been a fair price to pay? Her silent guilt for his life?

Instead, she'd told him what she'd done, and her confession had been part of his undoing.

Confession couldn't wash all sins clean, at least not in this life. Maybe God would still allow her into heaven. She'd be a pauper there, and still she'd have gotten off easy.

She turned and aimed for a quiet tone that couldn't be over-heard outside the office. "The only reason I would talk to you about this would be if it could bring him back."

"What if talking about it brought *you* back?"

Impossible. Nothing could restore the innocence she'd lost. Anyway, she never wanted to go back to being a person who would utterly fail the way she had. "You might not understand being happy in a life like mine, but that doesn't mean there's anything wrong with how I'm living."

Frowning, he pulled a scrap of lined paper from his pocket and held it out to her.

She took the slip. Another phone number. "What's this?"

"My direct number. The other one was Tim's, but if you change your mind about talking to me, I don't want you to have to go through someone else."

"And you trust me with it?"

"Do whatever you want with it. I'll get a new one if you share it." He took his helmet from the desk. "I hope I'll hear from you, but if I don't, I've said my piece. I'm staying in the area, but I'll leave you alone." Without another glance in her direction, he let himself out.

Loss pulled at her like an undercurrent. He'd thrown her out into the deep with all he'd said, then he'd left her to swim against the current alone. And for once, she couldn't blame him.

6

The July sun soaked into Adeline as she stood on her front lawn with a painter. When he'd done some work at the church, he'd done good work on schedule for a reasonable price. If she could afford to hire anyone, he would be the guy.

He made notes on his clipboard, then walked up to one of the windows, squinting at the frame. Bruce must've been watching from inside, because when the painter got close to the glass, the dog started barking. After a surprised jump, the man made another note about whatever had required closer scrutiny.

Her Saturday lunch shift at Superior Dogs started in a couple of minutes, and the longer he inspected and measured for the quote, the more she imagined dollar signs adding up. "Do you have a ballpark number?"

He stopped at the worst corner of the porch, took off his glasses, and looked the column up and down. "Needs more than paint."

"You wouldn't have to paint the deck or railings. They're being replaced." She was getting a quote on that work too, despite Drew and Chip's offer. She hated the thought of inconveniencing friends.

"How about the ceiling?" He motioned up with the clipboard.

No one had mentioned a structural problem with the section of roof over the porch. "I could paint that. Can you quote the job with and without?"

Another note for the clipboard.

"Do you have everything you need from me? I have to get to work."

"Sure, I'll finish up here and get you the quote in a couple of days."

"Okay." She hated the suspense, but the delay would give her time to get the bass appraised. She might be able to do that this afternoon, between the lunch and dinner shifts. Once she had dollar amounts from the music store, the painter, and the carpenter, she could make decisions. Did she have to sell the bass? Did she have to accept the church's help with the porch? She'd rather not do either, and she certainly hoped she wouldn't have to do both.

Even with no special gallery event today, plenty of tourists wandered the streets between her house and the lake. Without taking much notice of the line at the window, Adeline let herself in the trailer. Thanks to the cooking surface, the temperature hovered several degrees warmer inside the trailer than out. Asher stood by the grill, blotting his forehead.

After a glance over the orders Asher had taken so far, she moved to the window. One couple stood about eight feet back, not making eye contact, so theirs was probably the order in process. Closer, a big gray pit bull sat politely. Another pit bull, this one brown-and-black brindle, stood by the customer at the menu who had both dogs' leashes clipped around his waist like belts. Sunglasses shaded his eyes, but a recognizable full sleeve tattoo of a forest covered his right arm.

"John?"

His gaze shifted from the menu, and a grin split his face. He pulled off his sunglasses and hooked them on the neck of his T-shirt. "Hey, Addie. Long time, no see."

"You just got in?"

Before he could answer, a little boy approached the gray dog. The mom snatched him back, but John waved him forward. "Trigger's nice. Camo too."

The kid's hand was tiny on the dog's broad head, and when the brown one moved in with kisses, the boy retreated to his mother, giggling.

After they moved on, John glanced back at the menu. "I'll have a Super Superior and two plain hot dogs, no buns. Cut them up in bowls."

The unusual order brought Asher to the window. "Now those look like a couple of superior dogs."

John chuckled. "Ought to be after living with their trainer for so long."

Her boss stuck his hand out the window. "I'm Asher."

"John."

They shook, no recognition flickering in Asher's face. John kept a much lower profile than Gannon. No TV shows, no actress girlfriends, no solo magazine covers. "Once I get this order up for you, do you mind if we take a picture? We never let our canine friends go without one."

"Absolutely."

Asher went back to the grill, clearly oblivious.

John winked to Adeline. "You were saying?"

"You just got in?"

"Haven't even been to the cabin yet."

So the band was staying in a cabin. It was a wonder the whole city wasn't talking about them. Maybe everyone assumed Gannon had left. She'd find out tomorrow when she faced Olivia and the other teenage girls at church.

She took another customer's order while John lingered by the window. As she handed the other man his change, John asked, "Have you seen much of our boy?"

Our boy? The phrase made Gannon sound like someone who belonged to her in some way, but with their ugly history, Gannon wasn't and could never be hers, nor she his. She shrugged and glanced at Asher and the other customers. "Ran into him a few times."

"Small-town living." John watched the people walking by, but his dogs garnered more attention than he did.

"All right. Here you go." Asher handed over John's Super Superior and two diced hotdogs, each in its own boat. "Still have time for the picture?"

"Yes, sir."

Asher handed Adeline his phone, and they met John and the dogs on the sidewalk. She snapped the picture, and then John gave his phone to Asher.

"Get one of us?" He removed the sunglasses again. "Addie and I go way back."

As Asher took the picture, John tugged her into a side hug that threw off her balance. When Asher showed them the shot, John's arm was around her and she was laughing with her hand braced on his chest and one of her legs flung out for balance.

"That's a keeper." Smirking, John pocketed his phone and put the dogs' hotdogs on the ground. He only got in one bite of his own food before the animals had devoured theirs. "All right. Addie, we'll have you out, okay? Don't be a stranger."

She nodded, but how could she take him up on the offer to visit without seeing Gannon?

He walked off toward the public parking lot, the dogs trotting after him, content to ignore everything but their master even as they drew everyone's attention away from him. How long would that last?

~

MOSTLY OBSCURED BY trees and a bend in the island, the peach color of the closest lighthouse marked the spot where, at night, a beacon slowly pulsed. Another sightseeing boat meandered between there and the cliff, too far out for Gannon to see if anyone lingered on the deck.

There was a song in there somewhere. A distant light. Faceless people. He brought his notebook to the great room, and the pages opened easily to the next blank space, but before he touched pen to paper, the door swished.

He leaned back to see if it was Tim.

When John appeared, Gannon got to his feet. John clapped him in a brief hug, then turned, taking in the room. Doors to bedrooms lined the second-floor balcony. The ceiling with its cedar beams stretched far overhead, and a two-story wall of windows looked out onto the patio and the lake. The dogs, who had followed John in, trotted from one place to another, sniffing.

John's gaze fell on Gannon's notebook. "Working?"

"I haven't gotten very far."

"It's Saturday. Let's enjoy it." John opened one of the patio doors, whistled to get the dogs' attention, and then led the way out. They walked to the overlook and back before settling on lounge chairs in the sun. As the dogs stretched out on the patio rug, John intertwined his fingers over his stomach. "Remind me why we live in LA."

"Because we might as well. LA follows us wherever we go."

"Does it?"

"Yeah. We're here to work. There's never a break with Matt or Harper." He scrubbed his fingers through his hair. Harper had called again this morning. "She's always in trouble but never ready to change."

"So you have noticed that about her."

"Of course I have. But once she hits bottom, maybe she'll be ready."

"To do what?"

"Come to Christ. She's a seeker." Maybe not all the time, but given her abusive father and the agent who took advantage of her when she first came to LA, Gannon couldn't blame her for looking for attention in all the wrong ways. He was out to show her a better path, and for it, she called him her rock. "When God does change her, it'll be a testimony that reaches far and wide."

"She is seeking," John agreed dryly, "but not God."

They'd had this discussion before to the same result, but if anyone understood Gannon's motives with Harper, John ought to.

Despite opposing Gannon's move to fire Fitz, John had stuck by him. Once Fitz died, Gannon broke and confessed the whole story. John had quietly but unwaveringly represented truth, not downplaying the wrong he'd done but talking about forgiveness when Gannon was sure he'd disqualified himself from ever being usable to God. Years later, Gannon was being used—in the lives of fans, who wrote in often enough to tell him so, and in Harper's life.

"I'm trying to be for her what you were to me, a friend who's not easily scared off and is there to point the way when she's ready to listen."

"This isn't the same."

Gannon sighed. At least John had stuck with him through thick and thin. Gannon would pay that forward with Harper, and someday, John would understand. For now, he veered from the subject. "Seeing Adeline again has been something else."

"Yeah." A smile twitched John's mouth as he pulled out his phone. After poking the screen a few times, he passed it to Gannon.

John had managed to get an arm around her and had been rewarded with a gigantic grin.

"Nice." Gannon gave the phone back.

John snorted. "Don't be bitter."

Adeline deserved to be as happy as she'd looked in the picture. What he wouldn't give to the be one who could bring out that smile.

It'd already been days since their talk in the church office, and she hadn't reached out. He'd claimed that day that he'd said his piece, but he hadn't. They had so much more to discuss about grace, the band, the songs he'd written about her and what to do with them. John was right that Matt could use a project to focus on, and given Gannon's trouble writing much else lately, Awestruck needed the songs like never before.

"I gave her my number and told her I would leave her alone unless she reached out."

"And she hasn't."

Which meant he needed to keep his word. This obsession with Adeline needed to stop. He was forgiven, free and clear to continue with his life, even if losing Adeline was a consequence of his sin.

Impossible regret pummeled him. He'd rather have lost a limb than her.

He'd have to draw even closer to God to cope with that.

Focusing on work would help him too.

He stood to get his guitar and paper. He could write about the lighthouse. The distant people.

Inside, the notebook lay open to the blank page, but too much history with Adeline packed the other sheets to do him any favors. He carried the notebook to the kitchen as he hunted for a replacement. The drawer next to the silverware contained a legal pad. He swapped one notebook for the other and pushed the drawer shut again.

Out of sight, out of mind.

7

_T_he dark shape of the bass filled the back half of the spare bedroom closet. Adeline slid away boxes of Christmas decorations and leftovers from discarded hobbies. Pressing winter coats and floor-length dresses back, she gripped the case and lugged the bass out.

In high school, when she'd flexed, the guys had laughed and made squeaky-toy noises before showing off their own biceps. However unimpressive her muscles had been then, they must be worse now. She couldn't imagine carrying this around everywhere the way she once had.

But after today, she'd no longer have to handle this weight.

Grief lapped at her toes.

You used to love playing.

Oh, how right Gannon was.

Between the band and orchestra class, she'd once spent most of her free time on music. Though she no longer played, her ear picked out the bass line in every song she heard.

She could play one last time. What better way to get closure before selling? To say goodbye to an old friend?

As she felt along the seam for the zipper pull, thudding

sounded downstairs. A few moments later, Bruce panted into the room and immediately sprawled onto the carpet.

"Taking it in today?" Tegan dropped into the chair at the desk. Her forehead shone with a layer of perspiration. She and Bruce must've been running.

Adeline retracted her fingers from the zipper. Why did she feel guilty, as if she'd been caught kissing Gannon? Instead of confessing she'd meant to play first, she nodded.

"You know, you and Gannon ..."

Her stomach pulled into a tight knot. Tegan was thinking about them too? She fastened her focus on the bass and waited, hoping against hope for relief.

"Maybe if he's sorry for firing Fitz, he ought to pay for your home repairs. I mean, the money would be nothing to him. It's the least he could do."

As disappointment washed over her, she realized she'd hoped Tegan would say something different. But, given the way Adeline had represented him to her friends, of course Tegan would never say something positive.

The blame she'd cast, on top of everything else, smoldered to be confessed. "I'm not asking him for money."

She'd accept help from the church long before that.

"I figured you'd say that. But you aren't interested in the campus job either, are you?" Tegan had printed off the job description and left it on the table.

Adeline had read the information and left the pages where she'd found them. She already had work.

"Doesn't the idea of helping college grads find their way sound rewarding? The posting has been up for a while now. Maybe God's holding the job for you."

Adeline shook her head. Why was everyone on this kick of telling her that her life didn't measure up?

"I'm not trying to be difficult. I just ... are you sure you want to sell this?"

She was certain she *didn't* want to. She also didn't want to keep walls up between her and Gannon. But being an adult and taking responsibility meant enduring loss. Tegan would never understand the stakes, the motivations behind her actions, until Adeline explained. The time had come to tell the truth.

The whole truth.

Even if she lost Tegan's good opinion of her.

She leaned the bass against the wall and sat on the bed. "He came to see me Monday at church."

"What? Gannon? And you didn't tell me?"

"I don't like to relive my history with him. He's hard to talk about."

"But when something this big happens, you have to find a way. I mean, you knew him in high school and if your experience as a teen was anything like mine, every little thing was intense. The feelings were all so ... big. Seeing those classmates again is a time warp. It's like they have a special hold on me. If that's what Gannon showing up here is like for you, how can you process it if you don't talk?"

Adeline picked at her nails, the familiar pain in her throat. "He's always had a kind of special hold on me. Even shortly after we met, our friendship felt easy and comfortable."

Tegan chuckled. "Good for you. I *never* felt comfortable around attractive guys in high school."

The playful humor helped just enough that Adeline could continue. "Maybe I was okay because I didn't consider anything happening between us a possibility. Lots of girls liked him, he didn't show interest in me beyond friendship, and I was dating Fitz. Fitz was talented, a thoughtful boyfriend, and the whole reason I met Gannon and John to begin with. We didn't really have problems between us, so I wasn't going to break up with him over a friendship with someone else." She lifted her feet and dug her heels into the ridge of the bed frame. "Gannon says Fitz was depressed all along."

"Is that true?"

"He wouldn't have lied about the examples he gave." Even if she still couldn't fathom how she'd missed it. However, both of his suicide attempts had been in California, when all Adeline had to go on were phone calls spaced further and further apart.

And before that? What had she missed?

"He didn't do well in school, so when a test or semester grades came out, he would get down. I'd help him study for next time, but our work didn't improve his grades or his self-esteem. I guess I always felt like he needed me, and I felt like I owed him loyalty or something. And like I said, Gannon and I were strictly friends. But I'd be lying if I said I never had moments when I ..."

Tegan waited a few beats. "Wished for something more with Gannon."

She pressed a hand to her forehead. Either she was burning up, or her fingers had turned to ice. "Gannon never did much about the girls who hung around, and even when the two of us got together to work on music, I never felt like he was flirting with me. We'd start with lyrics and melodies and end up in long conversations. In retrospect, we shouldn't have met so often while I had a boyfriend, but Gannon ... He gave good advice, seemed to have genuine faith, and when he talked about his problems, he didn't fall in a black hole of discouragement the way Fitz did."

"You liked him."

She'd been in denial about her feelings back then, but thoughts of those lingering afternoons pulled her into a current of longing now that made disputing the statement impossible.

She'd liked Gannon then, and she liked him now, but those old days were over. They'd ended badly. Very badly. "When Fitz was doing well, he was fun to be around. He got me goofy anniversary gifts and ..." She shrugged again. How could she have cheated on him? It'd been the last thing he'd deserved.

"Right before California, he had so much hope for Awestruck. He was the happiest I'd ever seen him. So, when he proposed, I said yes."

"How old were you?"

"Eighteen."

"That's really young." Tegan spoke gently, as if Adeline's age excused what came next.

"After he'd been gone six months and things weren't going well for Awestruck, he got down again. We were growing apart. I was a college student living with my parents, and he was a starving artist, waiting for the big break with less and less hope."

"That's a heavy load for an eighteen-year-old to deal with. That would be heavy for me at twenty-five."

"Yeah, but I made terrible mistakes."

"You're not a psychologist. There's only so much you could've done for him."

"I could've been faithful."

Tegan drew her mouth into a line, but she didn't look as disapproving as Adeline had expected. "What happened?"

"After they'd been gone a year and a half, Gannon came home for Christmas. He wrapped me in this gigantic hug. It was like all the time we'd spent together, all the conversations we'd racked up, the ways he'd matured, the fact he was there, flesh and blood and present and interested in my life ..."

"And at that point," Tegan said, "you hadn't seen Fitz in over a year."

"That doesn't make what I did okay."

Tegan shifted in her seat, settling in, ready to wait her out.

Adeline pushed herself ahead. "I went to a classmate's party, knowing Gannon would be there. I hitched a ride home with him. Kissed him in the car."

When he'd responded in turn, she'd realized her crush wasn't as one-sided as she'd assumed. Neither of them had wanted to stop, so they hadn't. But they should've. The kiss never should've happened, let alone everything after. She deserved now for everyone to know she was that kind of person. The kind who'd done that. But her throat closed against the truth.

"I'm not saying it's okay," Tegan said. "I'm saying it's understandable."

"I betrayed Fitz. And God. When I told you and Drew the story the other day, I made Gannon sound like he was the one to blame, but I'm just as guilty."

"What Drew said is still true. You've carried this too long."

She didn't argue, but she couldn't bring herself to signal agreement. If God had forgiven her like Gannon promised, why did she still feel so ashamed? Why was her life so difficult that she had to sell the bass to fix her house?

That wasn't the picture of God's forgiveness. He didn't want her prayers, and He didn't want her music.

She stood and clutched the handles on the instrument case.

"Let me help." Tegan rose, steadied the top, and navigated with her down the stairs. They loaded the instrument into the back of Tegan's SUV. "Do you want me to come with you?"

"I've got it from here."

"Are you sure?"

"Yes." But as she got behind the wheel, her heart pounded and her breath went shallow. With shaking hands, she shifted into reverse and took the trip to the music store one block at a time.

Once she'd parked and wrestled the bass inside, business mode took over. She went through the motions, told the man behind the counter why she'd come.

He laid his glasses on the paperwork he'd been reviewing. "I remember you having the bass serviced here. Getting something new?"

"I haven't been playing, and unfortunately, I'm a little short on cash."

"Ah. Well." He scratched his chin and came out from behind the counter. "I wish you'd called first. We don't go through many basses here. Most students rent one of the school district's instruments."

"Oh." She looked over the case, remembering each curve of the bass underneath. "It's in excellent shape. Maybe a school would buy it."

He wobbled his head with doubt. "I could make some calls, but if we bought it to resell, we could only give about a thousand for it."

"It's worth twice that. At least." Would one thousand dollars even cover the cost of the painter?

"But who knows how long it'd sit in our inventory, and we have to have a margin on it. You might do better taking it to a larger city. I can give you the name of a shop in Green Bay."

Since selling the bass for so little was out of the question, she numbly accepted the slip of paper he offered her.

"Call before you make the drive. Mention me and that your service has been done by the same luthier they use. Hopefully they can make a better offer." He seemed to assess her and then the bass. "Can I carry it back out for you?"

She shook her head and lifted the weight.

The neighborhood association had given her ninety days, and a couple of weeks had passed since she'd received the letter. As drained as she felt by this trip, once she slumped back in the driver's seat, she forced herself to call the other shop.

The salesperson took a message and promised someone would be in touch on Monday, but the girl's tone hit the point home: her most valuable possession wasn't the commodity she'd hoped.

~

AT THE SOUND OF GIGGLING, Gannon rose from the couch and went to the foyer. Matt had caught an evening flight and then driven up from Green Bay. Gannon and John had expected him hours ago. As the night progressed, their theories about the condition he'd arrive in had grown grim.

The laughter bubbled from two blond women. Or girls. They wore enough makeup that they might be seventeen-year-olds hoping to look older. Their clothes were as skimpy as the women wore in the clubs Matt frequented in LA, but they weren't the same designer quality. He'd found these two somewhere else.

"You waited up for me?" Matt laid his hand over his chest as if flattered. Alcohol wafted off his breath. He had no luggage, but one of the girls lowered a leather duffle bag to the stone floor. Had he let her carry his bag for him?

"We're not here to entertain guests, Matt."

"I wasn't planning to share anyway." He drew the women closer, eliciting more giggles. Matt's clothes hung off him. With his sallow complexion and the circles under his eyes, he couldn't have picked up women this attractive without the help of his role in Awestruck, which meant the women knew who Matt and Gannon were. As if the staring and the coy smiles hadn't already confirmed that.

"They need to leave. Send them back with the car."

"I got a rental. It doesn't drive itself."

Gannon brushed past them and opened the door. A bright red supercar glittered under the lights of the carport, though a car service had been scheduled to pick Matt up from the airport. "You're lucky you didn't wrap that around a tree."

One of the women whispered something in Matt's ear.

He chuckled. "She wants to know if you're always this uptight."

Gannon focused on the blondes. "Where are you from?"

The one with longer hair twirled a lock around a finger. "Milwaukee."

"Originally," the other girl said. "We go to Lakeshore College."

Local girls? Matt must've stopped at a bar once he'd arrived in town. At least they'd be easy to send home and, if they were college students, they probably weren't minors.

Keys jangling, Tim approached, his hair sticking up as if he'd rolled out of bed and into a pair of jeans. "Someone needs a ride?"

John, who stood nearby with his phone, must've texted for help.

Matt dropped his arms from his guests and swiped the back of his hand under his nose. Always with the runny nose and bloodshot eyes. "You can't be serious."

"We're minimizing distractions around here." Tim's gaze swept the women up and down. "And you two look like marvelous distractions."

The women all but batted their eyelashes as they gravitated toward Awestruck's manager. They probably thought he was in the band too.

Matt made a grab for Tim's shoulder to stop him, but John and Gannon stepped between them. In moments, Tim had ushered the women out the door.

Matt hit his palms against Gannon's shoulders, shoving him back. "You heard what I did to that guy last week."

Gannon's anger soared, but he had better recourse than returning the blow. "Try it. You'll be gone, and not just from the cabin."

Matt jerked back, stooped, and slung the duffle bag over his shoulder with a grunt. "This isn't a convent, and I'm not a nun."

Gannon let the ridiculous statement go unanswered as he shadowed the bassist into the great room and pointed to a door on the second floor. "That one's yours."

Matt climbed the stairs, trailing his hand along the railing until he reached the bedroom.

Once Matt shut the door, John dropped onto one of the couches. "Nice room assignment."

The idea had been that Matt would be easier to supervise if he was near the common living areas, but with the door closed, he could do anything up there. What kind of war would Gannon start by checking on him?

"About what you said"—John brought his gaze down from Matt's door and met Gannon's eyes—"I agree. If he crosses the line, I'll be on your side this time. We'll fire him."

This time.

Gannon and John had only discussed firing a band member once before, when the label told them to drop Fitz. Pain spread through Gannon's chest. Behind that closed door, Matt wasn't who he used to be, but he didn't deserve an end like Fitz's.

"It'd better not come to that."

John nodded. "But we have to be prepared."

Gannon retreated to his room, the reminder of Fitz squeezing his lungs. After everything, Gannon had no right to harbor feelings for Adeline. He sat on the bed and peered into the darkness that had settled on the lake. From the edge of the island blackened by night shone the beacon of the lighthouse.

He took the fresh notebook he'd started and worked for about an hour before turning in. But despite the distraction, despite knowing he had no right, as he tried to sleep, thoughts of Adeline plagued him. She was the only woman he knew who'd have his phone number and not use it.

8

When Gannon made his way to the kitchen in the morning, Tim sipped coffee at the island, a laptop open in front of him.

"Get the women home all right?" Gannon put a mug of water in the microwave.

"Yeah. They won't be talking, but I can't say the same for everyone else."

"Everyone else?"

"Matt met them at a party, which he found by posting about being in town and looking for something to do."

Gannon turned from the cabinet to lock eyes with Tim. "You're kidding."

"Lina reached out as soon as she saw it, about twenty minutes after he posted."

Lina, Awestruck's social media manager, had been working for the band almost as long as Tim had. Judging by her quick action last night, she had a better handle on Awestruck's goals than Matt did.

"I had her take it down, but enough people know you're

here, and with *this* all over the Internet"—Tim swiveled the laptop to face Gannon—"it's a good thing the security team starts today. Expect a mob next time you go out."

An image of Gannon and Harper covered the screen, him in a tux, her in a backless, silver gown. His hand rested on her waist while one of hers lay on his chest. Despite his lackluster smile, the way they peered at each other in the picture had been spawning rumors for months.

He'd been doing an interview on the red carpet when Harper tripped on that fancy gown, slamming into him. A dozen pictures had been snapped in the three seconds it took to untangle from each other.

He shrugged at the headline and tried to hand the laptop back.

Tim shook his head to refuse it. "Keep going."

He scrolled the article to a picture of Harper leaving his building. Her hair mostly hid her face, and what wasn't covered by her locks, she'd held up a hand to shield. The article claimed it was a walk of shame.

"Well?" Tim asked.

His mouth went dry, but he refused to flinch. "I let her stay one night while we were here."

Tim continued watching him.

"There's nothing going on. Harper and I are friends. Period." He went back to making his tea. "She's with Colton, and there's a lot more photographic proof of that than anything with me."

Tim tapped the laptop's touch pad, intent on the article. "You know there'd be no shame in it."

"In what?"

"You and Harper ..." Tim shrugged.

"If there's no shame in it, why don't you want to finish that thought out loud?"

"Hanging out with you too long, I guess."

If only that were the case, but Tim's years with Gannon and John hadn't changed his theology. Back when they'd signed with Tim, the man hadn't said a word one way or the other about God. He was well known in the industry and had played a key role in Awestruck's success. As their fame grew and Tim devoted more and more of his time to them, he'd grown less tight lipped about disagreeing with Gannon and John's faith. They discussed whether to find someone new but decided they didn't have to share the same beliefs to work together, provided Tim stayed ethical. Plus, Gannon hoped to eventually win Tim for Christ.

Tim's phone pinged, and he typed a reply, taking care of who-knew-what detail of Gannon's life. "Sex is a basic need. No more wrong than eating."

"It's a gift for the right time, and I'm treating it that way."

"I'm sure people do crazier things in the name of religion." Tim pocketed the phone. A smile snuck onto his face. "None come to mind, though."

"So indulgence is the path to happiness?"

"All you have to do is say the word, and I can get you whatever you want. You've got a golden ticket, and you think you're obligated to waste it."

"Matt's not golden. Did you make him the same offer?"

"I'm the one who got the women out of here, aren't I? But since you asked, I think this God of yours does more harm to you than good. Religion limits your music, your lyrics, your life experiences. Without those limitations, would we need to be up here, trying to find whatever peace of mind you need to produce new music? And you and Matt would have a lot less to squabble over. You're risking the next album and the contract beyond that."

"God's the only reason Awestruck has gotten this far. I'm not jumping ship now."

Tim folded the laptop under his arm and retrieved his

phone from his pocket as he left the room. "You're doing this rock star thing all wrong."

~

GRAY CLOUDS DARKENED the water to the color of steel. Not the prettiest day for a boat tour, but a small cruise ship churned the surface of the lake as it ventured toward the lighthouses. As the ship cleared the breakwater, Adeline turned onto Main Street, on her way from church to her lunch shift at Superior Dogs.

When she stepped in, Asher paused in rotating hot dogs on the sizzling cooking surface to glance her way. "That guy wasn't a dog trainer."

"Guy?" Outside the window stood Olivia and a couple of her friends.

Olivia grinned and stepped up, putting both hands on the windowsill. The teen had painstakingly styled her hair and makeup and wore a tank with a low neckline. "Hey, Adeline. How are you?"

"I'm good." She glanced back to Asher, but he worked without explaining his comment. She returned her attention to Olivia. "What can I get you?"

"I already ordered." Her glossy lips pulled into a smile. "Isn't it a nice day? Don't you have any plans?"

"Just work."

"Oh. Well, we're going for a drive." She glanced at her friends, who watched from a few feet back. "Have you seen anyone today?"

Asher nestled a beef frank into a bun and left it on the corner of the food prep area.

"I've seen you." She passed Olivia her hotdog.

"I know. But ..." She tipped her head. "They are still here, right? Awestruck? I know you've seen Gannon Vaughn, and

Matt Visser was at a party on Saturday. And there's a picture of John Kennedy with his dogs taken in this very spot and posted this morning."

Adeline looked back to Asher, but he stirred the chili, probably purposely avoiding this. The revealing clothes and makeup suggested Olivia and her friends wanted to interest Awestruck in more than giving them autographs. She ought to ask if they realized the guys were at least a decade older. Would that burst their bubble, or would the rock star thing outweigh age?

"I just started for the day. You're the first customer I know about."

"So you won't tell me anything?"

"Do your parents know what you're up to?"

Enthusiasm dampening, Olivia stepped back. "I'm just hanging out with my friends. We're not doing anything wrong."

Adeline nodded slowly. "Make sure it stays that way, okay?"

"Sure." Olivia's lips quirked. "See you around, I guess."

Once they'd gone, she turned back to Asher. "What's this about a dog trainer?"

He snapped his tongs open and shut. "I posted the picture from Saturday this morning. The one of the guy with his dogs."

"When did he say he was a trainer?"

"He said his dogs live with their trainer."

"Oh. He probably meant while he was traveling with ... for work. John's away more than he's home."

"The picture got over a hundred shares." Considering their photos rarely got more attention than a couple of likes, Asher's reaction made sense now. "He's Awestruck's drummer?"

She should've warned him, but a viral picture could only help business. "The other guy, the day of the art show, was Gannon Vaughn."

"So I've heard."

Her pulse thrummed. "Are you angry?"

"No. I've only been open an hour and already two groups walked down from the college, which means they went right past Bryant's Subs and two burger joints. I might need you more hours, if you're interested, but I wonder what this is going to turn into."

"What do you mean?"

Asher took out the scraper to clean off the grill. "Some big movie was filmed near here years ago. Crowds showed up everywhere the stars did. Press, fans. A girl almost got hit because she threw herself in front of the actor's SUV."

"I won't do anything like that."

"You can't always help what the people around you do." He hit the warning home with a serious glance before his countenance brightened again. "But how about it? Extra shifts?"

GANNON STEPPED ONTO THE PATIO, sat next to the chaise where Matt lounged, and kicked the sole of his bassist's shoe. Matt lifted the arm he'd draped over his eyes and took a drag off the cigarette he held in his other hand. He tapped it, and the ashes piled on the metal edge of the chair.

Respect for property. Yet another topic they'd have to discuss today. "I want to talk to you about why we're here."

"You've got writer's block." Matt's Adam's apple moved under his scruffy skin. He needed a shave and a shower. And fresh clothes. "You think sequestering us is going to solve something."

Gannon struggled to remind himself of who Matt used to be. A daredevil, intense about everything except maybe school, he'd moved with Awestruck to California on only two weeks' notice. In the months that followed, Matt had gone from mediocre to playing bass almost as well as Gannon played guitar.

Even his drift from faith had been fast and furious. One week on tour, he was challenging them all during Bible study. The next, he skipped. When Gannon checked on him, he found the bassist doing lines of cocaine with fans.

"We're here to get back to our roots. Remember what's important."

"And what's that?"

"God and the music."

Matt scoffed. "God doesn't write the hits or put in the practice time."

"And that's why you figure your lifestyle doesn't matter?"

Matt propped himself up on his elbow. "You brought me here for an intervention?"

"Have you seen yourself lately?"

"Yup, and you know what I see?" He let the cigarette tip into the cushion of his chair. "Someone who's living his life. Time's short, and nothing's guaranteed. You live by your code, I'll live by mine. None of us knows how long this is going to last, so I'm enjoying the ride."

Gannon took the cigarette before it burned the fabric. "That's a collection of bumper stickers, not a code to live by." He tossed the butt into the firepit. "What are you into?"

Matt flopped his arm back over his bloodshot eyes. "Don't you have enough to worry about?"

"You're toward the top of the list. The women, the drugs, the alcohol. That's a lot that can fly sideways."

"You do you, man."

"Fine." Gannon stood, letting his shadow fall over Matt. "I can't control what you do other places, but nothing illegal and no women here. If you're going to smoke, do it outside and be careful. You're paying for any property damage."

"Anything else, boss?" Matt dug his cigarettes and lighter from his pocket.

"Be ready to rehearse tomorrow." They could go over their

sets for the upcoming shows, or, maybe by then, Gannon could make enough progress on the lighthouse or the addiction song to present something new.

he painter must've mailed a written estimate on Saturday, right after meeting Adeline, since a thick envelope arrived from him on Monday. Adeline took the mail into the house and greeted Bruce. Once she'd let him into the backyard, she braced herself and tore open the flap.

Her eyes stopped on the number at the bottom of the page.

That couldn't be right.

The itemized portion of the quote included removing loose paint, filling cracks, sanding, priming, and painting. Selling the bass at a slightly higher price than the local shop had mentioned might cover the first of those, but not the rest.

How could new paint cost so much?

Bruce barked at something, and Adeline called him back in.

In the momentary break from the estimate, she assured herself she'd misread a decimal point. Instead of thousands, the amount must only be hundreds. Surely.

As they returned to the kitchen, Tegan came downstairs. "The carpenter came by this afternoon."

She resisted rechecking the painter's quote, because if it

really said what she'd thought ... Well, she'd cope with that in a minute. She doled out a scoop of food to Bruce. "And?"

Tegan motioned at a sheet of paper on the counter. "Before you read it, remember, the church offered to do it for free."

To the soundtrack of Bruce chomping his kibble, Adeline picked up the second price quote. The total wasn't as high as the painter's, at least, but if she couldn't pay the painter, she certainly couldn't pay the painter *and* the carpenter.

She took another look at the painter's paperwork. The decimal point remained firmly where she'd initially thought.

"I get why you wouldn't ask Gannon for money, but you can accept the church's help with the porch."

"I'll have to. And how do you feel about painting?" She passed over the painter's quote.

Tegan pinched the paper as she read each of the line items. "It's a big job. Maybe he'd take installments? Or the youth group could help as a service project."

More charity. "If I do a little at a time and keep working at it, I could get it done in three months." But did she want to spend every spare moment painting for the rest of her summer? She'd have to sacrifice her annual kayak trip—that cost money anyway—and regular lakeside hikes.

"If the concern is curb appeal, could you just paint the front?" Tegan asked.

"The letter said anything visible from the street, which includes both sides." Even if she'd planted a few trees when she'd moved in, they wouldn't have grown large enough to shield much from judging eyes.

She should've gotten a smaller house instead of this mammoth, two-story fixer-upper, but she'd been so enamored with the view of the lake, she hadn't considered the cost of upkeep.

"Unless I want to have to redo the work every couple of

years, I'll need to do it right. Strip as much of the old paint as I can. Sanding. The whole nine yards."

"That'll take until October."

"It might."

"I'll help, but I can't make a full-time job of it. Though speaking of jobs, the college position is still open. They did a bunch of interviews, but they weren't happy with the applicants."

Adeline tossed the quotes onto the table. To change her life so drastically sounded like an even bigger task than painting the house. Could she handle the responsibility of the university job? What if she made the change and got fired for underperforming a few months later?

Superior Dogs and the church weren't glamorous, but she knew she wouldn't let anyone down there. "Asher's offering more hours to deal with an increase in sales. College students have been walking down in hopes of spotting famous people."

Tegan snorted. "Who shall go unnamed."

Her last talk with Tegan hadn't left her feeling much better. She hadn't come clean about how far she and Gannon had gone, nor had she confessed the ocean of feelings she still had for him—one wave of which had prompted her to program his number into her phone. But at least she'd started talking. If she kept it up, eventually she might get the whole thing out. "All three members of the band are here now."

"Because of you?"

"Gannon, initially, but this is something else. Vacation, I guess. Once they leave or people get bored, it'll be back to business as usual."

"How long do you think that'll be? Even my summer readers are talking about him. Before class started today, they were playing the acoustic version of one of his songs."

"Sixth graders?"

"Sixth-grade girls. I doubt they listen to most of his music, but even you have to admit the way his voice sounds in that song ..." She lifted her eyebrows as if Adeline would finish the thought. "It's the one about surrender that's on all the time lately."

Adeline could only shake her head.

"You haven't heard it?"

"I don't listen to the radio."

Tegan's chin dipped with suspicion. "Just to avoid Awestruck?"

"I hardly drive anywhere, and I play Christian radio at church."

"You aren't curious what your friends are famous for?"

"I already know, remember? I used to be part of it."

"I'm sure their sound's changed over the years. And that new one is like listening to Gannon read a page from his journal. Add in how raw but strong his voice is ... If you'd heard it, you'd know why half the women in the country are in love with him. He writes his own stuff, right?"

"That doesn't mean it's actually a page from his journal." But the song was most likely something similar. He'd never been able to get into work that didn't hit close to his heart.

She'd listened to everything Awestruck put together until that winter she'd gotten too close to Gannon's heart herself. After that, she hadn't wanted to hear what he had to say about her or Fitz.

"'I meant to be more than what I am,'" Tegan said. "'But what I am, I surrender.'"

"From the song?" Her skipping heart already knew the answer.

Tegan nodded. "And all the women went weak in the knees."

"I'd bet you the cost of the paint that's about his faith, not a woman." The inside knowledge slipped out on the desire to prove that she knew him, on the high that came with hearing his words after all this time and finding them familiar.

"You're on." Tegan pulled out her phone and started typing. A moment later, she turned her screen toward Adeline. She'd found an article that listed "Yours" by Awestruck as one of the top love songs of the year.

"That doesn't tell you the intention behind it."

"We'd only know if we asked him." Tegan lifted an eyebrow.

Adeline had taken this too far. She struggled to keep her voice even. "John will know."

Tegan shook her head. "The paint is going to cost a lot. I want to know from the source."

"I wasn't serious. It's my house. I'll pay for it."

"I won't let you pay all alone anyway. Find out from Gannon, but don't you dare tell him which one of us is counting on which answer, because we both know who he'd side with."

"You're overestimating my pull." Adeline dug her phone from her pocket with tense fingers.

Gannon had said he hoped she'd use his number. He hadn't specified that it needed to be anything important. Was texting this question worth the possibility that he'd start trying to talk to her again once she made contact?

He had said a lot of true and helpful things in their last talk. There was nothing wrong with having a couple of conversations every eight years, was there? Soon, he'd be back in LA, forgetting about her for another decade.

"A CAR of teenage girls tried to come up the drive."

Gannon's phone pinged with a text as Tim made the announcement. He would've left the message unread for a couple of hours while he worked on the lighthouse song, but Tim lingered in the studio doorway, an inevitable interruption.

Gannon steadied his guitar with one hand as he leaned to get the phone out. "And?"

"They waited about five minutes at the gate, then turned around. Someone from security saw the same car coming back down someone else's drive a few minutes later, so they're taking shots in the dark."

"Or they were lost."

"You're not that naïve."

Gannon nodded and lit up the phone screen as Tim wandered off.

Adeline had messaged? He held his finger over the button to unlock the device and read the text.

Is the song "Yours" written to a woman or God?

Since she had been inside his creative process, she ought to know he'd only give complete allegiance like that song expressed to God. Had she even listened to it?

Cut by the realization she hadn't, he put the guitar on a stand.

There could be another explanation. Maybe so much time had passed that she wondered if he'd changed.

He threaded his fingers together and stretched his hands before taking up the phone. *It's to God, and it's true.*

Adeline could use the message of the lyrics, but if she hadn't heard the song despite that it was in heavy rotation on the radio, she must've purposely avoided it.

But now she'd reached out to him. Maybe she was softening. Maybe he could get the song's message to her simply by asking.

Do me a favor and listen sometime.

Sure. The one-word response didn't exude enthusiasm, but if she said she'd listen, she would. And when she did, maybe he'd hear from her again.

～

ON TUESDAY AFTER WORK, Adeline arranged tarps along the side of her house and powered up the pressure washer. Her plan to prep and paint one side of the house at a time from start to finish would break up the task, giving her smaller milestones to reach for and celebrate along the way. If all went smoothly, she'd strip the chipped paint from this side tonight and return the rental in the morning, then move on to the next step.

After only a small section, her aching shoulders threatened the whole schedule. If she couldn't distract herself from the discomfort, she'd never finish.

What could be more distracting than Gannon's song?

Similar flimsy reasoning had carried her to that party all those years ago. She'd known then, as she knew now, she had much stronger feelings for Gannon than she ought to. But at least, working alone, she couldn't act on those feelings in a disastrous way.

She popped in her earbuds and opened her music app. She'd listen while she worked.

No big deal.

Except her stomach jolted when she saw the cover of Awestruck's latest album, a grayscale close-up of Gannon's face. His chin was tilted down and to the side, but his eyes locked on the camera as if the photographer had asked him the meaning of life.

She scrolled past the cover art to the list of songs. Icons indicated the popularity of each. All were popular, but some, "Yours" among them, had skyrocketed beyond the rest.

She centered the song in question on her screen.

She had to hit play.

She shouldn't have agreed to do this.

His music and voice played key roles in how deeply she'd

fallen for him. She couldn't breathe new life into those feelings. It wouldn't be right to Fitz.

But everyone knew this song. How personal could it be?

It was just a song.

Her heart thumped in her chest. Forget trying to work simultaneously. She wouldn't be able to continue with the pressure washer until this was over. Staring at chipping blue paint, she hit play, and her earbuds piped the sound directly to her.

The guitar started, Gannon in his element. He didn't have to be before her for her to know how he held the guitar, how he shifted his heel with the beat.

In high school, Awestruck had used his basement as their rehearsal space, and she might as well have been curled up in a corner of the old couch there, fitting in homework while he obsessed over a few bars he didn't like. He invited her to join him because she was better at lyrics than Fitz or John.

That was the reason she'd believed, anyway, until a couple of years later when she'd pressed her lips to his. His fingers found their way through her hair to her neck, his breath warm on her cheek, and his mouth—

Gannon's voice cut in. "The mistakes I've made stretch two thousand miles into a past I can't take back."

His voice seemed so close, the words so spot-on, her breath caught. What had started as soft picking of the strings grew to rhythmic strumming by the chorus, his voice unleashing pent-up power. "The past I can't forget, you don't remember. All you ask is that I surrender. Hands up, weapons down, I let you in and breathe again. You make me better than the man I've been. I meant to be more than what I am, but what I am, I surrender."

Adeline rubbed her eyes. Still, she could see images of the time they'd spent together. The way he'd looked at her during shows to signal a transition or the way he'd swung her around at graduation. The awkward hug he'd given her before getting in the van with Fitz, John, and Matt—awkward, in retrospect, because Fitz had stood right next to them.

Her core had tightened when their eyes met at that party the year he visited home, not long before Awestruck's big break. Her face tingled when he crossed the room to greet her with a hug that was anything but awkward, though he'd gained a couple more inches on her since he'd left.

One of her earbuds yanked out, and she snapped her eyes open.

"I knew I should've asked what you wanted the ladder for."

Face blazing, she turned toward Drew's voice. Good thing she hadn't been using the pressure washer, or he would've caught its full force right in the chest of his polo.

Drew grinned. "Working hard or hardly working?"

"Just a quick break." To fantasize about a man she had no business thinking about. She tugged out the other earbud and stuffed the pair in her pocket.

Drew surveyed the couple of feet of siding she'd covered. "Where'd you get the idea to do this?"

"I watched a video. It sounded a lot faster than using a scraper." Her voice sounded high and breathless. Any moment, Drew would ask what in the world had her so worked up.

He eyed the ladder he'd lent her, which lay in the grass. "Who's going to steady that while you work?"

"Tegan, if she's home when I do the top, but the middle section will be fine." Her laugh sounded like something from a haunted house.

Drew frowned at her progress, pointing a finger along an indent in a piece of siding. "You've got to hold it farther back so you don't gouge the wood. I'll show you."

In his nice shirt and khakis, he hadn't dressed for the work, but holding the power tool hadn't allowed her to shut off Gannon's song yet. She needed to turn it off. To forget she'd ever opened that door again.

She released control of the pressure washer, and he fired it up and aimed at the house.

While he shouted instructions she ought to pay attention to, she stepped back to stop the music. Once she'd backed out of her music app, she moved forward to retake the washer.

Drew kept at it, his progress much smoother and quicker than hers had been. "This is fun."

Maybe to him.

She fiddled with the phone as he continued spraying everything in arm's reach. She owed him for the help, but even more so for the interruption. She and Gannon had had their chance, and someone had died.

End of story.

Drew reached the end of the house and turned off the machine. "I promised the Bordens I would stop by tonight. I can come back tomorrow so you don't have to stand on the ladder alone."

She took the wand of the power washer from him. "The work will do me good, I promise."

He angled his head, eyeing the top of the house. "Once you get up there, the ladder is going to feel a lot taller than you expect."

A group of college-age women dressed to go clubbing appeared on the sidewalk, faces turned toward her house. One craned her neck, and the others slowed.

Adeline shook her head.

Even if they didn't know Gannon was a little taller and worked out more than Drew, the pastor's blond hair should've been different enough from Gannon's brown to get them to stop staring.

Drew waved hello. As the women moved along, he tucked his hands in his pockets. "Got a call at the church today asking if it's true Gannon Vaughn attends."

"Everyone's going a little crazy, including Olivia and her friends."

"I did some research on him."

Adeline laughed. Studious Drew, whose radio was never tuned to anything but the easy-listening Christian station. "You're getting into this too?"

Drew's light skin flushed, and his mouth blipped an embarrassed smile. "Not for the normal reasons. Olivia's friend Sophie wanted to use one of his songs during worship, said it was about God. I shut it down, but you know how high schoolers are. Lots of questions, and 'because I said so' isn't a good enough reason for anything. I wanted to be prepared to talk about what makes a worship song and a worship leader."

She could see "Yours" making a good worship song for those who knew its true meaning—and weren't too in love with Gannon to stop thinking about him while singing one of his songs. "And what'd you conclude?"

Drew shrugged as if they were talking theory or the politics of a foreign country. "Awestruck's lyrics are clean. Some, if you're listening for it, paraphrase Scripture. Psalms, especially. And Gannon is quick to credit God with his success in interviews, claims to be a Christian. But the band is with a secular label. None of their marketing, songs, or concerts are overtly Christian."

"Not all Christians work in ministry."

Was she defending him? Yeah. Because she found it comforting that Drew could pick out the influence of faith in Gannon's lyrics. It seemed that, after all this time, Gannon hadn't left his roots of faith.

"True. And not all Christians live consistent lives either. I'm not sure what to make of his relationship with Harper English. He's said they're friends, but she's been less cut and dry on the matter, and she stays at his place sometimes."

She may as well have slammed blindly into a wall. "She does?"

Drew's blue irises focused on her, brows raised.

Too much emotion had surged through the question. She'd sounded too much like a horrified girlfriend.

"The story may be nothing more than a rumor." Drew spoke quickly. "All I meant to say is we can't know exactly what kind of life he's living behind closed doors."

No kidding. If he was sleeping with Harper, it wouldn't be the first time he'd crossed that line with someone who was supposedly only a friend.

She picked up the ladder and tilted it against the house with a *thwack*. Before she could pull the cord to start the power washer, Drew laid a hand on her shoulder.

She straightened to face him.

"I don't know if the story is true. I shouldn't have brought it up." He lowered his hand.

She forced herself to breathe deeply. She was falling for Gannon all over again, and she'd needed the reminder of who he was. She ought to talk to him directly. If she could get him to admit his relationship with Harper had turned intimate, she'd know he hadn't changed. Her crush would be crushed.

That would be good news. Not a reason to be angry.

Still, pressure built in her chest.

Beyond Drew, another pedestrian stood on the sidewalk, this one a man. He lifted a camera.

"This isn't Gannon." She motioned at Drew and started for the sidewalk. "There's nothing to see here."

Drew jogged out in front of her but stopped after a couple of steps because the man retreated to his car. Adeline turned her back, as she should've done as soon as she'd seen the camera. Tabloids weren't above posting unflattering photos, and she'd been well on her way toward giving them some.

Drew rejoined her. "They ought to recognize I'm not him."

"Why else photograph us? Unless it's to report me for more violations with the neighborhood association." She eyed her yard. Should she have a permit to paint the house? She'd better call tomorrow and find out before she faced another fine.

"You're upset."

Of course she was. She had a chore as big as a house, she was falling for Gannon though he might still be up to his old tricks, and now she was being gawked at and photographed at her worst. "I'm not sure what would be worse—paparazzi or the neighborhood association."

Drew squinted at the now-deserted road. "You're in the clear with the neighborhood association. Since you finally agreed to let us help, we're organizing a group to remove the old porch the weekend after next, with the new one going in shortly after, and you're working on the paint. What else is there?"

"I don't know." There was the crack in the house's foundation, but that wasn't affecting the structure of the house, and the neighborhood association would have no way to know about it.

Even so, every time she thought she was doing all right, some surprise issue surfaced. Gannon. A letter from the neighborhood association. What would it be next? She picked up the power washer and yanked the pull so the motor roared back to life.

She climbed the ladder and got to work, her thoughts louder than the machine. Drew left without saying much, and shortly after, Tegan appeared at the foot of the ladder. He must've asked her to help.

Night had fallen by the time they finished the job.

Inside, Adeline shut herself in her room.

So Gannon mimicked Psalms in his music. She flipped open her Bible to the book and paged through a few of the songs David had written.

Her eyes fell on a verse in Psalm 33 about playing stringed instruments to worship God.

If God would tolerate a man with a past like Gannon's quoting Psalms in his music, maybe she, who'd been working so hard to be a good Christian, could play her bass again. If, that was, she didn't have to sell it to keep her house.

10

*A*deline held the phone to her ear and peeked between the curtains. The window from the second-floor spare room looked out over the porch to the street. In the dim glow of the streetlights, she couldn't be sure a photographer didn't sit in one of the cars parked on the narrow road. "Is it far-fetched that someone would take a photograph of me because of you guys?"

"Why do you ask?" John, forever easy going, might as well be talking about the weather, not paparazzi.

"Last night some guy took a picture of me talking with a friend, then went running off. I thought maybe it had to do with the house, but ..." She wouldn't worry him by saying she'd received a fix-it letter. She'd checked today, and her painting project didn't require a permit, so that wasn't the reason for the attention. "More people are coming by the food trailer. The picture of you there went viral—maybe not by your standards, but by ours. And Matt went to a party last weekend? That didn't help anything. I can't tell you how many people I've seen milling around, looking for Gannon."

"No photographers since last night?"

"For which I am eternally grateful, since tonight I sanded my house to prep for paint." Despite the belt sander she'd rented, the work had gone slowly. She'd made herself persevere until she'd completed the bottom third of the side she was working on. She'd have at least two more days of sanding to finish the wall. "I would've made quite a picture, covered in dust."

John laughed weakly.

"You don't think anyone would've taken one." When she'd removed her safety glasses afterward, she'd had clear patches around her eyes while light powder coated the rest of her. She'd showered and then, dressed in her pajamas, had taken her dirty clothes to the back stoop to shake off the dust before loading them in the wash.

John still hadn't replied, and his silence fed her fears.

She didn't know which would've been worse—a picture before or after her shower. "Why take pictures of me? I was working on my house. What does that have to do with anything?"

"Gannon's love life is a tabloid favorite."

"His love life?" She stepped back from the window. "That's Harper English, not me."

"You think so?"

"Yes." The photos that supposedly proved Harper had more than a casual relationship with Gannon didn't make a strong case. Still, Adeline knew him capable of compromise and cover-ups.

"You should talk to him, Addie."

"Why? There's nothing going on between me and him, and I don't know why they'd think otherwise, especially since Drew and not Gannon was helping me with my house when the guy photographed us."

"Drew?"

"My pastor. A friend."

"Huh."

"What?"

"You need to talk to Gannon."

"Why? This probably has just as much to do with me being seen with you."

"I don't rate paparazzi."

"Then I don't understand. There's nothing between me and Gannon."

"They don't know that."

"Could Gannon tell them?"

"You'd have to ask him."

She resisted the urge to growl in frustration. "Aren't you and I friends? You must know why he's here. And this Harper stuff. Does she really spend the night?"

"Harper's in his blind spot, not his bed."

"Oh." She pressed the back of her hand to her cheek, embarrassed at the blunt wording. "What do you mean about a blind spot?"

John was quiet for a moment. "These questions are the real reason you called tonight. The photographers were just an excuse."

"I ..." She groaned. "It's all of it. I don't understand him, and I don't like the attention."

"If you want to understand him, go to the source. Besides, record companies ignored us for years. Guess who was undeterred."

Gannon. He'd always dreamed bigger for the band than any of the rest of them. And he'd pushed until he'd made those dreams a reality. Now he'd turned his persistence on Adeline.

Maybe she ought to do as John said. Have the conversations Gannon wanted so badly. He might be satisfied enough to leave before the press dug up their secrets. Besides, she wanted the truth about Harper.

"Okay." She leaned her back against the wall of the hallway. "I'll call him."

"Good. And Addie?"

"Hm?" She bit her tongue between her lips, stomach tumbling at the thought of the call she was about to make, of hearing the voice from that song. Could she keep her guard up, remember who he was?

"If you need anything, I'm just a phone call and a couple of miles away."

She thought of the high school girls and wondered if they'd found where the band was staying. It didn't sound as if they'd have to go far. If she asked, John would give her the address. She could go, have the conversation with Gannon in person, but she'd never wanted to be a fangirl, and she wouldn't start behaving like one now.

She'd call him. She'd get answers. But she would not fall for him.

Not even a little.

GANNON PARKED along the side of the road and peered between the houses. In this section of Lakeshore, gardens of annuals and wildflowers filled the tiny yards. A shadow moved among the leaves and plants, rounding the side of the two-story Victorian he'd parked in front of.

Adeline's house was one block over. In case the press was watching, he'd suggested she cut through the yards to join him here. Her reluctance to agree to the rendezvous tempered the hope that otherwise would've hyped him up like only the biggest shows did.

When she cleared the shadows and he could make out the gentle lines of her face, he breathed a prayer of thanks. She'd come to him instead of the other way around. Finally.

When John had told him to expect Adeline's call tonight, the drummer added that this was as close as he'd get to playing matchmaker.

Gannon hadn't wasted the opportunity. He'd promised to answer any of her questions as long as they could have the conversation in person.

It'd taken some insisting, but here they were.

He put the rental in gear as she jogged around to the passenger side. When she dropped onto the seat, she buckled herself in wordlessly.

Gannon locked the doors and pulled away from the curb. "Ideas of where to go?"

"Turn right at the end of this road."

He glanced over to gauge her expression, but the hood of her sweatshirt blocked his view, another precaution he'd suggested. "Sorry about the cloak and dagger."

"Is this what your life is like now?" Judgment edged her tone, as if she couldn't understand why he'd wanted this much attention.

He hadn't. He'd wanted to share his music, not his whole life, and certainly not moments like this one. Still, it came with the job.

He turned as she'd directed, recognizing the two-lane country highway that led from one town to the next along the southern shore of Lake Superior. As they exited the residential area, clumps of trees and fields of tall grass lined the south side of the road. The lake, boat launches, and parks lay to the north.

With the city behind them, he took off his baseball cap. She pushed back her hood, and a light scent, shampoo or perfume, filled the cabin. A few minutes later, when the lake was out of sight behind some woods, she instructed him to turn on a narrow road. The trees, graphite in the deepening night, crowded the lane.

After a quarter of a mile, the road ended in a parking lot.

Forest crowded in from the east and west, but ahead, afterlight glowed over the watery horizon. Adeline unbuckled and got out.

Gannon locked the car and followed her, though she veered to the side instead of straight to the lake. They took a dim path a few yards through the woods and ended up at a stream, which Adeline followed to a large piece of driftwood propped along the shore where the brook emptied into Superior.

As she sat, he stopped nearby. "John told me about the photographers. I'm sorry I brought this on you."

"Is there anything you can say to stop them?"

So she wasn't giving him an inch. No opening for him to sit down beside her and put his arm around her. Tim would heckle him for how satisfying Gannon would find something so innocent.

"Ignoring them's probably best. The alternative is to try to control the narrative. We have shows coming up that'll be paired with radio interviews. I could say something then. Or I could post that you're an old friend who was part of the band when it first started. They'd eat that up, but feeding them comes with its own risks."

"Exactly. We don't want them digging into the original band members. Into Fitz."

He shoved his hands in his pockets. It would always come back to Fitz, wouldn't it? Gannon couldn't sit next to her and wrap an arm around her because she was entangled in the arms of a dead man. "Then the best thing to do is let it blow over. If the attention gets too intense in the meantime, you can stay at the cabin with us where they can't get so close to you."

"I can't hide out. I have a house to take care of. And work."

"I'm sure they'd understand."

"My bosses? Yeah, but I need the money."

He could cover the lost wages. A food truck and a church. Neither could pay much more than minimum wage. But the offer would offend her. "The press won't get that bad anyway. Lakeshore is secluded."

"It used to be."

"I'm sorry." Would he ever say the words enough to garner her forgiveness?

She clasped her hands in her lap, her shoulders rounded under the oversized sweatshirt. The gentle curls at the ends of her hair looked so soft. Maybe he did want more than a hug. He wouldn't mind running his fingers through that hair, smelling her skin, kissing her.

"Why are you here?" she asked. "Why now?"

He swallowed, chiding himself for entertaining the daydream. "Why not now?"

"Harper English."

So she had seen the same headlines his mom and the people back home questioned. At least she was giving him the chance to explain.

"Harper and I aren't together. Never were. I did let her stay at my apartment one night while I was here, and that might've been a misstep. It definitely fed gossip, but I wasn't in the state, and Harper's dating Colton Fremont."

Surely she'd heard of the actor. Had probably watched a few of his movies. Hopefully had never developed a crush on the guy.

Gannon pushed that thought aside. To prove the relationship between Harper and Colton, he could pull up a montage of pictures—the couple wasn't shy about PDAs—but that'd be stooping to the same level as the tabloids.

"So you're not sleeping with her."

The question stung. Mostly because, from her, he deserved it. "No. There's never been anyone else."

She moved her foot, and a rock clacked. "For nine years?"

"Never, Adeline."

A wave washed in and out.

"Then why is your love life such a tabloid favorite?" She stressed the last two words, but he couldn't guess why.

"Because I say Christ has made me different, and when they claim they can prove that's not the case, it sells. Every time I'm seen with a woman, it's reported as a scandal."

She turned her face toward the parking lot. "So tonight ..."

"That's why I was careful about picking you up." And hopefully the precautions would be enough. If this veered off course in the press, he'd never get to talk to Adeline in person again, let alone hold her or earn that kiss.

"You know what the worst part is?"

That he couldn't sit next to her? That he couldn't seem to get past her anger?

"They would never guess something as bad as the truth."

A thorn of shame twisted. He'd prefer to blame Fitz or Harper, but the truth was, his own actions caused the distance between them. And yet ... No. He wouldn't bow to shame. Wouldn't let the past define him.

For him and Adeline to have any hope of a future together, she had to live in forgiveness too.

"We've sinned, yes, but I believe in the God of David and Bathsheba, the God who forgives and uses us anyway. In Christ, we're not defined by our sin. We're defined by grace, and we can't waste years on regret or in fear of what people might think if they choose to believe the tabloids."

Her tone rose to match his. "If they choose to believe *the truth.*"

"Sin is ugly, Adeline, but the truth coming out is not the worst thing that could happen to me. The *truth* is that God is better than all our sin. Even if it doesn't make us look good, owning up to our mistakes showcases how great the grace of God is. We can't be afraid of facing that, and honestly, owning up to the past is a big part of the reason I'm in Lakeshore."

She sat perfectly still and silent.

He picked up a rock and let the smooth weight of it press against the hollow of his palm. "There are things I've considered too private to talk about in my music, and that was okay for the first few albums, but each one's gotten harder. Art depends on openness—on truth—and after John told me about seeing you …" He hesitated, but he couldn't argue the case for truth if he couldn't own up to his own feelings. "You saw John at Christmas. He came back and told me you were having a hard time. After that, you were all I could think about, the subject of all my new songs—and plenty of old ones too. But I can't use any of them because I left our relationship in shambles and using them would only do more damage between us. In shelving those songs, I've buried all kinds of truth, and I can't get past it. Other music won't come. I can't focus. I think the lack of inspiration was God's way of telling me to make things right."

"So that's why you came. For permission to use me in your songs." Her gaze was trained on him, a dark combination of lashes and brown eyes that blurred together in shadow.

He chucked the stone into the murky water. The air was so clean here compared to in LA. If only changing his location had cleared the smog from this relationship too. "This is our fourth conversation and the first time I've mentioned the songs. If I wanted, I could publish them without your blessing."

"So why don't you?"

"Because you've always been more important than music."

She crossed her arms, and her face dipped toward the ground, like maybe she'd heard him. Believed him.

He continued, "We're completely forgiven and free. You and I don't have to let a nine-year-old mistake define us anymore."

"I wish it were that simple." Sadness dragged her tone low.

"What if it is? What if you and I—?"

She shot up from the log and spun toward the path as if she planned to leave, with or without him.

"Adeline, wait."

She halted, back to him.

He longed to read the nuances of her expression. "Did you listen to the song?"

"I did." Her voice scratched.

"And?"

"You feel bad. I get it." A nasal undertone meant her nose was running. Which meant she was crying.

And he'd thought he wanted to hold her badly before. "You don't get it. The point of the song is that God forgives. Restores us when we come to Him, no matter our sin."

She faced him, but darkness shrouded her features. He could see little but that she had her arms crossed. "If you think somewhere in that definition of mercy you claim to live by, there's a line about you and me, maybe all you're doing is abusing grace, living by a fairytale you made up. Grace doesn't mean a grand do-over."

A grand do-over? As if Fitz and the pain of his severed relationship with Adeline were nothing?

She used to know him so well, and now she misunderstood him completely.

"I don't know what God has planned, but I do know He's the only hope for a grace abuser like me. And if you're honest, you'd admit He's the only hope you have too."

"Of course I need grace, but I'm not going to trample it, running around without remorse and repentance. Without changing. If we go back to what we were—"

"I'm not suggesting we fall back into sin, Adeline." He managed to keep his voice even, though hers continued to escalate.

"I'm not risking it. The book of James says we're supposed to show our faith by our works. You know what your works leave people with? Questions about who you are and what you stand for. My pastor isn't sure if you're a real Christian or not."

Anger flared. "Based on what? Tabloids?"

"You're not perfect. You admitted as much."

"And you are?" He clenched his teeth, summoning all his self-control to calm his tone again.

"No, but I'm not dating as if I'm completely unaffected by the past."

"Are you dating at all?" The question came out measured.

"No, because I've changed."

The answer he'd desperately wanted to hear—she wasn't dating—but she'd paired it with a riddle.

"You've changed into what?"

"A better Christian."

So he was a grace abuser, and she thought closing herself off to love made her holier.

If he said more now, he would insult her as much as she'd insulted him. "Let's get you back."

They made the drive in silence. When he pulled up to the curb a block from her house, he left the car in gear. Because of it, when she tried her handle, the door was locked.

He found the unlock button but hesitated to press down. "Maybe the reason you're so afraid of people finding out about our past is because if they knew, they might ask the same questions about you that they ask about me. You're afraid of the scandal, afraid grace won't catch your free fall. You'd rather make redemption about works and how people perceive you because you have some control there, but whatever scaffolding you're rigging to get yourself to God won't reach. Only the cross of Jesus will do that."

She glared at him with her head at an angry tilt, her fingers clutching the door handle.

He peered into the backyards as he hit the unlock button. As angry as he was, he hated the thought of her navigating those shadows alone. "Can I walk you home?"

"And risk them catching us together?" She opened her door, and the light in the car came on. She moved fast to get out.

"Text me when you're in."

She shut the door, and darkness returned as she disappeared into her neighbor's garden. Gannon stayed at the curb until his phone pinged.

In, she'd texted.

Lock your doors 24/7. And don't do anything you don't want photographed and analyzed by people you've never met.

Will do and never do.

She had once. He shifted into gear and pulled away.

11

*A*deline could message Drew instead of walking down the hall to his office, but she needed a distraction from her thoughts about the night before.

Gannon still had feelings for her after all these years. She hadn't expected that. Nor had she expected him to find fault in her theology. Her stomach had been tight and uneasy ever since.

She tapped on Drew's open door. "Darlene called. The hospital is keeping Henry another day."

"Okay." He typed something on his computer, then rolled his chair to reach his planner on the door-facing side of his L-shaped desk. He made a note, probably to visit Henry.

With Drew's neatly ordered bookshelf of spiritual wisdom nearby, this seemed like the place to talk about what Gannon said, but she wasn't sure how to word the worries that had kept her from sleeping. Most of what she'd said, she believed, but she didn't know what to make of Gannon's answers, and she'd gone too far saying Drew thought Gannon might not be a Christian.

Unaware of the words she'd put in his mouth, Drew

dropped his pen on his planner and folded his hands. "What else is going on?"

"At what point do you think the things we do disqualify ..." No. That wasn't right, and voicing the full question would've had her in tears.

The left side of Drew's mouth quirked into a smile as he waited.

She gulped and looked for a way into the conversation that bypassed emotion. "Gannon says he's right with God, that he repented for what happened with Fitz and is forgiven."

"Ah." He pointed to a chair opposite the desk. "Talked to him?"

She sat and scraped the textured armrest with her thumb. "Last night. He says he isn't dating Harper and never has. I believe him, but I'm not sure about the part where he repented over what happened with Fitz. If he regrets it, why does he talk about it so easily? It's like he's not embarrassed or anything."

"You think he should be?"

"Of course." Because her sin was the same, and her face flamed with shame, even though Drew didn't know what she'd done. He did know Gannon fired Fitz. That ought to be enough for this conversation. "It was so bad. Such a blatant sin."

"That's the only kind I know of."

Oh. Right.

"But I just ... How good is grace? I mean, can we really expect to get back everything we lose when we sin? Or is that asking too much?" Her heart pumped overtime. She longed for him to say restoration was possible. But she'd been striving to get right with God since she'd so utterly failed. If Gannon was right about grace, wouldn't she have seen progress by now?

Drew studied her, and her defenses failed.

She wiped tears from her cheeks.

He slid her a box of tissues. "God's grace is better than we can comprehend, and He is in the business of redeeming and bringing good from even the worst situations."

"But even once we've repented, there are consequences."

"Sure. Forgiveness doesn't cancel consequences, but the opposite is also true. Consequences don't mean we're not forgiven. When we're covered in grace, we don't have to walk around in shame anymore."

How was it possible to not be ashamed of something that had contributed to someone else's death?

"You said you aren't sure he's sorry. The right heart tends to lead toward the right works." He picked the pen back up and turned it in his hands. "We all fall short, though, so it's impossible to judge someone by their actions alone. Only God knows a person's heart, and that's what's important to Him."

He spoke gently, but her conscience pinged like a rubber band. She'd been too hard on Gannon. She'd been a hypocrite.

If hearts were what mattered to God, what did He think of hers, as tainted as it was?

Emotion built into a tidal wave. Before she could lose all composure, she murmured her thanks and hurried out.

AFTER NOT SLEEPING WELL FOLLOWING his fight with Adeline, a day of rehearsing with John and Matt left Gannon spent. He reached past John to power down one of the amps.

John stepped out of the way but lingered by the sound-board. "Last night didn't go well?"

"Not particularly." Gannon scanned the equipment. No red lights blinked at him, indicating he'd shut everything down. He moved to the door, and John followed him to the kitchen.

There, Gannon grabbed them each a bottle of water. "Every time we talk, it ends with her hurt and angry."

"So spend less time talking. Go help her with house stuff."

"The last thing she wants is anyone getting pictures of us together."

John drained a third of his water and raked the back of his hand across his mouth. "Have it your way. I'm sure Drew will help her."

"Drew?"

"A friend of hers."

"What kind of friend?"

"The kind that helps her with her house."

A man could do that out of the goodness of his heart, but if John thought that was the case here, he wouldn't have brought him up.

"I'm not going to steal her away from some other guy." Not again.

"For now, he's a friend. But you have a point about pictures. Paparazzi followed Matt home last night."

Great. Gannon stretched his arms and interlaced his fingers behind his head. Following his every move would be easier now that they knew the band's home base. A couple of close calls over the years had necessitated tightened security. The guards at the gate were armed, but Adeline had no one to protect her and wouldn't take kindly to needing someone, even if Gannon footed the bill.

"What am I supposed to do? She only called because you ordered her to. I've been pestering her since I got to town, and it's gotten us nowhere. I have to wait, don't I?"

John's mouth quirked. "Not your strong suit."

But as long as she was safe, he didn't see another option. He screwed the cap back on his water and started for Tim's office to find out how much of a scene Matt had made last night in town.

When he reached the doorway, Tim looked up, froze, then stood.

If Matt had done something bad enough to warrant this

odd hesitation, Gannon should have heard about it by now. Unless, thinking they needed to prepare for the show, Tim had hidden the news.

"What happened?"

Tim pulled him far enough into the room to shut the door, then stood behind the desk, fingers touching the work surface as if it were a rising problem he could suppress. "Harper stayed at your place."

"We already talked about this."

"More pictures of her leaving surfaced, these from inside the lobby. The lady who took them didn't realize what she had for a while because she was only trying to take shots of her kids, but when she had prints made, she saw it. Harper's in the background, clear as day. She didn't have bruises going in, but she does on the way out."

At least this wasn't another romance rumor that would work against him with Adeline. "She fell on the stairs."

Tim exhaled through his nose, patience seeming thin. "Someone told the press they saw you with her. Your doorman confirmed just now that he saw Harper with a man, but he swears he didn't talk to anyone about it." He paused there, as if to let the story sink in.

Gannon lifted his hands and shook his head.

Tim crossed his arms. "The press is reporting the bruises are from a lovers' quarrel gone wrong, that you and Harper have a secret relationship, but she won't leave Colton. She went to your place that night. You beat her up."

His body went rigid. Suddenly he missed the romance rumors. He hadn't known how much more offensive claims against him would get. "It's bogus. Start to finish."

And Tim should know that.

"It's spreading like wildfire. Trolls are blowing up your accounts, calling for this weekend's show to be canceled."

Gannon's mouth went dry. Some accusations left more of a

mark than others, and domestic violence had to be one of the bad ones.

But he was innocent. People had seen him here, in Wisconsin, a whole country between him and Harper.

What truly mattered was Harper's real circumstances. "Is it true? Not the part about me, but did someone do this to her?" Gannon trusted his building's doormen. If one of them said a man had come, it was true or an honest mistake.

Tim motioned at his laptop screen. "Do these look like they came from falling on the three stairs in your living room?"

Gannon stepped around the desk. The first set of photos of Harper from that morning, the ones that had been paired with claims of an affair, had been taken from the other side when she was out on the sidewalk. Her hand and hair had hidden her face. Apparently she hadn't thought to shield herself inside the lobby.

Brilliant red and purple marred her skin.

If Gannon hadn't seen the same marks, faded by a couple of days when she'd video called him, he'd say the image had been altered. "She could've hit one of the end tables or the corner of the couch on her way down."

"Or she let a man in, and he did this," Tim supplied. "People saw them together and assumed it was you. I can try to get my hands on the security footage. We can leak it to prove who was there that night instead of you."

"Leak it?" How would that help Harper?

"First choice would be for Harper to make a statement, but she and her people aren't returning my calls." Tim leaned forward, his hands fisted on the desk. "We've got to save the booking."

A bitter taste to match his frustration flooded Gannon's mouth. If Harper was dealing with an abuser, she needed privacy and support, not a media blitz. "We're not leaking anything."

"She's covering for someone at your expense. At *Awestruck's* expense." He stabbed a finger at the desktop, as if the income they could lose were a figure he could point to and change Gannon's priorities.

"Then I'll deal with her. You deal with the venue and get the footage. If someone hurt her, I want to know who, but we're not making this into more of a circus than it already is."

Tim's face flushed an angry red. "Am I the only one here who cares about your career?"

"People first."

"Too bad Harper doesn't see it that way, huh?" He clenched his jaw but couldn't seem to stop himself from continuing. "Can you imagine how fast you'd make a statement on her behalf? And she's letting this happen to you."

"Good thing I didn't follow your advice to get more involved with her."

Tim grunted and his mouth skewed as if he were barely containing retorts.

Gannon left before the restraint broke.

12

*G*annon sat on the floor against the door of the studio as if blocking the exit could contain the Harper situation from exploding further.

Despite their different priorities, Tim had been right about two things.

Harper wasn't returning calls, and the online reaction to the accusation had been volatile. Long rants in all caps and laced with profanity demanded Awestruck's music be taken off the air and this weekend's show canceled. Fans fired back, defending him. If the clash happened in person at the show, it would get ugly.

Gannon worked with Carol and Lina, Awestruck's publicist and social media manager, to post a picture of Lake Superior with a caption that read, *The truth will set you free. I'm not in California and haven't been since June, but I wish all my friends there a safe and happy summer.*

Fans and skeptics battled it out in comments there too.

Tim was working with Carol on a more straightforward defense. Only time would tell if they could save the weekend's booking.

"I don't get how so many people are willing to believe I'd do that to her."

Because Gannon had chosen the floor, John sat in the desk chair at the soundboard. "Domestic violence tends to be a well-kept secret." John's sincerity pulled Gannon from his own concerns long enough to focus on his friend.

The drummer didn't talk about his childhood often, but Gannon should've realized sooner this would hit close to home. And John might be uniquely qualified to recognize someone who'd faced abuse.

"You think her boyfriend's been beating her?"

John took a big breath as if to give an uncharacteristically long answer, but when Gannon's phone interrupted, he let out the air without speaking.

"It's her." Gannon answered the call on speaker. "What really happened at my place, Harper?"

"Nothing." Her voice came over the line, airy and carefree. "What do you mean?"

If his people were all over this, so were hers. The only reason to play dumb was to hide something.

Heaviness seeped into his limbs. "How did you get the bruises?"

"I told you." Her voice grew defensive. "I fell on the stairs."

"People say a man was there. Did someone hurt you?"

"Karina says the foundation of any relationship has to be trust. You should try it." She'd avoided answering. Also discouraging was how quickly she jumped to quote Karina, the quack of a life coach Gannon had long been encouraging Harper to fire.

He got up and paced, holding the phone in front of his chest. "I did trust you. I gave you access to my apartment, but you got hurt, and I want to know how. Was Colton there?"

"Of course not. He was the whole reason I called you that night."

"Someone else, then. Who did they see you with?"

"How should I know?"

Another evasion. Suspicion hummed like a malfunctioning speaker. "You were the only person who was supposed to be there."

"We haven't all taken chastity vows. You wanting to miss out doesn't mean that's the right choice for me."

Gannon rubbed his temple. There had been a man in his home when he'd let Harper stay there specifically to keep her from making more mistakes. "So it was someone else? You're not going to see him again, are you? He doesn't have a way to get to you?"

Harper tsked. "This is going nowhere. I told you, I fell on the stairs, and just because I might've had company doesn't mean that's not still the truth."

Sitting behind the soundboard, John drummed his fingers against his thigh in a fast rhythm. He did that whenever he was lost in thought, and Gannon wished he could put Harper on hold to ask what his friend made of her claim.

"Fine. You fell on the stairs. If that's what happened, you've got to tell the press. This is a PR nightmare."

Harper let out an exasperated sigh. "The truth doesn't matter. Only what people believe matters, and that changes every week. Like all the times they say I'm pregnant. If they won't believe me about what's going on in my own uterus, how am I supposed to clear up anything else?"

"You've got to try. By saying nothing, you're allowing them to run with whatever story they make up."

"Right. Talk to the press when even you don't believe me? I don't think so."

John tapped a driving rhythm that mirrored Gannon's mounting frustration

Harper hadn't quit talking. "... business and everyone else

should too. It's not like I issued a press release. It's not like I asked for this."

"Press coverage? You did ask for it, and I did too. These are the jobs we chose. No one forced us to live in the spotlight, but we do, and the choices we make don't go unnoticed. In your case, that could be a life saver. If someone's hurting you—"

Harper scoffed. "See? Even you. Call me back when you figure out how to trust." She disconnected.

He narrowly resisted throwing the phone at the wall. "I should've told her we'll find out from the security tapes soon enough. She might have spilled the whole story."

"Not if she's enjoying the attention."

Gannon froze. "You think this is a stunt?"

John stood, his right hand still moving to a silent beat. "She was all over the place. *If* she was attacked, you can only help if she cooperates."

"If I keep offering, eventually she will."

"Like she cooperated by staying at your place?"

The question hit its mark, and Gannon couldn't argue. Harper's efforts to clear his name would help immensely. Even if she were protecting an abuser—Colton? Someone else?—she didn't have to let Gannon take the fall.

"Distance yourself from her." John crossed to the door, a line on his forehead indicating worry. "Otherwise, she'll take from you, but not the help you're offering." He let himself out.

But what did it look like to distance himself from Harper now?

She might need him, and she might even be ready to admit she also needed Jesus if he stuck this out.

The truth would set them all free, like he'd written in that post.

No one was in a better place to tell the truth of what happened that night than Harper.

He texted her one last plea to tell the press the truth, slumped back down against the door, and started praying.

～

WHEN ADELINE LET herself into the living room after her evening shift at Superior Dogs, Bruce greeted her, then plopped back down in front of the couch where Tegan sat, watching a movie. Adeline had planned to sand the next portion of the exterior wall but joined them instead.

"You might regret that." Tegan didn't take her eyes away from the screen as she scooched over to give Adeline room. "I'm just waiting for this thing to end. It's one of those big misunderstanding movies where, if they all just sat down and had a conversation, everyone would be happy, and it'd be over."

Adeline nodded, numb. Was that what she was doing with her past with Gannon? Making it into a bigger and bigger deal by not confessing it?

A paparazzo had shown up at the food trailer today. As his camera lens snapped nonstop, he'd asked what it felt like to be Gannon Vaughn's new lady and whether she was sad he would be traveling this weekend for a show.

Asher had scared him off, but with the increasing attention and Gannon showing no signs of leaving any time soon—at least, not for more than a weekend—odds were getting better that someone, sometime would dig up the story of Fitz.

Gannon said that wouldn't be the worst thing in the world.

Drew said she didn't need to be ashamed.

The Bible said believers should confess sins.

Telling Tegan the full truth might be a good way to find out what kind of reaction she'd get from everyone else when it got out. She'd also benefit from having an ally who wasn't surprised when that happened. Plus, confessing it would prove she knew she was a sinner saved by grace, not works, and that she didn't care who knew it. It'd prove Gannon wrong about her.

Except, he wasn't wrong. She did care. She pulled a throw pillow onto her lap and picked at it until the movie credits rolled.

This was her chance.

Tegan leaned forward for the remote.

"I slept with Gannon. It wasn't just a kiss. That's the part of the story I never told you."

Tegan sat back without the remote and turned to face her.

"That year he came home for Christmas, and I saw him at that party, and I was engaged to Fitz. That's why Gannon fired him. That's why Fitz broke up with me. That's why ..." Her voice cracked, and she watched Tegan without blinking. Her eyes were so wet she didn't need to.

"I guessed. Whatever happened majorly impacted all three of you, and I couldn't imagine a little kiss doing the damage that came after."

The whole ugly truth, and this was the response? "It was that obvious?"

"Not when you talked to me and Drew, but when we talked after." Tegan shrugged. "Do you feel better now that you said it?"

"Not really. What if the press starts digging and everyone finds out about me and him and Fitz?"

"If you're worried what people will think, we all make mistakes. Unless you've been hiding a lot from me, that's not how you live now."

It wasn't. She worked in a church now. She volunteered all the time. She didn't date. "I'm not sure Gannon and I can even be friends now."

Tegan tilted her head. "Is that what you want?"

Adeline's breath solidified in her lungs. They'd been good friends once, and even in their recent disagreements, he'd proved himself grounded and loyal. So much had changed, but if anything, his best qualities had only gotten better. "I miss him. But with our history, and with Fitz ..."

"Fitz is gone, Addie, and your history is forgiven."

Her fingers tightened around the side of the pillow. "And God's forgiveness means Fitz doesn't matter anymore?"

"Fitz matters. He does. But nothing you do will change the past or the fact that he's gone."

Nothing would bring him back, as she'd told Gannon when he'd come to see her in the church office. But Gannon's question haunted her. What if talking about Fitz brought *her* back?

She caught herself biting her nails. "Do you think I haven't been living my life?"

"What makes you say that?"

"Something Gannon said."

Tegan lowered her gaze and said nothing. Meaning she agreed with him.

Adeline's hand dropped across the pillow in her lap. "Why haven't you said anything?"

"I encouraged you to apply for that job."

"That's not the same as telling me my life needs an overhaul."

"Maybe it doesn't. It's just ... you don't seem to dream or reach for things. I don't think I've heard you ever say what you want to accomplish—other than paint the house. And maybe, just now, to be friends with Gannon Vaughn."

The ache to see that happen sank deeper, an anchor she might never be able to haul back up. "Do you think that's possible?"

"Yes." Tegan had proved herself a true friend in this conversation. She hadn't judged. She'd encouraged.

A friend like that deserved Adeline's trust, which meant Adeline needed to consider that Tegan could be right.

Adeline could be friends with Gannon again.

She'd have to start by calling and apologizing for the whole grace abuser thing and for the words she'd put in Drew's mouth. That would be as hard as this conversation had been. "I'm going to work on the siding for a while."

LEFT TO HIMSELF, Gannon wrote rough versions of two songs in the eight hours following his conversation with Harper. Music hadn't come this easily in ages, but powerful emotions had always served his creativity well.

His phone lay face down on the desk near where he sat with his guitar. He flipped it over to check the time. Only five thirty in the morning, and notifications covered the display. Their flight to Minnesota for the weekend's engagements would depart in a few hours, assuming the trip hadn't been canceled.

He'd chosen a bad time to go dark, but if anything had needed his immediate attention, Tim knew where to find him. Gannon scrolled through the backlog.

His publicist had left a voicemail about the radio interviews scheduled for the weekend. "I told them to ask about Harper. Here's what you'll say: 'I don't know how a simple friendship has fueled so many dramatic rumors, but the truth hasn't changed. Harper English is a friend. I'd never dream of hurting her, and with a little fact-checking it'd be obvious I've been nowhere near her for weeks.' Don't confirm the bruises or the stairs or the fact that she was at your place. We're keeping it simple. Friendship, truth, fact-check."

He repeated the words she'd supplied to the equipment-filled studio before moving on to his text messages.

The oldest was from Harper. *You owe me.* She'd followed up with a string of emojis, all blowing kisses.

What had she done now? Hopefully something helpful instead of something that would throw more gas on the fire.

Before he resorted to searching online to find out, the next text, from Lina, Awestruck's social media manager, caught his eye. *Harper posted a video, in case you haven't seen it.*

Gannon hurried to tap the link.

"Hi, darlings." Harper's fingers fluttered as she smiled at the camera. "You've all been so concerned about me. It's the most touching thing, how you're all these wonderful people who are so ready to stand up for me."

Had she summoned tears? It looked like it, but she blinked quickly and moved on. "It's the sweetest, and I'm beyond flattered. So I'm hopping on to let you know that I'm totally okay."

She moved the phone farther out to include more of her body in the frame. She gave a shrug with a coy smile, then brought the camera closer again. "I did take a little tumble when I was at my dear friend Gannon's house, but he's off in Wisconsin. He wasn't even there, friends. He didn't hurt me. He let me stay at his place even though he wasn't there because, you know, we have a very special relationship, he and I."

She wiggled her eyebrows and seemed about to burst with a secret.

Gannon glared at the screen. She might be clearing up one rumor, but she was on a mission to ignite another. What would Adeline think of this? And Colton?

But wait. Was she once again at it with her evasion techniques? Harper had cleared his name, but she'd never said she'd been alone. She'd never said someone else hadn't been involved in that "tumble."

She praised her fans some more, thanked them for their concern, told them she loved them, and signed off.

Gannon heaved a sigh and ran a hand over his face.

He still had doubts about what had happened, and he would've given her a different script, but what she'd said seemed to have done the trick. Most of the comments on the video were positive.

Thank you, Lord.

He clicked back over to his messages.

The next one came from Tim. *Harper's video did some good. There are still skeptics, but they don't appear to have organized a protest at the show.*

Despite his relief, Gannon knew better than to believe this would be the last he'd hear of the accusations. Most likely, tabloids would still run with it. Some fans would doubt Harper's sincerity in the video—Gannon couldn't blame them when he had questions of his own.

Tim had messaged again a couple of hours later, in the middle of the night. The guy had been up late, if he'd gotten any sleep at all. *The venue's agreed to go ahead.*

Thanks for your work on this, Gannon typed. *Any progress on the surveillance tape?*

Tim's reply arrived immediately, confirming Gannon's suspicion that he hadn't slept. *Didn't think we still needed it.*

I'd like to see it. The situation still didn't sit right with Gannon. Finding out whether Harper had been alone that night would either put his mind at ease that she'd been alone or get him that much closer to the identity of the abuser.

He made quick work of his other messages.

Somehow, he'd hoped to find something from Adeline, but of course, there was nothing.

She'd already had questions for him about Harper. He could only imagine the events of the last eighteen hours alienating her further.

13

On Wednesday, Adeline pulled a crumpled shopping list from her pocket to make sure she had everything Asher had asked her to pick up for Superior Dogs. Water, soda, a variety pack of chips, and two bottles of barbecue sauce. She leaned her forearms on the handle of the cart and plodded to the checkouts.

She didn't mean to browse the tabloids, but a picture of Gannon earned a double take.

Olivia had stopped by the food trailer to announce that she and her friends had found the cabin where Gannon was staying. It wasn't a cabin at all, but an estate with over a dozen bedrooms in the main house, usually rented out for corporate retreats. Awestruck had flown out and played a show this weekend, but now that they were back, Olivia and company planned to more or less camp at the estate's gate.

By now, they may have seen Gannon, but he hadn't reached out to Adeline since their disagreement at the lake.

In the picture featured on the tabloid, he looked angry—angrier, even, than when she'd told him Drew thought he wasn't a Christian. A separate photo showed Harper English with bruises, and the headline made the connection, accusing Gannon of beating her.

Adeline's muscles hardened with offense.

Gannon? Beating someone? His response to Adeline's poor behavior the other night had been to deliver her home and give instructions to help her stay safe. She'd never felt threatened by him.

Quite the opposite.

She was drawn to him, and the only thing keeping them from friendship was Adeline's reluctance to call and apologize.

She finished loading the groceries onto the belt and then slipped the magazine from the rack. The article contrasted the ever-popular picture of Gannon and Harper laughing in each other's arms on the red carpet to a shot of a bruised-up Harper leaving his apartment.

He'd said he'd let her stay at his place once while he was in Wisconsin.

If that was when they snapped this picture of a bruised Harper, the writer of this article twisted Gannon's actions, using his hospitality to make him look bad. The nerve of the tabloids, accusing someone of something as serious as abuse.

"That too?" The cashier's question drew her attention to the empty checkout belt.

"No. Sorry." She returned the tabloid to the rack. She wouldn't fuel an industry that hounded her and featured such ridiculous headlines against Gannon.

Conviction stabbed her belly.

She shouldn't have accused him of not being a Christian because of something she'd seen in the press. The judgment and criticism aimed his way came from enough directions already. He hadn't needed more from her.

She finished at the register and loaded the food in the car. When she got behind the wheel, she took out her phone. Her nerves hummed like horror movie violins, but she hit the button to call Gannon.

After a single ring, his voice came on. "Leave a message. I'll call you back when I can."

She had expected to reach him directly, and the brevity of the recorded greeting didn't allow time to plan a voicemail. The beep sounded, but what could she say on a machine?

"Um, hey. It's Adeline." Should she ask him to call her back? No. No, leave the awkwardness of admitting she'd been wrong here, in a message, and be done with it. "I am calling to apologize. I shouldn't have said the things I did the last time we talked."

Did she need to give more details?

No. He probably wasn't sitting around, waiting for her to get her act together.

Maybe he'd thought he liked her, but after the things she'd said, he would've abandoned the notion. Moved on.

He had bigger problems like the tabloids to worry about.

She hung up and stared at the phone.

What nonsense.

He wouldn't have simply moved on, her words forgotten.

She'd seen his expression. She'd hurt him worse than any rumors could in her rush to tamp down her own feelings and not betray Fitz's memory. If only he had answered her call, she could have tried to smooth over what she'd said.

She should've admitted she'd put words in Drew's mouth, should've said she was sorry for how the tabloids dragged his name through the mud.

She could call again, but doing so would reveal how much she cared. He'd know she wanted to be more than friends and wouldn't understand why the memory of Fitz made that impossible. He'd push, and she'd either give in or alienate him forever.

Maybe if she left it at her fumbled apology, he'd eventually return her call.

They could be friends.

That was what she wanted.

Wasn't it?

Ugh. Her life had been so much simpler before he'd shown up.

She drove to the food trailer and got to work but found herself constantly checking her phone with a mix of hope and dread.

GOLDEN CLOUDS FLOATED at the horizon, signaling Wednesday's end. Adeline needed to hustle if she wanted to finish sanding this wall tonight. Already, this part of the project had stretched a week when she'd allotted three days.

The ladder was fully extended beneath her as she raced sunset to finish the last section under the roof. All the way down on the ground, her phone waited. She hadn't heard from Gannon before she'd climbed up here, and the one nice thing about her full hands and the loud sander was the forced break from constantly monitoring the device.

She sneezed on the dust, jerking the sander. The gritty belt propelled itself sideways. Leaning to keep her hold on the tool with one hand, she reached with the other for the ladder.

Caught only air.

She swiped again, this time catching a rung. Her safety glasses dropped two stories to the tarp. Righting herself, she hugged both arms around the rails, sander still running in her hands.

Thank you, Jesus.

The ground was so far below. If she'd fallen, she would've been seriously injured. Killed, maybe. Why had she risked her balance to save a power tool? She pressed the switch, and the machine stilled, but her hands buzzed as if it were running. Her heart buzzed too. She should never have ignored Drew's advice about getting help.

Then again, what good would Tegan do if Adeline fell from this height?

Stupid house. Stupid neighborhood association. Stupid paint.

Just a couple more feet to go and this awful job would be finished—but only on this side of the house. She needed to move the ladder to continue working, but that would mean climbing all the way down and all the way back up again.

Worse, though the street had been empty all evening, a sporty motorcycle rumbled up to the curb. The sound died. Still hugging the ladder, she turned her head as the rider dismounted and started her way.

If this was a photographer, she was a sitting duck.

He wore black from helmet to boots, long sleeves and long pants despite it being the height of summer—though in Lakeshore, that meant seventies.

Her biceps and forearms hurt from being pressed into the rails, but easing up would be no less uncomfortable. Maybe she could lower the sander by its cord, freeing both hands to hold the ladder as she descended. The photographer might have a field day taking pictures of her this shaken up, but so be it. Better embarrassed than dead.

"Are you okay?"

At Gannon's voice, her pulse went from nervous and shallow to galloping like a runaway horse. She renewed her grip on the sander and turned only her head.

He stooped and laid the helmet on the ground without breaking his pace toward the ladder. He gripped both rails and peered up at her. "Do you need help getting down?"

"What are you going to do? Climb up here?"

"Would that help?" He put one foot on a rung.

"No." She couldn't picture them trying to descend from this rickety thing together.

"Drop that and use both hands. You can get a new one."

"It's not mine. I'll lower it down."

He didn't reply, but he also didn't protest as she lowered the tool, one hand over the other. If the process damaged the power cord, she'd have to pay the hardware store extra, but it had to be less than her medical plan's emergency room deductible. Finally, the tarp rustled as the tool settled, and she dropped the plug.

Another car pulled up by the house. Adeline adjusted her grip on the ladder and took the first couple of steps down before checking the vehicle again. Two females got out.

"Hey, Addie!" Olivia Cullen shouted.

Three more girls joined her on the sidewalk for a total of five.

"You should leave." Adeline looked between her arm and her body to see Gannon, who continued to hold the rails, attention locked on her.

"Not until you're okay."

The girls hesitated, whispering and pushing each other forward. One rushed back to the car. Now that they'd found the person they'd sought all this time, they became shy?

Adeline white-knuckled the rails and watched her feet as she descended. She was about eight feet from the ground when the girls approached, talking over each other.

"Are you Gannon Vaughn?"

"We're huge fans."

"You're the best singer I've ever heard."

"'Yours' is amazing."

Gannon didn't reply. She descended another couple of steps, and his hand reached her waist, firm and warm and reassuring. When her feet hit solid ground, she didn't immediately peel her hands off the ladder. Safe on the ground, Gannon's chest against her shoulder, his hand still on her waist, protective.

"You okay?" He gently turned her from the ladder.

She nodded and ducked her face away from the staring high schoolers to brush sawdust from her cheeks and forehead. How humiliating.

Gannon shrugged out of his jacket and placed it in her hands. "Put this on."

"But—"

"Fast." He scooped up her phone and his helmet.

She scanned the scene as she obeyed. Another car had pulled up, and a man emerged.

The jacket emanated Gannon's body heat and smelled like sandalwood mixed with something sweeter. Orange, maybe. The coat had fit him snuggly without looking cumbersome, but on her, the fabric proved heavy and stiff. The sleeves did their best to swallow her hands. She must look like a clown, and the latest arrival had a camera.

Her phone landed in her hand, and she slid it into the jacket pocket. Everything went black for a moment as Gannon fit the helmet over her head. His hand closed around hers, and he led her, half jogging, half stumbling, past the still-jabbering teens to the bike. He was on the seat in seconds. The photographer raised his camera, so she hopped on behind him. Her first motorcycle ride.

Gannon said something she didn't catch through the helmet and over the throaty engine. He caught her hand and pressed it against his abs, then the bike surged forward.

She locked her hands together, lowered her chin to the side, and let the helmet rest between Gannon's shoulder blades. Though she couldn't make out the words, she felt the vibration of him speaking as they ripped down the street. He hooked a right onto the country road that linked the towns along the lake.

~

THE WIND RUSHED over Gannon's face, through his hair, across his arms. Adeline's arms, clamped around his torso, and her warmth on his back were fixed points. Just what she'd always been to him. Something solid in a rushing world.

When she'd lurched sideways on that ladder, he'd barely managed to park without crashing.

But she was safe now. In his care, and he wouldn't let anything happen to her. She'd looked so cute with the dusting from the sander on her nose before he'd plunked the helmet on her. And then there'd been the slight impression of her wide eyes blinking at him through the dark visor.

He didn't see anyone following them, but then he had thought he'd lost the photographer before heading to Adeline's house. He should've resisted such a direct approach, not put her in their sights, but once he'd gotten her message, he'd lost most of his common sense.

With her this close against him, he didn't miss it.

He checked the mirrors. Still no one, but even if he were willing to end this adventure, he couldn't take her to either of their homes, as both were likely being watched. She may have called to apologize, but that didn't mean she wanted to be front page material with him.

They needed a second helmet for safety and so identifying them in photos would be impossible. He'd drive until he found a place to buy another helmet. The next city would take about half an hour to get to, if he remembered right, but he could drive all night with her clinging to him like this. And how he wanted to.

Too soon, the edge of town welcomed them with a restaurant, two hotels, and a large farm and outdoor goods store. He pulled in, his body cooling as soon as Adeline let go and climbed off.

She pulled the helmet straight up. Her hair clung to it for a moment, then dropped, sending dust particles into the light that poured from the lamp overhead.

"You might want to …" He rubbed his fingers through his own hair.

Adeline brushed her free hand over her hair and face. Once he took the helmet, she removed his jacket, shook the dust off, and gave it back. That done, she crossed her arms. Her frown wasn't happy, but her expression wasn't angry either.

Time to start talking before she decided she didn't like this.

"I'll get you gear here, if they have it. Then no one will be able to take a good shot of us on the way home."

"Gear?"

"Jacket, pants, helmet. Riding is dangerous enough with the right gear. Without …" He'd intended to put her at ease, not worry her. "It'll make getting a shot of you more difficult."

She uncrossed her arms, a step in the right direction. Now, when he'd just ridden half an hour without a helmet, wasn't the time to ask why she'd taken on such a dangerous job as sanding way up on that ladder.

Once they'd stepped inside, she motioned toward the restrooms. "I'm going to clean up."

"All right. I'll text when I find the right section."

The store was bigger than he'd anticipated, and camouflage hunting clothing hung to the left. He waded through that and was rewarded by a few racks of motorcycle gear and a selection of helmets. He picked one off the shelf and turned to see the clothing options.

Adeline pushed her way through the crowded section, her eyebrows and the hair around her face damp. Half her makeup had come off with the dust, revealing a smattering of freckles on her cheeks. She lifted an eyebrow at the helmet. "All black for me too?"

"They don't have a lot of options. For clothes, you get to choose between black and white or black and pink."

"What about the blue?" She turned the tag on a hoody that hung closer to where they stood, then stepped back, shock skewing her features. "Or how about jeans and a regular jacket? This stuff is way too expensive."

"At highway speeds, you need the right gear. Especially with the wild cards of photographers and fans in the mix." He steered her to the rack with the armored jackets and pants. "Besides, I'm buying, and I was thinking we could ..." No. She'd never go for it.

"Thinking what?"

"We could hightail it for a visit home. Spend the night at our parents' houses, come back tomorrow." The trip would extend their time together, and it'd provide solid alibis that he and Adeline hadn't done anything inappropriate, should the press get ahold of this.

"Fox Valley's a two-hour drive from here."

"It'd be a shame to get the gear and not break it in."

She blinked, eyes fixed on the clothes, probably still too distracted by the price to consider other outlandish ideas.

A voice came over the store speakers, announcing they would close soon.

"Either way, the gear is nonnegotiable. White or pink?"

She snatched up the nearest price tag. "This will cost hundreds of dollars."

He adjusted his grip on the new helmet, hoping the price tag wasn't visible. "Nonnegotiable."

She had no idea how much she was worth to him.

With a sigh, she collected the gear with the white accents and turned toward the checkout.

"Gear has to fit right to do its job." He pointed toward the far wall of the store where a sign indicated fitting rooms.

When Adeline emerged with the clothes on, the thick material wasn't formfitting, but she looked ready for adventure. Though he'd rather stretch it into a cross-country road trip, even the prospect of the half an hour ride back to Lakeshore with her lifted a grin to his face.

She extended her arms to the side. "How am I supposed to know if this fits right?"

"You look great."

She'd been looking down at herself, but at the slip, her focus rose to his face.

"I mean the fit looks right." He fought against letting his gaze skim back over her. "It's supposed to be snug, but you should be able to move. Bend like you're on the bike to make sure the knee pads hit in the right place."

She made a face, but she tried the idea and straightened again. "I guess we have winners. I'll wear it out of the store?"

He nodded, and she pulled the tags off and handed them over as they made their way to the front. As the sleepy cashier scanned the barcodes, Gannon glanced at Adeline. "Have you been to Fox Valley recently?"

"I go a couple of times a year. Holidays, mostly."

"How's the family?"

"Good. My sister took a job in Chicago." Her eyes widened when the cashier scanned the helmet, and she slanted a look of protest at Gannon.

"Precious cargo." He tapped the side of her head. The gesture was meant to be light and teasing, but the silk of her hair under his fingertip almost stole his ability to withdraw. He clenched a fist as he returned his hand to his side. "And your parents?"

She frowned, apparently too miffed about the price of the helmet to have thought anything of the touch. "My parents are more and more excited about retirement the closer it gets. There's talk of an RV. Your mom?"

"She had a bout with breast cancer a few years ago."

"I didn't know."

Gannon paid for the purchase. "I came home a few times, but people didn't care about Awestruck so much then, so word didn't really get out. She's been cancer-free for five years now." He took the helmet and the receipt, and they started for the exit. "She came out in December, tagged along to watch us play for one of the late-night shows, made more Christmas cookies than LA has ever seen, and delivered them to all the neighbors like it was the most normal thing in the world."

Adeline laughed, and she didn't even know one of his neighbors was a hulking pro wrestler. He'd tell her, but this was such a normal conversation. Why derail their connection by pointing out how different their lives were?

He handed her the new helmet and zipped his jacket as they stepped back into the parking lot, that much closer to returning to Lakeshore. He didn't want to go. Didn't want this to end. "Her expression would be priceless if she woke up in the morning and saw me on the couch."

Adeline lit up her phone, probably checking the time as they walked toward the motorcycle, and his hopes soared. She hadn't immediately dismissed the idea.

He had already done the math. "We'd get to Fox Valley a little after eleven. Your parents would still be up. Unless they're early birds now?"

She shook her head. "Up until midnight, at least. You think breaking into your mom's house while she's sleeping is a good idea?"

"I have a key. Besides, the worst she'd do is scream."

"Or call the police."

"I'm willing to risk it. Surprising Mom usually takes more than a two-hour trip, and I don't know when I'll be back up this way."

She gazed at the helmet as if the answer of what she should do would surface in the visor. "I'm supposed to be at the church in the morning, but I could call Drew. I'd need to be back for the food truck in the afternoon."

Drew. The name John had mentioned. "Who's Drew?"

"The pastor. He'd understand. I never call in, and there's not a lot going on anyway."

So the man who'd been helping her with her house was also the pastor who'd planted the seed that Gannon wasn't a Christian. And the church job didn't sound reliable, if she wasn't busy. No wonder she had been doing her own work on her house.

"You got my message?" she asked.

"I did."

Her voice in that recording had been the sweetest sound he'd heard in a long, long time.

She pulled her gaze up from the helmet. "I misrepresented what he said about you. Mostly, he was positive about your music and interviews. He just mentioned that you being in a relationship with Harper would be inconsistent with your beliefs."

"He's right. It'd also be inconsistent with my tastes." He never would've said such a thing to a reporter, who'd take the statement as an opening to ask what his tastes were. But he regarded Adeline evenly. If she needed him to elaborate, he would. Happily.

Her eyes widened, and flattered surprise flickered over her features.

She understood.

Good.

As her expression fell, her lips seemed to form a word and then abandon it. She passed her helmet from one hand to the other. "I'm sorry."

"You're forgiven."

She chewed her lip, regret lingering. If she couldn't understand forgiveness over something minor, how would she ever understand it from God over what had happened between them and with Fitz?

She shifted. "I also saw that story about Harper. The abuse one." The corner of her mouth dipped. At least she looked apologetic instead of suspicious.

"I wish it were easier to clear up that kind of thing. We checked the security footage and confirmed no one else came or went to my apartment that night. She just fell."

Adeline nodded. "I'm sorry they're saying otherwise."

Lots of people had had sympathy for Harper. In response to her video, they'd piled on affirmations.

Though Gannon's inner circle had never doubted his innocence, mostly, from them, he'd faced frustration. Adeline's sympathy marked a first, and his fingers ached to reach for her.

"Where to?" he asked.

Adeline studied him, and doubt crept in. She'd never go along with this.

"Lakeshore?" he asked.

She pulled on the helmet. "Let's visit home."

14

*G*annon paused on the front step to text his mom. If she was awake, she'd get the message and meet him at the door. If not, hopefully she'd see it in the morning before calling the police about the man in her house.

After a minute without an answer, he let himself in. He left his shoes by the door and took a quiet tour of the first floor. Not much had changed in the last eleven years, including the lingering scent of savory cooking spices. He lay down on the couch instead of in the guest room upstairs so he'd wake when Mom got up.

Or at least, that was the plan, but when he opened his eyes in the morning, light drifted through the windows, and the scent of bacon and eggs meant she'd snuck by him into the kitchen. His phone told him it was only six o'clock, but he made himself sit up. Adeline needed to get home before her lunch shift at the food trailer, so they didn't have much time.

The sight of Mom at the oven, checking what must be an egg bake, brought a smile. He leaned against the doorjamb and waited while she refilled her coffee. When she turned and saw him, a grin broke across her face.

He wrapped her in a hug.

When she stepped back, she patted his cheek. "You stinker." She lifted her coffee mug, her smile marking her eyes. "How's Lakeshore? And Adeline?"

"I brought her with, dropped her off at her parents' house." If only all those years ago, giving her a ride home had been so uneventful. Last night, there'd been no good-night kiss, hardly anything but a quick "see you tomorrow." He'd watched until her dad opened the door and welcomed her in.

"It's good you two are talking again. Fitz was a nice boy, but even weddings that do happen are only binding until someone dies."

"She took it hard."

"We all did." She dipped her chin and met his gaze pointedly. She'd been the one to rub his back while he lay on the couch crying after the funeral, where the only words Adeline had spoken to him were, "We did this to him."

Coming home always dredged up memories like these. Maybe that was why he usually flew Mom out to LA and why Adeline had never gotten over Fitz's death—she lived so much closer to the loss, came home to reminders of the tragedy a few times a year. If he wanted to understand her, understand how their mistakes could be so fresh in her mind after all this time, he ought to go see Fitz's grave.

His stomach hardened at the idea, but by resurfacing in her life, he'd made Adeline face feelings like these and worse. The least he could do was go remember. Seeing the grave again would confirm for himself and for Adeline that, even when confronted with the ugliness of the past, he could cling to belief in God's forgiveness.

"You still care for her."

He rubbed his face. Mom wasn't supposed to know. He'd never spoken to her of his feelings for Adeline. "It's complicated. Don't read too much into it."

"Wouldn't dream of it. You've got an entire industry of people to do that for you."

True, and they'd be hard at work today.

ADELINE TURNED the mug tree her dad had made. Her favorite, a white mug dripping with teal glaze, came into view. She put it under the single-serve coffeemaker, then pressed the button. Her parents had been thrilled to open the door and find her on the step. So thrilled, the three of them had stayed up until two playing board games, which had been fun until her alarm sounded that morning.

Mom made her own selection from the mug tree. "The roses are lovely this year, if you'd like to pick some for this morning or to take back home with you."

For this morning meant she could cut flowers to take to Fitz's grave. She visited every time she came to Fox Valley. The whole reason she'd agreed to this trip was to freshen her memory of the stakes, and following through with a visit to the cemetery would dampen the building anticipation for the ride home.

She smiled to thank her mom for the offer, then went back to watching the coffee gurgle into her mug.

"Unless you're not going to the grave this time." Mom wrapped her fingers around her own mug, one with a logo for the church Adeline had attended for years before she'd moved. "Time is short, after all."

"What does that mean?"

"Whatever you need it to, sweetie." She rubbed Adeline's arm. "Fitz won't notice what you do. At some point, you've got to let God take care of the dead."

We're completely forgiven and free.

Free to enjoy being with Gannon, though? She'd wanted to

reestablish their old friendship, but now that she had it, a longing for more had entwined around her heart, immune to the barbs of regret that should've repelled the desire.

"Life's short," Mom continued. "This visit too. I guess the question is, who do you want to spend your time with? The living or the dead?"

Dad wandered in. "Is Gannon going to say hello?"

Her dad had always liked Gannon and Awestruck. He used to mortify her by bobbing along to the music at the back of their shows, but at least she'd known how genuinely he supported them. His encouragement these days, a side hug while scarfing down a hotdog or a comment on how good office help kept a church running smoothly, was nothing in comparison.

For bringing her home for a visit, Gannon had gained bonus points with her parents. Even more, she suspected, for being the first man they'd seen her spend time with since Fitz.

"Unless he's running late, I think he'll say hi." She claimed her coffee, doctored it with sugar and milk, and sipped as she readied herself for the day.

Less than an hour later, she parked the car she'd borrowed from her parents on a dirt road shaded by mature oaks and surrounded by stone crypts. Fitz's parents had secured him a plot in the prettiest cemetery in town, not that she was supposed to enjoy anything about this. She set off on foot around the big, old monuments to the smaller markers on the more recent graves.

She lifted her focus from the uneven grass to locate Fitz's gray headstone among the sculptures and other markers, but between her and the grave stood a man. His back was to her, his black jacket was fitted across his shoulders, and his brown hair was disheveled. A helmet dangled from his right hand.

Her stomach plunged, and she inhaled sharply, freezing. It

had never occurred to her Gannon would be here, the very place she'd determined to go to cool her feelings for him.

She looked back toward the car, thinking of leaving. A crypt hid all but the rear bumper, but the vehicle wasn't that far away. Gannon didn't seem to have seen her yet, and she could probably leave before he did.

But then Gannon lifted his hand to his face and dropped it again. Was he crying?

Could the loss have affected him more powerfully than she'd known? Curiosity and an instinctual desire to offer comfort pulled her forward.

She saw no tears, but when he looked at her, grief pulled at the corners of his eyes and mouth. He fixed his gaze back on the grave marker with Fitz's full name, Gregory Fitzwilliam. After a deep breath, he stepped away. "I'll give you space."

When it came to her grief, all she'd had for years was space. The last thing she wanted was to be alone again with the desolate emotions. Maybe that, rather than curiosity or a noble hope of offering comfort, was the real reason she hadn't run when she'd spotted him here. "I didn't know you would come here."

He slowed, then stopped. His hazel irises lifted her direction before he took another step away.

"Weren't you afraid someone would photograph you?"

He halted again but kept his back turned. "I already told you, Adeline. The truth coming out isn't the worst thing that could happen to me."

"What is?"

He lowered his face as if the weight of a headstone had been loaded onto his shoulders. "I'm only here for the summer. The worst thing would be having to leave you still broken." As if to block her from stopping him with more conversation, he pulled on the helmet and walked off. A minute later, the growl of his motorcycle hammered against the tombs as he pulled out.

Broken. He thought her broken.

Her mom did too or she wouldn't have been trying to talk her out of this visit.

Tegan did, or she wouldn't be trying to get her to apply for a new job.

Adeline studied Fitz's name, engraved in granite. They were all correct. She was broken.

Gannon wasn't letting the past define him. The idea of that freedom was intoxicating, especially now that she'd seen him here, seen that he wasn't denying the cost of his sin, wasn't immune to regret.

Also, he'd shielded her from trouble last night. He'd been so attentive in helping her off the ladder, had hidden her under the helmet, and had paid hundreds to ensure she would be safe on the bike.

There was something to him, to his belief that, though she was broken, she was worth protecting and making whole again. The longing returned, squeezing so hard, breathing took effort. She wanted that wholeness, and it seemed the closer she got to Gannon, the more possible it became.

WHAT WOULD BE *the worst thing?*

Prior to Adeline's question, Gannon had put no thought into what he'd most hate to experience, but as soon as she asked, the answer had flashed through his mind, and now that he'd seen the truth, he couldn't erase the realization.

Having to leave you.

He'd almost stopped there, almost hadn't added those last couple of words. He'd rented Havenridge indefinitely. He'd bided his time, letting days slip between conversations with

Adeline, but when she'd asked that question, he saw how much time he'd wasted.

He couldn't stay indefinitely. He had commitments that required he return to LA at the end of summer. What business did he have trying to ignite her old feelings for him? He'd still leave, and then what? They lived separate lives.

He hadn't come to Lakeshore to win her over—that was a goal he'd added when he'd seen her. Maybe it was for the best that she wasn't interested. If a relationship didn't work out, the disappointment would be on his end, and he'd shouldered that pain before. Like the possibility of seeing their past splashed across the front page, he didn't relish the idea, but survival would necessitate he cope again.

So, he'd added the "still broken."

Having to leave you still broken.

She'd suffer until she found healing—something the last nine years had proved she wouldn't find on her own. The clock had been ticking for weeks already, and though Adeline was finally softening, true healing took more time than he had.

The inevitability of the worst happening dropped even more heaviness over him than seeing Fitz's grave had. It pulled at him all the way back to his mom's house, lingered in the back of his mind as they visited and eventually said goodbye, and he dragged it with him when he went to the Greens' house to collect Adeline.

The sky was overcast, but the cloud cover was thin enough to glow in the general direction of the sun. In her new pants and jacket, Adeline stood with her mom at the side of the house. Mrs. Green clipped gigantic collections of blue flowers off a thigh-high bush, but Adeline smiled his direction.

He got off the bike and hooked his helmet on the handle-bars as his phone went off. For most people he wouldn't have answered, but John's name showed on the display.

"What's up?"

"Matt hit Tim's rental in the garage last night."

"Fantastic." Gannon turned away from Adeline. She already had enough to not like about him without knowing about the drama within the band. "Is he all right?"

"Yeah. He was as surprised as the rest of us this morning."

"I assume Tim's working it out?"

"The things Tim can do are too little, too late. I'm not sure keeping Matt on is helping him."

So John was back to the idea of firing Matt.

Adeline would be uncomfortable around Matt, and she'd hate getting caught anywhere near the bad press his behavior could lead to. But what would she think if Gannon fired someone? They'd just come from Fitz's grave.

"We can talk when I get back." He disconnected and pivoted back toward the house.

The front door opened. Adeline's dad emerged, and her mom rushed inside with the flowers. A happy family scene.

Would he ever have that?

"Gannon, how you doing? Long time no see." Adeline's dad gave him a firm handshake.

"I'm good, Mr. Green. How are you?" His PR training spoke for him—never complain, be grateful, care about people. Under normal circumstances, these things came naturally.

"Lance. Call me Lance. You're not a high schooler anymore." He chuckled. "Your last record won quite a few accolades, I understand. We're beyond proud of you."

Adeline picked up her helmet from the front stoop and approached.

Her dad slung his arm around her as he continued. "Sort of wish we'd never kept Addie from going with you boys. Bet with her, you would've gotten that record deal faster."

Adeline gave him a helpless smile that seemed to say, *Parents, right?*

But her dad's belief in her wasn't misplaced. She had talent.

"We hated to leave her behind, but we were just stupid kids. The move could've turned out badly."

Adeline bit her lip at that.

Gannon tipped his head, silently acknowledging that in important ways, the band's early days in California had turned out badly. If she'd come, everything might've played out differently—but for the better or the worse?

"But it didn't." Lance slugged his shoulder, then circled the bike. "This looks like fun."

Gannon followed him into conversation about the motorcycle until Mrs. Green came outside again, holding the flowers. She handed them to Adeline, and Lance laughed.

"Janie, how's she going to get those home on this?"

Mrs. Green dropped her hands to her sides, and her mouth popped open. "You rode here on a motorcycle? All that way? In the dark?"

"There were hints, Mom." The helmet in one hand and flowers in the other, Adeline lifted her arms the way she had when she'd exited the dressing room last night.

Lance pulled Janie to his side, gaze kind but serious as it focused on Gannon. "Gannon's a good driver, right? He's going to be careful."

"Yes, sir, but I'm afraid the flowers probably wouldn't survive the trip."

Lance clapped Gannon's hand into a second handshake while Adeline said goodbye to her mom.

When they switched, Janie squeezed Gannon's arm. "Treat my baby well."

"I'll get her home in one piece."

She held her focus on him an extra beat, conveying she hadn't meant for her directive to apply only to the ride. Clearly, she had the same ideas about them as his own mom.

Though they were wrong, he nodded. He'd wronged Adeline years ago, but he'd do everything in his power to treat her well now. That meant seeking her healing above his own desire for a romance that he'd have to leave behind when he went back to his normal responsibilities. In return for his nod, Mrs. Green pulled him into a hug, the flowers damp and fragile against his neck.

15

A pair of picnic tables sat on a concrete slab beneath a metal roof in the wayside. Adeline tightened her arms around Gannon for the bump as he steered the bike up between the tables, under the shelter. As she pulled off her helmet, the noise of rain pounding the roof reached her ears.

Gannon jerked his own helmet through the air, sending a spray of water out toward the grass. "I'd rather not keep going in this."

Her front, where she'd been leaning against him, was dry, but the arms and back of her jacket were soaked. She removed the outer layer and took her phone from one of the zippered pockets. Thankfully, the device hadn't gotten wet. "I'll text Asher. If the weather's the same in Lakeshore, the food truck won't be busy."

A notification reported Asher had already reached out to her.

She dialed voicemail.

"You don't have to come in today. Some guys with serious cameras are hanging around, and it's gloomy anyway."

Gannon whisking her away last night must've made her

seem worth watching. She didn't mind as much as she might've a couple of days before. Dealing with some attention came with the territory of life among the living—when Gannon was involved, anyway.

She texted Asher and focused on Gannon. He'd shed his jacket and taken a seat on the picnic table, feet on the bench, elbows on his knees.

"Photographers are waiting at the truck. Asher said to take the day off."

He sighed heavily. "I'm sure they're at your house too. I'm sorry."

Her nerves threatened to raise her voice an octave as she searched for a way to admit everything he'd helped her realize this morning. "Maybe it's like you said. Maybe the press and the stories they write aren't the worst things."

He hadn't shaved that morning, and coarseness marked his jaw. Still, he was fit for a photoshoot. Nothing could mute the golden-brown ring at the center of his blue-green irises. "And what would be?"

"Maybe a new fear doesn't have to replace the old one."

His hazel eyes followed her as she sat beside him.

Her vision flitted away from his face. His short sleeves revealed the mysterious characters on the inside of his left forearm.

She tilted her head. "I've been meaning to ask about that."

He glanced at the tattoo. "Hebrew. Psalm 51:14. Basically says, 'Forgive me for the blood I've shed, and I'll sing of your righteousness.' Got it after Fitz died."

More confirmation she'd been unduly hard on him. She longed to reach out to him, but could she just do that? Touch him? After everything?

The air flashed with lightning, and a few seconds later, thunder reverberated like a falling drum. The trees that surrounded the shelter swished with rain and wind.

"I almost didn't go to his grave this morning," she said. "Next time I'm home, I don't think I will." The admission took almost as much courage as touching his arm would've. "Up until now, I've gone each time."

Gannon brought his gaze in from the greenery to study her face. His mouth hinted at a smile before his line of sight roved back to the trees. "That's quite a change."

"It's because of what you said about us being forgiven and free. And my mom said something this morning about life being short and did I want to spend it with the living or the dead."

"And you chose the living." He checked her expression.

"I did. I do." She straightened her fingers, meaning to touch his forearm after all, but he stood.

At the edge of the shelter, he stopped with his back to her. "That's good news. A good choice."

He didn't understand what she'd meant, and was she sure, absolutely sure, she wanted this? A romance with Gannon Vaughn? She'd glimpsed his life, the fans, the photographers, the constant attention. But that storm didn't scare her as much after what she'd seen at the grave that morning. She'd thought him blind to the consequences of their sin. He wasn't, and he had freedom she wanted for herself. Freedom that said they could be together.

The rain eased as her heartbeat increased.

She longed to enjoy a relationship with him.

But she'd been burying her feelings for him for so long, she felt helplessly exposed at the thought of revealing her change of heart. Paralyzing fear told her the possibility of a future together was too good to be true. She couldn't say how disaster would come about, but in the shadows, she saw the vague shapes of possibilities. He'd reject her. God would determine she didn't deserve this happiness. She'd make another mistake and end up more broken.

But this time would be different. Right?

She played possibilities in her mind so long, the rain let up entirely.

When she realized a good twenty minutes had passed in silence, she rubbed her cheeks, embarrassed. Even if she couldn't know the future and didn't know how to proceed with Gannon, she could've made normal conversation.

Of course, he could've too. What had he been thinking that whole time, staring off into the woods so quietly for so long?

A minivan exited the highway and splashed through puddles in the gravel lot. It stopped beside the shelter, and the doors slid open. A kid jumped from the van to the gravel.

Gannon grabbed his coat. "We need to get moving."

The family lined up along the edge of the concrete slab, holding what must've been their lunches, waiting for Gannon to get his motorcycle back where it belonged. She turned to find Gannon already seated on the bike.

In Lakeshore, he pulled over a few blocks from her house. "Sorry, but it's best if you walk from here. Cut through the back-yards, and maybe they won't get a shot of you."

She pulled off her helmet, wishing he'd do the same. Instead, his head swiveled as if he were watching for photographers. The moment she'd missed at the wayside wouldn't happen here.

Maybe it was better this way.

She stepped back with a wave and let him go.

THE NEXT DAY, Gannon found John studying the lake from the overlook on the cliff. Brown and gray tinged the waves under the cloudy sky. His dogs played nearby, deep in a game of tug-of-war.

Gannon took a seat on the bench that ran along the three-foot-tall wall. "This thing with Adeline's doomed, isn't it?"

Amusement tugged John's expression. "Is there a thing now?"

"No." Though he'd almost tried to start one. He'd narrowly resisted kissing her at the wayside yesterday, telling himself he had to leave her better than he'd found her. "In a few weeks, we'll leave. Between the press, Matt, our schedule, and distance, I don't know how it could work long term. If I start something more than a friendship, isn't that making promises I can't keep?"

Trigger, the gray pit bull, barked as Camo lay down, chewing on the toy they'd battled over. John stepped away long enough to throw the toy and restart the game, then returned. "You've got cold feet."

"We went to the cemetery. If I've got cold feet, it's from standing on a grave."

"Stand on *grace*."

Grace and grave. A one-letter difference that could change everything—or stand between him and Adeline forever.

His phone sounded, and he scrambled to pull it from his pocket, hoping to see Adeline's name.

John chuckled as he and the dogs wandered off.

But the caller was only Harper.

He lifted his phone and answered. "Where've you been?"

"Who's this girl?" Harper sounded as if she'd opened her dressing room to find it occupied by someone else.

The "girl" had to be Adeline. His pleasure at getting to talk about her proved one more time how much of a goner he was. But with Harper, he had to be careful. He scanned the lake. "What girl?"

"This small-town mystery girl I'm looking at."

"I don't know what you're looking at." But he could guess.

Harper was addicted to gossip sites, the kinds that could get miles of copy out of one blurry photo of him and Adeline on a motorcycle.

"Adeline Green." Harper pronounced the name as if she had to sound it out one syllable at a time. "She's cute, I guess, if you're into plain."

Plain? Adeline's silky hair could beat out Harper's teased and heavily sprayed styles any day. Instead of makeup, all it took to bring out Adeline's eyes was that smile he saw so rarely or a little sunlight, which highlighted her brown irises with honey.

"She's a hot dog vendor?" Harper's laugh rang like a wind chime. "You can't be serious about this, Gannon."

He put the call on speaker to search for the article, see what they'd written, and decide if he ought to warn Adeline or not. "Why does it matter to you who I'm serious about? You've got a boyfriend."

"Don't you hear anything? Colton dumped me. He wants nothing to do with me. No one does. I'm disposable to everyone."

"Don't talk like that."

"What? I am. You can't prove otherwise."

He'd find the article later. The breakup could only be good news. Though he doubted Colton had attacked Harper since he hadn't been on the security tape, the relationship had been responsible for many of Harper's ups and downs. Once she got past the sting of it, maybe she'd even out.

He switched off speaker and brought the phone back to his ear. "My texts and calls prove I care, but you chose to ignore them until you got jealous."

"Don't pretend you mind the attention. We've been dancing around this for months. With Colton out of the picture, you don't have to settle for less."

He bit back his response. If he defended Adeline, Harper would take that as confirmation of a romance, and she'd share the news publicly in ways that would hurt Adeline. He had to stay focused on himself and Harper. "You and I would never be happy together."

"You're my best friend."

Maybe, but she wasn't his. "You know I'm here for you, Harper—"

"I do. Think of how much you've helped me. And I love what you believe. I want to know more about it. I'll come up. We can talk for hours and hours."

"You're not coming here." He mimicked the tone security used with fans. "If you need something, you can call, but if you keep after more of a relationship, I'm done."

"So there's more to you and this girl."

His phone beeped, and the display showed Adeline's name. Joy rushed in. Yes, there was more. Always had been, and if he could find a way, despite all the reasons he told himself it would never work, there always would be.

ADELINE SAT on the back step and watched Bruce sniff the grass. Since the phone had rung four times already, she started planning a voicemail for Gannon. She didn't want to leave another fumbling one.

"Adeline." His smiling voice—not a recording—gave her a thrill that alone justified the call.

"Hey." She gulped. What had been her excuse for calling? It wasn't just to indulge her crush. "Did you have something to do with the sanding being finished when I got home?"

"I'm not sure what you mean."

"Funny. Tegan, Drew, and Chip all said the same thing. Only they were more convincing."

Gannon's rich voice rumbled with laughter, his lack of further denials admission enough.

"Thanks." She brushed dust from the step beside her. "I appreciate not having to go back up with a sander. The caulk gun and paint shouldn't be nearly so hard to control."

"I hired them to prep and paint the whole thing. They'll be back Monday."

"Gannon, that's too much. You can't—"

"Let me do this." His tone warmed. "I don't like the possibility of you falling while you're holding a paintbrush any more than I liked it while you were holding a sander. I promised your mom I'd take care of you. I can't let you risk your life over paint."

She'd reached home without incident yesterday, but when she'd circled her house to check on the worksite, a photographer had shouted questions. Where had Gannon taken her the night before? Were they officially a couple? What was it like to date him?

She'd ignored the man. Still, her stomach tightened every time she thought about the questions. What *would* it be like to be Gannon Vaughn's girlfriend?

Nervous energy fluttered in her chest. "My mom asked you to take care of me?"

"She said to treat you well."

"And you agreed to." She fought it, but he had to hear the smile lift her voice.

"Of course. You know that's been my intention this whole summer."

The tenderness in his tone eased past her defenses. Not a difficult task. She'd waited to call him about the work he'd hired out, but the extra time had done nothing but make her miss him more.

"I do know," she said.

A beat, and then when he spoke again, she heard notes of gentle happiness. "What are you up to?"

Her stomach hopped like a bow against taut strings. "I'm

getting ready. The crew from church is coming, and we're working on my porch tonight." Should she invite him to come too? If he'd asked about her plans because he wanted to get together, he probably hadn't envisioned a group activity. Even less, a group activity that involved manual labor.

"What's wrong with your porch?"

Oh. She'd never told him about the letter from the neighborhood association. "It needs to be replaced. A contractor from church will make sure it's done right. Apparently with everyone's help, it won't be that big of a deal."

Just as she was about to invite him, he spoke. "You should call it off. We can hire someone to do the work. Paparazzi will be there. They've already started writing about us."

Of course they had. Why did Gannon sound so frustrated?

Bruce sat beside her. She rubbed his warm ears. "They've been out front since I got home. What are they saying?"

"I haven't looked yet, but I hear they're making us out to be a couple."

"Oh." So he didn't want to look like a couple. Had she taken too long to come around? He'd given up on her?

"I'm sorry. I wish I could stop them, but people buy it. The less we give them, the less they have to run with."

She pulled Bruce a little closer, earning herself a kiss that didn't do much for her nosediving hopes. "Wouldn't we look more like a couple if you paid people to fix my house?"

"They wouldn't know who hired the contractors."

"Everyone knows I don't have the money for it or I would've hired someone myself. The church is helping because I couldn't do the porch myself or afford a carpenter, and they don't want me to have to pay the fines."

"What fines?"

He might as well know. He was already unhappy, and with press digging around, her standing with the neighborhood association would come out eventually.

"My house isn't up to the standards for the neighborhood, so the association gave me ninety days to fix it. The porch and the paint."

His silence stretched. He was probably thinking about how different they were, him on top of the world and her barely keeping a grip on a rundown house.

"Anyway. None of that's your problem. If they stop seeing us together, they'll lose interest."

"Adeline—"

"No, it's fine." Good thing she'd hesitated to reach out to him at the wayside. This rejection, subtle as it was, stung enough. "They're writing rumors. I'm more concerned with reality. The big waste container is here, Chip has the materials, and a team of deacons is coming. Plus, Drew's bringing the youth group over to help. I'm not canceling such a big production."

He sighed. Maybe he was as disappointed as she was by the course this conversation had taken. "When are they working?"

"Four until dark, and they'll come back tomorrow if they need to, but I have to work then, anyway."

"And if your boss tells you to stay home again?"

"He didn't order me to. If I'm such an attraction, I'll bring in extra business." And work would help keep her busy and prevent her from thinking about Gannon.

"Okay. Good luck. Let me know if you run into trouble."

"Thanks." She kept the phone to her ear a little longer, but only dead air followed.

16

*A*deline helped carry a chunk of her old porch, but the men on either end probably could've moved the debris without her. As the boards thudded into the large trash container, she stepped back to let a couple of the boys hoist another section of rotting floorboards over and in.

The porch was mostly gone already, and two or three hours of daylight remained.

Three photographers lingered on the sidewalk, but their interest had waned since they'd confirmed none of the thirteen males on the premises—Chip, Drew, five deacons, and six high school boys—were band members.

Good. They didn't need to snap any more unflattering pictures of her.

She'd found the article Gannon had mentioned. The piece featured a shot of Gannon leading her to the motorcycle. His jacket had, indeed, made her look like a clown.

But in that picture, he'd held her hand and looked back at her.

All eyes were on him, but his eyes were on her.

Or at least, for that moment, they had been.

The article had been kind enough to end with a reminder that the last woman Gannon had been involved with was Harper English.

Beautiful, famous Harper English.

Olivia and her friends advanced up the sidewalk to join the work. Judging by their meticulous hair and makeup, they would be even less help than Adeline had been to that point. Tegan seemed to have made herself useful, though, so Adeline would too.

She turned to find something to carry to the waste bin, but as she did, Olivia slid her slender arm through Adeline's. "So where did he take you? You didn't come home."

A few of the boys' heads swiveled their way too. Had everyone read that article? The piece had called their trip a "romantic getaway" and had listed resorts in driving distance where they could've stayed. How mortifying.

"We went to visit our parents. I stayed with my mom and dad. He saw his mom. Not everything on the Internet is true."

Olivia shrugged, her shoulder brushing Adeline's. "Amy saw him drop you off."

Gannon had been more serious than she'd known when he'd texted to not do anything she didn't want the world to know about. "We're old friends. We went to high school together. Nothing romantic has happened."

"Do you think we could meet him? Because he just left, and—"

A crash interrupted her. They turned to see Drew and two of the adults stepping back from the waste container. On spotting Olivia and Adeline, Drew waved them in.

"Olivia, can you find a rake and take care of that?" He motioned to the collection of leaves and sawdust exposed by the disappearing porch.

"There's one in the shed at the back of the yard," Adeline said. "And yard waste bags."

With a heavy sigh, Olivia plodded off.

Drew smiled. "I'm not sure what she was expecting. I made it clear this was a service project, not a meet and greet. But more of the boys showed up than I expected too, so she's in good company hoping it'll turn into that."

She checked on the photographers again, expecting to see more of the same, but all three had their cameras up and pointed at her and Drew. "Speaking of ..."

"Let's get drinks for everyone." Drew tilted his head toward the house, and Adeline led the way around the back and through the entrance by the kitchen.

Bruce ran up, whining. She kneeled to pet him. The fur on his paws was wet with pink skin showing through. He must've been licking them for quite a while.

"Poor baby. The noise must be stressing him out."

A loud creak sounded, another part of the porch coming off the house, and Bruce buried his head against her shoulder. He was melting into a puddle of fear.

The skin around Drew's eyes creased. "How about you? Are you doing okay with the press and everything?"

"Yeah. Fine. It's just frustrating, the things those people will write. All we did was visit home." She stroked Bruce's thick fur.

"You two must be getting along better."

Better? Yes. But not as well as she'd like. The proximity on the bike had been a shock to her, but he'd placed her arm around his body, pulling her even closer, allowing her to hold on. This from a man who paid his staff to prevent others from getting that close.

She felt special around him. She felt special just thinking of him. As long as she didn't think about how he'd dropped her off or his tone on the phone earlier.

Drew studied her.

She left Bruce and retrieved the lemonade mix she'd

bought for volunteers. "I had to go with him. A photographer was here."

"You don't seem to mind them too much today."

He had her there. She'd seen what they'd written. Though the pictures and the description of her jobs weren't flattering, the article hadn't mentioned the past at all. Maybe she'd been wrong to assume they'd dig deep. Why bother when they could sell tabloids without sorting through years of history?

A puff of lemony sugar lifted from the mix as she poured it into a pitcher.

Bruce leaned against her leg, still whining.

"Can you take over?" She stepped from the pitcher and went back to keeping the dog company. Maybe she ought to stay in for the rest of the night for his sake. How would he fare tomorrow if the guys had to come back to finish the footings while she was working?

Drew poured water into the pitcher. "Does it worry you that they keep taking pictures of us?"

There'd been no mention or pictures of Drew in the article she'd seen, so she shook her head. "Does it worry you?"

"It's definitely an escalation from what I'm used to, but any pastor has to put up with scrutiny." He turned off the faucet and took a spoon from the jar next to the oven. "I dated a woman at the church where I youth pastored before coming here. Someone told her she was a bad example because she wore skinny jeans, someone else insisted we needed to bring a chaperone on our dates, and a lot of people thought she should do as much with the youth as I did, but she had her own full-time job."

"I hope you defended her."

"I did, but expectations have a way of stomping out flames. It takes a certain type to date a pastor, someone with thick skin and the kind of relationship with God that lends peace and discretion in the midst of varying opinions."

Peace? All that to date a pastor. She looked into poor Bruce's brown eyes. She'd felt happy and excited yesterday before beginning the journey home, but since then, she'd been on a rollercoaster. She feared it would take a lot more to date a rock star, and she might not have it.

THE PAPARAZZI TURNED their cameras on the car as soon as Gannon opened his door, but he and John continued. They'd come prepared for the attention—autographed T-shirts for the teens at the worksite and two guards to keep the photographers at a respectable distance. For all they'd see, this was nothing more than a community service project.

Behind closed doors would be another story, if Gannon could help it.

Adeline had interrupted when he'd tried to tell her he did consider her problems his own. He wasn't sure what had prompted her change in tone, but the only way to undo it would be an in-person conversation.

First, he'd pitch in with the porch. If he'd already worked for her an hour or two before he tried a conversation, guilt—if nothing else—would earn him an audience. Besides, if he went inside now, they'd have two minutes, tops, before the teens came in to seek him out.

When he and John stepped into the yard, the porch was already gone. The old columns had been replaced by makeshift supports to keep the porch roof aloft as it waited for the new structure. The adults were in various stages of digging holes for footings with an auger and hole diggers. The youth group kids bagged brush in large paper sacks.

No Adeline.

That would make this next part, focusing on the crowd, less

a test of his patience than if she hung in the background the whole time, in sight but out of reach.

One of the boys spotted them and nudged the kid next to him. A girl squawked and jumped, tugging her friend forward and beginning the onslaught.

After twenty minutes of handing out T-shirts, posing for selfies, and giving the local paper a statement, he and John secured the job of mixing and pouring the concrete.

High schoolers rushed to assist them. They'd finished their first batch when the pastor came from behind the house. Had he been with Adeline this whole time?

Gannon tipped the wheelbarrow of concrete, and John used a shovel to guide the slop into the cylindrical form. Meanwhile, the boys who'd helped mix the ingredients waited for them to bring back the wheelbarrow for the next load.

Drew stopped by his students. "How long have you guys been standing here?"

"We're helping mix concrete, right, Gannon?"

He'd lost track of how many times the kids had ended sentences that way.

The boy wore a proud smile, but if he wanted to impress the pastor, he'd failed.

Drew's head swung toward where Gannon stood with the wheelbarrow. He seemed to study him, the tattoos exposed by the tank he wore, and maybe the quality of work he was doing. After a few seconds, he gave a slight, unenthusiastic smile and walked over to talk with the project leader, Chip.

"Drew?" John timed the question to coincide with the noise of his shovel grating against the wet concrete. When Gannon nodded, John smirked. "Probably wants to know who does your ink."

Gannon chuckled, but when he looked a few minutes later and found Drew watching again, he felt as though he might as well be sinking in concrete. If Drew had been with Adeline and he'd come outside with a grudge, she might be inside not because she had a project there but because she was upset.

A window looked out onto what used to be the front porch. Did she know he was out here? Was she happy about it or grumbling?

The work dragged on an hour before Chip pressed the last of the brackets into the wet concrete and smoothed the surface with a trowel, finishing the footings.

Drew raised both hands to get the kids' attention. "The deacons have offered to take the cleanup from here. Adeline's got snacks ready, so we're going to head in for a devo and worship before calling it a night."

Olivia, the girl with the light brown hair who'd been among the first to greet him, peered at Gannon. "Are you coming, Gannon? John?"

He had no intentions of leaving without seeing Adeline, so he nodded. With that, the kids swept them along into the house. He was in the back entryway when his phone buzzed with a text from Tim.

Harper missed an event. They're asking if you know where she is.

No. Why would I? He stepped into the kitchen.

Adeline and her roommate had added fanciful touches to the plain, worn space. A fox salt-and-pepper set curled together on the counter. Brushes for washing dishes stood in a vase by the sink. A floral-print square of fabric decorated the center of the table. A matching hand towel hung from a cabinet handle.

His phone vibrated again with Tim's response. *These people are as dramatic as she is. Don't worry about it.*

He didn't plan to. He turned the phone to silent and pocketed it.

A double-wide doorway allowed a view of the living room. The gray carpet and sectional couch appeared newer, but the coffee table had seen better decades. It sat on a teal rug, and someone had placed a stack of teal and blue books and a vase with silk flowers on the surface.

The kids shifted toward the food on the kitchen table, and John followed them while Gannon entered the living room. A small flat-screen sat on a cabinet that, judging by the marks in the carpet, had been pushed against the wall to make room for the kids tonight.

"Gannon." The pleased surprise in Adeline's voice brought a smile before he turned. So she hadn't been shooting daggers at him out the window this whole time.

She stood at the mouth of a hallway to his left. Her hair was pulled back in a ponytail, and shorter pieces framed her face. She wore a T-shirt and jean shorts. No pretense. No trying to make herself something she wasn't. If anything, she was a lot more than she made herself out to be.

An old black dog threaded around her and sat in front of him. He petted the dog's head, but his focus wandered back to Adeline.

"I didn't know you were here." She hooked a thumb through a belt loop on her shorts, then pushed her fingers into her pocket. Was she nervous? "You were helping?"

"For a little while." He stopped rubbing the dog's head, but then it scooted closer with a whine, so he kept it up. "I like your place."

Her eyebrows curved skeptically as she glanced around, but before she could reply, John came in with a plate of food and three of the high schoolers.

The kids plunked onto the couch, but John slung his free arm around Adeline's shoulders. "There's our girl." His attention landed on the dog. "And who's this?"

"I'm watching him for the shelter. His name is Bruce."

When John dropped to greet the dog, Gannon studied Adeline. "We need to talk."

She must've been able to read at least some of his intentions because pink tinged her cheeks. Her focus dodged his to follow movement behind him. Drew had entered the room carrying a guitar case and a Bible.

"After?" She lifted her hand toward an empty section of the couch, the last piece of furniture open.

"You take it. I'm fine here." He settled on the floor by the wall.

Drew's ten-minute devotional used the disciples as examples of how encounters with God should change people. He wound down with lists of good and bad behavior from a passage in Galatians 5.

The kids' interest held all the way through the prayer, but when Drew flipped the latches on the guitar case, Olivia leaned forward. "Gannon, you should play!"

Others quickly agreed.

Drew hesitated, his grip on the neck of the guitar visibly tight.

Suspecting he knew how this would go, Gannon didn't move forward.

But all the kids watched him, hopeful.

"I can," he said. "I'm sure I know enough of the same songs as the group."

Drew cleared his throat and fit his right arm over the instrument, preparing to play. "I'd like this to be a time of worship that's about God, not the musician."

One of Olivia's friends bounced in her seat. "But he knows the songs about God, he said."

"Yeah." A boy pushed his hair out of his face as if eye contact would be more convincing. "We should find a drum too. Music is their job."

"And leading worship is your pastor's job." Gannon motioned to Drew to send the attention in his direction.

Drew nodded his thanks, then focused on the kids. "Rock stars and worship leaders aren't interchangeable. They're

different jobs with different qualifications. Let's focus on God."
He started a song.

Different jobs with different qualifications? Okay, but what
did leading worship require besides a love of God and an
ability to carry a tune? Which did Drew think he lacked?

Gannon glanced at Adeline, but she stared at her hands as
if to avoid his gaze. John shook his head slightly and opened his
hand, telling Gannon to drop it.

17

*A*deline went on tiptoe to reach her arms around John's shoulders for a hug.

"See you around." He lifted her off the ground for a moment. "I'll send the car back for Gannon."

He nodded to Drew, who hovered by the dining table, then left.

Drew bumped the table, which he'd lingered to help clear. "You look tired." His tone was flat.

She certainly didn't feel tired. Her pulse buzzed, a mixture of excitement and guilt she hadn't experienced since the night she'd gone to that party looking for Gannon. That night, their relationship had been nothing more than hints and a wild crush, and here she was again.

But whatever happened, they would not repeat their mistakes. Experience had been a harsh teacher.

At the door, she thanked Drew for all the work and bid him good night.

Back in the living room, Bruce lay curled in his bed in the corner.

Gannon stood at the wall, studying a painting she'd done

on a piece of plywood. He'd either ripped the sleeves off his T-shirt or had bought it distressed that way. Whatever the case, she had a full view of his tattoos.

The detail in the lion made it a work of art. On his other shoulder, a tree burned with orange flames so realistic they looked painful. A simplified version of that design had marked the cover of their first album. He also had a compass on the side of his calf, exposed by his knee-length shorts.

No cross, which would've been the first tattoo she would've guessed he'd have. Perhaps one spanned those broad shoulders?

Before he could turn and catch her staring, she stepped up next to him. The painting he studied was nothing more than swirls of blues and yellow with a touch of pink here and there. He'd know she'd painted it by the initials in the corner. What did her simplistic art look like to him? What kind of art did he have in his house?

"Inspired by the lake?"

"A happy accident, but that's what it reminds me of too."

Nodding, he turned, eyes focusing on the front window.

The sheers had been pulled, but not the curtains them-selves. She kneeled on the couch, drew the curtains in case photographers remained outside, and turned to sit.

He took a place next to her, angled so their knees were an inch or two apart. "I hope you don't mind that I came. You said something about the paparazzi losing interest if they didn't see us together, but I didn't get the feeling that was what either of us wanted. Not at that price."

"Even if they write about us like we're a couple?"

"I never said I minded that."

Hadn't he?

No, not directly. She'd assumed, based on his tone.

She smiled. She couldn't help it.

A smile played at Gannon's mouth too. "What I don't want

169

is you in the middle of a media circus you want no part of. The opinions and rumors can get nasty."

"Like the ones about you and Harper."

"Exactly."

"Well. I'm more concerned about the reality than the rumors."

He didn't break eye contact. However intricate his tattoos, they were nothing compared to his eyes. That golden ring around his pupils got her every time. "The reality is that Harper and I are hardly even friends, and I never hurt her."

She ought to ask what he wanted the reality of his relationship with her to be, but she dipped her head and studied her hands instead.

"Does Drew believe the tabloids about me and Harper?"

"I think he knows not to put a lot of weight on what they write."

"Thoughts on what he said, then?"

Had Gannon been bothered by Drew's devotional too? She'd managed to squelch the guilt the passage had raised, but now the discomfort returned, burning in her throat.

She gulped. "The verses in Galatians say the sexually immoral won't inherit the kingdom of God."

His forehead knotted. "But you said he doesn't believe the tabloids, so why the speech about me not being qualified to lead worship?"

Oh. So Gannon had been offended by that comment, not convicted by the devotional as she had been. She gripped her hands together, hanging tight through the disappointment and embarrassment. "He probably wanted the kids to pay attention to God, not you."

"They were paying attention to me, regardless."

She nodded and shrugged.

Gannon watched as if he knew he'd lost her somewhere along the line.

Maybe she should just face it. The embarrassment, the vulnerability. Why carry her burning conscience any longer? If she didn't deal with this, she'd never fully enjoy time with Gannon, even if their attraction was mutual. "I don't think Drew was trying to give either of us a hard time, but passages like what he talked about tonight always leave me feeling unsettled."

"Why?"

He didn't know? Looking for something to focus on other than him, her gaze landed on the guitar case across the room. Drew must've forgotten it.

"The way I understand it," he said, "that passage is about ongoing sin, and you told me you haven't had any relationships." His eyebrows lifted as if to ask if he was correct.

"True." And in more than the way he meant. She hadn't slept with anyone, and she hadn't had true friendships either. Only recently had she started talking with Tegan.

"So this unsettled feeling is because what we did nine years ago is still separating you from God."

Tears jumped to her eyes, but she shook her head. "That seems like a strong way to put it."

Gannon pressed his elbows on his knees and massaged his thumbs against his temples. She blinked and blinked, but the tears wouldn't evaporate. He and her emotions were taking this so much more seriously than she'd intended. Why couldn't this not be a big deal? Why did she have to be on the verge of crying? When she'd found him in her living room tonight, she'd wanted this evening to go so very differently.

Gannon cleared his throat, then brushed her wrist, bringing to life every nerve within three inches of his touch. "I've made a big assumption."

"What?"

"I assumed you thought you were right with God."

"I am. I just …"

His hand covered hers. "You're not, Addie, and I think you know it. That passage is about who gets to be with God eternally and who doesn't. If it leaves you unsettled, you must feel some degree of separation that even you sense is a problem."

The burning in her throat ate her oxygen. She struggled for calm breaths, clenching her fingers into a fist under Gannon's hand.

"Tell me the story." He pressed his thumb gently against the side of her fist until she held his hand instead of digging her fingernails into her own palm. "What happened between you and God after that night?"

She didn't want to get into this, but Gannon wouldn't give this up. She'd already said enough to ruin their night. She might as well confess all.

"I avoided church. I told my parents I was sick. The next week, I said I was going to a service with a friend, but I went to a park instead." A park on the small lake that bordered their hometown. She'd stared at the other shore and wished she could move to get away from her mistakes, her messed up life. Maybe all those hours spent gazing at the water had been the reason she'd chosen Lakeshore when she finally relocated. "I did that for months. I felt like a complete failure. A fraud."

He flinched, and his hand felt heavier around hers. "And when Fitz died?"

"I switched. I'd been playing bass up until then, but when he died, the bass went in a closet, and I went back to church. Just to be there. To do what God wanted."

"You didn't think He'd want you to play anymore?"

"He wanted me there—at church. He wanted me to be a better person. But He wouldn't want praise from someone like me, and I had no right to ask Him for anything."

Gannon waited, and the last confession burned its way out.

"I stopped praying too."

"You still don't?"

"Except when I was up on that ladder." She laughed.

Pathetic.

His smile wilted as soon as it rose. "The only time in years?"

"Why would He want to hear from me? Because I know it's not so much about one sin or another, but what if my heart isn't in the right place? Can we ever be repentant enough or loyal enough to God?"

"No, I don't think so."

She'd expected him to say yes, to tell her she just had to believe. At his unexpected answer, her fingers tightened around his.

Another smile flickered, his gaze on their hands, before his expression sobered again. "I don't think our hearts can be right on their own, but we can follow David's example and ask God to create clean hearts in us. He can do for us what we can't do for ourselves."

"That seems like a lot to ask."

"Asking is the only way. And He's happy to rescue us."

She nodded, though she hadn't thought of God as happy in ages and still couldn't picture it.

Gannon rubbed his forehead, and she glimpsed the Hebrew script. He'd said it essentially meant, *Forgive me, and I'll sing your praises.* A fitting verse for a lead singer, and a prayer God had obviously answered. But would He answer a prayer from her? She didn't deserve it. She couldn't offer anything comparable to the huge platform Gannon had.

She ran her finger over one of the symbols and then checked his face again. Did her touch do to him what his had to her? If so, the timing probably wasn't appropriate.

But he stared at the tattoo too. "The clean heart passage and this one are both in the same psalm. Psalm 51. David wrote it after having Uriah killed to cover up what he'd done with Bathsheba."

"Oh." Shock lifted her hand.

When he'd told her the reference of the verse at the wayside, she hadn't bothered to look it up.

"Remembering how God restored David was the only way I could live with myself after Fitz died."

She slid her hand back over the symbols, maybe to absorb their truth. They were a link across the ages to someone who'd found hope in a situation similar to the one that had been drowning her for years. And it didn't hurt that the inscription was on Gannon's forearm.

"Addie, I'm sorry."

She lifted her gaze. His pained expression startled the tears from her eyes.

"I had no idea what I was doing to your faith that night."

"I made my own decisions. I think there was a fault in my faith all along."

"Whatever fault was or wasn't there wouldn't have turned into what you're experiencing now if not for me. To know what I did cost you so many years of peace ..." He shook his head. "You said you were ready to live with the living. How can I help you do that?" The plea in his expression told her that she could ask anything.

Like a piccolo straying from the score, the idea to ask for a kiss screeched through her mind, but she quickly quieted it. Hormones had gotten her into this mess.

"You already have." Who else could she have had this conversation with? Drew had knowledge and faith, and Tegan could listen, but only Gannon had walked the same road she had.

He withdrew his arm and stood. Bruce lifted his head, watching, as Gannon crossed the room and kneeled before the guitar case. The latches snapped up, and he lifted the instrument.

Her pulse roared. "It's been a long time since I've heard you play in person."

"Just don't tell Drew."

"He's not a bad guy. He probably honestly didn't want the kids distracted." The words tumbled out, nervous chatter. She closed her mouth lest something else pop out—something about the mosh pit of excitement that had broken out in her when he'd picked up the guitar.

"There's no way they weren't distracted." He returned to the couch and pulled the guitar close. "When I'm in a room with another human being, my job is in play. There are very few exceptions. John, my mom, and you."

"I make the shortlist?"

He already held a pick, though she hadn't noticed him find one. In high school, he'd usually had one in his pocket. Maybe some habits didn't change.

The first notes rose as he adjusted the tuning. "Do you have your bass?"

Bruce nestled his head back down into the fleece of his bed, settling in as Adeline's breath, already shallow, caught. She swallowed. "My upright, not the electric bass guitar anymore."

"Let's make a deal." He adjusted a peg. Even before starting a song, he was in his element, coming alive in ways he didn't any other time.

"Sure." As if she could say anything else to him right now.

"I'll play something for you, and then we're going to get the bass out, and you're going to play too."

"With you?" Her voice rose an octave. She remembered the fingerings, didn't she? But she'd never be able to feel her way through a song as she'd done back when she'd practiced hours every day. Did she even remember the music they'd played at gigs? He'd be as disappointed with her skill as he'd been with her confession that she no longer prayed.

"With me. Alone. Whatever you want. But you have to play." He ran the pick across the strings one more time. Apparently satisfied with the sound, he fixed his gaze on her. "Deal?"

The last chord he'd strummed faded from the room. Her heart beat such a fast tempo, she might never find a sense of rhythm tonight. Was that at the prospect of listening to him or at the prospect of having to play?

Both, and then some.

To get him to put his fingers back on those strings, to hear his voice in person after all these years—singing just for her, no less—she'd agree to almost anything. She nodded.

Gannon returned his attention to the guitar. The strings responded to his touch the way her nerves had, singing. The air filled with music. She breathed it in as she tried to commit the moment to memory, the sound, the shifting muscles in his arm, the way his shoulder blade moved under his shirt, his eyes slanted toward the guitar as if it were a partner and not a tool.

Then his chest rose with a breath, and his voice came in strong, like when she'd listened to "Yours," only now she could watch the way he winced at painful words. And the song was painful, a breakup song from the perspective of a man whose failure had cost him the woman he loved. The lyrics pleaded with the woman's new lover to do for her all the romantic things the singer thought she deserved.

But this was Gannon, who wrote his own songs and only from a place of deep feeling. The lyrics weren't some random man's perspective. They were his. And he'd chosen this song for her. For tonight.

The meaning fell into place.

This was his version of what happened after that night, and it was entirely different than hers. He'd written this song to commit her to God's care.

The chorus circled one more time. Gannon really thought God would hold her each night as she fell asleep? And that God would always greet her with a smile? That He'd sing for her, and He'd protect her heart? That He would love her like no one else ever could?

No uncertainty dimmed the delivery, but what he described wasn't at all what she had experienced. How long had he been singing this? Did everyone know this like they knew "Yours"? More importantly, was he wrong about God, or had she shut out the greatest lover she could've had?

GANNON LET the last note fade before glancing to gauge Adeline's reaction. Her eyes were wide, but her gaze pointed away, toward the painting. She started to open her mouth, then bit her lip. When she raised her hand to scratch her neck, her fingers trembled.

She couldn't keep up her end of the deal shaking like that, but she'd understood the song, and that was enough. He picked the strings in a quieter melody.

"Should I know that song?" Her voice sounded wet, as if she'd fished it out of the lake to use it.

"No. I'd like it on the next album, but I wanted you to know about it first." He focused on the guitar because that was easier. "I've always kept the music about you to myself."

"How many songs are there?"

"Enough."

"About how stupid I am?"

"Not one."

"I don't understand how you could care. All I've ever done is alienate people. Fitz, you, God. And apparently all any of you want is for me to be loved and in love."

"It's a lot less selfish in God's case than mine." He thought of revisiting a song they should both know from the early days, but how many reminders of Fitz could she take? He stuck with the more recent melody, another of the songs he'd never shared before. But no lyrics. She didn't need to know yet every thought he'd ever had about her. "You've always understood me. You knew me before I got this job. You know the best and the worst of me. That you might find a way to fit me into your life anyway ..."

"Scares you?"

"No. I told you my greatest fear."

She stretched one of her arms and rolled her shoulders. "I read that article about me. They got horrible pictures."

"They're good at that." He watched her, trying to judge if he could lose her over the rumors after all, or if she was only trying to shift the subject further and further from God.

She pushed her hair back from her face and looked at the curtains. Her brown irises held more than their share of concern. The article had upset her.

He set the guitar aside and rested his arm along the back of the couch so he could touch her cheek. "No one else's eyes do to me what yours do."

When she focused on him, he lowered the hand. Even such simple contact packed more of a high than hearing thousands chant his name. But what had he expected? He still remembered the vanilla mint taste of their first kiss. He was as much of an addict as Matt, but he had to operate by a new code. If he kissed her now, he'd have nowhere further to take the relationship when his feelings for her somehow deepened.

Was such a thing even possible?

What did it mean that he didn't think it was?

She intertwined her fingers with his. "If we're going to keep being seen together, I'll have to learn to ignore them."

Her hands were so small and smooth compared to his, the crescents of her fingernails delicate. He ran his thumb against the tip of one of her nails. Back when she'd played bass, she'd kept them trimmed down to nothing. She'd have to cut them when she started playing again, but that would be a small loss compared to everything she'd gain. Maybe she'd pulled herself together enough to give it a shot.

But she waited for him to respond to something. What had they been talking about? Right. The press.

"A local reporter stopped by to write about the project here. John and I gave her a quote about communities pulling together and the church being a family that pitches in. That should start a story that won't go bad on you. I posted about visiting my mom to counteract rumors about where we went. As for tonight, if we give them an inside glimpse that tells the story we want, they're less likely to make up something on their own."

"What are you going to say?"

"Here." He took the guitar again, angled away from her and took a photo with his phone, him and the guitar in the foreground, Adeline behind him, the soft smile she offered a little blurry, but her hair glinting, as silky as ever.

Jamming with an old friend and a borrowed guitar.

Her breath warmed his arm as he typed, so she probably read along as he entered the caption, but he tipped the phone toward her when he finished.

She rested her head against his shoulder as she read. "So we are just friends." Her voice was neutral, curious maybe. She angled her face up, the corners of her mouth lifted in a smile that nearly made him drop the phone so he could cup her chin, close the gap, and show her how much more than a friend he wanted to be.

She glanced back at the phone. "I suppose it'll always be true that we're old friends, even when we're more than that."

She'd said *when*, not *if*.

He fought to stay calm. "We are more."

She laced their fingers together and rubbed her thumb over the hollow in the center of his palm. Like a voice carried through an auditorium with perfect acoustics, every circle of her thumb echoed through him. At this rate, his resolve to save kissing at least a little longer would expire in about two seconds.

"You make it hard for a guy to think."

Smile broadening, she leaned away from him and released his hand.

The distance gave him enough space to breathe. He added hashtags and the filter Lina, the band's social media manager, insisted he use, then shut off his screen. "I'll post it on my way out."

Adeline rested her head against the back of the couch. Maybe she wasn't signaling she was tired, but the clock read eleven thirty, and he was headed for trouble if he stayed longer. He returned the guitar to its case. "I'll send you a recording and the chords to a new song. Play around with a bass line, and next time, we'll work on it together."

She followed him into the kitchen, toward the back door since only the preparations for the new front porch had been completed today. "You're letting me off the hook."

"Not for long." He wrapped her in his arms and felt her exhale. "I'd like to see what it looks like for you to live with the living."

"Me too." Her touch on his waist was tentative, but she peered at him with such focus, she had to be thinking exactly what he was. One kiss wouldn't be wrong.

But this was so new, the hug itself a big step. He'd done so much damage last time. This time needed to be different. So instead of finding her lips, he let her go.

18

The flashing reds and blues contradicted the calm of nighttime in Lakeshore and the happy buzz of Gannon's evening with Adeline. He had planned to get back to Havenridge and work on the recordings for her tonight, but because of the strobing lights, he leaned to see down the road that jutted off Main Street.

Was that a red sports car beside the police vehicle?

"Can you slow down?"

The driver wordlessly complied.

Glowing signs hung from a couple of the buildings. One featured a woman in a corset and stockings holding a bottle, the other a bundle of dynamite and a beer logo. Whatever nightlife Lakeshore had must happen here. The squad car had double-parked near a car with a low, cherry-red tailgate. A small crowd gawked from the sidewalk, a few holding phones up to capture the commotion.

A man Gannon hadn't spotted at first straightened. Had he been on the ground?

Gannon's stomach registered the truth an instant before his mind did. "Pull up. That's Matt."

The bassist's leaning posture and exaggerated gestures signaled he was drunk. Or high. As soon as Gannon climbed out of the car, Matt's raised voice met him. Something about leaving him in peace.

The officer stayed in Matt's space. "When we get a call about a man lying in the street, we can't leave him in peace."

Gannon jogged the last couple of steps, joining Matt and the officer between the cruiser and the sports car. "Matt, your ride's here." Gannon motioned to the waiting sedan with one hand and grabbed Matt's arm with the other.

The officer rested his hands on his belt. "And you are?"

The man had to know. Everybody knew, including the crowd of onlookers. Yet neglecting to answer would be a sign of disrespect that would play out badly. "Gannon Vaughn. I can get him home right away."

Unless Matt had done something Gannon didn't know about and the officer wouldn't let him go. He resisted a glance at the raised cell phones. This would look great all over the Internet tomorrow.

Matt jerked free. "I'll take care of myself."

The officer shined his flashlight at the ground, illuminating a set of keys. "He's under the impression he's driving home."

At least that was the worst the officer had to say about him.

"That won't happen." Gannon hooked Matt's arm again. "Sorry for any trouble, Officer."

"I don't know what you gentlemen are used to in LA, but everyone, including our teenagers, is watching and deciding how to act based on the precedent you set. We won't give you special privileges here."

Uh-oh. Was this guy the father of one of the kids they'd met? His name tag read Officer Cullen. He'd have to ask Adeline about him later. "I understand. Again, I'm sorry. Matt's going to be using a designated driver from now on." He squeezed Matt's arm, but the guy didn't apologize. Maybe it'd be best to get him out of there before he opened his mouth, anyway.

Gannon pulled him toward the idling sedan, but the officer's voice followed them. "This car will be ticketed if it's left overnight."

"You can't tow my car." Matt lurched to circle back, but Gannon held tight and delivered him to the rear seat of the sedan.

"Get him home." Gannon slammed the door, the locks snapped, and the car pulled away, threading around the cruiser at a crawl, then disappearing around the first corner.

Gannon made his way back to where the officer stood near the car and scooped up the keys. "Thank you. If these had gotten into the wrong hands—"

"I'm more concerned about what would've happened if he'd gotten in the vehicle."

"You're right, sir. This won't happen again."

"We'll be watching for this car."

"I understand." Tracking the only exotic sports car in Lakeshore wouldn't take much effort. "Am I free to go?"

Officer Cullen shined the light over the car, then gave a nod and stepped back. Gannon let himself in and started the engine. The officer moved the cruiser so Gannon could get the car out. With a glance to the right, he grabbed the shifter. Wedged between the seat and the center console was a tightly folded square of wax paper.

If it'd been visible from outside the car, Matt would be in cuffs right now.

Gannon set his jaw and pulled away from the curb.

OUT OF RESPECT for her roommate, Adeline wouldn't try her bass so late, except that an episode of one of their favorite shows sounded through Tegan's closed bedroom door. She was still awake and would wholeheartedly second Gannon's request she play again.

Upstairs in the guest bedroom, the bass leaned against the wall where she'd left it after visiting the music store. She flicked on the light. This was the front of the house, and anyone watching from the street would see the glowing window. Were photographers still out there? She wouldn't part the curtains to check because if she saw them, they'd see her, and what she was about to do needed to be private.

We're free and forgiven. We don't have to let a nine-year-old mistake define us.

Free and forgiven.

Free and forgiven, despite the undertow of attraction when Gannon had hugged her.

"God, give me a clean heart so I can please you." Speaking the words aloud should've made them feel more real, but the sound evaporated.

She tugged the zipper of the case, revealing the scroll, a rich chestnut brown, and then the pegbox, the fingerboard, and the table, a face as familiar to her as Gannon's or John's—maybe more so, since they'd grown up in the years they'd been apart while the bass had remained unchanged.

"I've missed you." And she hadn't realized how much until now. Holding it felt like embracing a friend.

Maybe Gannon was right. Maybe she never should've given this up. Maybe she had something to offer that not only brought her joy, but would benefit her church too. She'd told Gannon talking wouldn't bring back Fitz. It hadn't, but avoiding music wouldn't bring him back either.

With a deep breath, she placed the fingers of her left hand on the strings. Had it always felt this awkward to get her hand in place?

With no music before her, she determined to attempt a scale.

A thud sounded against the house. A voice hit one surprised beat, and a murmur followed. Had photographers come into the yard?

She abandoned the bass and crossed to the window. Parting the curtains, she could see the roof of the porch. Shadows—people, she was pretty sure—fled from the side of the house out toward the road, but the neighbor's trees blocked a clear view.

The paparazzi should've seen Gannon leave and wouldn't have had a reason to come near the house. At least the fans, whoever they were, had left now. She watched another minute. Spotting no further movements, she returned to the bass.

Before hesitation could turn into surrender, she plucked a note and then depressed the string with her left hand and plucked another. The cord felt tough against her skin, the fingerings awkward, and the notes not quite in tune with her intentions. She'd kept the instrument in working order, never realizing how her talent would deteriorate.

On the other hand, being out of her depth felt right. She didn't deserve what she'd once had. Did she want to do the work it would take to gain it back?

She struggled to complete the scale. Up and down, with mistakes each time. By the end of the third attempt, her fingertips had turned tender. When she missed her mark with the last note, she didn't retry. Instead, she wrapped the bass in its case once more.

As she lay in bed, trying to sleep, snatches of Gannon's song haunted her. If she could find it somewhere and listen again, she would, but he'd said he hadn't shared it publicly.

He had, however, shared other songs. Years' worth of them.

Her phone glowed in the dark as she downloaded all of Awestruck's music, dating back to the first album. She wouldn't get through the hours of songs tonight, but she'd listen until she fell asleep, and if she could concentrate on work well enough, she'd play more in the office tomorrow. Maybe along the way, she'd absorb his way of thinking about God, which was as different from her current perspective as her halting scale was from his moving living room performance.

With the bass, if she practiced enough, she could get back what she'd lost, what Gannon still had. But God was a being, not an instrument. If she showed up, would He do for her what He seemed to have done for Gannon? Would He do for her the things Gannon had asked?

One of his requests in the song had been for God to hold her as she fell asleep. She didn't feel any divine presence—she hadn't in years—but for once, she didn't miss the connection. How could she when she had Gannon's voice?

When Gannon pulled into the garage, the headlights revealed Matt. Gannon let the car roll within inches of his legs before he shut off the engine.

"I'll take those." Matt extended his hand and waved his fingers toward the keys.

"You're done for the night."

"Fine. Give me the keys so I can get my stuff."

"Be my guest. It's not locked." Gannon went inside, the keys closed in his fist. He'd stopped along the private drive, out of sight from both the gate and the main house, to search the car. He'd emptied the packet onto the shoulder and had used his shoe to mix the contents with the gravel and dirt. Now, he flushed the wrapper in the first bathroom he passed.

Tim lay sprawled out on a couch in the great room, head propped on an armrest, headphones on, and phone on his chest, about eight inches from his face.

"You know we have TVs for that." An entire home theater, in fact.

Tim pushed the headphones off one of his ears. "Hear from Harper?"

"No. She hasn't turned up?"

"Missed a charity dinner. She had a dress commissioned for it, so they thought there was no way she'd no-show, but my guess is the dress is why she skipped out. Probably too small or something."

"Did they check her place?"

"She's not there. Took her must-haves with her, so it's not like she was kidnapped. If one of you went AWOL, it'd be a lot longer before I started calling your exes looking."

Touching. "Harper and I never dated. Her people must've had a reason to think I'd know something."

"She was talking about you earlier."

"What'd she say?"

"Didn't specify."

Gannon found Harper among his contacts and hit the call button. Her voicemail picked up.

"People are calling looking for you. Let someone know where you are." He disconnected as Tim's focus settled behind him.

Matt had followed from the garage, face flushed. "You've got it, don't you? Probably going to use it yourself. Playing all high and mighty when you're no different than me."

"I don't have anything of yours."

"Yeah? Prove it." Matt pushed forward and started patting Gannon's pockets.

Gannon lifted his hands from his sides to give him an easier time of the search. "Matt here's going to need a ride when he goes into town from now on."

Matt pulled Gannon's socks at the ankles, as if he would've

hidden the drugs there. Sober, the guy would never stoop like this. "I don't need a babysitter."

"A driver. Hire a limo for all I care. If it weren't for me, you'd be in a cell right now."

"I'm fine to drive."

Gannon crossed his arms, looking down at Matt's dingy hair. If the guy could've seen what he'd become, would he still have signed on with Awestruck? "Then why'd I find you crawling around, looking for your keys in the street in front of a cop who would've arrested you as soon as you got behind the wheel?"

"He wasn't going to arrest me." Matt straightened, and his gaze shot toward his room.

Gannon had gotten rid of what was in the car, but Matt likely had more on the premises.

He shouldn't have intervened with the police officer. Only serious consequences would convince him to reconsider his choices.

As Matt proceeded up to his room, Gannon tossed the keys to Tim. "The police are watching for his car to make an example of him. Unless you want him in jail for our next show, he gets a babysitter whether he wants one or not."

"I'll do what I can." Tim pocketed the keys.

Gannon continued to the studio, but when he set his phone on the desk, it buzzed with a text.

I'm not all right at all.

Harper. Despite the words, the fact she was sending texts ruled out the worst possibilities.

He sent a reply. *People are concerned. You need to let them know where you are.*

I'm letting you know.

Because he'd shut her down earlier, she was turning up the dramatics. If he bit by continuing the conversation, she'd think he was coming around. He abandoned the phone and powered up the equipment he'd need to make the recordings for Adeline.

His cell lit up again.

I'm coming to Lakeshore. I need to see you. I don't know what else to do.

That, he couldn't let slide. *You can't come here, Harper.*

Something special had happened tonight when he sang for Adeline, but their relationship remained fragile. He finished his set up, chose a guitar, and pulled the strap onto his shoulder before glancing at the phone again.

I'm two hours away. Please. I wouldn't ask if this weren't an emergency.

She was that close? She must've gotten on a plane not long after their last conversation.

This windowless room, with its closed door and sound-proofing, gave the impression of privacy. An illusion. Word about Harper's visit might already be spreading. If he allowed her on the property, the speculations would have teeth.

Adeline said she cared more about reality, but she'd care about those rumors.

You're not welcome here. Strong wording, but he had to guard what he had with Adeline. He dropped the phone onto the desk and drew a breath to clear his head.

The screen lit up again.

He glared at it, but she'd said this was an emergency. What if it was?

He picked up the phone.

There's nowhere else I can go.

With the text, she'd included a selfie, one of her pretty blue eyes staring at the camera, the other swollen by a bruise that extended halfway down her cheek. A ragged line of broken skin ran along her temple.

How was that possible? She'd claimed the last injuries were from falling, and he'd seen the footage. No one had entered the apartment. But here she was, injured again, looking for a place to go. Was it abuse after all? If so, how had the guy avoided the security camera the first time?

Gannon hit the call button, but she didn't answer.

Another text hit his phone. *Please.*

19

A piece of equipment malfunctioned with a crash in the middle of Awestruck's concert. Screeching beeps pierced the music with such ferocity that Adeline could no longer make out the words Gannon sang. Then a dog started barking, and someone jostled her arm.

Adeline opened her eyes to find Bruce next to her bed, forcing his head under her arm as the high-pitched beeps from her dream continued. The fire alarm? Was the battery dying? She struggled to interpret the noise through the haze of sleep.

Bruce trotted from the bed to the closed bedroom door, barking again. Her phone still played, audible between the alarm's shrieks. She grabbed it and paused Awestruck's music. The smoke alarm didn't beep like this over a low battery. Either it was malfunctioning, or there was a fire.

She went to the door. A snatch of fire safety training from elementary school resurfaced, and she touched the back of her hand to the doorknob to test for heat.

Normal temperature. She turned the knob.

The window in the living room, straight down the hall from her bedroom, burned orange with flames, both outside and on the curtains inside. Bruce, still barking, made a break for it, but she caught his collar.

Tegan's door opened between Adeline and the living room, and her roommate rushed toward the flames.

"Tegan!"

"It's only on the curtains."

Even so, the fire was too much for one person. Adeline struggled to keep a hold on Bruce's collar. "We can't do this ourselves."

Tegan grabbed a chair from the kitchen table and set it in front of the double-wide window. The curtains on the left flamed from the halfway point up, near where the end of a burning piece of wood protruded through the broken glass. From her perch on the chair, Tegan grabbed the center of the curtain rod, then hopped to the floor and shoved the curtains outside. The fabric caught on the jagged edges of the glass, but what had made it out whooshed into a cloud of orange.

The flames would spread back inside if the blaze outside wasn't extinguished. Adeline led a still-struggling Bruce to the front door. She yanked it open as Tegan lifted the chair and used the legs to break the window further so she could dump the rest of the curtain.

"I'll call 911!" Tegan's call parachuted after Adeline as she jumped to the dirt where the porch had been.

Bruce didn't jump out after her, but she couldn't leave him in the house in case the fire spread. As she pulled him from the house and into her arms, all seventy or eighty solid pounds of him squirmed. He fell and sprinted away.

"Bruce! Come back!"

But the dog was gone.

She could either chase him or save the house.

Hopefully, at this time of night in this quiet town, he'd be okay. The burning house wouldn't be unless she acted now.

God, please keep him safe.

She rounded the corner as the piece of flaming wood, a six-foot ladder, fell to the ground, a result of Tegan forcing the curtains out. The yard waste bags, which had been lined up along the house, under the window, blazed so high and hot she couldn't tell whether the siding had lit too.

Adeline sprinted past, the heat warming her skin though she gave the fire a wide berth. She cranked the outdoor faucet and threw her weight into pulling the hose. As she approached the ring of heat surrounding the fire, another long-lost memory told her to aim at the base of the flames.

The fire hissed and steamed. She adjusted her thumb over the hose opening to sharpen the spray, focusing on the bags. At first, the fire seemed to hold its own, but then the orange tongues shrank. As the fire dimmed, the siding sparkled with embers, but no open flames. Small ones still licked the ladder, but away from the main blaze, those lost momentum.

Tegan appeared in the window, the phone to one ear and a pitcher of water in hand. She splashed the liquid up toward the ceiling, and it doused a gasping flame and washed down the remaining glass.

On the street, spectators assembled, but maybe because the fire was dying, no one moved forward to help. Sirens rose in the distance, soon enough to suggest a neighbor had called before Tegan managed to.

Her roommate came back with another pitcher, sloshing water over the side and bottom of the windowsill before joining Adeline. The soggy, smoldering bags reeked of smoke and burned leaves.

"How bad is it inside?" Adeline asked.

"We must've found it the moment the curtain lit. Smoke blackened the woodwork and the wall and ceiling over the window, but it doesn't look too serious. It'll be a trick to get the smell out, though."

She wanted to ask how this had happened, but Tegan

wouldn't know any more than Adeline did. There were more important issues, anyway. "And you? Are you okay?"

Tegan nodded, and a smile blipped to her face. "And you?"

Adeline shook her head. The smile seemed so out of place.

"Up until this, you had a good night, didn't you?"

"Oh." Ashes seemed so incongruent with the time she'd spent with Gannon, the fact that she'd prayed again for the first time—and a second time, come to think of it—and that she'd played her bass. "I guess I did."

"I tried to respect your privacy, but Gannon's not exactly quiet when he performs, and a bass pipes out a lot of noise too." The firetruck pulled up, and Tegan turned toward it. Her expression darkened. "Speaking of your privacy ..."

Adeline followed her line of sight. A man with a bag over his shoulder and a large camera in hand hustled up the sidewalk. She turned her back to take stock of her clothes. Pajama shorts and a tank with a lacy bralette underneath. She crossed her arms and kept her back turned as she and Tegan spoke with the firefighters.

Once the initial questions were answered, Tegan started off in search of Bruce while Adeline let two firefighters inside to see the damage there.

When she moved to step inside after them, one held up a hand. "Wait outside while we check to make sure it's safe."

"There's a man on the sidewalk taking pictures of me in my pajamas." Calling him paparazzi sounded too outlandish. These things didn't happen in Lakeshore. "I need to get dressed so I can help find my dog. I'll stay away from the wall where the fire was."

The firefighter, a man in his forties who stopped occasionally at the food truck, frowned but waved her in. "Stay behind me until we get a look."

Almost immediately on spotting the window, he motioned Adeline to proceed and turned his attention toward the alarms.

No wonder they continued to sound; lingering smoke made her cough as she crossed the living room.

In her room, Adeline scrambled into blue jeans, pulled a sweatshirt over her tank, and jogged to the back door. The firetruck's strobing lights reached the trees, but other than that, the night was still. She peered at the maze of fences, bushes, and trees that made up the center of the block, but nothing moved in her yard or her neighbors'.

"Bruce! Come here, boy!"

Nothing. She rounded the house.

Two more firefighters and a third man, this one in a police uniform, stood where the fire had burned.

"Adeline, what happened?" The lights of the emergency vehicles flashed over the officer's creased forehead. Joe Cullen. Olivia's dad. In other circumstances, it wouldn't have taken her so long to recognize him.

"I don't know. There weren't any power tools or anything over here, so I don't understand how it lit on fire. Or how a ladder went through the window."

"Do either of you smoke?" A firefighter had crouched next to the sooty pile that had once been the yard waste bags.

"No." She leaned to see the spot illuminated by the man's flashlight. Four or five cigarettes, all in various stages of being smoked, lay in the grass. "I heard a noise out here earlier and saw someone crossing the yard. Did they do this?"

The firefighter straightened up with a shrug.

She pointed toward the photographer, who snapped photos from the sidewalk. "Even if he wasn't involved, if he's been watching, he may know something."

Officer Cullen marched across the yard. The photographer retreated, but Joe stopped him before he'd made it more than a few steps. In the darkness, she couldn't make out their expressions, and they stood too far off for her to hear.

She looked back to the ashes. She'd seen the ladder leaning

on the center post between the windows earlier. It wouldn't have gone through the glass on its own, would it? Adeline lifted a shaking hand to her forehead.

The firemen who had been inside rejoined the group.

"You'll want to board up this window until you can get it replaced. The structure is sound, but the fire inspector and insurance adjuster need to go through before you start any clean up." The man handed Adeline a card with the fire inspector's information. The business card was white, small, and orderly in her hand, such a contrast to the mess of ash and emotion.

What was she supposed to do? Find Bruce and then go to sleep as if nothing happened? She needed help that firefighters, police officers, and even Tegan couldn't give. She took out her phone and dialed Gannon, but the call went to voicemail. Maybe he silenced it overnight. She tried John.

"Hey." John cleared his throat, his voice thick. "You know even rock stars sleep, right?"

She checked her phone screen. Two thirty. "I'm sorry. There was a fire at my house. It's okay, but a window broke, and my dog ran away, and there's a photographer here."

"A fire?"

"Someone was smoking next to the house, by the yard waste bags." Would she sound paranoid if she voiced her suspicion that the ladder had been pushed? Was she overreacting by calling him?

"You're okay?"

"Yeah. Shaken up. It didn't spread much." But what if they'd been sixty seconds slower about getting the curtains outside? Whoever had done this could've burned down the house. And there was still the matter of Bruce, running through the neighborhood, terrified. "An officer is talking to the photographer to see if he knows anything. But what if he started it? Who would've been smoking next to the house?"

"I'm on my way."

"I tried Gannon first. He didn't answer."

"I'll wake him up. Be there soon."

Adeline disconnected. Could the fire have been set on purpose? Paparazzi might want to drum up dramatic photographs and draw Gannon out. Or what if some fan had gotten jealous of Adeline's supposed romance with Gannon?

Would anyone go to these lengths for a story or a celebrity crush?

Joe Cullen returned. "He said he's staying at Ida's B&B and saw the flames, but not how they started."

The bed-and-breakfast was across the street and a couple of doors down. The fire would've been visible from some of the windows, so the photographer might have been telling the truth.

Officer Cullen scanned the mess. "Do you have supplies to board up this window?"

"In the shed." Adeline led the way, and they found a square piece of plywood left over from before she'd purchased the house. After she'd supplied him with a hammer and nails from the basement, Officer Cullen tacked the board in place, the rap of the hammer knocking against the quiet night.

Joe took the last nail from between his lips. "I'll take pictures, collect the cigarette butts, see if I can find anything else. We'll cordon off this part of the yard until after the inspection tomorrow."

"Who'll watch the property until you find the culprit?"

Adeline turned at the man's voice. John slid his arm around her shoulders as he fastened his gaze on Officer Cullen.

Joe lifted his chin as if he didn't take kindly to orders. "We'll do drive-bys."

"I'll send someone, then." John wore a T-shirt and athletic shorts, either what he'd slept in or something he'd thrown on, and stubble textured his jaw. His eyes seemed to follow the shadow the smoke had left trailing toward the second floor before he turned his gaze to her. "You're staying with us."

"You think something else might happen?"

"Let's not risk it." His attention seemed to sharpen on the photographer. "Ready to go?"

The man had his camera raised again. Maybe that's why Gannon hadn't come onto the street. He must be waiting in the car. Seeing him would make everything so much better.

She looked to Officer Cullen. "Can I?"

"Let's finish up some details inside."

"Okay. I have to pack a bag anyway, and Tegan is out looking for Bruce. She can come too, right?"

John nodded and lifted a hand to motion her toward the back entrance.

She hesitated. "Will Gannon wonder what's taking so long?"

John's expression clouded, and he shook his head.

Right. She ought to prioritize her house and dog right now.

The next half hour dragged by. Tegan returned, unsuccessful, and once they'd finished talking to Officer Cullen, they packed overnight bags. Tegan opted to drive her own vehicle, but Adeline wanted to be near Gannon more than anything, so she followed John down the sidewalk to a sedan. He pulled open the front passenger door while Tegan backed out of the driveway and into the road.

As John placed her bag in the trunk of his car, Adeline scanned the interior of the vehicle. No one waited inside.

"Gannon?"

John frowned and motioned her in. "Let's find Bruce."

So he didn't want to explain Gannon's absence. What did that mean?

Tegan pulled up next to them. "I'll look this direction." She pointed through her windshield. "Text if you find him?"

John nodded. "Do the same. We'll meet up so you can follow us to the cabin."

She gave a thumbs-up and then pulled away.

Adeline considered going for her own car, but exhaustion and disappointment dissolved the idea. She slipped into the car and tugged her seatbelt into place, fingers shaking again. John pulled away from the curb and navigated the streets, looking for a black dog in the black night.

~

GANNON SAT behind Tim in the SUV, where window tinting had shielded him from the photographers at the gate as they pulled out of Havenridge. When they'd gotten clear of the press, he'd moved to the front passenger seat.

Twenty minutes down a two-lane country highway, he spotted the headlights of an idling car.

Tim huffed. "This is a setup for a horror movie. Any chainsaws or guns and I'm out of here. You can fend for yourself."

Gannon's phone lit up in his hand with a question from Harper. *Is that you?*

To the rescue. He plunked the phone into a cup holder. "If I die, you're out a job."

Tim parked the nose of his car close to the front bumper of the other. "True. We should've brought security."

Gannon left his phone in the cup holder and climbed out of the SUV as the driver's side door of the other car opened.

Harper wore a loose tank, cotton pants, and heels. Despite the late hour, gigantic sunglasses covered half her face. The combination of those and her hair hid the bruise. He hesitated. What if the whole thing—the bruise picture and, an hour and a half later, the picture of the blown tire—were an elaborate ruse?

As if sensing his doubts, Harper removed the glasses. The headlights hit on the purple and red that swallowed her right eye.

How could this have happened? He'd been so sure no one else had been in his apartment. So sure she hadn't been attacked. Maybe she hadn't been. Maybe this was something new. But so soon after those rumors of violence?

He met her where she stood, still by her car, and she clung to him. Her chin against his shoulder felt off. Adeline was shorter, and her hair didn't brush his neck like this when they hugged. He returned the embrace, but as he did, he checked the car's wheels.

Sure enough, the back tire was shredded.

She sniffled. "I can't believe this would happen tonight, of all nights."

He untangled himself from the hug. "How far did you drive after you hit the board?" He didn't see anything in the road resembling the two-by-four she'd described.

"Not far. It sounded awful."

Then where was the board? But the tire was undeniable evidence that she'd hit something. "What happened?"

"There was a board in the road. As if this night needed to get worse."

"I mean to you."

"Oh. I"—she slid the sunglasses back on—"fell."

This story again? "Eye first?"

"Into a chair."

"Did you have it checked out?"

"Nothing's broken."

"If you're not worried about it and it was a simple fall, why are you here?" In her messages, she'd implied she was running for her life.

She frowned and focused down the dark road as if to control tears.

Fine. It was after two a.m., too late to play twenty questions. Especially on a deserted road in the dark.

"Pop the trunk. Let's get your luggage and get out of here before the tow comes."

"Why? Embarrassed to be seen with me?"

Yes. Hence the SUV to hide in, Tim to act as a driver, and the tow instead of putting a spare on and having her drive herself to Havenridge. "Do you really want to deal with a tow truck driver right now?"

"If he's cute."

He lifted the lid of the trunk and found it stuffed full of luggage. With a bag in each hand, he started for the SUV.

Harper trotted after him. "Maybe you don't know how to change a tire."

"I know how." Fitz had taught him when they'd gotten a flat on the way to LA that first time. He stood clear as the tailgate of the SUV opened.

"Who taught you?" Her tone was playful. Somehow, she thought this was flirting. "Your dad?"

One of Awestruck's first hits was about how he'd been raised by a single mom, and Gannon had discussed it in hundreds of interviews. Everyone knew about it, but Harper, who claimed to be a friend, forgot?

He swung the luggage, letting it thud too hard into the vehicle.

Harper sucked in a breath and glared at him as he stepped back so Tim could shut the tailgate again. "What?"

"My dad? Really?" He shook his head and forced a deep breath.

Harper followed him around the side of the SUV, her towering sandals grinding stones against the asphalt. He opened the door for her to get in.

She drew a ragged breath as if he'd given her a second black eye. "Tonight has been awful, so whatever chip you've got on your shoulder ... Look, I'm sorry about the flat. I'm sorry I'm here. I'm sorry I'm such a burden to you, that I didn't know who to go to after Rob attacked me. I thought this would be safe. And then I hit something in the road in the dark in the middle of nowhere, and I'll never be good enough for you. I'm sorry, okay? Leave me here with the luggage and the car. I'll go with the tow driver. You'll never see me again." She stomped to the tailgate.

So there was a man.

Gannon held a deep breath, then pushed it out. Body suddenly heavy, he joined her at the back corner of the vehicle. "Come to the cabin. We'll get you set up for the night and figure everything out tomorrow. Okay?"

"You hate me."

"I don't hate you. I'm sorry I lost my temper. My dad left before I was born." And Gannon couldn't blame Harper for the part about Fitz. It was his own fault a question about changing a tire brought on guilt like this.

"Oh." She tucked her hair back. "I forgot."

A true friend wouldn't have. But this wasn't about a friendship. This was about being a decent human being to someone in need. This was about all the people watching Harper who needed to know there was a better way, people who would listen to her testimony when they wouldn't listen to anyone else.

But first, he'd have to stick this out long enough for her to change.

"Let's get going."

She slid her glasses on again and followed him, head down, into the backseat of the SUV. Tim steered toward Havenridge, but Gannon couldn't shake the horror-movie feeling that said he was still walking into a trap.

20

$\mathcal{A}$deline made out the shape of people standing next to the dark country road.

Something tapped her arm, and she found John holding his sunglasses toward her, even though it was dark out. "Might be best if they don't get a clear view."

As he slowed the car to turn toward the waiting people, she slid them on. When the first flash went off, she lowered her head and lifted her hands to block her face. The car muffled the photographer's calls, but as John steered through the fray, it sounded like they crowded close to the windows.

Had the car stopped? She peeked to see an iron gate suspended between massive posts, each made of a trio of logs. Bruce, whom they'd finally found fifteen minutes ago, whined from his spot in the backseat. John let the car crawl forward, advancing as quickly as the gates' slow-motion movement would allow. A man in black pants and a gray polo stood nearby, making sure no trespassers dashed onto the property.

Once the photographers were behind them, Adeline removed the sunglasses and glanced in the side mirror. Tegan's vehicle hovered behind them, apparently unscathed.

Now on the private drive, John accelerated. Two minutes later, they rounded a bend, and Havenridge came into view.

The material proof of Awestruck's success left her craning her neck. The house towered three stories high and was made of thick logs and stretching windows. The drive split, offering the option of stopping under a hotel-like carport by the front door or pulling into the six-car garage. Lights shone onto the house and washed the front door in golden, welcoming light.

John hit the button to open one of the garage doors. He parked between a fancy red sports car and a black sedan like the one they rode in. She got out of the car and spotted Gannon's motorcycle parked nearby, as well as another car.

Bruce scrambled up from the backseat and vaulted out. Tegan, who must've parked outside the garage, entered with her bag slung over her shoulder, expression marked with a mix of awe and uncertainty.

"Don't let the money fool you." John retrieved Adeline's bag and shouldered Tegan's too.

"Fool us?" Adeline asked.

"Into thinking we're more than just some guys with guitars and drums." He whistled, and Bruce followed him to the door leading inside. John pulled it open, and Bruce trekked in, sniffing along the hardwood floor of the hall toward whatever lay ahead.

"WHO'S ROB?" Gannon crossed his arms and leaned against the doorframe as Harper opened one of her suitcases. To keep her away from his own room, he'd brought her luggage here, to a room along the great room balcony. Though he longed for sleep, what she'd told him ought to be dealt with.

"A fling. It wasn't supposed to be anything serious, but he saw it differently." She withdrew a smaller bag from her suitcase and set it on the bed. "I stopped by his place, and when I tried to leave …" She chewed her lip for a moment, frozen, then shook her head and went back to unpacking. She lifted a silky slip.

He turned his gaze away. If she wanted a reaction, she wouldn't get it here. "What happened?"

She left the slip and rounded the bed to stand in front of him. "We were arguing about what our relationship is and isn't. I put my hand on his arm"—she touched Gannon's arm where the honor tattoo ran—"and he pushed me off."

"Hard enough to do this." He lifted his hand but stopped short of touching her cheek.

Her bruised and red eyelid half covered her blue iris. She held eye contact for a moment, then nodded and shrugged away. "I got out, him screaming behind me that he'd find me. You don't think he'd come all the way here, do you?"

That depended on the man's resources and determination, and given this new information, Gannon wondered if this man had both. What if he'd also caused Harper's injuries at Gannon's apartment?

"Was this guy involved the first time you got hurt?"

She cocked her head, expression troubled. "Oh. At your place? No. I fell, like I said."

That lined up with the security footage. It was easier to believe she'd fallen the first time than that her fling had erased his presence on the video. And one attack was plenty serious. "You ought to press charges."

She eased past him and onto the balcony, as if considering what he'd said. But then she asked, "How many dogs do you have here?"

"Just the two." Trigger and Camo had greeted them when they walked in, so John must've left his door open.

"But this one's different."

Gannon joined her on the balcony. A black dog with white

on his muzzle explored the great room. On spotting them, the dog barked once and wagged his tail.

"Bruce, be quiet."

Sick pressure built in his stomach. Bruce and Adeline? Here? Now?

Harper arched an eyebrow. "Bruce? What kind of dog name is that?"

"You should call it a night." He started for the stairs. He'd descended only a couple of them when he caught sight of Adeline, Tegan, and John coming down the hall from the garage. Though dressed in jeans and a sweatshirt, Adeline appeared to have just rolled out of bed, her hair a gorgeous tangle of waves.

Behind her, Tegan gazed at the room as if she was touring Versailles, and John carried two bags. His gaze hooked firmly on Harper, who stood at the railing. If the drummer were the type to give lectures, Gannon would be in for one.

Adeline didn't seem to notice her. She met Gannon at the base of the stairs and leaned into him, arms finding their way around his waist.

He held her, but confusion, regret, and worry kept him from enjoying it. Was that smoke he smelled on her? "What's going on?"

"Called and texted you, man." John glared at Harper another moment before fastening his glare on Gannon. "Someone started Adeline's house on fire."

"What?" His stomach filled with acid as he studied what he could see of Adeline for damage. Her forehead was smooth and pale, her hair glossy, the shoulders of her top unsinged.

"It wasn't serious." She stepped back from him and snuggled her arms across her body, as if she still needed a hug. "It was probably an accident, but John thought we should come here."

Tegan's gaze locked on the second-floor landing. It was only a matter of time until Adeline noticed Harper too, and what would she think? She'd been concerned about his relationship with the actress already.

John handed Gannon one of the bags. "She heard someone messing around in the yard earlier. Cigarette butts next to the yard waste bags. Could've burned the whole place down."

"On purpose?"

Instead of replying, John caught Tegan's eye and tilted his head toward the kitchen. "There are rooms this way."

Tegan offered Adeline a glance loaded with sympathy, then left. Bruce trotted after them.

"Some of Gannon's fans are the jealous type, aren't they, honey?"

Adeline's big brown eyes angled up to the balcony. Her lips parted as she spotted Harper, who'd hidden behind her sunglasses again. The differences between the two had never stood out so strongly. Harper, intent on controlling appearances with sunglasses, styled hair, designer clothes, and aloof comments, versus Adeline, who remained authentic and vulnerable with raw beauty that didn't come from surgeons, stylists, or makeup.

He pulled his focus away to check his phone. Adeline had called once, and John had texted and called, all around the time he'd left his phone in the SUV to grab Harper's bags. He hadn't thought to check for messages when he got back in the car because it was so late. Everyone should've been sleeping. He'd left Adeline safe and sound just hours before.

Now she gaped at him, displaced, looking lost and hurt.

Harper was talking again. "... in a bag that size. Clothes for tomorrow, something to sleep in, hair and makeup products, styling tools. If you need to borrow anything, I'm sure I have extra."

Adeline's bottom lip disappeared, and her line of sight

settled on her bag as if she'd discovered it contained a rattlesnake. She must've forgotten something.

Harper's musical laugh fell from the balcony. "Come on up, honey. I'll lend you whatever you need." She pivoted and disappeared into her room.

Adeline eyed him with pain and suspicion. He couldn't blame her. To make matters worse, Harper was right. One of his fans probably had done this to her.

Harper was apparently so confident they'd come to her that she remained in her room. They could round the corner toward the other bedrooms before she came out and discovered they'd gone.

"I'll get you set up." He motioned her to follow him upstairs.

ADELINE STEPPED from the hardwood of the living room to the wood of the stairs. The risers, fashioned out of logs cut in half the long way, were wide enough that Gannon could've walked beside her with space to spare. Instead, he rested a hand on the small of her back as if Harper's being here changed nothing.

The log steps, the exposed beams in the ceiling, and the stone fireplace matched the feel of the exterior, but as soon as they were up the stairs and around the corner, the hints that this was a cabin disappeared.

Gannon's hand brushed over her back, drawing her attention to his concerned expression. "I'm sorry she's here. Some man in LA attacked her, and she ran here. I didn't know she was coming until she texted on her way from the airport. She got a flat tire. Tim and I were out, picking her up when you called."

"Okay." She was too tired and numb to deal with the overload of emotions. Her house. The search for Bruce. Harper. Being here with Gannon.

His frown said he knew nothing was okay.

Her phone beeped, and she paused to check the screen. Her battery was at two percent. Gannon watched her.

"I forgot a charger and cord."

"Micro USB?"

She angled the phone so he could see the charging port.

With a nod, he continued down the hall and past a study. He opened a door on the right and clicked on a lamp, revealing his hat on the desk. Next to it, a black leather duffle and a guitar case.

The bed frame was made of driftwood, understated and naturally beautiful. The plush carpet reached over the thin base of her flip-flops to touch the edge of her toe. Over the desk hung an oil painting of a storm-tossed ship, exquisite light detail on the waves.

Gannon set down her bag and crossed to the nightstand. He lived here with no comfort spared, while she struggled to hold on to her rundown house.

Her rundown, smoldering house.

"What's the truth about you and Harper?"

He turned from the drawer he'd opened, forehead knit. "I told you. Friends. If that."

"But she's here."

"How could I send her away?" He took a black cord from the drawer.

She picked up her overnight bag. She'd been attacked too. Why did Harper get the same treatment, the same level of protection? Wasn't Adeline's relationship with Gannon different? Couldn't Harper fend for herself? But those were selfish thoughts, weren't they? Fatigue blurred all the answers.

Gannon set the cord on the desk and put his hands on her elbows, his touch firm. "I don't know what I would've done if something had happened to you. I'm sorry I wasn't there. If I'd known you needed me, I would've been there."

He would've known she needed him if he hadn't been with Harper. She stepped backward, into the hall.

With a heavy sigh, Gannon picked up the cord and her bag again. "This is all it'll take. The outlets have USB chargers built in." He studied her in the dim light that spilled into the hall, then sighed again. "You want a lake view?"

"What?"

"From your room. Do you want it to overlook the lake?"

"Sure. Yes."

He motioned her to continue down the hall. They passed a couple of more rooms and climbed another staircase.

"John's staying up here too. Take this hall around that corner. I'm sure you'll find Bruce there, if you want him. But these are the lake-view rooms. The best is probably the third door down."

The one directly above his own room. She nudged open the door. A wall of windows overlooked the lake, a feature Gannon's room had boasted too. On the dresser, a tray held orchids growing from a piece of driftwood. The comforter bulged, inviting her to flop in and sleep like she'd never slept before.

He laid the cord on the writing table by the door. "Harper—"

Adeline lifted her hand. "Let's talk tomorrow."

He swallowed, tense, and nodded. "Do you need anything else?"

She shook her head. How could she begin to name the things she needed right now?

"If that changes—"

"—John's right around the corner."

He lowered his head and rubbed his neck, then retreated into the hall without putting up a fight.

Adeline eased herself onto the bed and stared at the empty doorway. She should've let him explain. She'd thought it'd be better to wait for a fresh day, a little sleep to renew her perspective, but she wouldn't sleep with all these unanswered questions between them.

Something in the hall rustled. He must not be able to leave their relationship so shaky either. She scanned the room. Two armchairs waited for a conversation by the windows, but they probably ought to talk somewhere other than a bedroom. The study they'd passed would suffice. She stood to head him off.

Harper appeared in the doorway, still wearing sunglasses, a tote over her shoulder. She pranced into the room, more agile in her platform wedge sandals than Adeline could ever dream of being.

With a giggle, Harper held a tote toward her. "Here you go, hon."

Hon? Adeline almost corrected her, asking her to call her by name, but she stopped. A little pink was visible below the rim of the glasses. Harper needed grace. She could let a pet name slide.

Harper extended the tote closer. "I just saw my stylist, and he had all kinds of goodies for me, so I'm sharing." She emphasized the last word as if Adeline would be impressed she had the manners of a kindergartner.

Adeline took the tote. "Okay, thanks. I'm going to get to bed, so ..."

The sunglasses made Harper's face unreadable, but she smiled sweetly. She sure was peppy for someone who'd been attacked earlier. "Aren't you going to look?"

Adeline didn't bother to hide her sigh as she retrieved the bag and parted the handles. The bag contained full-size bottles of shampoo and conditioner. Something black and lacy pooled at the bottom. A headband? She hooked the fabric with her finger and lifted it.

Lingerie.

She let it fall back into the tote.

"Brand new. Tags and all." Harper touched the lip of the tote and peeked inside, the baby powder scent of her perfume nauseating. "I won't be needing it, and Gannon likes that kind of thing."

Adeline's stomach rolled at the implications.

Harper smiled and withdrew to the hall. "Have a good night. Don't do anything I wouldn't."

The bag fell from Adeline's fingers.

Is this how you clean up my heart, God? You dismantle the relationship most likely to make me stumble?

No. She needed to be doubting Gannon's goodness, not God's.

And even that ...

Harper was probably lying, but if she was that kind of person, why would he have let the actress onto the property? Surely there were other safe places for her. Unless Gannon had feelings for her. Unresolved feelings, like the kind that might linger after an intimate relationship.

The bag lay at her feet. She should've sent the offering away with Harper. But even if it were gone, the image of the lingerie would've remained. This was ugly. A relationship she resented and certainly hadn't wanted to see the inner workings of. Was that how God felt about Adeline's own past with Gannon?

Lord, I'm sorry. Please forgive me.

It wasn't a permanent solution, but with her foot, she shoved the bag under the bed and got ready to sleep.

She needed a step back. Gannon had taken a misstep here, but she shouldn't assume that misstep included intimacy with Harper. He deserved the chance to defend himself. But first, she needed rest, or she'd never think straight about any of this.

God, I'm going to need Your peace if I'm ever going to sleep.

21

*H*eavy fatigue discouraged Adeline from opening her eyes. It was still dark, and nothing the day could hold would be as wonderful as the sensation of this soft bed, this quiet room. But uneasiness slithered into her limbs. The bed was too comfortable, the room too silent. She moved her arm, and a pillow plopped to the ground, though one remained under her head.

Where had the second pillow come from? Her eyes opened to darkness, not her bedside clock. When she twisted, sheets softer and smoother than her own slid against her skin.

The fire and the search for Bruce and the trip to Havenridge hit. Harper and the lingerie. She'd lain in bed, praying for peace. God must've answered, or she wouldn't have slept.

Lord, could you top me off again?

The anger from last night had turned to an ache. As she'd fallen asleep in her own bed before the fire, she would've sworn she loved Gannon and he loved her, that the vulnerability of opening up to him had paid off with healing. But what was going on with Harper?

She groped for the bedside table where she'd left her

phone. Once she found it, pressing the button didn't illuminate the screen. The device must've died before she'd plugged it in. Powering up would take it a minute.

Her gaze found the blue numbers of a clock. 11:38? That didn't make sense. She couldn't have slept all day and into the night. She sat up and felt for the switch on one of the bedside lamps.

Her bag, a large canvas tote she'd gotten free on Black Friday, slumped in a corner like a runaway who'd snuck into a luxury hotel.

A ping rose from the phone. Tegan had texted.

I'm at class. Let me know if you need anything.

After untangling herself from the sheets, Adeline crossed the room and slid her fingers between the thick layers of curtains. Light answered, washing through the crack. She'd slept until almost noon, not midnight.

Sunlight bathed the lake all the way to the horizon. Tiny white flashes—gulls—rose and fell along the tree-heavy shore of Liberty Island. Beneath the window, the pristine lawn and flagstone patio rested empty, lending no hints about who she might run into first if she ventured from the room.

She didn't belong here. Didn't want to face any of them. Not Harper with her lingerie, not Gannon with his explanations. Not even John, since he always saw more than he commented on. He would know in one look that she'd fallen completely for Gannon, and Harper's presence meant it wasn't as mutual as she'd thought.

Or maybe Harper's presence meant something else.

Lord, bring the truth to light and show me what to do with it.

Going downstairs and interacting with people was the only way to find out what was going on, but she didn't want any of these people witnessing her pain if the worst was true.

It probably wasn't.

But just in case, she'd do everything she could to protect

herself. She would clean up, apply makeup, style her hair, and wear the dress she'd packed—originally to impress Gannon but now to act as armor.

GANNON WENT to the kitchen for lunch and found Harper at the stove, a wok hissing over a burner.

She'd muted the bruise with makeup, but she couldn't hide the swollen eyelid or the cut. "Orange chicken. You want some?"

She could cook, and her rendition of the dish didn't sit like a brick in his gut the way the takeout version did, but he shook his head. Eating her food would only encourage her to stay longer.

He opened the fridge and pulled out ingredients for a sandwich.

"Suit yourself. Do you think Sleeping Beauty will want some, or is she going to sleep all day?"

"Save her some. She gets to sleep as long as she wants." When he'd given up on rest at seven, he'd gone and stood outside her door. All had been silent, so he'd told Tim to let him know if she came down.

Meanwhile, he'd retrieved his notebook of songs about Adeline from the drawer in the kitchen and closed himself in the studio.

Probably shouldn't have left such a vital, vulnerable piece of his heart in a drawer where anyone could've found it. Tim would've pushed to move ahead with the songs regardless of Adeline's opinion, and if Harper realized what a hold Adeline had on him, her next move wouldn't be pretty.

He would take more care with the notebook moving forward, but as he'd tried to pick a song to record for Adeline as he'd promised, he found he had the opposite problem. Instead of wanting to keep all the songs from her, he struggled to narrow his choice to just one to share.

He chose three from the notebook and added one more, thrown together that morning, and recorded them all.

Afterward, he'd stowed the notebook in his room and now carried a drive with the songs in his pocket.

Adeline probably wouldn't play for him, but that was no longer the point. The point was keeping his word by making the recording and letting the lyrics apologize for missing her call. And for Harper's presence.

Though surely Adeline could understand giving shelter to someone who'd been attacked the way Harper had been. Or she would once she saw the bruises.

"Where are you going to go?" he asked.

Harper stared at him as if he'd just strangled a small animal.

"I'm sorry about what happened to you, but I ... this ..." He couldn't say this put too much strain on his relationship with Adeline, or Harper would find a way to make things even worse. "Where I stand hasn't changed. I want you to be safe, but there have to be boundaries. I don't want your staying here to muddy the waters."

Red tinged the whites of Harper's eyes, and tears lined up to fall.

"Look, I'm sorry, but yesterday you had all these ideas about us, and then you, what? Ran to this other guy because I rejected you? You've got to see how messed up this is."

"Of course I see it. I'm doing it to myself, right?" The tears cascaded down her cheeks. "You want me to go right back to LA where he's waiting for me."

"I care, Harper, but this isn't healthy. You need help I can't give. There are places set up specifically for women in your situation. Safe places with trained staff—"

"You think I need a shrink. You think I'm crazy."

She needed professional help. He'd leave the why to someone else to diagnose. "How long did you expect to stay here?"

She stabbed the spoon into her food, tossing the chicken around in the skillet. "Let me stay a couple of days until I can open my eye."

"Two days. Tops."

"Fine. Two days."

He stacked his sandwich as Harper turned off the burner, pushed food onto a plate, and left the room, either for the great room or the patio.

"Finally!" Harper's voice and clapping broadcast from the great room. She bounced from one emotion to the next like a tennis ball. "I've been waiting for you all day. Did you see what I got for you?"

He abandoned his sandwich and reached the great room as Harper—sunglasses back on—grabbed Adeline's hand and dragged her toward the room next to Tim's office.

"Harper." Gannon dodged a couch and the table where the actress had left her food. He should've made her promise to keep as far from Adeline as the property would allow.

Ignoring his advance, Harper pushed open the small room. "If you're going to be here for a while, you'll need more than you brought, so I went out first thing this morning to be your personal shopper." She lifted her hands like a game show model introducing a contestant to their new car. Three display racks stood crowded with clothes. Below, the assortment of shoes belonged in a store. She must've picked up multiple sizes of everything.

"Pick what you like, and we'll return the rest. But I think you'll like everything. If I weren't an actress, I'd be a personal shopper."

Adeline stared at the selection. Her black sleeveless dress

cinched at the narrowest part of her waist and fell easily over her hips, the fabric simple and soft. Touchable.

She shifted as if she might bolt. "I can still get in my house for my own things. In fact ..." Her gaze darted to Gannon and then away. "I'm going back. I'm sure the fire was an accident, so, thanks, but I'm all right."

Gannon focused on Harper. "Take off the glasses."

Both women looked at him, Harper's mouth ajar.

Gannon repeated his order with a hand motion.

Harper licked her lips. "You may trust this woman with all your personal stories, but my business is my business."

"It was until you came here. Take off the glasses."

Jaw set, Harper obeyed, revealing a glare. Its effect was diminished by the swollen skin and the gash beside her eye.

Adeline's eyes widened, and she looked Gannon's way.

Harper tossed the glasses on a nearby table. "So what? No secrets between you two? Is that it?"

Gannon focused on Adeline. "I told her she could stay two days until the swelling is down. That way, when she leaves, she'll cause less of a media fiasco. That's also why we went out and got her last night. To keep this quiet."

"You know they saw me when I went out this morning."

Somehow he hadn't put that together. "I thought you were worried Rob would follow you."

"You have security."

"You didn't think it'd be safer for him to have no idea where you are?" Besides, his security team couldn't protect their reputations. The press would've also seen Adeline arrive. He rubbed his temples, imagining the spawning rumors.

Harper tossed her head, too proud to admit she'd made a mistake.

"What car did you take?" Tim would've known better than to give her the keys to one of their rentals after they'd gone to all the trouble of keeping her from view last night.

"The rental company delivered a replacement for me first thing. So I paid it forward." She gave Adeline a smile that almost looked gracious.

Adeline swayed. Was she imagining the rumors too? Her focus lingered on the clothes. "Thanks for all of this."

"At least someone appreciates me." Harper brushed past him and swiped up the sunglasses. Abandoning her lunch, she veered toward the garage.

Finally.

Gannon touched Adeline's forearm. "You understand why I didn't send her away."

She eyed the clothes as if they might eavesdrop and report back to Harper.

"But you're still upset. About her or your house?"

"About you."

"Me?"

"What is the truth about your relationship with her?"

"I told you. Friends. Never more, usually less."

"She stopped by my room to give me a bag of her castoffs."

He crossed his arms as a blush crept onto Adeline's face. A blush?

She raked her fingers into her hair, avoiding eye contact, then dropped her hand and shook her head. "Can you explain how she knows what kind of lingerie you like?"

"How she knows what?"

"In the bag. She included lingerie she swears you like."

"No. She's—" Harper would do that? Really do that? He looked out into the great room, but the actress was out of sight. "Harper and I have never had that kind of relationship. Never. She's ... she's playing so many games, I don't even know what she hopes to accomplish anymore."

John had said Harper would take from him. When would Gannon learn to listen?

Adeline stared at the clothes. "I don't belong here. If you

think I'm in danger at my house, I'll call the church and find another place to stay."

He couldn't let her run to Drew. "If someone is running around with a serious grudge, this is the safest place for you. You do belong here. I'll send Harper away."

"Don't. You obviously think she should be here. And maybe you're right. I got out of the house safe and sound. She didn't. Maybe she needs this more than I do."

He heard movement in the great room, but he continued. Even Harper could overhear this. The truth might do her good. "No. If she would lie low here, that'd be one thing, but I didn't let her in to cause this kind of trouble. Harper English has resources and friends. She doesn't need to be here."

"Got that straight. You said no women here, and now Harper—" Matt's voice ground to a halt as both Gannon and Adeline turned to face him. Body odor indicated he needed a shower and fresh clothes instead of the torn jeans and faded green T-shirt he'd been wearing for three days now. He jacked his thumb toward Adeline. "What's she doing here?"

Was that fear in his eyes?

He couldn't have Matt making Adeline feel even more unwelcome. "Did you need something?"

"Yeah." Matt twitched his nose and sniffed. "You were in the studio all morning. We've got that show next weekend, and then we're recording the album, right? Practice time matters."

Not to Matt, it didn't. Not usually.

But he was talking fast and fidgeting with energy. High. Again.

"I'll grab John. We shouldn't waste time."

Gannon stepped up to block Matt's glare toward Adeline. She'd been through enough. Once Matt exited the glass doors to the yard, Gannon turned back to her.

"He's changed." Her worried eyes focused beyond him, on the view of the patio.

"He's using."

"Using what?"

"You name it, he's into it."

"Oh. So I'm just one of three charity cases."

"What?" Was this what it felt like to be thrown overboard in a storm? One wave of disappointment washed over him after another, and anytime he felt like he'd gotten his head above water, the current swept him and Adeline farther apart.

"Harper's been abused, Matt's an addict, and someone might've tried to kill me."

"Harper's a charity case. Matt's a coworker."

"And me?"

Adeline was the only person he wanted here, but she'd never believe him. Even if she did, she wouldn't reciprocate the feeling. "You're the guest of honor."

Skepticism tightened her lips. "Can I borrow a car?"

"That depends."

"On?"

"If you're going to come back."

"So I'm a prisoner now?"

"Of course not." How could he get their relationship back on solid ground? "Where do you need to go? I can take you."

She tilted her head, expression flat.

So accompanying her wasn't an option. "I'll arrange for someone to go with you." He took out his phone and texted Tim.

"Like a bodyguard?" Adeline asked. "Did you get Tegan one too?"

"Tegan isn't the target."

The phone vibrated, signaling Tim's response. *We're short-staffed as it is since we've taken on watching her house. If I send someone else away, this place will burn next.*

Gannon typed a reply. *A house can be replaced. Adeline can't.*

You have twenty minutes to figure it out. "They'll pick you up out front at twelve thirty."

Matt approached the door, returning from the patio with John and the dogs close behind.

Gannon wouldn't leave it like this, but Adeline was already exiting, unwilling to stay and talk. "Adeline?"

She turned, her dress swaying with the movement.

"Please come back."

She studied him until the patio door swung open. Bruce ran up, tail wagging. She greeted him and John without responding to Gannon's plea.

"Come on, dude." Matt pressed Gannon toward the studio.

Gannon shrugged him off.

"You sleep okay?" John laid a hand on Adeline's shoulder. "Need anything?"

She gave him the grateful smile Gannon had been wishing for all morning. "Yeah, slept great. I'm getting a ride into town to figure some things out."

That sounded ominous.

"I'm here if you need me."

After Adeline nodded, John turned to Gannon, made eye contact, then silently proceeded to the studio, the message clear enough: if she had been able to reach Gannon when she'd needed him, she wouldn't have nearly so much to figure out.

22

*A*deline waited on the red stone step outside the front door and gazed up at the gigantic beams that supported the carport high overhead. Under other circumstances, she'd happily hide away in a place like Havenridge. The property was peaceful, the building luxurious. How many bedrooms must the place have? A dozen?

Too bad Gannon had filled so many of them.

She'd never imagined what his life was like behind the walls of his own house. Not only was Harper a surprise, but she also hadn't put enough stock into the rumors of Matt's drug addiction.

Did she truly know Gannon? And did she have what it took to live in his world? Yesterday, she would've insisted yes to both. Today, her attraction to him had been replaced by uncertainty, and this trip into town wouldn't be long enough to sort it all out.

A black car with tinted windows came down the drive, turned under the carport, and stopped before her. Adeline pulled her purse over her shoulder and stood as a man in black pants and a gray polo got out. "You must be Adeline."

"Hi."

He came around to her side of the car, and Adeline saw the gun holstered at his waist. Armed security? Another surprise.

"I'm Michael." He opened the back door for her and waited until she was in before returning to the driver's seat. "Where are we headed?"

"My house." Since talking to Gannon, she'd gotten a call that the fire inspector would be arriving in half an hour to determine the cause of the blaze. She'd texted Chip, and he'd also promised to stop by to advise her on whether she needed to open a claim with her insurance company for the damage.

After those meetings, she'd pack more belongings to take with her, but where should she stay? Was it necessary to remain at Havenridge and have an armed guard driving her around?

The car slowed as the gate came into view. The crowd had multiplied to about twenty people—five of whom were Olivia and company. Most onlookers didn't hold fancy cameras, but many did have cell phones. At the sight of the car, they strained to see around each other.

The gate rolled open, and Michael steered through much the way John had last night, slowly progressing, though a couple of women, probably in their twenties, came right up to the windows. So did a man with a camera.

Michael accelerated.

The window tinting would've prevented any photos, but Adeline would be fair game when she got out at her house. Good thing she'd chosen to bring the dress and had taken time with her hair and makeup.

She leaned forward. "Do you think I'd be in danger at the house?"

"Caught a couple people trying to climb the fence, but no one's gotten by us yet."

Her house didn't have a fence, so Michael must be referring to Havenridge. "Teenage girls?"

"No, men in their twenties. One of them shouted the whole way back to his car about how he'd be the best thing to happen to Awestruck, that they needed him as a second guitar."

Second guitar. Fitz's old role.

"And your gun? Have you ever had to use that?"

"Only in training. And Afghanistan."

A soldier who'd seen combat.

"Thanks for serving."

"You're welcome." He didn't so much as glance in the rearview mirror and clearly wasn't looking to get into it any further.

She hesitated to return to her point. How silly would the concern for her safety sound to someone who'd been in a war zone? "I'll be okay at my own house, right? If people are only interested in Gannon and the band, and if the fire was accidental, there's nothing to worry about."

"At best, careless trespassers caused the fire, and carelessness on that level can be as dangerous as malice."

"Oh." So the danger was more serious than she'd hoped.

She watched as they passed Lakeshore's outlying businesses. She was stuck at the cabin, and the proximity would be make-or-break for her and Gannon.

Could she believe him about Harper? Did she want to? Because if their relationship got back on track, she'd still have to figure out how to deal with fans lighting her house on fire, Matt, and who knew what other problems.

Michael turned onto Main Street. They passed two blocks of shops and restaurants and then had to slow for pedestrians who were crossing to Superior Dogs.

Her stomach lurched. "Oh no. Can we stop here?" She angled to see how much of a line waited while Michael parallel parked with expert precision. She hopped out, ran over, and opened the trailer door.

Startled, a teenage boy froze, hands in the till. Equally

surprised, it took her a moment to connect the short, dark hair and light brown eyes the boy shared with Asher. This was his nephew, Noah. Asher glanced away from the sizzling grill as Noah went back to counting change for a customer.

Had he replaced her? She gulped. "I'm so sorry. I completely overslept, and there was so much going on I forgot to call in."

Asher gave her an understanding smile as he used tongs to rotate the cooking brats and hotdogs. "The fire's all anyone's talking about. I assumed you wouldn't make it in. You're okay?"

"Yeah." She eyed Noah, who was taking another order.

He braced his hands on the window as she had so many times. "Want to upgrade that to a brat? Only fifty cents more."

As the customer agreed, Adeline bit her lip. A kid could do her job as well as she did.

"Don't worry." Asher chuckled. "He knows it's temporary."

"I'm glad you have help." She forced a smile. "I'd stay, but I have a meeting with the fire department."

"Good. Get to the bottom of it."

"I don't suppose you've heard anything helpful. Did anyone mention seeing something?"

Asher plucked a hotdog off the cooking space and plopped it into a bun. "I've heard a lot of theories but nothing I'd call credible."

Asher would have to hear news directly from Joe Cullen or the fire inspector to consider it believable. Asking him to repeat anything else would be a lost cause, so she put her hand on the latch to leave.

Noah finished with the customer and jotted the order down on the list for Asher. "Someone asked if you did it yourself to get out of paying for the work the neighborhood association wants."

"As I was saying"—Asher handed the boat with the hotdog to his nephew, who hustled back to work—"nothing credible."

"Who said that?"

Asher shook his head. "No one you need to worry about. Go meet the inspector. It'll all be sorted out."

With the authorities, yes, probably, but they were no longer the only concern. Everyone knew how much of a struggle the repairs were. Though she'd accepted help, nothing had been completed yet, which could add some credibility to the gossip. If a tabloid got hold of the rumor, they could run with it. Everywhere she went, she'd be the woman who'd chosen arson over getting a better job and paying for her own home upkeep.

"Okay, so you know the lighthouse song?" Matt held the neck of his bass guitar with one hand and pushed the other into his hair until his fingers tangled. "I have an idea."

Gannon fought for an expression that didn't show his exasperation. Matt could have a good idea—he used to offer them all the time and had even written a few of their songs early on —but they'd been in the studio for hours, and Gannon needed to get out.

Harper had been smart enough to leave while he'd talked with Adeline. The actress's things were still in her room, though, so she meant to come back, and when she did, Gannon would kick her out for good. He'd rather complete the task before Adeline returned. If she returned.

He'd asked security to notify him the moment either woman pulled up to the gate, but he'd feel better if he could go keep an eye out himself. "Will this idea keep?"

Matt passed his wrist under his nose. "Sure, I guess."

"Let's come back to it tomorrow, then."

John shook his head and exited the studio. The drummer had been extra quiet all day, a sign that he disapproved of

Gannon's choices last night. But how could Gannon have known how it would turn out?

All he could do now was try to fix it.

"So, um ..." Matt ducked out from under the shoulder strap of the bass and set the instrument aside. "Look, I wanted to talk to you."

Who was this and what had he done with Matt? Gannon could only wait to see what the man had to say and hope that in the meantime, security would alert him to any developments.

Matt passed his hands over the thighs of his jeans. "I think you're right, man. Things, um, have gotten a little out of hand, and maybe I want to get clean."

Gannon stared. Matt was a wreck, his need to beat addiction broadcast in every move he made, but he'd been nowhere near ready to admit that last night. "Why?"

His fingers disappeared into his hair again. "I had a come-to-Jesus moment, you know? I don't wanna—well, there was that cop last night. That was a close one, right?" He chuckled uneasily. "I was standing here today thinking it's time. Time to get serious. To pull my weight again and that's gonna mean cleaning up, so I thought you should know."

Just like this, God?

Matt *had* always done everything suddenly.

"You'll go back to rehab?"

"Ah, well." Matt cringed. "We're all here, and I know I've made bad choices, but I thought this place could be my rehab."

Okay. Maybe this wasn't the change Gannon had been waiting for. "You've been using here the same as anywhere else."

"I'm done now. Here on out." He lifted his hands parallel to each other as if to indicate the straight and narrow. "I've done this before, remember? Work will help distract me, and this way, the album doesn't have to wait on hold for weeks."

"Detox will be brutal. You won't be in any shape to rehearse. Will you be able to play next weekend?"

"I'll manage. It won't be as bad as me leaving for a month. I'd miss the show then for sure. And, I mean, are we even still going to be here a month from now?"

No. Summer would end, and Awestruck was due in the studio to record an album Gannon still hadn't written—unless he could supplement what he had with the songs about Adeline.

"If I fall off the wagon, you can check me into rehab yourself."

"It's one thing to say that now and another to follow through when the time comes."

"Then do something else to me. Have me thrown in jail. You've wanted to do that forever."

"If I wanted that, I would've left you with the officer last night."

But Matt's suggestion did reveal an option. Gannon could stop protecting him if he went back to using. He could even take it a step further, do what his mom had suggested all those weeks ago and fire Matt. But given everything Gannon had been forgiven for, wasn't he obligated to show mercy?

"Won't matter, anyway. I'm done. Cold turkey. Alcohol too."

The near miss with the police officer last night wouldn't have been enough to inspire a sincere change, and maybe this wasn't sincere. But on the chance Matt would surprise him, Gannon didn't want him failing. "Stay close to me or John, so you've got backup when it gets bad."

"Or Tim. Or just here."

"No. With me or John." Not that Gannon wanted to be saddled with Matt right now, but the cravings would be intense, and as Tim had pointed out, Matt had a golden ticket—he could get whatever he wanted, wherever he wanted. Tim might even arrange the delivery for him if it meant keeping the performances and the recording schedule on track.

"What's up with John, anyway? The way he was acting, you're lucky you don't have a drumstick through your eye."

Gannon opened the studio door and motioned Matt through. "Let's hope he feels more charitable toward you."

On the way through the great room, Gannon scanned the couches. Tegan was there, but no Adeline.

She rose. "I need a minute with you." Her chunky necklace and black short-sleeve sweater reminded him she'd gone to work today. Teaching. She hadn't looked this tense when she'd left.

On the other side of the patio doors, John was doing something on his phone as the trio of dogs trotted off onto the grass. Tegan's and Bruce's presence suggested Adeline hadn't left permanently, unless Tegan's tight expression meant she was about to break bad news on Adeline's behalf.

He pointed Matt toward John. "Go tell him what you told me. I'll be out soon."

Tegan lowered herself to her seat and folded her hands. How long had she been sitting here, waiting for him?

He sat across the coffee table from her and laced his hands together. "What can I do for you?"

"I need to thank you for letting us stay here." Her tone was formal with undertones of disapproval, maybe even aggression. The treatment he'd expect from an interviewer bent on blowing apart everything he stood for. She kept her gaze level, no gratitude cracking her serious expression.

"It's the least I could do."

"I agree." She kept her voice as even as her eye contact.

He waited. No sense guessing what had angered her and speaking to the concern preemptively. If he guessed wrong, he'd give her more ammo.

"The fire inspector told Adeline today that the ladder was

pushed through the window. The fire could've been accidentally caused by the cigarettes, but the man you sent with Adeline told her something about carelessness being as dangerous as someone who's out to get her, so she feels like she has no option but to stay here."

Gannon would have to make sure that guard got a raise. "I'm happy to put you up in a hotel, but I'd rather know you have good security, and this is the only place I can guarantee it. You're both welcome here. If this is about the damage—"

"It is about damage. To Adeline. She called and begged me to stay here with her because she doesn't want to face this place alone."

So she was upset. He'd rather talk this through with Adeline than with her proxy. His bet? Adeline had no idea what Tegan was up to and might even be angry her roommate had stepped in. But if Tegan would confront him, she'd also speak against him to Adeline, straining things even more. "I'm telling Harper to leave as soon as I find her."

"That doesn't solve the problem. Every time I see Adeline, she's reeling from some monumental change between you and her. And that's sad because I see her a lot, and this isn't who she is. One minute she breaks out the bass for the first time since I've known her, the next she's crushed and begging me to stay here as if her life depends on it, all because you're toying with her."

"She played her bass?"

"Is that the only thing you heard?"

"If you don't realize how good a sign it is that she played again, you don't know her or our relationship well enough to judge. You might know Adeline as someone who works in a stuffy office and serves hotdogs, but she's been burying her talents, pulling into herself instead of thriving."

"And you think the way you're treating her will somehow help her realize that?"

So Tegan wanted more for Adeline too. At least they had that in common.

"Harper shouldn't be here, but if Adeline played again, my showing up in her life hasn't been a complete waste, and if you think I would willfully hurt her ..." He wanted to tell her to find another place to stay, but that would only work against him. "It's a good thing you're here, so you'll have a front-row seat to see how much that isn't the case."

"Maybe you wouldn't willfully hurt her. But it's like that bodyguard said. Carelessness can be equally dangerous."

Anger stretched tight in his chest, about to snap. "How long have you been her friend?"

"A few years."

"And you only heard her play bass once?"

Her silence answered.

"Then my being here a few weeks has done something for her that years before haven't." Years Tegan had been in the picture. Did he need to spell that out for her? "I'm not perfect, but I'll do whatever it takes to help Adeline live with the living again."

"Live with the living?"

"Adeline can fill you in. I have other business."

23

An immense lawn stretched from the parking lot to the red brick building. Mature trees reached higher than the roof three stories up, somehow making the university building more imposing, even now, after Adeline had done what she'd come to do. She clicked her seatbelt as she heard the snap of Michael doing the same.

Tegan would flip out with joy when she found out about this. Getting the job would be a relief for Adeline too. She might not know what to do in her relationship with Gannon, but she could improve the way her life looked apart from him. Or at least, she could try.

God, please bless this, but only if You want me to work here. If You think staying in the church job is best, let me know.

How she'd know God was trying to tell her something was anyone's guess, but making the request calmed her worry over that one aspect of her life.

Let me know what to do about the rest of it too.

Unfortunately, immediate peace didn't follow.

"Where to?" Michael started the engine. He hadn't said much all day except to answer her questions, but he'd done his job. He'd walked through her house to make sure everything was in order and had waited for hours while she dealt with the fire inspector and opening an insurance claim and packing and resume writing. When a photographer tried to follow them from her house to the college, he'd lost the man in a matter of turns.

"To Havenridge, I guess." Tegan had texted she was there already, a small comfort.

Less than ten minutes later, Michael pulled to a stop under the carport.

Adeline unbuckled and looked up at the door through the tinted window. As soon as she walked in, Gannon would be there, wanting to talk. Harper might linger nearby too. She hadn't scared Adeline off the property with the lingerie or bought her favor with the personal shopping. What might come next?

And then there was Matt, dingy and abrasive.

Michael opened her car door. The rest of the day, she'd gotten out when he had, never giving him the opportunity. Had she been expected to wait all those times? She didn't even know how to get out of a car in Gannon's world. She gathered her purse and the large tote she'd filled with toiletries and shoes.

Michael handed her a business card. "If you decide to go out, call or text day or night. I've been assigned to you specifically."

He opened the trunk and lifted out the suitcase she'd packed. Before she figured out how to protest, he'd taken it in through the front door. She pressed her index finger against the crisp edge of the card. She'd been assigned a bodyguard. What was the etiquette of that kind of relationship?

To her relief, he came back out immediately, so he hadn't acted on any grand ideas of delivering her luggage all the way up to the third floor.

"Have a good afternoon."

"You too." She watched him get back behind the wheel before mustering her courage to move forward. But as she approached the front door, she heard another car in the drive.

She got a glimpse of Harper in the driver's seat before the vehicle parked by the garage.

Great.

Adeline found her suitcase just inside the door. She adjusted her tote, lifted the handle of the rolling suitcase, and then pulled it behind her into the great room.

"Welcome home." Harper flounced in from the garage. "How are you? How was your day?"

Through the windows toward the lake, she spotted Gannon, Matt, and John sitting in a loose huddle on the patio, heads bowed. Were they praying together? Beyond them, the dogs played on the broad lawn.

"You changed." Harper breezed to a stop next to her and rubbed the material of Adeline's sleeve between two fingers as if to judge its worth. Without betraying her verdict, she grabbed Adeline's hand and tugged her toward the stairs. "Let's chat. Away from the noise." She wiggled her fingers at the patio, as if they could hear anything from there, and pulled Adeline toward the stairs. "It's personal."

Adeline's shin bumped the first step, and the weight of her tote and purse made her turn her attention from Gannon to prevent a fall. "Talk about what?"

"Life. Love." She shrugged one shoulder with a helpless smile. "The pursuit of happiness."

Wasn't the phrase from the Declaration about liberty, not love? Either way, their pursuits of happiness were at odds with each other. "I should get my bags up to my room."

"That thing is as big as you are." Harper waved her hand again. "One of them will carry it for you."

John and Gannon were definitely praying. Matt had his gaze pointed at the ground, eyes open. It was hard to tell if he was waiting the other two out or if he was a willing participant.

"It's not about Gannon, if that's what you're worried about." Harper gazed at him, undermining her words. "Well, it is about him a little bit. I've never known anyone else like him. I mean, look at him."

Adeline watched Gannon's mouth move. What was he saying? Every time they'd spoken, he'd had so much to say to her that rang truer than most of what she told herself, but they hadn't prayed together. What would he say if he were to pray over her as fervently as he appeared to be praying now?

"Well, I mean, don't *stare* at him. He's hot—right?—but that's not what I'm talking about. It's the Christian thing. You're like that too, aren't you? I read that you work at a church. That's probably why he likes you."

Adeline wasn't *like that* at all. Her meek prayers were nothing compared to whatever Gannon poured out now.

Harper watched her, plainly hopeful, though the bruised swelling still dimmed one of her eyes. "I can't hide out here forever, but I don't know what to do, and no one wants anything to do with me—not that I blame them, really—but I'm so alone and I need ..." Her bright manner faded into something tremulous, and her nose turned pink. "What does it take to become a Christian?"

Adeline had walked in expecting something from Harper, but not this. Could she refuse this conversation?

With a sigh, she let the actress usher her into Harper's room. Harper closed the door most of the way, then sat on the bed, leaning against the elegant curves of a driftwood headboard similar to the one in Gannon's room. She motioned, and Adeline took a spot against the footboard.

"So? Can I be one?"

"A Christian?"

Harper nodded vigorously.

Did she seriously want to turn her life over to Jesus here and now? Was she in any place to do that? For that matter, was Adeline's faith in any condition to lead someone else to Christ? "What do you know about God?"

"I know about Jesus dying. John three-sixteen—God loves us."

"That's a start. God loves us, but we also have to love Him, and if we do, we'll change the way we act. Jesus died to pay for our sins, and for us to be right with God, we have to repent and turn our lives over to God."

"The whole sex thing, right? But you can still be a Christian and do that stuff because—"

"No, you have to change." The words came out harsh. She softened her tone. "I mean, if you love Him and want to follow Him, you'll obey what He says to do—and not just in your relationships with men." She pulled her hair away from her face and breathed deeply. "Another example might be considering what films you act in. How do your characters behave? What do the films encourage your audiences to do and believe? Do you see what I mean?"

"Oh. Like how Gannon refuses to take his shirt off for photoshoots?" Harper giggled. "But then they follow him around on the beach until they get what they want, so the whole thing is silly. If anything, it makes them more curious. He works out. He has nothing to be shy about."

"And you would know."

Harper gave a guilty smile but no explanation.

Unless she was bluffing, Harper would know if Gannon had a cross tattoo. Though Adeline hadn't realized he'd drawn a line at shirtless photos, she could understand why he had. Even the photo of him in a tank had been pretty steamy. Shirtless ... Her throat tightened. "If he believes he's doing what's right, then that's a good thing."

"Sex scenes are part of, like, every good role. But it's just pretend. I'm sure God doesn't mind. A girl's got to pay her bills."

Men's voices sounded from the great room. The guys must've finished on the patio.

Adeline pressed her hands over the thighs of her pants. "I don't know specifically what Christ will ask of you, but putting Him first instead of money is part of having faith in Him." She heard fast, clicking steps—one of the dogs.

Adeline needed to wrap this up. She wasn't doing any good anyway, wasn't presenting things right, though she didn't know what to change.

"Is that why you're poor? God wants you to be?"

Poor? She had food, a house, two jobs. She wasn't poor, though to Harper's point, she had taken the modest jobs because she'd thought working for the church would please God. She'd done it out of duty. But had God asked her to take that rather than finding a better fit?

A sudden wave of guilt made her feel seasick. Since she hadn't been praying when she'd taken the secretary role, she'd acted on an outward idea of holiness rather than on a relationship with God. She'd been struggling to get by for so long, but maybe God had never called her to that.

Bruce's fur brushed against the door and pulled Harper's attention away. "Look who missed his mommy."

Bruce whipped his tail as he approached, but Gannon called him, and the dog hesitated halfway to Adeline. The sound of something rolling across the hardwood of the balcony toward the bedroom door got louder, and then Gannon stood in the opening, her suitcase handle in hand.

His line of sight tracked from Adeline to Harper and back.

Adeline passed her hand over her upset stomach. He'd be disappointed in her for focusing on works with Harper, the same as she had in her own life. Repentance and works and grace and faith all balanced together somehow, though, so what she'd told Harper might not have been wrong.

Anyway, she was disappointed in Gannon. What did it matter if he was disappointed in her?

For her part, Harper didn't appear troubled. "Having a little chat." She rose from the bed and crossed the room, laying her hand on Gannon's chest as she passed.

He stepped backward.

Harper moved on to primp her makeup in the mirror. "We're done now. You can have her."

The actress behaved with such familiarity with him. She knew how to navigate this life. She belonged in a way Adeline never would.

She stood and thought of telling Gannon she could take her suitcase from there, but as soon as he saw her struggling with it on the stairs, he'd reclaim the task. She pulled her tote onto her shoulder and looped her purse strap around her hand. Bruce kept pace with her as she started down the hall behind Gannon.

Even without the suitcase, she was carrying too much. The realization that she'd taken the church job to please God when she hadn't even consulted Him on the decision. The knowledge that she hardly knew God well enough to present Him to someone who asked to hear. A day ago, she would've turned to the man who walked ahead of her for help, but today, she couldn't deny she hardly knew him either.

ONCE THEY WERE around the corner, away from Harper, Gannon glanced back at Adeline. He'd resisted sending Harper packing only because it would've led to a fight and prevented him from taking this opportunity to talk to Adeline.

Her change of clothes looked crisp and professional, but he

missed the dress she'd worn this morning, if for no other reason than that her choice to go business casual was a mystery to him. "What did Harper want?"

"She was asking about Christianity."

"Figures."

Adeline drew her eyebrows together.

He started up the stairs to the third floor. "That's how my relationship with her started. She knows we won't refuse to talk to her about our faith, so she fakes interest to get us to let her hang around."

"It didn't seem impossible that she was genuinely interested. She's beaten up and camping out here. She needs hope."

And Harper was exactly the type to manufacture some for herself by conning Adeline into feeling sorry for her. "If you think she's seeking God, I'll connect her with Drew." They reached the landing, and he set the suitcase on its wheels. "How did everything go today?"

"The damage to the siding and woodwork isn't bad, but because of what it'll take to get the smoke smell out, I have to open a claim. The work on the porch can continue. The painting on the other areas of the house can too, but I'm not sure yet if insurance will want to pay your painters for repairing the fire-damaged portion or if they'll want to bring someone else in. It's a mess."

Gannon rolled the suitcase a foot or two into Adeline's room, then retreated to the doorway. "Let me pay the deductible and whatever other expenses come out of this. I'm the reason someone was on your property. In fact, I'll pay the whole thing. You don't even have to go through insurance. Make it easier on yourself."

Adeline stood just inside the room, the tote and purse still weighing her down. "I'm working on something that'll cover the deductible."

He'd expected her to refuse, but had she dressed up to go to the bank and ask for a loan? That would explain her forlorn expression. "Don't go into debt over something I caused."

"I turned in my resume for a job at the university. Tegan knows someone there. She thinks I have a good chance." Though from her unenthusiastic smile, Adeline wasn't as confident.

"You know that anything you need—"

"You've done enough." She deposited her tote and purse at the foot of the bed, crossed her arms, and turned back to him. "Michael's nice, but why does he carry a gun? That seems intense."

Michael must be the security detail Tim had arranged, the one who'd said something to convince Adeline to stay. "They have to be prepared. I've had some close calls."

Sadness, rather than concern, shrouded Adeline's expression. "Like what?"

Those details might cause her to wheel that suitcase right back out of his life.

"People have tried to hurt you?"

At this rate, she'd imagine something worse than it'd been. "Someone pulled a knife on me backstage once. Another time, a woman carried a pocket revolver into a music festival, also with the intention of finding me."

"Why?"

"Which one?"

His question seemed to deepen the lines on her forehead, so he gave up holding out. "The knife was a disgruntled husband. His wife came to one of our shows, met us backstage, and never went home. She filed for divorce. Not because of us, but that's how he saw it—hence, the knife."

He waited to see if she'd let him stop there, but she moved a little closer, watching for him to continue.

Closer. That had to be a good sign, even if her forehead remained furrowed.

"The pocket revolver lady called in to a radio interview I was giving. She went on about how she and I were meant to be together for eternity. I said Jesus had dibs on my eternity, and she came to the festival to introduce me to Him. She didn't get to use it, but that's more than enough close calls for me, and I won't gamble with you."

Adeline ran her finger over the surface of the desk near the door, less than two feet from him now. "Can I ask you something?"

"Don't you know the answer to that by now?" He touched her elbow, hoping she might step nearer.

Hurt seemed to pool in her eyes.

"Yes, Adeline. You can ask me anything."

Frowning, she focused on the desk. "How close are we?"

"To what?"

"Each other." She shifted away. Only a few inches. A movement that didn't look conscious, but it warred with his impulse to reach out and pull her closer. Why hadn't he kissed her when he'd had the chance? Then she wouldn't have to ask questions like this.

She must've taken his silence to indicate confusion because she dove into an explanation. "We have history together, and I wonder if that has led to a false sense of closeness. Maybe I'm a lot like that woman with the gun, thinking we're something when that's not at all what it is for you. In the past, we were close, but now, we're just a couple of weeks into getting reacquainted. We're barely friends."

"I thought we were past this."

She backed farther from him. "You didn't tell me about Matt. And people have tried to kill you? Being here is a wake-up call. I hardly know you."

She might as well have planted her hands on his chest and shoved him away.

Hardly knew him? After everything? "Tegan and John seem

to think your heart needs to be protected from me, but you pack a few punches of your own."

Her shoulders drooped. "Be honest, Gannon. Harper knows you better than I do."

"Harper doesn't know herself, let alone another human being. She pays enough attention to manipulate us, but *knowing* someone? That takes more than she has to offer. She asked me last night if my dad taught me to change a tire."

She winced, but her frown persisted. "I'm not sure I trust you where she's concerned."

"I'm not one to hide my sins like that. I wanted to tell Fitz about us. Why wouldn't I be honest with you?"

"You didn't want to tell Fitz enough to follow through. For all I know, you have reasons for not telling me the truth about Harper."

"You're throwing in my face the time I was loyal to you against my better judgment?"

"You were loyal to yourself. You didn't want to look bad. Nobody does."

"Fine. You want me to look bad? You want me to name all my sins? Lust, lying, anger, selfishness. I've been proud and judgmental. I've failed to devote the time to God that He deserves. You want me to keep going? I could, but I'm never going to say what you want me to say, because I won't confess a sin I didn't commit."

Adeline retreated to a spot by the foot of the bed. "Maybe too much doesn't feel right. Maybe it's the timing. I've got a lot going on, and so do you."

"Don't blame the timing. This might be the only chance I get to take this much time away for years. Between recording, touring, and *Audition Room*, my schedule's impossible. I saw an opening, and I took it. Maybe the problem is that you're afraid because real life isn't neat and tidy. That's why you haven't been living it—because you tried once and it went badly and now you think every imperfection will turn into the same thing."

"Or I don't fit in your life and never will. If your schedule's that hectic, how would our relationship work? You'd want me to move to LA? Or go on tour with you? Or you'd fly here once in a while? None of that sounds practical."

"I can afford impractical." His exasperation had spilled into his tone. He paused and measured his next words carefully. "The question is whether you can forgive imperfect—in me and in yourself."

Her back straightened. "I do forgive you, but I can't act like it didn't hurt to find Harper here. I care about you. I love your faith and how you stand by people, but what else about you am I going to find out that's going to end up hurting?"

"Does it matter? You're taking shots in the dark, trying to hit an artery and kill this so you can go back to life without me and ignore or avoid anything that makes you uncomfortable. Is that what you want? To run back to your comfort zone?"

She blinked rapidly.

What if she started crying and wouldn't let him give her a hug? He was being too rough, in danger of nicking that artery himself.

"Look." He infused his voice with tenderness. "I know this isn't ideal, and I'm sorry I hurt you."

She sat on the foot of the bed, shoulders rounded as if they were still weighted down by the luggage she'd carried.

"You're one of the few people who doesn't judge me by my fame or my reputation, someone who truly knows me. Hearing you say you don't know me ...?" He pulled a flash drive from his pocket and laid it on the writing table. "For me, there is no going back to a life without you. Since the day we met, you've been a huge part of my life, even during all the years we spent apart. That's when I wrote these, except for the last one, which I wrote this morning."

Adeline's eyes fixed on the small black drive. "Lyrics?"

"Recordings." Maybe he should give her the whole note-book, go all in. But if she wouldn't accept what she heard in the four recorded songs, having the whole collection wouldn't make a bit of difference. "I promised you music last night so you could practice. You'll find an electric bass downstairs in the studio, if you want it."

"Matt's? He wouldn't like that."

"Matt waltzed into Havenridge with little but the clothes on his back. Except the drums, what's in the studio is mine, and you're welcome to it, whether or not you like what you hear." He stepped back into the hall.

She stared at the drive without moving.

"You have the say over whether we can use these. If you let us, I can't say which songs, if any, will make the cut—we offer a lot more than what makes the album—but they have potential. My most successful work has always come from my most personal experiences and emotions, and it doesn't get any more personal than that."

If she listened to them and rejected him anyway, she'd be rejecting the best he had to offer. He'd never win her over.

"Okay." She studied her hands, picking at the nails she still hadn't trimmed.

"Okay." He pressed his palm against the doorframe, waited another beat, and left.

24

*A*deline dug her laptop from her suitcase. Once it powered up, she loaded the flash drive and hit play.

She returned to the bed, lay back, and let the comforter cradle her.

The quality of the recording was good—no noticeable white noise, just guitar and Gannon's voice—but her laptop speakers playing from ten feet away should allow her to listen without feeling immersed. It would be like getting a voicemail message. Removed. No immediate reply expected.

The theory washed away when she teared up during the first song, the one he'd performed for her last night. As beautiful as it was, the idea of God holding her seemed so much less important than that He might direct her in what to do. When she spoke with Harper, she'd made it sound so simple to determine what God asked of a person, but that wasn't the case at all.

If His guidance were easy to discern, she'd know what to do about Gannon.

Gannon was right about one thing: pursuing a relationship with him would put her far outside her comfort zone. Security details, paparazzi, fans, hectic schedules. Harper. Taking their connection deeper would also mean trusting Gannon the way she had last night when she'd told him about the rift in her relationship with God. A romance meant risking that he'd hurt her again, and worse.

The second song started. Though he used no names, the song said enough for her to recognize he'd been missing her when the lyrics came. He sang of hoping to spot her face in the crowd, of how she followed him everywhere but was never there when he turned around. The song gave no indication of when it had been written. From what he'd said, this may have come to him any time over the last nine years—or even before that—but had he honestly thought of her that much?

She'd thought of him often, but he was famous. Reminders of him were everywhere. Once in a while, she'd done what his song described—mistaken someone else for him and done a double take, heart pounding. She'd felt foolish each time, assuming he had forgotten her the way she had told him to.

She'd spent so much time blaming Gannon for what happened to Fitz that she'd considered herself the one who'd been rejected. But that wasn't true. Gannon had wanted her to pick him and had only stopped calling when she'd told him she was staying with Fitz. He'd called again when he somehow heard—maybe through John?—that she and Fitz had broken up.

Again, she'd rejected him.

And then, at Fitz's funeral, Gannon found her sitting out behind the funeral parlor and tried to comfort her. She pushed him away. What had she said? Something about how they'd killed him.

She wasn't the only one who'd been hurt. He'd said she'd thrown some punches, and she had. She'd hurt him, and in a relationship, odds were she'd do so again. Why was he so willing to accept the risk?

Silence, and then the third song started, the beat driven with a bitter tension the other songs had lacked.

You can't hurt me now so go ahead and try. You can't win or wound a missing heart, and mine's been laid to rest. I buried it at nineteen, I sent it packing with a girl who's long, long gone. Beneath your hand's an empty chest. You came too late, and you're only second best.

The moment when Harper laid her hand on Gannon half an hour ago flashed to mind. The inclusion of a song that expressed something other than selfless love or longing made the collection ring with authenticity.

The fourth song started. There had only been four files on the drive, so this was it, the song he'd composed this morning.

The house burned down, I'll take the blame. The sparks keep catching, an open flame. Kerosene on my hands, and you're a girl on fire. The ashes swirl higher, and I watch for a phoenix to rise. The story here will define our lives, and I'm praying a phoenix will rise.

Though it was the roughest and most incomplete of the songs he'd recorded, she could imagine the music fleshed out better than the others. By the third and final time the chorus repeated, she was tapping the rhythm she'd use for the bass line. Maybe she ought to go down to the studio and see if she could get anywhere close to the sound she had in mind.

"Look at you."

Adeline started and sat up. The song had ended, but she hadn't heard Tegan take up station in the doorway.

"Superior Dogs changed their dress code? Or ..." Tegan slanted her head, eyes on the teal top Adeline wore. "Isn't that mine?"

Adeline smoothed her hands over the fabric, stalling as her mind switched gears. "My church clothes didn't seem quite right, so I raided your closet before I dropped off my resume for that job you've been telling me about. Since it's the weekend, I was lucky they were open at all. I doubt any decision makers were there, but I figured better safe than sorry."

"You applied?" Tegan perched on the edge of a nearby armchair.

Adeline lay back on the bed again. Gannon had accused her of wanting to retreat to her comfort zone, but those were all gone. The press hounded Superior Dogs, fangirls attended church to gather details about Awestruck, and her house had become a target for crazy fans. Adeline herself had changed. Even if she and Gannon didn't move forward, she was dreaming up bass lines and applying for jobs. There was no going back.

"Asher replaced me with a high schooler—temporarily— but maybe it's time I stop hogging a job a teenager would love and take my place in the world."

Tegan hesitated, probably searching for something to say other than, *It's about time.* "A high schooler couldn't do your job at church."

"I'm not so sure. I prayed a little bit about quitting, and I'll take any changes one step at a time, but if the college job comes through, church will find a replacement easily enough. Anyway, I'm ready for money to not be so tight." Pain slithered through her again at the memory of what Noah had said. "There's a rumor I tried to burn down the house because I couldn't afford the repairs."

Tegan uttered a *pfft.* "People are unbelievable."

"Yeah. Well ..." The fire inspector might not think the rumors were so far-fetched. He'd asked again and again about what she'd done when and why. Maybe she ought to accept Gannon's offer to pay for the repairs without an insurance claim. She'd rather endure romance rumors than accusations of arson. "You talked to Gannon?"

Tegan sighed, drummed her fingers on the armrest, and

gazed out the window. "I'm not his biggest fan. Harper shouldn't be here."

Adeline studied the recessed ceiling over the bed. "I agree."

"But?"

"He apologized. Gave me some of his songs to listen to."

"And?"

And she was still hurt, afraid of more pain for both of them, but more in love with the man behind the songs than ever.

"I take it they were good songs," Tegan said.

"I keep thinking about a bass line for one of them. It's like playing for five minutes yesterday cracked open a door to music that I have to walk through now."

Music and a new job—these had become needs that outweighed the discomfort of having to change. Could she add more change to the list? How long would it be until she felt peace dealing with the difficulties of being associated with fame? And could she safely rely on Gannon to help her through?

"I like him." Adeline almost laughed at the understatement. "A lot. But I'm worried too, and his life is complicated. I'm praying about what to do, but do you think God will answer clearly enough for me to recognize Him?"

"I do, but you'll have to be willing to hear, even if the answer isn't what you want."

DESPITE AN ONGOING BREEZE, the sun shone. Gannon stood at the wall on the cliff and watched the crests of waves foam and fade back to turquoise. A group of kayakers bobbed about sixty feet from the rocks, their progress slowed by the choppy lake. Farther out, a tourist ship rounded the side of the island on its way from the lighthouse to the marina.

He'd spent twenty minutes searching the cabin after his

latest fight with Adeline so he could tell Harper to leave. She'd disappeared again. Somewhere in the cabin this time because security said she hadn't left. To avoid him, she must've been purposely hiding.

When Gannon last looked back at the cabin, Matt, John, and Tim had been on the patio, lounging near the grill as dinner cooked. The sharp footfalls approaching wouldn't be one of them, nor would it be Tegan or Adeline, who never wore heels tall enough to make this racket. He braced his hands on the wall and refused to turn.

Harper had called way too many of the shots as it was.

"You look so lonely out here." Harper leaned against the stone an inch from his left hand, her back to the lake.

He didn't turn his head. "I want you to leave."

"Is this about Adeline? All I did was talk to her, and not even about you."

"If you want to know about God, I'll set up an appointment for you with a local pastor, but you can't force me into letting you stay by winning Adeline's sympathy."

"That's not what I was doing."

"So you want that appointment with the pastor?"

"No, I found out I don't need as much help as I thought I did." Her chipper tone grated on him.

"You need to leave. Now."

She chuckled. "Go ahead. Play that game. I'm onto you." She laid her hand over his.

He pulled away, crossing his arms. Maybe his glare would tell her what his refusal to look at her hadn't—he wasn't playing any games.

Her mouth twitched with a smile. "You're in love."

Was that what these mangled emotions were? Frustration, desperation, concern, protectiveness. A longing to see Adeline happy. "Then you know why you need to go."

"Why can't we be open about it? She'll get over it." Harper

flicked her fingers through her hair. "She can't honestly think she can steal you from me."

Adeline?

Harper adjusted her top, then folded her hands and stilled as if he were a photographer and she was now ready for her photoshoot.

"You think I'm in love with *you*?" He let disdain coat his voice. How else could he get through to her?

"You wrote a song about me."

"You're delusional."

She waved dismissively. "You're so cute. I was in your room. I found your notebook."

He rubbed his hand over his heart. In his search, he hadn't thought to look for her in his own room. "You have no right to be here at all, Harper, let alone to trespass in my room."

Her shoulders lowered. "But the song—"

"Whatever you saw was about Adeline. The entire notebook, all of it is for her, songs dating back to before anyone outside your little hometown knew your name, let alone before I heard it. Understand? What you're up against here isn't something you can flirt into submission. For the hundredth time, you and I have. No. Future."

"So that's it? You never loved me? Never even cared about me?"

"How many times do I have to tell you?"

Though the glasses hid her eyes, her seething glare was obvious in the lines that formed around her mouth. "I hate you. I really hate you."

He bit back the reply that the feeling was mutual. He stepped from the overlook to the yard. "I want you gone. Tonight."

"What about everything that's happened to me?" She flew up next to him, sank her nails into his arm. "What if he catches up to me again when I leave?"

She shouted the questions, but Gannon kept walking. Kept his eyes turned away. The performance would end when she realized she had no audience.

Except they did have one. Tegan and Adeline had joined the group on the patio, and all five faces had turned to watch.

"Fine. Well." She whipped off her sunglasses, revealing the bruise, which had darkened. "We're already on a cliff. Maybe I should take a step in the wrong direction, right? For all you care?" She loosened her grip and stepped back toward the short wall.

Gannon caught her wrist. "Call Karina."

As much as he disliked Harper's misguided life coach, Karina pandered to Harper's ego and got her through her worst mood swings. He and Adeline already had one too many suicides on their consciences.

Harper glared at him, chest rising and falling fast.

"Now. Call her now."

Harper yanked her hand free. "Why do I put up with you?"

Another sentiment he could parrot back to her. "Make the call."

Anger set her jaw as tears welled in her eyes. Harper punched her index finger against her phone screen as she marched toward the cabin. She lifted the device to her ear as she stepped onto the patio. Though Gannon had stayed where he was, halfway between the cliff and the house, he heard her shout into the phone.

"He's throwing me out on the street. He says I have to leave after I came all the way up here." She stomped into the house.

The door slammed behind her.

All five faces turned back to him.

Then, as if nothing had happened, Matt and Tim resumed their conversation. Tegan looked at the door Harper had used. John focused on Gannon with an expression that seemed to say he'd done the right thing.

But Adeline dropped to a seat with her back to Gannon. If she'd listened to the songs, they hadn't made enough of a difference.

There was too much to navigate here, too many conflicting opinions, too many eyes.

He let himself in the house, changed into riding gear, and tore off on his motorcycle.

---

25

*T*he phoenix song played so fast, Adeline had to keep hitting pause and backing up the recording. It was hard to hear if she hit the right note at the right time because the bass guitar played through an amp, but the song played through her laptop.

She had ducked out of the home theater, leaving Tegan, John, Matt, and Tim watching a movie. Equipment more sophisticated than anything they'd had back in high school packed the studio. There must be a way to play Gannon's recording through the speakers, but she'd barely been able to get the bass plugged in and working.

Then again, her inability to use the equipment was an excuse. The truth? She'd dreamed up an advanced part too complex for a beginner.

She could feel it—what the song could be, what she intended to play—like a desperate need, the way a person hungry for air felt pressure in their lungs. But her fingers on the strings brought dissonance, not satisfaction. She replayed the first ten seconds of the recording and hit pause. As she fit her fingers back on the strings of the bass, the studio door cracked open.

She hadn't seen Harper or Gannon since the two had fought on the lawn. Had Gannon returned from his ride? If so, he would be disappointed at how poorly she played. It'd be one more step toward an answer from God that didn't result in them being together.

Matt entered instead. His forehead furrowed when he saw her, and he seemed to assess her setup—the computer, the bass. "You lost?"

She bit her lip. "Gannon said this would be all right."

"You think you have a right to be here?" He stepped in, shut the door, and leaned against it. "Prove it."

He was going to stand there and watch? He wasn't this confrontational or challenging to Gannon, but Gannon also had a confident presence she couldn't muster while holding a bass she couldn't play right.

She replayed Gannon's recording again, delaying the embarrassment a little longer. When it ended, all she could imagine was flubbing up the notes. She pressed the play button one more time.

The song ended all too soon. Matt crossed his arms, blue eyes icy with interest.

Maybe she could nail it. Maybe the music she felt would come out this time. After all, she'd once been good at this. The knowledge had to be there somewhere. She hit replay and tackled a few notes.

One of them hit where she'd meant it to. The others fumbled and fell.

Matt pushed away from the door, took a cable from somewhere in the maze of cords, and plugged it into her laptop. He leaned over the jumble of equipment that crowded the desk and pressed a few buttons.

"Try that." When she didn't, he came around behind her and tapped the touch pad to play the recording again. This time, Gannon's voice and guitar sounded steady and clear through the speakers.

Her wrong notes grated against the melody.

"I can see why they left you behind."

Gannon wouldn't allow him to speak to her like that, but Gannon wasn't here. No arguments about her former skill would help when none of it remained.

Matt extended his hand, demanding the bass.

She handed it over, praying he'd do even worse than she had.

He fit the strap over his head and shrugged, settling the instrument where he wanted it before he gave a nod to start the recording. What he played varied from what she'd envisioned —the notes were simple and repetitive, but they fit the music, grounding the song. And this was the first attempt of a drug addict. If she let him keep working, he could probably build from there, elaborating. Or maybe such a thing wasn't necessary—bass lines didn't have to be complicated.

That was her problem. She made everything complicated.

The song ended, and Matt set the bass in its stand. "You'll never replace me."

"That's not why I'm here."

"Great." He smirked as he opened the door. "'Cause you couldn't if you wanted to."

Shortly after eleven, Gannon pulled through the gate at Havenridge. Halfway down the drive, he spotted headlights through the trees, moving fast. He swerved to the inside of the curve just as Matt's car roared past, taking the turn wide.

Gannon's headlight flashed through the windshield, revealing Matt in the passenger seat. The driver seemed to have trouble straightening out after the curve, and then the lights disappeared down the road.

Gannon pulled to a full stop. John was an expert driver, and Tim a good one. Adeline and Tegan wouldn't have experience handling a supercar, but they'd also never team up with Matt for a joyride.

That ruled out everyone but Harper, who wasn't as good of a driver as she thought she was. If she was out with Matt, she probably planned to come back to the cabin afterward, but that wasn't happening. He'd already told her to leave and had given her space to do so. She was out of chances.

He texted security and asked them to pack her bags and have those and her rental waiting for her at the gate when she returned. If she wasn't in shape to drive herself, a team member could deliver her to a hotel, but he wouldn't allow her to terrorize his relationship with Adeline a moment longer.

Harper English was not coming back on this property.

Gannon proceeded down the drive. The cabin's exterior lights glowed, but the windows were dark and blank. He parked and pulled off the helmet and jacket as he let himself into the house. Moonlight fell through the windows into the great room. Along the balcony, Matt and Harper's bedroom doors stood open, black rectangles.

He climbed to the third floor and resisted turning toward Adeline's room to see if she was still awake and had anything to say about the songs. Instead, he made his way toward John's. Before he got close enough to knock, one of the dogs sniffed loudly from the other side of the door. Must've sensed him coming. Shortly after, John opened the door, the light of a lamp and TV casting shadows around him.

John backed up and settled against the headboard, his arm

behind his head, eyes focused on the television, where a documentary about migrating birds played. "Feel better?"

"Not really." Gannon sat at the desk and scratched Trigger's gray fur while the other dog jumped up next to his master.

John leaned out of the range of Camo's tail as the dog circled twice before dropping into a curled-up ball. "Addie holed up in the studio most of the evening."

"I gave her recordings of some of the songs to work with. I wasn't sure she would." But she had. Would she let him hear her, or was accepting his music separate from accepting him?

"Matt's losing points fast. I went down to check on him about twenty minutes ago. He was already wasted. When I asked what happened to straightening out, he said, 'False alarm.' They got a good laugh out of that."

"Was she drinking too?"

"Looked that way."

"Now she's driving. They were leaving when I pulled in. Maybe we should try to catch up with them before they do real damage. Or land in jail." If security hadn't packed Harper's things already, Gannon could throw it all in her luggage, take it with, and deliver her to a hotel himself, then bring Matt home before he made more trouble for himself or Awestruck. He stood and moved to the door.

John scoffed and shook his head, eyes still on the TV screen. "You want to go there? Playing Harper's hero last night meant not being Adeline's."

"Isn't she sleeping?"

"That's exactly what she was doing when her house lit up." He switched which arm was behind his head without looking Gannon's direction. "Every time you try to save Harper, you're telling Adeline another woman has a hold on you. You're going to have to choose whose hero you want to be. Let the others fend for themselves."

"It's not just about Harper. She could hurt anyone they

meet on the street, not to mention the fact that Matt's risking a lot of bad press—or imprisonment. Or worse."

"We've given him chance after chance. We agreed we might need to replace him."

"And what? Let him kill himself like Fitz did?"

That drew John's attention away from the screen. "Matt isn't Fitz."

Though the door was open, Gannon twisted the knob one way and the other. Matt and Fitz struggled with different problems, but both were life-threatening.

"Fitz didn't deserve to be fired," John said, "but Matt's only hope of changing is in experiencing consequences for his addiction. And Harper needs to be let go more than anyone."

"And if something happens?"

"This is a stunt to get your attention. Intervening will reinforce that she gets her way by being reckless. You've got to cut her off. Sit this one out."

"I don't think I can."

"She's a drunk driver. Call the cops. Let them handle it."

Objections swelled in his chest. Each of these episodes brought her closer to the point of changing. Everything he'd put up with before now would be useless if he missed the moment when she was finally ready.

But a drunk Harper wouldn't be ready to make any changes or commitments, and he couldn't knowingly let her endanger the public.

Fine. He'd sit it out. Call the police.

But even once he'd made the call, a sick ache permeated his chest. He lingered at the patio doors in the great room. Once Harper went back to LA, he'd feel a lot less responsible.

Lord, keep her safe. Break through to her. Matt too.

He shifted, and the lighthouse beacon came into view. Only then did he realize something on the lower patio by the cliff had blocked the light a second ago. He leaned his head, trying to discern the shape outlined by the dim lighting out along the wall. Was that a person?

The figure lifted a hand and moved as if to pull long hair over a shoulder. He'd seen Adeline do that exact thing. It had to be her out there, gazing at the lake.

Gannon pushed open the patio door and stepped outside.

26

*L*ovely. Just how she'd wanted to be discovered. Adeline ran her hand over the small of her back to ensure the hem of her sweatshirt reached the waistband of her sweatpants as Gannon's footsteps drew nearer. She sat cross-legged on the bench of the lower patio, elbows on the wall, staring at the lighthouse beacon. Her sweats were comfortable and warm enough for the fifty-degree weather that had rolled in with nightfall, but if she'd expected company, she would've pulled on jeans and a jacket instead.

Or not come out at all.

Unable to sleep, she'd taken up station here about half an hour ago, figuring that at nearly midnight, no one would notice. She'd wanted to think and pray, just her and God. If she was going to talk with Gannon instead, she ought to tell him what was on her mind.

She didn't know how to navigate the risks of a relationship.

But how could she cut off the potential between them? The knowledge he was walking up behind her had turned her breath shallow and distracted her so thoroughly, she couldn't focus on a single point of light. Stars? Lighthouses? What were those?

She forced a deep inhale, the air clean with the first chills of impending autumn, and pivoted, putting one foot on the ground as Gannon descended the two steps that separated this outlook from the rest of the yard.

Lights set under glass among the flagstones glowed like candles across a smile that told her he thought the sweats were cute. "Mind if I join you?"

She motioned to the bench. "Plenty of room."

Littered with pillows, the bench ran the entire length of the outlook. Gannon didn't take advantage of the space but sat close enough for the warm sandalwood notes of his cologne to mingle with the crisp air.

He still wore motorcycle pants, but he'd shed the jacket. He leaned back with his elbows on the wall. His face angled toward the sky, expression clouded.

She rested her arm on the wall and supported her head. "What's on your mind?"

A smile lifted the corner of his mouth. "I should be asking you. You're the one sitting out here alone in the middle of the night."

No, not so soon. She'd already hurt him enough. Why couldn't she go along with him on this? See where romance took them?

God, how do I know for sure what You're saying?

Crickets chirped, waves fell against the cliff, and aspen leaves shimmied, none of it whispering an answer. She skirted the subject. "Hardly feels like the middle of the night, since I slept until noon."

He nodded.

She nudged his arm, hoping to get him to answer her question. He turned his head with more intense focus than she'd intended to draw.

She folded her hands in her lap. She could tell him she'd played, but then he'd want to hear, and she'd rather wait until she'd reclaimed more of her skill. Besides, what would trusting him with music say about their relationship? That she was as in as he was?

"Harper and Matt went out together, drinking," he said.

Of course something new had happened with Harper. The development served as a reminder to keep her head, not get carried away. "You're worried?"

"I called the police because I think she's driving drunk. It's in their hands and God's now. I brought it up because you've had enough surprises. If their escapade turns into something, now you know."

"Thanks."

"Whatever happens, she's not coming back here. Staff packed her bags and are keeping them at the gate to send her off when she arrives."

"She won't take that well."

"She had warning." He pulled his arms off the wall and crossed them over his chest. The movement was steady, more like a defense mechanism than a response to the cool air. "What'd you think of the songs?"

She'd loved them, loved everything about them. But telling him as much would be committing to a relationship she wasn't sure was best. For either of them. He deserved someone who could give her whole heart with no lingering worries about navigating his world. "You can use them. I have an idea for a bass line for the phoenix one, but I can't make it work."

"Rusty?"

She nodded. She'd expected more of a reaction when she'd dropped the hint that she'd played again.

"It'll come."

She'd practiced, driven by the same conviction, but to hear him say it, low and calm and full of confidence, renewed her hope. "When Matt heard me work on it, he seemed relieved I'm not here to replace him."

"Replace him?" Gannon scoffed. "He got it in his head today he was going to quit drugs, drinking, the whole nine yards. I knew there had to be a reason."

"I was the reason? Then when he found out I wasn't a threat ..."

"He lost his motivation." Gannon shook his head, clearly annoyed. "One of the high schoolers' dads is a cop, isn't he?" Arms still folded over his chest, he looked her way, annoyance fading. Points of light reflected off his eyes as he studied her, but not enough that she could lose herself in the color of his irises again.

It was probably better that way.

"Olivia's dad, Joe Cullen. He showed up at the fire."

"Matt and I had a run in with him after I left your house last night. Matt was about to get behind the wheel drunk, even with Cullen right there. I sent him home with my driver, took his car myself. He had drugs in there. The officer didn't see, but he said he'd watch for the car in the future." Gannon tightened his arms, biceps flexing. "I hope he does, because this needs to stop. Better with an arrest than an accident or an overdose."

"Any of those could cause problems for the band, though."

"Yeah, but an arrest is one of the best outcomes I can see for Matt. He was onto something when he mentioned replacing him. The next album is our last chance to make a mark before our contract is up. We need it to be the best it can be, and he hasn't been his best in years. We should have someone waiting in the wings to take his place." He slid her a loaded glance.

"Not me." Playing with the band would mean spending so much time with Gannon that she'd never get the rest of her life in order. Besides ... "You need someone better."

"Nah. It's bass. Doesn't take that much skill to play the same three notes over and over."

She whapped his shoulder, and he laughed.

"When I conquer that song, you'll change your tune."

His smile turned gentler. "And how does it feel?" His eyelashes sloped toward the ground instead of toward her, but he waited, listening as intently as she imagined he would if she offered to pluck a few notes for him.

"On the one hand, it's frustrating because I can't play the way I used to."

"On the other?"

A deep breath filled her lungs. "Playing again feels like freedom. Or like music will be freedom once I get back what I lost. I've been stuffing down a lot—emotions, my story, my personality—for years now." She paused, realizing he'd said something similar when he'd first mentioned the songs he'd written about her. If she hadn't already given her blessing to share the songs, she would now. "Returning to bass makes me feel like I'm on the verge of being able to express all that again."

"Sounds like living." He tilted his head, gaze climbing to the sky.

Lakeshore didn't emit much light pollution, so here, a mile or two from town, a generous canopy of stars shone. "I think it is."

"Are you praying again too?"

"I am." And it felt almost as good as sitting here talking to Gannon, but shouldn't God mean more to her than a man? "I was praying when you came out."

"About?"

"You."

He returned to studying his feet. "You haven't said much about what the songs mean."

"They're flattering."

She'd intended it to be a compliment, but his smile turned rueful.

"Musically, the phoenix song pulls me the most." When had

music become a safer topic than their relationship? "The song about thinking about me ... I've thought a lot about you too."

"You haven't missed me, though, have you?"

"I ..." She'd been about to insist she had, but looking back, she hadn't missed him the way his song said he'd missed her. She'd thought a lot about what-ifs—what if he showed up again, what if he'd forgotten all about her, what if she attended one of his shows? Longing tinged all of it, but the flavors of guilt and anger had been too strong to call it missing him. "I couldn't, Gannon. I was too caught up in what had gone wrong and trying to not go off course again. But if it helps, when you leave now, it'll punch a big hole in my life."

"I'll fly you out whenever you want."

She'd gone too far, and now she had to backtrack. This was why she hadn't wanted the conversation to go here. "Do you do that for all your friends?"

He stood and turned toward the lake. "Are we on that again?"

"I'm sorry."

He stared silently over the water as if there were no more to say. Maybe there wasn't.

Adeline slipped off the bench and took the first step toward the house to leave him in peace, but he clasped her hand, turning her back. He was close—much closer than she'd realized—and she put a hand on his chest to avoid crashing into him.

He covered her hand, his fingers cool over hers, a contrast to the body heat that seeped through his shirt to her palm. His breath rose and fell. Contrary to those lyrics, his heart beat against the base of her thumb. If they kissed, would she feel it speed up?

He dipped his head, not for a kiss, she could tell, but to coax her into lifting her gaze to his eyes. When she gave in, his line of sight strayed. Down to her lips. Heat rushed her face.

This wasn't what she'd intended, but would it be so bad? Just a kiss. So the timing wasn't ideal. The changes she faced would be a lot more fun if she could sometimes escape into Gannon's arms.

Still holding her hand over his heart, he brushed her hair away from her face. "I'm running out of ways to show you what you mean to me."

"And I'm afraid of how much you mean to me."

"What's there to be afraid of?" His question brushed her cheek, and his fingers trailed under her ear and into her hair.

She parted her lips to reply, but she didn't know the answer. This wouldn't be wrong. She had nothing to be afraid of. There were obstacles, sure, the potential for pain, but couldn't Gannon help more than he could ever hurt her?

He glanced down to his side and smiled. Only then did she realize her free hand was at his waist, clutching the fabric of his T-shirt as though, if she lost her grip on him, she'd fall off the cliff.

"Tell me now you want to be friends, and I'll believe you." Even as he spoke, he moved closer.

The desire to kiss him hadn't been half this strong the last time, so many years ago. That version of her never could've held out this long, let him take this kind of time. This version of her had completely melted inside, wanted nothing more than to close her eyes and press into him, but getting involved physically wouldn't be right. Something was off. What? And why couldn't attraction erase her better sense this time?

Gannon's lips brushed her cheek, and in another second, her silence would be her answer.

"Friends." She whispered it.

She felt Gannon's sigh on her cheek. His chest rose and fell under her hand. Another breath. In and out.

What was wrong with her? Why had she cut it so close? She

couldn't tell if his heart rate had picked up because hers was beating so hard.

He stepped back, his touch sliding from along her neck, the hand that had cradled hers to his chest releasing. He started for Havenridge.

She ought to grab him the way he'd grabbed her, catch him and take it back.

God, what am I doing? How could that have been the right thing? He's helped bring me closer to You. Doesn't that make us a good match?

She didn't know God well enough to guess His response, and the one person who might've shed light on it for her was ten feet away and farther every second.

She'd hurt him again. She never should've let it get so close to a kiss.

"Gannon, I'm sorry." She jogged after him and fell into step beside him, the thick grass dragging against her canvas tennies.

His mouth was set, hints of a frown there and in the angle of his eyebrows. The pace he kept suggested anger, but he didn't lash out at her. If only he would, they could argue, and somewhere in the back and forth, she'd figure it out—why a romance didn't sit right.

"The timing is wrong," she said.

He didn't answer, and she didn't blame him. They'd already had the timing discussion. He'd explained why it had to be now or never. Did that mean she'd chosen never? Because of a reservation she couldn't even name?

He pulled open the patio door, let her through first, then started for the stairs.

She followed. "Gannon, we need—"

He stopped abruptly, and she ran into him. She stumbled back, apologizing, but he held up a hand for quiet.

She bit her lip, utterly confused until she registered the voices. And music. Who was up and making so much noise?

"They're back." Gannon headed for the stairs to the lower level, where the rec room was.

Laughter and voices ricocheted to meet them as they descended. Whoever had come, it wasn't just Harper and Matt.

When Gannon pushed open the door of the rec room, more than a dozen people mingled, drank, and explored the games. Meanwhile, music thudded through the stereo equipment.

Gannon paused at the doorway to send a text, then stepped into the room.

One of the few guys nodded to Gannon as though they were old friends, but Gannon's jaw pulsed with anger, eyes lasered on Matt. A woman sat on the bassist's lap, her hands in his hair, and the pair ignored everything around them.

Another woman kneeled across the coffee table from Matt and cleared a space on the glass surface. Adeline didn't need a good glimpse of what she held in her hand to guess what it was.

"Everybody out!" Gannon's command, issued from the center of the room, fell on deaf ears.

A man with a goatee and small eyes toyed with the hair of a thin, young woman who tried to shrug him off. He wrapped a hand around the waist exposed by her crop top, hindering her escape. Her beer sloshed over her fingers as she shifted again, but to no avail. She wore short shorts, showing miles of legs. Despite her smoky makeup, her small face looked immature and way, way too innocent to be in this group.

The girl's shocked and guilty eyes locked on Adeline, and realization dawned.

"Olivia?"

27

Gannon's fists tightened. One of the high schoolers was here? Worse, a man who looked a decade older nuzzled her neck.

"Addie." The teen squirmed away from the creep. "Addie. I can explain." A slur softened the words. Her eyes cut to Gannon.

As if she could sense the tidal wave of fury building in him, she took a step back, bumped into a chair, and fell onto the cushion. As she settled, her hands wrapped around her beer as if to hide it.

"You don't have to explain anything." The pig slid his arm around her as if to lift her to her feet and take her somewhere else.

"She's a minor." Gannon crossed the space and pulled the man away by his arm. "Touch her again, and her cop dad will be the least of your problems."

The man raised his hands, and the group quieted beneath the blaring music. The woman on Matt's lap twisted, puzzled concern on her face, then shifted to a seat of her own.

Matt rose. The telltale white powder by his nose explained where he'd found the nerve to throw this party. "She's twenty-one. She was in a bar. Drinking."

"She's a high school student." Gannon lifted his voice from the low growl to address the room. "Security's already on the way. You don't want to be here when they arrive."

The exodus began, as if they could leave the gated property without dealing with the team. The woman who'd been sitting on Matt's lap gave him one last look as she gathered her clutch and scampered out of sight.

As if to exit with the others, Olivia climbed to her feet, but she possessed all the grace of a kid trying out a pair of stilts. Had she sampled anything in addition to alcohol? She'd had options.

Adeline crossed to her, detaining her as the last of the others left. Olivia seemed to listen to whatever quiet counsel Adeline gave until the girl's eyes caught on something behind Gannon. Her chin shifted back with shocked dismay, as if she were witnessing a car wreck.

Gannon heard a deep sniff as he turned. Matt, seated on the floor next to the coffee table, swept the back of his wrist across his nose.

"Do you have no shame?" Gannon asked.

Matt tipped back against the couch, laughing.

A violent urge rocked Gannon. He could pull Matt to his feet, punch some sense into him. But Olivia had already experienced enough darkness tonight.

"If you're bent on ruining yourself, fine, but look what your actions are doing." He pointed to Olivia.

"You can't blame me for *that*."

Olivia shrank in on herself, shoulders hunched forward, collarbones thin and fragile, like bones that belonged on a bird and not a girl.

Gannon met Adeline's eyes. "Let me take care of this, then I'll get her a ride home."

Adeline ushered the girl from the room.

As they left, Gannon texted Tim. *911. Rec room now.*

When he estimated Olivia and Adeline would be out of earshot, he turned back. "In what world did you think this would fly?"

Matt climbed to his feet, a mocking smile on his face. "I didn't bring the girl. She was at the bar, so who's really to blame here?"

Gannon took a breath to answer but exhaled without a word of it.

They'd been doing this dance for years. The first time he'd found Matt throwing a party, lines of cocaine on the coffee table, Gannon had also cleared the room. Then, as now, fire burned in Matt's eyes.

But that time, like so many others, Gannon had let the offense slide.

No longer.

"You're out."

"Out?" Matt scoffed. "Over this? That girl was drinking all on her own, and she lied about her age."

"You think her cop dad's going to see it that way? I can't be responsible for this anymore."

"You can't fire me." Matt stepped closer, his hand drawing into a fist. "You need me."

If Matt would just throw the first punch, Gannon would be justified in returning one.

He crossed his arms to keep from doing something he'd regret. "Where's Harper?"

Matt snorted with laughter. "Security wouldn't let her in with us. Sent her away in her rental, just her and all her luggage."

They'd done as Gannon had asked. Except if she'd been drinking, someone was supposed to drive her. Would the team have overlooked that part of his instructions?

Had he been right to kick her out that way to begin with?

"Lover boy looks so sad," Matt crowed.

Gannon splayed his hand, then clenched it in front of his forehead before he could reach out to strangle him. The rec room door clattered open, and Tim stepped through in sweatpants and a T-shirt. "What's going on?"

Gannon stepped away from Matt before his temper could get the better of him. No sense earning himself an assault charge. "Matt decided to throw a party with a minor."

Matt rolled his eyes. "I was nowhere near her, and I had no way to know."

"Her name is Olivia Cullen. She's with Adeline now. Get her a safe ride home."

"Sure. We can do that." Tim's line of sight bounced from Matt to Gannon, as if he knew there was more.

"He's out."

"You need me." Desperation fluttered in Matt's voice, but Gannon didn't pivot to see it on his face.

"Will you go to rehab?"

"You can't bring in just anyone to replace me. Besides, without me, who're you going to blame for everything that goes wrong? You're going to have to take the blame yourself, and your ego can't take that."

That would be a hard no on the rehab.

Gannon's chest burned with retorts. He kept his focus on Tim. "I don't want to see him again."

Tim lifted his hands. "Calm down. We can work this out. Awestruck can't crumble right now. Keep it together."

"This isn't crumbling. This is standing up to an offense that's gone on too long. Call whoever you have to call, do whatever you have to do, but he's out."

Matt sputtered. "You can't—"

"John and I have already discussed it. You're done." He had to get out of here before he lost it. He moved toward the door.

"Gannon."

The serious note in Tim's voice made him turn.

The manager swallowed visibly. "A minute before I heard from you, Harper's people called. You had her sent away?"

He nodded once.

"Her assistant and that Karina lady, the shrink or whatever, are flying here as fast as they can. She posted a quote from one of her movies. The last thing one of her characters said before committing suicide. They think it's a threat."

Dread poured into his veins. He'd thought he had healed after Fitz. Thought he'd gotten right with God and could move forward. But if they lost Harper the same way, he wouldn't get past it. Adeline wouldn't, either.

The post could be another game, another bid for attention.

But he'd missed so many signs with Fitz, and he couldn't afford to do that again.

Everything was already falling apart. The band. Adeline. He couldn't allow any other disasters.

THE CLOTHES HARPER had bought for Adeline still hung in the little room off the main living area. Adeline sorted through them while Olivia huddled in the doorway, arms folded over herself.

"You don't have to call my dad, do you?" Tears smeared her black eyeliner.

Adeline found a slouchy cardigan that would cover Olivia from neck to midthigh and slipped it from the hanger. Gannon had said he'd find a ride for the teen, so Adeline didn't plan to call Joe. Better to break the news after he had her back safe and sound. "Were you really in a bar?"

"Well." Olivia clamped her mouth shut and exhaled through her nose. "It's not like, you know, we ... It was a special occasion. Not everybody gets to live here with them. How else was I supposed to meet him?"

"Matt? I thought you liked Gannon."

Olivia shifted. "He's into you, and John hardly leaves the property, so Matt seemed like the best bet."

Adeline held out the sweater. "Was he worth meeting at that cost? That guy who was with you was trouble."

He should've been suspicious of her age, regardless of where they'd met. Even if he'd believed her to be at least eighteen, Olivia had tried to push him off, yet he'd persisted.

"The drinking, the drugs?"

"I didn't do any drugs." Olivia pulled on the sweater, and the scent of cigarette smoke wafted off her before she folded the cardigan shut over her cropped tank.

"What if Gannon and I hadn't come in when we did?"

Olivia shrugged. "I was just hanging out."

"You were drinking, and you were in danger." Adeline's stomach churned. Given even just a few more minutes, the guy may have managed to separate Olivia from the group. And then what?

Lord, is that why I wasn't supposed to kiss Gannon?

If only.

The peace she didn't feel about Gannon was over something else.

"I was cool for once." Olivia's mouth trembled, and her nostrils flared. In her big, sad eyes, Adeline recognized the girl who'd squealed over meeting the cat her family had adopted earlier in the summer. The wide-eyed innocence was so incongruent with the outfit under that sweater, with bars and partying and Matt.

"I've always thought you were cool. You don't need any of this." Adeline guided her to a chair at the desk. She rubbed the girl's shoulder, thin and angular even under the sweater, until the door swung open.

Gannon stood in the doorway long enough to motion Adeline to join him in the great room.

As she did, she pulled the door shut behind her, closing Olivia in the office.

"Tim's getting her a ride home, but I'd like someone she knows and trusts with her until she's dropped off."

Adeline nodded, accepting the assignment.

"Harper's out somewhere. I'm worried she's in danger, so I'm going to help them look."

"Danger?"

His mouth settled in a grim line, but he didn't elaborate.

"Okay." She pressed her hands into her pockets. She'd rather go with Gannon—to be close to him, to see that nothing happened between him and Harper. But Adeline had insisted on being friends, leaving him free to pursue the actress in whatever sense he wanted to.

Gannon set off for the garage, and she returned to Olivia.

When Tim came, he wore jeans and a button-down that made Adeline wish she'd changed out of her sweats while she'd had the chance. "Let's see your IDs. Real and fake."

Olivia rifled through her clutch and extended a card toward him. "I only have this one."

The woman in the picture was obviously not her. How had she gotten into a bar with that?

Without taking the card, Tim snapped a picture. "Let's go."

He led them to the drive where an SUV waited. Two members of the security team hopped out and opened the back doors. Adeline and Olivia sat in the middle row, Tim in the back.

Olivia gave her address, and they were off. Other than the

teen's crying, no one made a sound the entire way into town. The SUV pulled to the curb by the Cullens' modest Cape Cod. Everyone piled out of the vehicle.

At the sound of more car doors, Adeline leaned to see who else was out at this hour. Photographers. Of course.

Tim appeared at Adeline's side. "We're here to bring her home, but we're not commenting on or apologizing for anything. Understand?"

His tone left no room for argument, as if he'd sue her if the Cullens pressed charges using anything she said.

Olivia bumped into her other arm and hiccuped. "My dad's going to kill me."

She wanted to correct her that the one he'd want to kill was Matt or the man who'd bothered her, but because of Tim, she refrained. "He'll be glad you're home safe." With her arm around the teen's shoulders, they climbed the concrete steps. Adeline pressed the doorbell.

As they waited, she peeked over her shoulder. The security detail had succeeded in discouraging the photographers. The two extra vehicles pulled away.

The door let out a short creak. Joe Cullen stood in the opening, rumpled in plaid flannel pajama pants and an old T-shirt. "What's this?"

Olivia covered her mouth and sobbed, shaking under Adeline's arm. Tim stood at the bottom of the stairs, silently observing. It would be ages before Olivia could speak.

Adeline couldn't stand silent that long. "Olivia was at a bar with a fake ID, drinking. She ended up at the cabin, so we're bringing her home."

"What cabin?"

Cabin. Right. No local would call it that. "Havenridge. Where the band is staying."

Lines bracketed Joe's mouth, and concern wrinkled his forehead. "Olivia?"

The girl inhaled a vortex of air. "I got invited to a party. That's all. Nothing happened." She coughed twice and lay a hand over her stomach. "I'm going to be sick."

Joe focused on Tim for a moment. When his line of sight moved on to the street, where the security detail stood, his expression hardened. He moved his mouth, but before he spoke, Olivia turned, gripped the railing, and vomited into the bushes along the front of the house.

She spat, groaned, and put a hand back on her stomach.

Joe glanced at Adeline. "You've done enough." He took Olivia by the arm and brought her inside, closing the door behind them.

Olivia was in for quite a discussion, if nothing else. Did Joe see Adeline as part of the problem?

Sadness more than anything swirled as she turned from the door to find Tim still stationed on the walk, watching her.

"What? Did I say too much for you?"

Tim wordlessly followed the walk to the SUV. He took the spot that had been Olivia's on the way there, and Adeline returned to her own seat. As the vehicle pulled away from the curb, she watched the dark neighborhood pass.

Tim took a breath, and she looked over.

"I have a daughter." He frowned and sighed, not making eye contact. "It's good that didn't go any further."

She nodded. Understatement of the year.

The whole thing left Adeline's stomach twisting, uneasy.

This was Lakeshore, Wisconsin, her serene, small-town home. It was supposed to be safe, but a seventeen-year-old had gotten into a bar and a party where someone was only too ready to take advantage. In only a few moments, Adeline had witnessed more drug use than she'd seen in a lifetime. And equally sheltered Olivia had been in the thick of it.

"Gannon fired him." Tim worked on his phone as if he hadn't spoken, but she was sure of what she'd heard.

"He did?"

"Matt has been escorted off the premises."

Adeline rested her head and returned her gaze to the window. The world may have lost some of its innocence, but at least Gannon had taken a stand.

28

On returning to the cabin, Adeline looked out at the patio and walked by Gannon's room, searching for him, but he hadn't returned from his hunt for Harper. Were they out talking somewhere? Was Gannon in danger of falling for the actress after all?

She typed him a text on the way up to her bedroom, asking how the search was going. She had no right to jealousy. She'd rejected him. She sent the message anyway, and he replied a minute later.

She's not at the bars and her rental's not parked at either of the local hotels. I'm combing the streets.

How can I help? she typed back.

Security's looking, and we notified the police. Her own people are watching social media and calling hotels farther out. Not much else to do.

Social media was one idea, but gossip sites could post instantaneously, couldn't they? With the paparazzi presence in town, it wouldn't be impossible. Adeline settled on her bed with her laptop and took a stab at a search.

The first result soured her stomach.

It's Complicated: The Status of Gannon Vaughn's Love Life. Gannon Vaughn's new love interest is rumored to be Adeline Green, but things aren't as straightforward as they seem.

She hadn't enjoyed the condescending tone or the unflattering photographs in the first article she'd read about herself, and whatever this one contained would unsettle her even more. She scrolled to other results. What she didn't read couldn't hurt her, and she was supposed to be looking for information on Harper, not some off-the-wall commentary on her own relationship with Gannon.

Her attention floated back to the headline, though. Even she didn't quite know why she and Gannon were so complicated, why she hadn't let him kiss her. Why she resented this search for Harper even as she tried to pitch in.

Pursing her lips, she clicked the link.

Friends.

Thanks to the silence in the car, the word echoed in Gannon's mind. He flipped on the radio to drown it out.

Didn't work.

"You're looking for Harper. She's the concern here." Stating his mission aloud helped.

Some.

This hunt was technically to save Harper, but it was also to spare his *friend* Adeline another brush with suicide.

However she labeled their relationship, that was vital. For everyone's sake.

He turned into yet another park along the lake and let the car coast the perimeter of the lot. Small trees reached over an empty bench, and sand extended to the black water. Maybe

Harper had checked herself into a hotel like he'd intended and was sleeping peacefully.

Somewhere else, Matt was either doing the same or looking for a high. Tim had reserved a room for him in a nearby city and had sent him off with a man from the security detail who would've left him at the hotel by now. He was on his own from here on out. Being fired would be a wake-up call to get clean, the space to fully succumb to his addiction, or another chapter in a slow decline.

God, You're his only true hope. Save him. He can't see what he's doing to himself. Same for Harper. Please show us where she is.

No one lingered in this park.

He pulled back onto the road to check the other public waterfronts.

Tim didn't need to worry that firing Matt would hamper Awestruck's future. The move would add complications, but they had enough connections to arrange temporary help until they found a match to add another member back into Awestruck.

He had names in mind, solid musicians who'd proved themselves with their roles in other bands. He just had to stop fantasizing about playing a show with Adeline again.

Friends.

He'd thought a kiss would stop the friend talk once and for all, but she hadn't been interested. The only card he had left to play was the notebook of songs. At this point, the lyrics wouldn't surprise or impress her. She'd tell him to go ahead and use them if he wanted.

He could pour his heart out for the whole world because Adeline Green didn't care if he had anything left just for her.

A wooden sign announced another park. Gannon steered in. Trees obscured the two streetlights in the lot, but some of the light that poked through landed on a sedan parked at the far end of the lot. Harper's rental.

He pulled up and found it empty. The waterfront was out of sight at the bottom of a brush-covered slope. Pulse quickening, he parked, climbed from the car, and pocketed his keys.

The moon turned the wooden steps to the lakefront into gray shadows. The stairs ended in matted grass. A few feet later, an old pier reached over the water, thirty or forty feet long and wide enough for a car, but occasional dark gaps warned him of the structure's frailty.

A woman sat out at the end. She looked over her shoulder at him and then turned away again.

Thank God. Gannon sent two texts, one to security and one to Adeline, both with the same four words: *Found her. She's okay.*

He illuminated his cell phone's flashlight and stepped onto the pier. The wood didn't give, so he proceeded, the sound of lapping water surrounding him as he left the shore and its crickets behind.

"Let's get you someplace safe." He or security could wait with her at a hotel until her people arrived.

Harper didn't move.

He reached down to help her up, but she pulled away.

"Leave me alone."

"You know I can't do that." She was lucky she hadn't fallen in. Could she even swim? And maybe that was the point.

"You keep insisting you can."

"That's why you're out here? To prove otherwise?"

"No ... Though I'm sorry about that post. I didn't realize how seriously everyone would take it. When I saw, I took it down. I guess I crossed the line. Believe me, I don't want to die. Not ever, and certainly not on a night when all I'm thinking about is how messed up I am."

He did believe her, but his relief was tempered by the pain in her voice. He couldn't just leave her here. He looked back toward shore. The only way to force her to leave would be to pick her up and carry her. The attempt would end with one or both of them in the lake if she fought him, which, in her mood, she probably would. He made sure his phone was securely in his pocket and then sat next to her, their feet off the end of the pier.

"I'll never be perfect." Her voice brimmed with melancholy, like the haunting notes of a low register wind chime.

Gannon waited for the theatrics to kick in.

"Your girlfriend told me I needed to quit doing all kinds of stuff if I wanted to be a Christian, and I can't, so why not show everyone how awful I can be?" In the moonlight, he couldn't judge the details of her face, but her speech was as clear as ever, and he smelled the wet, muddy scent of the lake, not alcohol. Their theory she'd been drinking had been wrong. She was sober. "But I didn't want that, either, because you'd never even look at me again. So I went out for the most boring night of my life, then found out it didn't matter. You wouldn't let me back in, anyway."

A decision he wouldn't rehash, though rejecting her as he had tonight meant he might never have another chance to share his faith with her. His hope. "What did Adeline tell you to change?"

"Doesn't matter. I can't live like a puppet, even for you. Anyway, why would I? You never loved me. You've only loved her. Right?"

There must've been a true but kind way to answer, but before he found it, she continued.

"There's nothing I can do. There's never anything I can do." Her posture curved, and she kept her gaze down and away instead of checking his reaction so she could adjust her act accordingly.

Harper English had broken.

John's warning rang in his mind. Even if she appeared to

need him, he couldn't be Harper's hero. As soon as he took on that responsibility, she'd pull herself together and infiltrate his life again. Had he already gone too far in seeking her out? He and Adeline were friends. Period. So this decision didn't depend on what Adeline needed or wanted.

It was about him.

About whether he could trust God with Harper or felt he had to do all the work himself. About acknowledging that enabling Matt and Harper with his energy and friendship would never make up for the wrong he'd done Fitz.

He'd tried to take on the role of hero to earn his redemption instead of accepting it as a gift. In the process, he'd saved Matt from a confrontation with Officer Cullen that could've led to an arrest before Matt had made any more poor choices. What would continuing to save Harper cost in the long run?

He sent another message to security, asking for someone to come take over, and then tried to make the best of the time he had.

"Jesus Christ loves you, Harper. He wants what's best for you, and He'll never fail you. Following Him does involve changing—constantly, for all of us—but He doesn't leave us to figure that out without His help. If you want a relationship with Him, it's got to be about you and Him, not you and me, because there is no you and me. The only thing that's permanent for any of us is God."

That last part was as true for him as for Harper. Adeline had labeled him a friend, but she might not even allow that to continue. Not when she realized he would never stop waiting for her to love him the way he loved her.

As he got to his feet, he prayed for the next right step.

"I did it to myself. Not the first time—I did fall in your apartment—but the second time." Harper didn't turn from the water, but she motioned at her face. "Everyone cared so much when they thought someone attacked me. I thought it'd make you care."

How could she say that like he hadn't come through for her time and again?

But he never would've let her come to Havenridge without those injuries, just like he wouldn't have ventured to this park if not for her post. She wasn't herself tonight, and he couldn't guess what she would've done if no one had found her. Maybe nothing. Maybe something awful.

Gannon could still recall the sound of Fitz's mom sobbing at the funeral.

"I do care." His voice had thickened. "There is help and there is hope, but you have to decide to take it."

She didn't reply.

Despite standing right behind her, he couldn't reach her. She needed a better hero than he'd ever been.

"Your assistant and Karina are coming to spend time with you. I'll make sure you're not alone tonight, and I can put you in contact with a local pastor tomorrow."

Still nothing.

He looked to the stairs and spotted a member of the security team descending. When the bodyguard reached the end of the pier, he paused, apparently waiting for Gannon's direction.

Okay, God. I trust you. Be the hero.

He motioned the guard to move in and walked back to shore alone.

GANNON TRUDGED TOWARD HIS ROOM. A sniffle drew his eyes to the top of the stairs.

Adeline stood on the landing, a laptop hugged awkwardly to her chest. She still wore the sweats she'd had on when he'd last seen her, but now she sounded like she was crying.

"What's wrong?"

She shook her head and tightened her grip on the laptop. "I'm going to see Tegan."

"Is she up?" What time was it, anyway? Still dark out the great room windows, but he'd lost track of the hour and wouldn't take his focus off Adeline long enough to check his phone. He took three more steps and stopped two shy of the top. When he touched her arm, she tucked her chin and looked away.

"What happened? Something with Olivia? Or Tim?" Gannon was on a roll tonight. So what if he had to fire one more person?

Shaking her head again, she sidestepped to the other end of the staircase and descended the first step. "It's nothing you can fix, Gannon." She took another step. "It's the way things are." Her socks padded against the stairs as she found a rhythm and stuck to it, leaving him alone and in the dark.

Everything in him screamed to go after her, get the story from her, and find a way to fix it.

Trying to fix everything had gotten him in trouble with Harper and with Matt.

God, isn't Adeline different?

Apparently not, or he wouldn't feel this conviction that he needed to let God handle this one.

This was what the better lover song had been about— letting God care for Adeline instead of trying to himself—but he'd tried that.

Tried it for eight years, since the funeral.

Not only had he not gotten over Adeline, but God hadn't done the things Gannon had asked in that song. Adeline had lived all those years without God breaking through her barriers and flooding her with love.

Of course, now that Gannon had returned and tried to

break through those barriers himself, she'd rejected his love too.

Maybe she would reject all love. Maybe that wasn't something he could fix.

He had to trust that God would heal her. In His own time, in His own way.

Tonight, that way wasn't Gannon.

29

"Adeline, can we speak with you, please?" Despite the polite wording, Joe Cullen's request rang in her ears like an order from a police officer.

She turned, the skirt of her favorite maxi dress brushing her legs.

Olivia, who squirmed at Joe's side, appeared as uneasy as Adeline felt.

Adeline glanced over her shoulder.

When she'd gone to the kitchen of Havenridge this morning for coffee, Gannon had asked if she'd mind him and John joining them for the service. They'd driven separately but had all sat together until the service ended.

After the closing, the guys had stepped away. Adeline had assumed they wanted to make a quick exit, but instead, they were crossing the sanctuary.

John ran interference by greeting those who approached, leaving Gannon relatively unhindered as he made his way toward Pastor Drew. The men shook hands, but she couldn't hear their conversation, leaving her to wonder why Gannon would seek out Drew.

She could, however, guess the line of questioning Joe wanted to put her through.

If only Tim had attended, he could handle this. By saying the wrong thing to Joe, she could cause trouble for Matt or the band. Then again, Gannon had trusted her to look out for Olivia and her family. If Matt got in trouble for what happened last night, it would only be because he had it coming.

"Sure, Joe. Should we step in the office?"

He gestured for her to lead the way.

She flipped on the light and held the door for Joe, who had his daughter's arm as if he were escorting an inmate into a cell. Only after Adeline closed them in did he release her.

Olivia chewed the inside of her bottom lip, forcing her mouth into a fish face. Her eyes focused on her dad before aiming somewhere near Adeline's knees. "Sophie and Amy and I were at your house on Friday night."

"I know. You helped with the porch."

"Yes." Her face lit up until she saw her dad watching her like a prison warden. "But we came back later a couple times. We were, um, well, we wanted to fit in, you know? So we were smoking."

"Fit in with who? Matt?"

Olivia shrugged. "We didn't know the cigarette butts would start a fire. When we saw it, we tried to put it out, but it was too late. We ran, but I bumped that ladder." Olivia's blue irises lifted to meet Adeline's eyes. The girl's entire face was red, and moisture had accumulated on her lower lashes. She gripped both of Adeline's hands. "I'm really sorry. I didn't mean to wreck your house. And it was stupid to run away because I could've killed you." With a sob, she leaned into Adeline's shoulder.

Adeline hugged her, too stunned to do anything else.

Joe sighed, shook his head once, and dropped his own gaze.

Olivia sniffed loudly. "My dad says it's up to you if you press charges or not, but that maybe you'll let me and Sophie and Amy pay you back."

The fire was bad. Running, worse. But Adeline felt awful for the teen who cried in her arms.

"I spoke with the other parents." Joe's no-nonsense tone continued, and his arms remained crossed, though the creases around his eyes softened. Pity was starting to take over. "I'm going to cover the repairs. The girls can pay me back as they earn the money."

Olivia stepped back and held both of Adeline's shoulders. "I won't ever do something that foolish ever again. I promise. I broke the law and that could follow me forever. And that would be fair." She gulped. "The laws are there for a reason, and I'm going to follow them from now on. I'm nearly an adult, and my actions have consequences, so I'll make restitution."

These had to be the vestiges of the lecture Joe had given. He uncrossed his arms. His frown seemed sad but not angry, as if he would hug Olivia if she turned to him now. She continued to wait for Adeline's verdict.

"Paying for the repairs sounds sufficient to me. But, Olivia ..." Adeline sighed. Was she, so in love with Gannon, one to talk? Yes. Because she'd said no to him, and that had ended up helping Olivia immensely. "Fame doesn't make a person more valuable, and it doesn't make people happy. If anything, the money and power result in a lot of temptation. You need to be grounded in God before you go chasing anything else. Look at everything you did to try to get close to Matt. It was dangerous and unhealthy and could've altered your whole life—and not for the better."

Olivia nodded vigorously, but only time would tell if she truly understood.

Adeline opened the office door, and Olivia and Joe filed out past her.

Once they'd gone, she closed it again.

What she'd said to Olivia had been for the girl's sake, but it rang true to her own situation. She'd been living a quiet life, but not a life where she let God fulfill her. She wasn't grounded. Gannon was, but that wouldn't be enough for both of them. They'd never be happy together if she expected Gannon to do for her the things only God could.

The door clicked, and she stepped out of its way.

Tegan stuck her head in. "Everything okay?"

Gannon had been right last night that Tegan was sleeping, so Adeline had waited to catch her up on everything until this morning. Adeline wouldn't have to say much to convey her latest realization—she needed space from Gannon if she was going to get right with God. But if she put that developing conviction into words, it'd be that much closer to being something she had to act on, and soon.

So, she nodded, though she felt as if the whole lake were damming up behind her eyes. Once she reconnected with God, maybe she and Gannon could try again, but he'd already made it clear that his visit to Lakeshore was a unique opportunity that wouldn't be repeated. Next time wouldn't be like this.

If he'd even allow a next time.

Tegan maneuvered around the door. "You sure?"

She nodded again. "Olivia and her friends were smoking in the yard. They caused the fire, and they're going to pay for the damage."

"Oh. Wow."

"Yeah." Adeline shoved her hands into the pockets of her jacket. Maybe there was no putting this off. "Knowing that, I suppose we can move back home."

Tegan studied her. "Let's not rush into it. The restoration company hasn't even started on extracting the smoke smell, and as long as the band's in town, you're a celebrity too."

Grateful, she sighed. She could stay a little longer, then.

∽

GANNON AND JOHN sat in chairs opposite Tim's desk.

Tim looked at his computer screen, shook his head, and frowned. "It's not feasible in Wisconsin. Sanders is an easy fix for Saturday, but he's still going to need rehearsal time. He can come up here, but Philip Miller leaves for Europe on Thursday. He won't be back for weeks. If he's your top pick for replacing Matt long-term, the sooner you hear what he's got to offer, the better. Unless you want to push back the recording schedule."

Which would also push back the tour. A nightmare.

Gannon's phone buzzed. He pulled it out and skimmed a text from Drew.

After the service that morning, he'd asked the pastor to meet with Harper, but apparently, she'd already skipped town.

"Are we interrupting something?" Tim asked.

Shaking his head, Gannon placed the phone screen-down on his leg. "Can Miller make it up here before he leaves?"

"Already asked. He's a single dad, so he's got to figure out childcare anytime he travels. An audition is going to have to be in the next couple of days in LA or not until October."

Gannon didn't have to look to know John was watching him. Firing Matt had been the right decision, but finding a replacement meant returning to LA.

It meant leaving Adeline still broken.

Tim rolled his chair closer to the desk and folded his hands on the surface, elbows spread wide. "Unless you two have a solution in mind you haven't told me."

John seemed to understand the solution Tim envisioned because he laughed and picked up a beat with his thumbs.

Tim didn't look amused. "Fans might mutiny."

Gannon didn't follow. "Over what?"

John continued to drum his fingers against the chair's armrests. "Bringing Addie back on."

Gannon looked to Tim. He'd never told him about Adeline's role with the band, and those days were so far behind them, it'd been ages since anyone had asked for details about who'd come and gone prior to their first record deal.

"I did my homework as soon as I heard you mention Fitz." Tim picked up a tablet and passed it across the desk. "And I'm not the only one who's been asking where this thing with Adeline Green came from."

An article covered the screen. The bold title read, *It's Complicated.*

He skimmed the predictable chatter about how often he and Adeline had been seen together. But then the story took a turn that made him read with care.

Exactly how does world-famous rocker Gannon Vaughn end up with small-town hotdog vendor Adeline Green? It's all about history.

Awestruck was originally a four-member band hailing from Fox Valley, Wisconsin. As high school seniors, front man Gannon Vaughn and drummer John Kennedy started the group with classmate Gregory Fitzwilliam on second guitar and none other than Adeline Green on bass.

"She was really good. Completely one of the band," says Heather Wolski, a high school friend of Green's.

But more than music was in the air.

"I always thought Adeline and Gannon would end up together," Wolski admits. "But she dated Fitz."

When the band relocated to LA to pursue a record contract, Green stayed behind and was replaced by current bassist Matt Visser. Green's relationship with Fitzwilliam turned serious, and they were engaged.

However, shortly before Awestruck signed its first contract with Wakefield Records, Fitzwilliam fell on hard times. He left the band and broke off his engagement to Green.

Wolski explains the reaction of their hometown. "None of us ever knew for sure, but we all suspected there was something going on between Adeline and Gannon."

Whether or not a love triangle played a role in his decline, Fitzwilliam appears to have struggled with depression. He died by suicide weeks after the release of Awestruck's debut album, *Burn*.

"It was a tragedy for everyone, especially Fitz's family, of course, but also Gannon and Adeline. He stopped visiting home much, and she moved away. I haven't seen either in years, but I hope it's true that they're finally together. Whatever happened in the past, they deserve to be happy. I think even Fitz would want that."

Unfortunately for Vaughn and Green, their days of love triangles don't seem to be over.

"Before he showed up, we were all kind of rooting for Adeline and Pastor Drew," says a Lakeshore local who asked to remain anonymous.

Despite Vaughn's presence in the small community of Lakeshore, Wisconsin, where Green now resides, Green has been spotted multiple times with Drew Hastings, who pastors a local church.

Vaughn's attentions are likewise divided. His ex, Harper English, traveled to northern Wisconsin. Both Green and English were photographed entering and leaving Vaughn's property over the weekend.

Perhaps this explains why Green's online relationship status remains "single" and Vaughn's only post regarding his relationship with Green refers to her as "an old friend."

It seems the most anyone can hope for is an update from "single" to "it's complicated."

This had to be why Adeline had been clutching her laptop and crying the night before. *Died by suicide.* And all the photos

—a picture of the original band performing in an outdoor amphitheater back home, one from Adeline and Fitz's engagement announcement, a shot of Adeline and Drew, a picture of Harper.

John took the tablet and started reading. "Who's Heather Wolski?"

"Nobody." Probably a classmate, but if she'd been close enough to Adeline to deserve to be quoted, the name would be familiar. He focused on Tim, who tapped a corner of his phone against the desk. "You can relax," Gannon said. "She's not interested in rejoining."

Stilling the phone, Tim leaned back into his chair. "So Plan A, then."

Plan A: leave Adeline behind. Again.

John laid the tablet on the desk. "It's time."

Gannon would argue if the article were wrong, but finding their tragic past spelled out so clearly last night must've only confirmed her decision that they could never be more than friends. "If we're going to catch Miller, it's got to be today or tomorrow."

Tim typed something on his phone. "Let's say tomorrow. Take today to pack up and say goodbye."

Goodbye. Right. As if he could bear that.

30

*A*deline forced herself to nod along with the conversation. What she wanted was to go inside and find out where Gannon had been hiding for the last two hours. And why.

Tim and John laughed at something Tegan said. Tegan looked over as if Adeline ought to appreciate the joke too, but she'd heard nothing. She smiled and hoped that would cover her cluelessness.

John made a show of dancing in his seat, and the others erupted again.

Sitting here was a waste. She couldn't enjoy the company while she wondered about Gannon and whether he was hurt or angry—or both.

She excused herself with a polite smile that faded as soon as her back was turned.

Gannon wasn't in the great room, the kitchen, or the studio. She climbed the stairs.

Pausing at his partially open door, she heard the crackle of paper. Tapping on the door pushed it far enough open to reveal him sitting against his headboard, a notebook in hand. He had one leg stretched out, the other knee bent up. On seeing her, he tossed the notebook to the comforter and rested his wrist on his knee.

Her heart plunked against her ribs like a child abusing a piano. "So, this is how a brooding rock star looks."

His brow furrowed. He must not understand the way his mood tempted her to give in, to kiss him in hopes of changing everything about how he felt right now.

Not her best idea.

She glanced at the chair at the desk. He'd asked before joining her on the patio last night, and that had been a much less personal space. "Can I sit?"

He nodded, but as he did, he rubbed his forehead as if he weren't in the mood for company. Too tired. Or hurt. Or angry.

She took the chair. If any more nervous energy infused her, she'd float away like a helium balloon. She gripped the armrests to keep herself in place. "I wanted to explain about the friends thing."

"I already know." He looked out the window, eyebrows still drawn.

"You do?"

"You still feel guilty." He worked his fingers. A guitar melody or simple, subconscious movement while he thought? He focused on her again, a hint of blue visible in his irises, but she was too far away to see the gold ring she loved so much. "What if God is better than you know, Adeline? What if He's perfect and forgives perfectly?"

Of course he had the right thing to say.

"You're right. Partially. I do feel guilty. Ashamed, even. I found an article last night that published almost all of our story, pictures and all, for anyone to read."

"I saw."

She gulped and nodded. "But that's not why I think it's best to be friends. It's more about what you asked just now. What if God is better than I know, and what if He forgives perfectly? Those are beautiful questions."

He watched her as if she were an act on *Audition Room* he still hadn't made up his mind about.

"He *is* better than I know. He *does* forgive perfectly, and He has a plan for me. I want to take the time to understand what that means."

The lines of pain and frustration lightened little by little, compelling her to continue.

"I want to stop assuming following Him means taking on work I don't love and volunteering every chance I get. I want to stop punishing myself by not playing bass and by keeping everyone at bay. But changing all that is turning my world on its head." Speaking her reasoning lightened her load, and examples poured out. "I applied for a new job, I started practicing again, I opened up to you and Tegan about things I've never told anyone. It's a lot, all at once, and I need a strong relationship to carry me through." Here, she hesitated. What would follow was a minor chord in an otherwise upbeat song, and it changed the entire feel. "But I don't think that can be with you."

He rubbed his forehead again, jaw flexing.

"I think it needs to be Jesus."

He laughed once, not looking at her. He laughed again, more convincing this time, and scrubbed his hands through his hair.

Though unsure what he found funny, a chuckle rose from her own throat. "In that song, you sang about God loving me and looking out for me, and I think I need to learn to rely on Him before exploring other relationships. Being grounded in God first is the only way I'll make a good life partner for anyone. I just hope you were wrong."

"About?"

"About this summer being a unique opportunity. By not being ready now, am I saying no to this for the last time?"

He'd focused out the windows again. Though the lines of pain and anger hadn't returned, he might not promise her another chance. How she longed for a quick reassurance, preferably paired with a hug. She'd memorize the feel of his arms around her, and maybe that would help through all the time they would spend apart.

She licked her lips. "It's occurred to me I'm the only one who's said no to a relationship between us. I chose Fitz, and I chose guilt, and now I'm choosing something else again."

He met her gaze, expression kind but sad, tired. "You're choosing well this time. I wish you all the best, Adeline."

His tone was gentle, but cues to cry flooded her face. "That sounds a lot like goodbye."

He swung both feet to the floor, giving her a view of his profile, and propped his elbows on his knees. When he looked at her, his mouth and the skin around his eyes tightened as if it took masterful control to keep from a look of all-out despair. "Our time here's up. We're going back to LA tomorrow."

GANNON COULDN'T STAND to watch Adeline's expression crumple into tears, so he stared at the floor. But he couldn't bear to sit by while she sniffled either. He grabbed the tissues and walked them to her. After she blew her nose and stood to toss the tissue, he pulled her against his chest, cradling her head over his heart the way he'd done with her hand last night.

"I have a problem, Addie." His voice came out rough with emotion he'd meant to suppress. This was too similar to saying goodbye to her when he'd left with John, Fitz, and Matt, bound for California, obligated to hide his feelings because she'd committed herself to someone else. "I've been trying to earn forgiveness too. On some level, I thought if I could keep Matt and Harper from destroying themselves, I'd make up for failing Fitz. But being one person's hero doesn't make up for failing another. Anyway, the only real hero is Jesus."

She held tight to him, and he felt her hold her breath. "You were trying to save me too."

"But it turns out I needed saving." If it weren't for her and the way events had unfolded this summer, Matt and Harper would still control swaths of his life. If it weren't for all the reminders that they couldn't earn forgiveness but only accept it, he might never have realized how hard he was trying to earn it.

But the woman in his arms was more than a spiritual realization. She saw him for who he was and gave him back as much as he invested in her. And where he'd had to turn Matt and Harper over to God, Adeline was running to Him all on her own.

Gannon would have to find the strength to let her. "You're making the right choice."

"This is harder than I thought it'd be." Her arms tightened, and her voice cracked.

"For me too." Even though he had information she didn't.

Chip and Drew had told him that morning they'd rallied the community—the church and those who knew Adeline from the food trailer and other places—to give her house a makeover. Tegan was in on it too. Though the work had yet to begin, they'd put down deposits with contractors to fix the basement, put on a new roof, and update the kitchen. They'd refused Gannon's offer to chip in beyond the painting he'd already arranged.

The old Adeline, the one he'd met when he'd first arrived, never would've accepted such a gift. But this Adeline? She might protest, but she'd give in, accept her friends' expression of love as a blessing. She was in good hands here.

He held her until the urge to hook his finger under her chin and tilt her face up for a kiss dominated his thoughts. Stepping back, he took the notebook from the bed and passed it to her.

Her damp eyes focused on the worn cover. "What's this?"

"A parting gift." One New Year's Eve, Awestruck had performed in front of a million people—more if those watching by television counted—and he hadn't missed a beat. Now, he had to clear his throat. "I told you I had a stash of songs I wrote because of you. The recordings I gave you barely scratched the surface."

She sniffed and blinked, clearing tears from her vision so she could study the notebook. Could she see from the places the red had worn off, letting white show through, all the time he'd spent with it? Did the stray pen marks reveal to her how he'd rushed to open it when a lyric came to mind or how he'd flipped it shut to hide his most personal thoughts when someone surprised him?

"You're going to let me read them?" She hugged it to herself.

"I'm letting you keep them."

"But you're leaving. Don't you need your notes for the album?" She held the notebook out to him, the expression on her face as if they were arguing over who should take the last lifejacket on a sinking ship.

Was that what this was? A sinking ship? If so, she was crazy if she thought he'd take something that might keep her afloat. "I have a copy of the recordings I gave you. Between those and what I've written since I arrived here, I have enough. Besides, the album was never the point of those songs. You were the point."

Adeline wiped her thumb against her cheek, clearing tears, then practically fell into him again. She wrapped her arms around him so the notebook pressed his back, her face against his chest.

He almost lost it, pressure building behind his eyes. He stared at the wall and let out a deep breath.

"This isn't goodbye forever, is it?" she asked.

"I hope not."

"Are you sure? I haven't been great to you. How many more chances are you going to give me to break your heart?"

He rested his cheek against her head and inhaled the floral notes of her hair. "At least one."

31

Six Months Later

*A*deline nudged an ice cube under the waxy leaves of her orchid plant and sat back in her desk chair. The visible edge of the ice turned glossy. The flowers had died a couple of weeks ago. Were ice cubes really enough to coax out another round of blossoms?

"Things are pretty slow, huh?"

Adeline swiveled toward the door of her cubical.

Tegan wore jeans and a light jacket that wasn't suited to February in northern Wisconsin. She must be dreaming of spring. She waved a glossy magazine with Gannon on the cover.

In the photo, he leaned against a gray wall, his thumb hooked in his pocket, a look on his face as if someone had said something marginally funny.

Tegan plopped the magazine on the desk and took the chair usually occupied by the university students Adeline advised in their job searches. "Any big Valentine's Day plans?"

Adeline shook her head. Tegan would've been the first to know if that had changed.

"Can you believe that when he showed up at Superior Dogs last summer, you told him to get lost?"

"I didn't exactly say that." She laid her fingers on the corner of the cover. She'd been so standoffish with Gannon back then. Now, she'd marry him in a heartbeat if he asked.

Wait. Would she? Marry him?

Tegan laughed. "Have you read it yet?"

She hadn't even seen it. *TMR* had to be one of the most famous music industry magazines, yet Gannon hadn't mentioned being featured, and she'd given up seeking out articles about him. Studying the photos and quotes was like finding comfort in a tub of ice cream. Satisfying in the moment, but a letdown in the long run. The things he spoke about to reporters gave only a glimpse into his true thoughts and feelings. His conversations with her were richer, but not enough.

They talked about music—she'd written and recorded the bass line for the phoenix song. They talked about the tour and her work, the day-to-day challenges and wins. But she sensed he'd put up emotional barriers. Either he was protecting himself in case she didn't come around or he thought she wanted distance. To a point she had, but she was in a good place now, wasn't she?

God, I trust you to bring him back to me if that's what You have for us.

She'd been praying it so much that the thought autopiloted through her brain. Now if only the mindset would permeate her heart.

Maybe it was all the tour. Maybe if not for that, he'd have come back already or at least would have had more time for deeper conversations.

But I trust you, God.

"So how's work?" Tegan thrummed her fingers against the

armrests and looked around the cubical as if she'd go stir crazy
if their roles were reversed.

"I heard today from one of the students I helped land a paid
internship in Madison. She's been at it a couple of weeks now
and loves it. She's over the moon."

"And so are you."

Adeline bit back a grin. The student had emailed a thank
you and credited Adeline with instilling her with the confidence she needed to take the big step toward her dream job.
"I'm making an impact."

"And the church hasn't fallen apart."

"Olivia's been doing a good job in the office."

Tegan moved to the edge of her chair. "I should let you go.
Just, I think you're going to like what he says in that interview.
It's not the same as a Valentine's Day date, but it's something."

She studied the cover again. Had he said something for her
this time?

She looked up as her friend reached the door of the cubical.
"Hey, Tegan?"

"Yeah." She stopped in the doorway.

"You didn't like Gannon."

Tegan lifted a shoulder. "I never would've guessed he was
serious enough to wait months for you, but here we are. Plus,
he affected good change in your life. You're happy, aren't you?"

Adeline nodded.

"Have you told him about the tattoo yet?"

Adeline turned her wrist and looked at the Hebrew characters on the inside of her forearm. She'd brought a picture of
Gannon's tattoo when she'd had hers done so the artist could
copy the style, though she'd picked a different verse. The idea
had been to tell Gannon about it right away, but then she'd
realized how brazen it had been, copying him in such a permanent way.

"You ought to."

"I don't know." The longer she'd waited to tell him, the harder it'd been to think of how to bring it up. Maybe it'd be better to just show him whenever they saw each other again.

Similar thoughts had kept her from broaching the topic of their relationship. So much time had passed. And it wasn't like she could ask him on a date when he wasn't even in the country.

"He'd like to know. I think it'd clarify some things for him."

Adeline smoothed her fingers over the tattoo. "Like what?"

Tegan smiled and turned to go. "Just tell him. And enjoy the article."

Adeline checked the time. She'd taken a quick lunch, and her next appointment wasn't for an hour, so she could spare a few more minutes.

She paged through the magazine until a picture of smoke and lights caught her eye. She pressed the pages flat on the desk. The photo had been taken at a show from behind at least a few rows of fans because silhouettes of heads and hands lined the bottom of the foreground. On stage, Gannon leaned toward the mic, midsong, gripping his guitar. Kyle, the second guitarist who toured with them, and Philip, the new bassist, flanked him. John sat behind the drums, one arm raised with a drumstick in his hand.

She looked over the other photos. Gannon and John talking, presumably backstage. Gannon and Kyle playing their guitars together. The guys walking down a hall, Gannon followed by Philip and the others.

So close, yet so far away.

This might not be the pick-me-up Tegan had intended, but she'd come this far. She lifted the magazine and settled into her chair.

Gannon Vaughn has the even, steady look of a man who knows what he's about. The powerhouse behind Awestruck's vocals and guitar, Vaughn turns everything he touches to platinum—or diamond, now that Awestruck's album *All I Asked* has sold over ten million units.

We caught up with the singer backstage in Pittsburgh, one of 80 stops in Awestruck's *Letting Go* world tour.

TMR: Thanks for taking the time to meet with us. This has been a big year for you. Adding bassist Philip Miller, releasing the new album, the tour.

GV: This year's been crazy, but the band is more solid than ever, and that simplifies everything. We're in a good place, operating and creating from a good place, and grateful for the opportunity our fans give us to do that. Without them, this wouldn't be possible, so I'm happy to say that I think they're going to like what's in store.

TMR: They already like your latest offering, *Letting Go,* which has been topping charts since its release. You've been quoted saying the album contains your best work to date. What makes this collection different from your past albums?

GV: You can't produce your best art when you're not honest with yourself about who you are. This album came from letting go of pretense and having those honest conversations. But the goal's always that when people hear Awestruck, the songs won't be about us anymore. *Letting Go* is about the fans, what's going on in their lives, whether the song is about addiction, redemption, the dynamics of relationships.

TMR: Speaking of relationships, in the past, you've stated that what people take for love songs are, in fact, inspired by your faith. You seem to have ventured from this with a couple of tracks on *Letting Go* in which the lyrics refer to a woman. Can you shed light on the inspiration behind songs like "If I Let Her Go" and "Phoenix"?

GV: They are love songs. As for the rumors, you mean the actress who claims I have feelings for her.

TMR: We weren't going to get that specific.

GV: I didn't write "If I Let Her Go" or "Phoenix" for that actress. I'll give her points for being right about one thing: I do still have feelings for the woman I wrote those for. She knows who she is.

TMR: Philip Miller wasn't available when Awestruck started recording for *Letting Go*, so a quarter of the songs include other bassists, including one name that stands out. Adeline Green, who wrote and recorded the bass line for "Phoenix," was a part of Awestruck at its inception. What was it like to collaborate with her again?

GV: She added to the song in ways no one else could've, and we were thrilled to work with her again, but the collaboration wasn't the reunion I wish it'd been. She couldn't join us in the studio because of other commitments, so the bass line was recorded separately.

TMR: There is speculation that she provided more than the bass line.

GV: I know what you're getting at, and yes, absolutely. Awestruck never would've gotten off the ground in the first place if not for her.

TMR: That isn't what I was getting at.

GV: I wish there were more I could tell you.

TMR: Okay, fair enough. The album offers a lot more than love songs. "One Man Left Behind" deals with grief, anger, and guilt after losing someone to suicide. The ultimate decision to move forward with life seems to be a reluctant one.

GV: When you lose someone like that, the tragedy changes you. To anyone fighting for their lives against depression, don't try to fight alone. There's no shame in needing help. No one can win a war alone.

TMR: And that's why Awestruck is donating some of the proceeds from the tour to suicide prevention efforts.

GV: Yes, we want to help. There is hope. There's a lot to

live for. Jesus loves you and put you on this earth for a purpose. I'm not saying faith results in automatic healing. Mental illness is real, and its consequences can be devastating. If you're struggling, reach out.

TMR: That's an important cause and just one song on an album that's marked with growth both musically and lyrically for Awestruck. It's hard to imagine topping this, but you alluded to being excited about what's in store. What can you tell us about your plans after the tour winds down?

GV: A lot of the growth is directly related to the time I spent away last summer, where the only professional commitment I had was the band. I don't mean to be ungrateful to my fans or to the opportunities available to me—I've got something special, and I'm grateful for that every day. But for me to continue without losing my bearings and my music, I need to be careful not to let the job take over too much.

TMR: Is there something specific you plan to cut back on?

GV: I don't know yet, but regular time away will be part of my future. That'll mean hard decisions about commitments aside from Awestruck, but our fans will appreciate that focus when the next album drops. And that's important to us. The fans make this possible. For them, we need to keep evolving and growing. This is the beginning of a new phase for us, and I'm excited about what's on the horizon, personally and professionally.

The din of fans flooding the building hums through the walls, signaling an end to the interview and proving that Vaughn's fans are as excited as he is about what's on the horizon.

Adeline scanned back up to the part where the interviewer had tried to get him to comment on their relationship. The way Gannon had said "Absolutely" before sidestepping was as close as he'd come to publicly admitting the song was about her.

I do still have feelings for the woman I wrote those for. She knows who she is.

After reading it again, she stood, paced her cubicle, then plopped back into her seat.

He'd also said he wished he had more he could say about their relationship. She rubbed her hand over the tattoo. Tegan was right. She needed to tell him about it.

And about her feelings.

His comments on taking more time away had to mean he planned to spend more time in Lakeshore, didn't it? The tour, which had started last month, went all the way through December and into next January, but maybe he could steal a week or two over summer again.

Maybe, but did she really have to wait that long?

32

Two Months Later

*G*annon pulled up the collar of his jacket and tweaked his baseball cap as he stepped over the cords taped to the floor of the elementary school gymnasium. Twenty or thirty rows of metal chairs bustled with movement and conversation between him and the stage. He advanced up the outside aisle. A glance revealed no one he knew in a row about halfway up, so he slid into a seat and watched his program, hoping that by being still, he'd draw less attention.

The discord of the musicians tuning tempted him to lift his head toward the makeshift orchestra pit, but he couldn't risk it. Any moment now, the house lights should go down, and he'd be free to look.

Young, overly loud laughter sounded from the center aisle.

Olivia had chopped and dyed her hair, and she wore dark eyeliner. Despite the edginess, her oversized flannel looked like it'd been chosen for comfort. He didn't recognize the others with her, a group of girls about her own age, maybe friends from college. Based on what Adeline had said, Olivia was within a month or two of finishing her freshman year.

The girls stepped into the row ahead of him, pointing to seats where they'd be a couple of chairs from him. Olivia's line of sight fell on him. She froze and blinked.

So much for keeping a low profile. He cringed, but instead of pointing and screaming the way she would've last summer, her head swiveled away.

"I don't like this spot. How about up there?" She lifted her arm and pointed to seats about as far from him as they could get. "It's so much closer. I want to see. And hear. Remember last year when the speakers went out?"

She waited at the end of the row until all her friends exited. When they were on their way to the seats she'd pointed out, she winked and hurried after them.

Gannon chuckled and fixed his attention back on the program until the lights went out.

Standing in front of the velvet curtain in the pool of a spotlight, the director talked about the musical and the cast. In the orchestra pit, musicians switched on the lights mounted to their music stands, the glow glinting against their white shirts and the metal of woodwinds and brass.

And there stood Adeline.

Only the conductor, the two percussionists, and she with her bass, were on their feet. She'd pulled her hair back in a ponytail with soft curls at the ends. Her variation on the dress code of black and white was classy, a silky short sleeve blouse and slim-fitting dress pants, probably paired with flats since she looked as short as ever, especially next to her instrument. Her expression was serious, but she didn't fidget. She was in the zone, ready to work, but not nervous.

He could applaud already.

The conductor lifted his hands and guided the orchestra into the first piece. Gannon heard nothing but the bass line and didn't glance at the stage when the curtain opened and the actors made their entrance.

Adeline was performing again, all in.

In many ways, the last eight months had been the longest of his career. Because Adeline wanted to be friends while she pursued other things, he'd known they couldn't spend hours and hours talking. Their conversations were semi-regular but never as deep as he'd like.

The ache to discuss their relationship and future grew no matter how he tried to curb it. He'd kept busy recording the new album, taping *Audition Room*, getting to know Miller, writing new music, the tour. The time had passed, but he was growing too tired to keep the pace much longer.

It'd gotten bad, this friend act. So many times he'd nearly ended one of their calls with an "I love you." Wherever he went, he knew how many hours it would take to get to her—how many flights, how long each would last, how far he'd have to drive.

He regularly played the recording of Adeline's bass line for "Phoenix." Once John discovered that, he'd started blaming any off day Gannon had on lovesickness, and both John and Miller had been laughing at Gannon's increasingly good mood the closer the calendar got to this trip.

"Why haven't you married this girl yet?" Miller asked as they boarded a plane for the US, the Asian leg of the tour over.

John had smirked. "She's just not that into him."

Was that true? When they'd said goodbye in August, he'd expected her to invite him back into her life long before this, but here he was, just another face in the crowd.

Now, he understood how his fans felt.

He'd promised to let her break his heart one more time, and for all he knew, she would when they saw each other. She'd say he'd respected her request for space so long and so well that she'd assumed they'd both moved on. She'd introduce her new boyfriend, who would've attended opening night of the musical.

Okay. Not a boyfriend. That would've come up.

But it'd been months.

A couple of weeks ago, she'd told him she missed him at the end of one of their calls. A first. He hoped it meant she missed him like he missed her, but he hadn't pressed to clarify in any of their conversations since. He wanted to have the discussion in person, especially given he'd already planned this trip.

Tonight, he'd find out what she'd meant. If she remained stuck on the idea of being friends, she'd never get unstuck from it. He'd have to move on.

He didn't want to. So he'd boarded that plane in Beijing, then another plane. And another. And then he'd gotten in a rental car. On arriving in town, he'd cleaned up at the hotel. Now, here he was, absolutely spent and not sure how she'd receive him, if he should even let her know he'd come or if she'd see this as an intrusion on a process she'd asked to complete without him.

All he knew was that listening to her play felt more like rest than anything he'd experienced in a long, long time.

ADELINE ROLLED the bass into the classroom across from the gymnasium. The case with wheels had been one of the best investments she'd made in the last year. She maneuvered around Mandy, the cellist, to fit her instrument into a corner.

Jessica cleaned her flute at a nearby desk. "Good job tonight."

"You too." Adeline couldn't stop grinning. The three hours had flown by. She'd wondered if the show would tire her. They'd practiced so much that she'd feared the music might start to bore her. Instead, she felt nothing but energy.

The last time she'd felt this way had been after performing with John, Gannon, and Fitz in high school. They'd made a habit of going to an all-night pancake house after shows. Up until tonight, she'd thought that had been teenage energy at work, but now she understood it as something else. If Lakeshore had an all-night restaurant, she'd get a group together. Maybe she could talk Tegan into staying up to make a batch of pancakes at home.

"Addie, Addie, Addie." Olivia dodged the last row of desks and clasped her arms. "You're never going to guess who's here. Did you know?"

Only one person would elicit this excitement from Olivia.

Gannon had come?

She'd mentioned the musical, but he'd last called from China. He hadn't breathed a word about seeing her. She couldn't blame him—he'd been sticking to the relationship she'd requested last fall. But she was ready for more.

So ready.

Maybe he'd lost interest, but Tegan assured her he wouldn't keep in touch if that were true.

Finally, she'd taken matters into her own hands. Told him she missed him. A lot. Waited to see how he'd respond.

"I miss you too." He replied quickly with warm relief, as if he'd been waiting to tell her.

They'd been ending their calls that way ever since, but nothing more had come of it.

Or so she'd thought.

Now he was here.

Olivia's eyes got wide and worried, and her voice dropped to a whisper. "You didn't know."

Adeline's stomach churned, but it was a little late to be nervous now. He'd already seen her perform. He'd sat through a three-hour, small-town rendition of a Broadway musical to hear her. "Where is he now?"

Olivia lifted her shoulders. "I don't know where he went for intermission, and he was gone before the lights came back on at the end."

"But you talked to him? You're sure it's him?"

"I didn't talk to him, but I spent a whole summer stalking him. I'm sure."

"Okay. Well." She glanced at the bass. It was safely stored, and nothing kept her except how little she trusted her legs. She linked her arm with Olivia's, and they left the classroom together.

A rolling bulletin board kept attendees from wandering into the area reserved for musicians, cast, and crew. Gannon would've had no qualms about sidestepping such a thing, but the hall was empty and gray, except for an eye-level line of children's artwork. Voices carried, audience members lingering outside the gymnasium to chat. She and Olivia stepped into the crowd.

"There she is!" Tegan hustled up and threw her arms around her. "Great job! I'm so proud of you!"

Drew moved in behind Tegan, blocking Adeline's view of the rest of the lobby. "That was excellent."

As Tegan released her, Drew moved in for a hug too.

Olivia weaved impatiently, scanning for Gannon.

Adeline stepped back from Drew. "Thanks, you two. I appreciate you coming."

"Of course." Tegan tweaked her elbow and took a half step toward the door. "Shall we?"

Olivia looked about to burst as she tagged along through the doors and into the night. Cool air washed Adeline's flushed face and bare arms, welcome relief. The gym had grown too warm toward the end of the show, and Olivia's news had added a few more degrees of anticipation and nerves.

Olivia made no effort to be discrete about looking to either side of the door and then, when there was no Gannon, along the side of the building. Unless he'd hidden in a recessed alcove, he wasn't there.

It'd been a little too good to be true, anyway. Adeline gave her a smile. "It's okay, Olivia."

"But I'm sure."

Wishful thinking could go a long way toward a false sighting. Adeline would know. "It's all right. He's on tour, and I wasn't expecting him. Have a good one, okay? Thanks for coming."

She joined Tegan and Drew on the sidewalk, and they started on foot toward Adeline and Tegan's house.

Technically, only Adeline owned it, though. Tegan only rented, and she was there less and less in favor of time with Drew. They'd officially call it dating one of these days. If these two got married, Tegan would move out and Adeline would either have to live alone or find a new roommate. Neither option appealed, but even without a roommate, at least she wouldn't be completely alone. She'd adopted Bruce, and he followed her from room to room. Also, with the job at the university, she could afford the mortgage by herself.

They turned the corner, but the neighbors' landscaping kept her from seeing her front porch until they were one house away. The tree she'd planted last fall obscured the view of the steps for a moment, but once she'd passed it, she had her answer. No one waited. With a sigh she looked toward the lake.

No good. She wouldn't be able to see over the pottery studio to the water until she was on the porch, and it was dark, anyway.

The driver's door on the car across the street opened.

Her body froze. Was that ...?

The man who climbed from the car wore a baseball hat. The glow from the streetlight failed to illuminate his features beneath the brim, but she recognized his confident movements. Not to mention the broad shoulders and athletic form.

Gannon. Here to surprise her. Here for her show.

She dropped her purse on the sidewalk and ran across the street. When she threw her arms around his neck, he picked her up and swung her around, his laugh reverberating with hers.

He set her back on her feet and used both hands to brush her hair away from her face. "I've missed you."

He was here, his voice so much richer for not being filtered over airwaves. The fabric of his shirt soft and warm beneath her fingers. Had he always smelled this wonderful? And his eyes. If only it weren't too dark to distinguish the color of his irises.

"I thought you were in China."

"Was I?" He focused on her so intently, she believed that he couldn't remember where he'd been and had no interest in thinking about it. He brushed his finger along her cheek, and the night air didn't feel so cool anymore.

If she went up on tiptoe ... but she remembered Drew and Tegan. She looked over her shoulder in time to see the living room light flip on. Drew was walking away down the sidewalk.

She and Gannon were alone, but how was this supposed to work, a reunion after so much time and distance? Could they rewind to that moment on the patio, to right before she'd said the word "friends" at the worst possible moment?

He laced their hands together. "Show me this remodel I've heard so much about."

Direction. Good. They could ease into it—as long as he kept holding her hand, a gentle promise that he'd come for more than a musical and a tour of the house.

"I planted a tree."

He chuckled as they crossed the street, hands linked. "I see that. Putting down roots."

Until now, it hadn't occurred to her that doing such a thing here, so far from LA, could cause problems for her and

Gannon. Could they be serious about each other if she wanted to live here? Or would she have to give up the home she'd only just started to love?

Still gripping his hand, she dipped to pick up her purse.

"The porch turned out nice."

This was the first time they'd held hands this way. Maybe she shouldn't try to plan the whole future.

She'd installed plant hooks. In June, she planned to put up hanging baskets of petunias, but since they remained empty now, she resisted pointing them out. "The painters added stripes on the woodwork that make such a difference." She motioned, but in the dark, the navy blue accents didn't stand against the white and sky blue the way they did in daylight.

Still, Gannon's line of sight obediently moved over the face of the house.

They mounted the steps, and she opened the door. Bruce passed her to sit before Gannon. He scrubbed the dog's ears, but when she moved on to the kitchen, the pair followed her.

Tegan stood at the sink, pouring herself a glass of water. Gannon retook Adeline's hand, and Tegan's attempt to squelch a knowing smile only half succeeded. "Gannon, long time no see. How's life treating you?"

"Can't complain." He turned his head, seeming to note the refinished cabinets, the white tile on the floor and backsplash, the countertops. Chip and his crew of generous volunteers had turned her worn, dated kitchen into something sparkling and white.

Tegan chuckled as she left the room, and Adeline understood. Gannon might've replied to her, but would he even remember greeting her now that she was gone?

"They put on a new roof, fixed the basement wall, and patched the ceiling of the upstairs bedroom where the leak was too. But the porch and this are my favorite parts." She lifted her hand to the room that surrounded them.

Gannon's interest sharpened on her arm. He opened his mouth, then shut it and met her eyes, his expression full of questions.

"Oh." She laughed nervously and rubbed the tattoo.

He turned her wrist and ran his fingers over the Hebrew characters. When she'd had the tattoo done, she'd learned how sensitive the skin on the inside of her forearm was, but his touch took it to a whole new level.

"What verse is it?"

"Psalm 33:3, about singing a new song to God and playing stringed instruments." The ink reminded her of her renewed relationship with God and also of Gannon, though seeing how similar hers was to his confirmed how bold the decision had been. "I probably should've asked permission first. People will think we're ..."

He leaned against the counter, his eyes fixed on her, golden and blue-green and intent. "You wanted space to focus on faith and making over your life."

Bruce shuffled up and sat, leaning against Gannon's leg like a seventy-pound anchor.

Good dog.

"I wanted to experience what you sang about."

His song "If I Let Her Go" had spent weeks as one of the most-played tracks on the radio. She wasn't tired of listening to it, and she wasn't tired of trying to realize it in her own life, but she'd come far enough alone, hadn't she?

"Everything is much fuller now. I've felt alone sometimes, but I've also seen God answer prayers, so I know He's holding me even when it doesn't seem obvious."

At some point, couldn't God use Gannon to hold her as she fell asleep?

He pulled her to his side and wrapped an arm around her. "When I had to trust Him with you all over again, I found out how much I'd still rather do everything myself." He inhaled, his mouth and nose against her hair. "I have to leave in the morning."

"Already?"

He rubbed her arm, confirming without repeating the bad news.

"I was hoping we'd have more time."

He lifted her wrist again. His thumb on the tender skin prompted an involuntary shiver he responded to by pulling her closer. "There's something I wasn't sure I'd tell you, but since you got matching ink ..."

She let her head rest against him, and the weight of his arm around her grounded her wild hopes. What could he say that was as brazen as her tattoo?

"I've been watching real estate listings. Havenridge went up for sale."

"You bought it?" She straightened to see his face.

His arm shifted on her shoulders but didn't release. "No, I didn't."

"Oh." She turned from him and braced both hands on the counter.

Of course he wouldn't have bought it. His life was in California. This would be long distance until they were serious enough for one or the other of them to move, and since she made a lot less and had fewer people depending on her, she'd have to make the sacrifice.

Gannon covered her hand with his. "I've realized how sick I am of the Harpers and the Matts, of people who'd give anything for a little more fame, a little more money, another high. People who look for happiness in all the wrong places."

She nodded. Harper had gotten engaged but was rumored to be having an affair. Matt had joined a band with three other guys who appeared to love their vices as much as Matt loved his.

"Even I did it, letting my life get too loud and complicated. I want things to be different. Quieter. This will be my last season on *Audition Room,* and I'm cutting down on other commitments. From here on out, I'm focusing on Awestruck and on building a life away from the noise."

She nodded again, following, but schooling her hope.

"I mentioned the cabin because it started interesting conversations. Turns out John has wanted to move back to Wisconsin for a few years now to be closer to his family again. Two of his sisters are married, and Kate just got engaged, but he barely knows his brothers-in-law. Miller's favorite season is winter—however that happens—and he's got two kids he's not crazy about raising in LA. He's open to moving too."

She waited for it this time, refusing to let her feelings soar and then be shot down again.

"Moving here, Adeline." Gannon lifted her hand from the counter, turning her to face him.

"So it's okay that I put down roots."

He rubbed the back of her hand with his thumb. "I wouldn't ask you to leave this place. This house someday, but only for one with the best view of the lake we can find."

Leave this house to be with Gannon in a house they found together? He wasn't just talking about living in Lakeshore. He was thinking of marriage too.

He pulled her back to his side. "It wouldn't look like it did last summer. With this as our permanent home, the guys and I would all get our own places. That's why I passed on Haven-ridge. Awestruck travels a lot, but you'd be welcome to come with us."

She tried to picture it, Gannon here year-round, attending the fall festivals, venturing to the ice caves with her in winter, getting lunch from Superior Dogs in summer, attending the little church. Locals would get used to him. If he lived the quiet life he seemed to have in mind, paparazzi probably wouldn't bother with him. Not much, anyway. Not here.

"You would do that. Move here?"

"Well, there's this girl ..." He trailed his fingers up and down her arm. "But if you think matching tattoos make us look like a couple, me moving the band will start real talk. Then again, you did say you care more about reality than rumors."

"And what's the reality?"

"I thought you'd never ask." He nudged her chin, tilting her face toward his. For once, his eyes couldn't captivate her attention. His breath was warm on her cheek, and a smile pulled at his lips. "Tell me now you just want to be friends, and I'll believe you."

She held her silence, closed her eyes, and inhaled his scent. Sandalwood.

He kissed the corner of her mouth, gentle.

Was he really waiting for her to reply?

"I want so much more than that."

He shifted, arms tightening around her. His mouth found hers. She lost track of everything else until he pulled back.

Then she found she'd moved her palm to the center of his chest. His breathing had picked up, rolling in and out like waves. His thumb was on her cheek, his hand resting on the side of her neck, the other arm still snug around her waist. He kissed her forehead and sighed.

There it was, discernible under the exhale. His heartbeat. Fast and strong.

She snuggled her head against him, listening to distinguish the sound of her heartbeat from his. "So this is what it is to live with the living."

"Is it worth it? All the time and trouble to get here?"

"Yes." She angled to see his expression. "And you? Is this worth the time and trouble?"

"I'd play my part again one hundred times over." He ran his fingers from her temple to her jaw and stole another kiss. "Whatever it took to bring you back."

~

Deliver me from bloodguiltiness, O God,
O God of my salvation,
and my tongue will sing aloud of your righteousness.
O Lord, open my lips,
and my mouth will declare your praise.
For you will not delight in sacrifice, or I would give it;
you will not be pleased with a burnt offering.
The sacrifices of God are a broken spirit;
a broken and contrite heart, O God, you will not
    despise.
Psalm 51:14-17, ESV

Spend more time in Lakeshore with an email subscriber exclusive.

Food trailer owner Asher has seen too many tears he couldn't dry. Determined to be part of the solution, he avoids romance and all the heartbreaking drama that comes along with it.

At least, that's the plan until his heart decides it has a mind of its own. If he can't rein it in, he's destined to break not one but two women's hearts.

Subscribers to Emily's email newsletters will have the opportunity to download *Between the Two of Us*, which is a prequel novella to the Rhythms of Redemption Romances, as a welcome gift.

Sign up at emilyconradauthor.com.

AUTHOR'S NOTE

Whatever you are facing, I hardily echo Gannon's statement that there is hope, Jesus loves you, and He put you on this earth for a reason. Gannon encourages those reading his interview to "reach out" if they're struggling, but what does that look like?

I think it can start by talking with trusted loved ones, but that's not always enough. In my own life, finding the right mental health professional at the right time has made such a difference.

If you're not sure where to start, Psychology Today's online therapist finder allows you to narrow your search by speciality or type, including Christian counseling. Results include an introduction, information on specialties and experience, and contact information to help you in your search. Check out their listings here: https://www.psychologytoday.com/us/therapists

If you are experiencing a suicidal crisis or emotional distress, call 988 in the US for free and confidential support from the 988 Suicide and Crisis Lifeline. For chat or more resources and information, visit https://988lifeline.org/.

You matter. If you are hurting, please seek help.

NEXT IN THE RHYTHMS OF REDEMPTION ROMANCES

An Awestruck Christmas Medley - Book 1.5, a novella - Four hundred miles of snow-covered terrain, not to mention troubled relationships, stand between the men of Awestruck and a Christmas spent with loved ones. Gannon's made a promise he's determined to keep, and he's not about to let a blizzard stop him.

To Belong Together - Book 2 - Drummer John Kennedy can keep a beat, but he can't hold a conversation, so he relies on actions to show he cares. Unfortunately, when he's instantly intrigued by a spunky female mechanic, he can't seem to convey the sincerity of his intentions. Could God intend this pair of opposites to belong together?

Learn about the rest of the series and new releases at https://www.EmilyConradAuthor.com.

DID YOU ENJOY THIS BOOK?

Help others discover it by leaving a review on Goodreads and
the site you purchased from!

DISCUSSION GUIDE

1. Which character did you relate to the most? Why?
2. Do you enjoy running into former high school classmates?
3. Gannon and Adeline went on a spur-of-the-moment trip home. Share about your last spontaneous adventure.
4. Portions of the story were inspired by the account of David and Bathsheba. What parallels and differences did you notice?
5. How did Adeline telling Tegan about her past help her on her journey back toward God?
6. Drew, Gannon, and Adeline are all on pedestals, though for different reasons. In what ways do you think those expectations and opinions helped or hurt them?
7. Gannon and Adeline experience both benefits and inconveniences because of his fame. Given the choice, would you opt for a life of fame and fortune?
8. How would you have answered Harper if she asked you about Christianity?

9. Adeline and Gannon both reacted differently to the same sin. How did those reactions limit or free them?

10. How did you feel about Adeline's decision to distance herself from Gannon while she righted her relationship with God?

11. How do you know when to step in and help a person as opposed to when to step back and trust God?

12. Was there a line from the story that stood out as especially helpful or meaningful?

ACKNOWLEDGMENTS

It takes a village to produce a book.

When I first dreamed of publishing novels, I never gave a thought to how many others would be intricately involved in the process. Looking back from here, I'm humbled by and grateful to the community of family, friends, readers, writers, and professionals who have made this book—and everything else I write—possible.

Thank you to my family for never rolling your eyes when I start a conversation by saying, "So for a story ..." You're always willing to brainstorm with me, talk me through the hardest discouragements, and dream big on my behalf.

Adam, reading these stories with you is one of my favorite things. Thank you for supporting me and this writing dream. There's something of you in every story I write.

To my beta readers and friends Elizabeth Yzaguirre, Jessica Bradley, and Kendra Arthur, thank you for talking about my characters as if they were real. Jessica, that you heard a voice on the radio and at first mistook it for Gannon remains one of the biggest compliments of my writing career.

I'm grateful for the expertise, guidance, and friendship of the many writing friends who have poured hours and heart into this story in big ways and small: Anne Carol, Jerusha Agen, Janet Ferguson, Robyn Hook, Amy Renaud, Katie Powner, Kerry Johnson, Rebekah Millet, Audrey Appenzeller, Jessica Johnson, and Janyre Tromp. I first drafted *To Bring You Back* in

2017, and I combed back through years' worth of emails to compile that list. I pray I haven't missed anyone!

My volunteer readers Erica Bostaph, Teresa Fritschle, Jane Bradley, and Joan Paterson helped catch typos and errors. Any mistakes that made it through are on me, but if you find a typo, be sure to congratulate it for evading so many sets of eyes!

Robin Patchen, thank you for taking this story on and for all the help and guidance.

Judy DeVries, I appreciate your expertise in proofreading and your enthusiasm for the story.

A few years ago, I wrote out that my dream is to publish books I love with a team that understands what I'm trying to do and helps me to do it better. And that makes working with each of you a dream-come-true.

Readers, thank you for coming along for the journey with these characters and with me. Special thanks to those of you who are always willing to brainstorm on my Facebook page. Chip loves his new name.

To the Quotidians. I couldn't ask for a better group of writers to hang out with. You all inspire me, and I wouldn't want to navigate the writing world without you by my side.

I didn't start my job at hope*writers until long after this story was drafted, but the team's positive, can-do mindset helped inspire me with the courage to pursue indie publishing. Thank you for all you do to help writers make progress.

Lord, You are truly better than I know. Thank You for the stories. May they bring You honor.

ABOUT THE AUTHOR

Emily Conrad writes contemporary Christian romance that explores life's relevant questions. Though she likes to think some of her characters are pretty great, the ultimate hero of her stories (including the one she's living) is Jesus. She lives in Wisconsin with her husband and their energetic coonhound rescue. Learn more about her and her books at emilyconradauthor.com.

facebook.com/emilyconradauthor

twitter.com/emilyrconrad

instagram.com/emilyrconrad

Printed in Great Britain
by Amazon